Letters and Lies

by

Colleen L. Donnelly

Letters and Lies

Cover Art by *Jennifer Greeff*

The Wild Rose Press, Inc.
PO Box 708
Adams Basin, NY 14410-0708
Visit us at www.thewildrosepress.com

Publishing History
First Cactus Rose Edition, 2020
Print ISBN 978-1-5092-3122-5
Digital ISBN 978-1-5092-3123-2

Published in the United States of America

"He wrote and changed your plans? Why didn't you tell me? You know I love hearing his letters."

Everyone loved hearing his letters. Or at least they'd pretended to. I glanced at my friends again, noting especially the one who'd first suggested I correspond with her husband's homesteading friend in Kansas who was ready to look for a wife. She dabbed at her eyes with a handkerchief while she flicked the fingers of her other hand in a weak wave. I dredged my soul in search of a smile, though the man she'd introduced me to truly had penned everything I'd ever wanted in a husband, months of letters which convinced Mama that Jim was my open door. Letters I'd foolishly carted from family to friend to blather every word like a desperate spinster. Drat.

"He didn't send his change of plans in a letter, Mama." I squeezed her forearm. "He sent them in a telegram." The only six words I would never share.

"Oh. Well, that's nice. I imagine your Jim has a surprise for you and didn't have time to send a letter before you left for Crooked Creek. How thoughtful to wire you instead."

Thoughtful...I felt poisoned, and Mama would too if she ever found out Jim had shut my open door. Which she wouldn't, since as soon as I got out there and found him, I'd wedge it back open again.

Praise for Colleen L. Donnelly

"I stayed up past my usual bedtime reading *OUT OF SPLINTERS AND ASHES*."

~Kathleen Buckly, BookBub

~*~

"You know the saying, 'If you love someone, set them free…' The quote summarizes *LOVE ON A TRAIN* beautifully."

~Kameron Brook, Reviewer

~*~

"Wow, Wow, and Wow…This morning at 8 AM I started your book [*MINE TO TELL*] and it is 2:40 PM and I have just finished it. It is the most enjoyable book that I have ever read…A JOB WELL DONE TO YOU. Thank you for a nice Sunday read."

~ZT Armstrong

~*~

"Just finished your book [*MINE TO TELL*]. I had to let you know it was beautifully written. I can't express how much I liked the book, the words are in my heart but won't go on the paper."

~Another Reader

~~~

Other Books by Colleen L. Donnelly
at The Wild Rose Press, Inc.
Mine to Tell - Amazon #1 Bestseller,
Readers Crown Award, and Crowned Heart winner
Asked For
Love on a Train
The Lady's Arrangement
Out of Splinters and Ashes -
Crowned Heart winner and Rone Finalist

Dedication

To my mom, who always encouraged me
to write a story and heroine like this.
She'll be enjoying the final product from heaven,
but without her help and encouragement this book
may never have been written.
I also want to thank my critique partners who gave me
advice I should have listened to sooner,
along with Kacee Everhart and Julie Daniels
who suffer willingly as my manuscript's extra eyes.

Chapter 1

Every promise Mama had ever believed for me radiated from her face. I wouldn't let her down. I'd board this train as if nothing had changed, then fix what had, once I arrived. Her hands cupped my shoulders. She pinned me in a spotlight of such admiration I knew I'd made the right choice—stick with my lie.

"Look at you, Louise," she said above the din of St. Louis's Union Depot. I let her look and held as steady as I could in the onslaught of passengers who bumped against us, hurried by the waiting locomotive's belch of steam and its conductor's call of the next several stops to the west.

Mama held me at arm's length and took in the tiny hat and new dress she'd bought me just for this day, this trip, this momentous open door she always knew would come. She let go of one shoulder, and with a frown at the soot collecting on my outfit, she brushed at the tiny black particles which fell like damp dust over the platform and those of us either standing or rushing across it.

Her glove blackened as she protected the latest style she'd been so proud to give me—less bustle and fewer cascades to the floor where the toes of my shiny boots peeked out. Mama stepped back and admired me once again. "My little Louise Archer of St. Louis, Missouri. Here you are, all grown up and on your way to become Mrs. Jim Baylis of Crooked Creek, Kansas."

Jim's last-minute telegram burned within my glove—*Don't come. I can't marry you.* I glanced from her to my friends clustered behind her and looked for "at last" on any of their faces while "maybe not" thundered in my mind.

"I told you your open door would come." Mama effused the promise she had never lost faith in, not even this year when I reached the age of twenty-eight. "I would love to see Jim's face when you step off that train in Dodge City."

"He…well…"

Trust shone on her face. She saw her only daughter married…at last…while I saw her future equally secure once my husband's name appeared alongside mine on the unsettled estate Papa left behind.

"Actually, Mama, I'm to take a stagecoach from Dodge City to Crooked Creek. Then he'll see me." After I asked directions to the Baylis homestead so I could find him.

Mama tilted her head, a tiny frown dampening the glow of her earlier light. "He wrote and changed your plans? Why didn't you tell me? You know I love hearing his letters."

Everyone loved hearing his letters. Or at least they'd pretended to. I glanced at my friends again, noting especially the one who'd first suggested I correspond with her husband's homesteading friend in Kansas who was ready to look for a wife. She dabbed at her eyes with a handkerchief while she flicked the fingers of her other hand in a weak wave. I dredged my soul in search of a smile, though the man she'd introduced me to truly had penned everything I'd ever wanted in a husband, months of letters which convinced Mama that Jim was my open door. Letters I'd foolishly carted from family to friend to blather every word like a desperate spinster. Drat.

"He didn't send his change of plans in a letter, Mama." I squeezed her forearm. "He sent them in a telegram." The only six words I would never share.

"Oh. Well, that's nice. I imagine your Jim has a surprise for you and didn't have time to send a letter before you left for Crooked Creek. How thoughtful to wire you instead."

Thoughtful…I felt poisoned, and Mama would too if she ever found out Jim had shut my open door. Which she wouldn't, since as soon as I got out there and found him, I'd wedge it back open again.

Mama stretched to her toes and neatened my hat, the woman who'd readied me for this day so close I inhaled a great draught of her trust to carry with me. "This shade of green is perfect for your hair. Auburn goes so well with green." She dropped back to the flat of her feet and clasped her hands. "You're beautiful, Louise, so tall, so slender…"

So like my father. The man we both missed terribly, and who had also trusted my open door so much he'd anticipated this marriage and built it into his will before he passed. I grasped her hands and held them.

"At least your father can watch you from Heaven," she continued. "He must be so proud."

I doubted that. I looked away. The grief and fury over being jilted probably wouldn't look like thoughts of Papa in Heaven on my face. I focused on Union Depot's commotion instead. Marveled at what had seemed a good idea a year ago, building a station where most railways entering and leaving St. Louis could converge. A good idea done in by poor planning, since already in 1876 the newest and largest depot was too small. If Papa did happen to be watching everything his daughter was up to, he could at least credit me with a foolproof plan.

"I can't wait to meet your Jim," Mama said. "He writes so well, I think all of us wanted to move out west and join him."

Jim had written well…until his last six words…so many wonderful letters as he'd courted me.

With my own hands, I've built a home worthy of and ready for two. And you and I have built two lives worthy of and ready to become one with our words in our letters. Miss Louise Archer, we've done everything except meet after months of correspondence. Please come. Please consider me. And please say yes that you will marry me.

I'd been pretty quick to write yes, I'd come, yes, I'd consider him, and of course I would marry him. What I should have said no to was his suggestion in one of his first letters that we share no photographs…only words, so we could truly come to know one another. Now I had to find a man I'd never met and only knew by his words. I glanced again at my friend who'd suggested Jim and I write. I should never have let her persuade me her husband's shy friend's idea was a good one. A romantic notion she'd called it, something which left me headed to Crooked Creek with only "tall, sturdy build, weathered skin, and dark brown hair" to go on.

The train blasted a warning, its deafening whistle

joined by a conductor's shout to board.

"They did load your trunk, didn't they?" Mama asked as my friends came close, smiling while dabbing at teary eyes.

My face warmed at the thought of the trunk I could have easily loaded myself, nothing more in it than two regular dresses, a few personal items, my wedding dress, and the album I'd made of Jim's letters to remind him of our courtship and plans. "Yes, they did," I affirmed to squelch any repeat of her earlier protest that I hadn't packed nearly enough for a wife as I'd slammed the lid on what it would take to become a bride first.

Would you be willing to come here, live in my world, and be my wife on this land that's nearly mine? You may visit first before you answer, come taste Crooked Creek's land before you decide. Meet me and see me. Let who I've tried to show you, through words, show you in real life.

Jim's words spoke again, the voice that had grown in my imagination as his, a tone in my thoughts, louder than the waiting locomotive's sudden burst of steam. More soot rained down on people who ducked as if they could avoid the blackened particles. Mama didn't flinch or swipe her glove down my dress again. Maybe she heard the same voice I did, her smile just like the first time I'd read aloud a letter from the Kansas homesteader to her and Papa. The rest of Jim's letters she'd heard alone, but her excitement, her determination I pass through my open door never wavered, even with Papa gone.

I glanced at my train, where tired officials in equally tired uniforms funneled people and their baggage to the right doors. Jim had been right about the flood of people and businesses headed west. He'd described Dodge City as a hive of activity ever since the cross-country rails had reached it three years ago. I could hear his voice again, his poetic phrases, flowing descriptions of his territory, the challenges of the Cimarron Cut, the hardships of homesteading, and the stage he'd told me the two of us would take from Dodge City to Crooked Creek...before he changed his mind.

Well, I would change it back. I needed what Mama had preached. I wanted to be someone's wife, carry his name, raise his children...and secure the family business for her. And Mama wanted it even more, bittersweet joy which loved yet hated to see me go.

"Lord knows I'll miss you, Louise, but I'm so happy at how happy you are going to be," Mama said at my side.

I nodded. Neither of us would be happy if the ruse I'd devised to get me to Jim without him or anyone else knowing I was Louise Archer, the jilted spinster from St. Louis, didn't work. I gripped my three bags, one with a ticket for Mrs. Penelope Strong, that I would surreptitiously hand to the conductor, hidden inside. People would believe my claims to be a once-loved widow on my way west to complete my late husband's unfinished business. No one doubted or bothered widows. My plan would get me there so I could study Jim's situation, figure out how to fix whatever had caused him to change his mind, then introduce myself with all of our answers in hand. All before our tentative wedding date Mama intended to buy a ticket for.

I glanced at her. I'd never lied to my parents

before. I fidgeted with the cords to the bag which held Mrs. Penelope Strong's ticket. "As soon as I reach Jim and we affirm our wedding date, I will wire you."

"No need to wire me." Mama dismissed my assurance with a wave of her hand. "I intend to come long before your wedding."

"You what?" Drat. My plan allowed me one week to find Jim and a day to fix whatever had gone wrong. Then a few extra to meet his friends and make our wedding arrangements. Plenty of time to send Mama a letter which assured her life in southwestern Kansas was grand and I would soon get married, before she began to suspect it wasn't and I wouldn't.

"I won't miss one second of your open door, my dear. I will come early and help you prepare everything."

"Wait, Mama. Wait until I write you. And don't come…" *Don't come. I can't marry you.* "I mean, don't come until I let you know when it's time." Goodness. Mama would be devastated to learn her daughter lied. Sort of lied, since once I found Jim and straightened everything out, I would wire her and I would wed.

The crowd thinned. Baggage previously strewn across the station's platform dwindled. Families and passengers who had swarmed around us could now be seen through my train's windows, a steady file from the cluster gathered in front of the nearest car's door, a conductor at one side and two men at the other—one tall, a sturdy comfortable ruggedness wearing a western-style hat next to a slighter man more finely dressed. The conductor across from them helped each person step up into the car, as Tall-and-Sturdy stood to the side and studied each person as they passed.

7

Drat. I hadn't counted on some stranger paying so much attention before I'd rehearsed my story.

"I should go, Mama." I squeezed her hands and pondered how to slip past the man near the train. *I am Mrs. Penelope Strong, widow, traveling west on my late husband's unfinished business...*

Don't go filled Mama's eyes while *Don't come* demanded I do everything I had to, to keep Mama from ruin, and her tears from spilling over forever. I threw my arms around her and held tight. "I love you, Mama, and I'll make sure I find that open door."

"Find it?" She tipped her head to the side.

"I mean...thank you for never wavering about my open door."

This time Jim filled her eyes, happy yet sad tears for the man we'd both waited for and needed. I gave her one last squeeze and hurried to each of my friends and hugged them as well. "I'll write," I promised each as I turned toward the train...and the two men who were still there. Drat. I ducked my head to hurry past. *I'm Mrs. Penelope Strong, widow...* The platform blurred as I crossed it. I swiped at tears with my sleeve. Mama would be so horrified if she saw such manners. The conductor's hand also blurred as he extended it to take mine.

Please come. Please consider me. And please say yes that you will marry me.

Mama called Jim my open door. He was her open door too. I fumbled with my skirts to board the train which would take me to the door that needed to be re-opened.

"Ma'am."

I stole a glance at the conductor, who nodded

toward the tall man to my left. I looked up as a weathered hand removed the western hat from a head of dark brown hair.

"I see you're headed west on your own." Equally dark eyes focused on my tears. "I could help, if you..."

I lifted my chin, wishing that I cursed so I could curse these traitorous tears away. "Yes, I'm headed west, but I don't need..."

"Oh, excuse me, my dear." Mama appeared between me and the stranger, and wrapped an arm around my shoulders. "I forgot to tell you your uncle Roy wanted to see you off, but something happened and he couldn't get away from the store."

"He what?" I glanced behind her, for once hoping to see Mama's inept and greedy brother. He should be nowhere near Papa's store unless he was pulling his hair out over legal paperwork I'd sewn up so tight neither he nor his slithering attorney would be able to scratch their name on any dubious-looking documents before I got myself married.

"You know Roy and how considerate he is." Mama let go with a soft smile.

"I certainly do know how he is," I said through clenching teeth. Mama's grief never let her see that Uncle Roy grinned too big and wore clothing too expensive for a brother who'd claimed to be only helping as he oozed his way deeper and deeper into Papa's hardware business and pockets after Papa became ill.

"He said not to worry. He will take care of the store just like it's his own." Mama backed away until she stood alongside my waving friends.

"Mama, we don't need Uncle Roy to take care of

the store. I already…" I paused at her furrowed brow, the same look that worried my knack for running Papa's business would frighten potential husbands away. I could see in her pinched expression the warning that no man wanted a woman who was smarter than he was. Goodness. Maybe Jim agreed. Maybe he cancelled our wedding after I'd written in great detail how I'd shadowed Papa since childhood and used what I'd learned to thwart Uncle Roy's antics. Drat. I shouldn't have told Jim that Papa's attorney complimented my aptitude as we'd signed off on a plan which would take effect as soon as Jim and I were married. No more of that. I'd be naïve and uninformed from this moment on.

Passengers from behind pushed past me to board the train.

"You might finish up, ma'am. Train'll be pulling out in a minute," the conductor said.

I looked at Mama. I'd worked hard to keep her brother's shenanigans from her and Papa. Such betrayal would have crushed them. My father may have been failing, but I wasn't.

"Ready, miss?" The conductor held his hand out to me.

I stayed where I stood. What if my plan to keep her brother's and his attorney's fingers out of the business failed before I married? It shouldn't…it couldn't…as long as I hurried. "Don't worry, Mama."

"I won't. Roy promised to help while you're gone." Mama waved. "You just go be happy."

I tried to wave back, a weak lift of my hand to a woman and friends who blurred.

"You look distraught," Tall-and-Sturdy said. His earlier studious observance narrowed as he gazed down at me. "Are you sure I can't…"

"Of course I'm distraught," I snapped. "I'm recently widowed." I ignored his, as well as the conductor's, hands as I took the first step into the train. I caught the shift of the smaller and more well-dressed man next to him and heard the subtle clearing of his throat. I reprimanded myself. Naïve. Less assertive. Widows may be distraught, but they would be kind. I turned back. "I'm Mrs. Penelope Strong, and I'm on my way to…" Drat. If I said Dodge City, this man…or his friend…might happen to know Jim. Drat that Jim's telegram arrived only yesterday. I should have spent more time working out the details of my plan and less putting together the album of his letters. "Larned, Kansas, to finish my dear late husband's business," I said as I prayed neither Mama nor my friends would shout a sudden goodbye to Louise Archer. I also prayed this man would do what I'd intended every person to do in the face of a widow—stammer, shy away, and leave me be.

"I'm sorry about your late husband, ma'am," he said with what sounded more like relief than awkward grief. He set his hat back on his head. "Larned's a long trip on uncomfortable seats. My seat…I mean, ours…" He nodded at the raised brows on his traveling companion's face. "Is far more comfortable. And private." He gave a poignant nod at tears I couldn't swipe with a sleeve now that I was up high where Mama could see. "You're welcome to it. We can make do somewhere else until then."

Until then? These two were headed to Larned? To some little dot on the map I happened to spout simply because it caught my eye as I'd stretched my sewing tape across two states to chart my trip? I should have said somewhere farther west, maybe even beyond Dodge City, so this man...these two...would have gotten off long before. "Thank you," I said with as much new-widow meekness as I could. "Your help is appreciated." I stepped back to the ground and took the proffered elbow to let comfortably rugged Tall-and-Sturdy—along with his friend—steer the distraught Mrs. Penelope Strong to their seat. Which I'd graciously thank them for, once we reached Larned, slip off the train and then back on, then stay out of everyone's sight the rest of the way to Dodge City.

Chapter 2

"Larned, Kansas," the conductor boomed, the same way he'd bellowed every other stop since St. Louis. "Fort Larned."

The train squealed as it slowed, a riot of noise the conductor managed to thunder over as he announced the one town I'd prayed the train would miss.

I dropped back against my seat...that tall man's seat. Maybe the train's struggle meant the brakes had failed.

"Mrs. Strong?"

I turned from the wall in front of me that I'd stared at all the way from St. Louis, straightened from what had indeed been private and comfortable, the last seat in the car, and looked up at the man who'd given it to me. Plus his traveling companion pinched tight against his side in the aisle.

"I believe this is your stop." He removed his hat. "You said Larned, if I remember right."

Yes, I'd said Larned, but I hadn't meant it. Drat the luck he remembered, and that this man had interfered with me to begin with. And double drat I'd lied that I had a ticket for a town I had no intention of staying in.

"So you will...both...be getting off here as well?" At least this seat could remain mine once they left the train and I slipped back on.

"No, ma'am. We're continuing on."

"Continuing on? I mean, oh, I see… So this is Larned?" I feigned fresh-widow confusion as the conductor bellowed, "Larned, Kansas," again.

"Maybe the lady needs a moment to collect herself, McCloud." The slighter man spoke, grace I certainly needed, though his expression said nothing of the sort.

"A moment would be nice." I glanced at the cushioned bench seat between me and the window as if I had a lot to gather. My three bags lay closed and in a heap, the window's glass still clouded with pipe smoke and crowded conditions. My face warmed. I pressed a hand to my cheek like a widow so forlorn I couldn't even bother to clear a spot to gaze at the scenery. I'd done nothing but worry about Mama and recalculate the legal scheme I'd left behind to hinder her brother. And think about Jim, where and how to find him, instead of preparing to disembark so I could slip back on.

"Take your time." The smaller man cleared his throat, and one of them shuffled his feet. "We don't need the seat until the train pulls out again anyway."

With a final squeal of brakes that hadn't failed, the train ground to a stop. Passengers stirred and struggled to their feet in relief, people apparently glad to see Larned.

"Rather unpleasant sitting out in the open where we were stared at, but—"

"My name's Everett McCloud, ma'am," the tall man interrupted his friend. "I'm not here for the seat. I have time to help you with your bags before I…we…head on west with the train."

West. Possibly the two of them were headed to Dodge City. I set my hands on my bags. I could confess that I'd lied and stay on the train and travel red-faced all the way to Jim. Who may, if he knew Mr. McCloud, hear what I'd done and be glad he'd refused to marry me. Or I could stick to my lie and get off the train here…but lose time while I waited for another.

I glanced at the window between me and the town my lie had landed me in. Larned could be larger than its little dot on the map made it seem. It lay right on the main tracks, so surely another train would come soon enough I could continue with my plan.

I faced the two men, at least one of whom wanted this seat back. I could figure a way out of this. I had managed to out-think, out-plan, and outsmart Uncle Roy and his crooked attorney, so I could handle a non-criminal's offer to carry my trunk.

"We just—"

"Want to help." Everett cut his friend off again. "A man finishes what he starts, especially when it involves a lady. I'm sorry, ma'am, that the man who started something with you is no longer around to do it."

I clapped a hand against my chest. Jim was still around…

"I'm sure he'd want to know someone stepped in and took care of what he couldn't," Mr. McCloud added, and this time he did look sorry I was a widow left on my own. My face warmed, and I dropped my hand at his genuine concern, the same care my Jim, who wasn't fictitious, but real and good, would have. The fiancé I'd come to know through his letters would finish what he'd started, if I could just get there. One look at the album I'd made of his letters, a re-read of the loving words he'd written as we corresponded, would set him straight. He'd likely created something similar with my letters. I just had to get there and see the man who would apologize, after which we'd marry, just like he'd asked and we'd planned.

"Need some help here?" the conductor bellowed as if he still called Larned's name. He came alongside Mr. McCloud and his friend—the loud and uniformed next to the tall and strong next to the slight and finely dressed. The air filled with a dampened swirl of tobacco, faint cologne, and warm fabric.

"The lady, who isn't quite ready, is getting off," Mr. McCloud's companion said.

"Off?" The conductor frowned at me. "No, ma'am, this isn't your stop."

Drat.

He scratched his forehead, his tired conductor's cap rising with each thrust of his fingers. "Your stop is…"

"Here." I swiped my three bags from the seat, untouched needlework in one, something I'd planned to practice while on the train to remind myself what every good wife knew how to do. Thanks to two years of Uncle Roy's shenanigans, my domestic skills had suffered. I could practice while I waited for the next train. I looped all three bags over my shoulder and faced Mr. McCloud. "You've been very kind—both of you—for allowing me to ride in your seat. Thanks to you, I rested. And worked out necessary corrections to my plans," I added over the confusion which clouded the conductor's brow. "I've left your spot neat as a pin, ready for you to have it back."

"Are you sure…" the conductor hedged.

"Of course I am…especially now that I've had time to think." I stepped to the window, smeared a circle in its grime, and surveyed the town I had no intention of staying in beyond the next train west. Brown. I saw brown everywhere, vertical brown buildings and horizontally blown brown dust. Even what little land I could see looked flat and plain with more brown—exactly as Jim had described his territory.

It's not much to the newcomer. But it's beautiful once you get to know it.

Jim's brown had to be more beautiful than this. And this brown was temporary.

"Yes, this is the place my late husband described. He had business here and intended to return to… Well, I'm trying to do homage to investments he so cleverly managed while alive. He was a genius. I'm merely doing the best I can, and unfortunately confusing things while doing it." I pressed my forehead like a flustered widow. "I'm sorry if in all my grief I've…"

"I understand." The conductor did what he was supposed to in the company of a recent widow. He reddened, took a step back, and bent in a nervous bow. "I'm sorry, ma'am. I'll see to your trunk. I'll make sure it's unloaded."

"Thank you." I wobbled a smile as he backed away.

He paused. "Of course you'll need to exchange your—"

"Thank you again." I waved him off with a flustered flap of my hand so he wouldn't mention the ticket he was right about, that I'd have to exchange.

"Yes, ma'am." The conductor turned and disappeared.

"You said your husband had some—"

"Mrs. Strong, since you have more than those three bags…" Everett interrupted his friend yet again. "A trunk, did he say? I'll be happy to help with it." He gazed down at me with the same dark-eyed attention that had caused me to blurt out, "Larned, Kansas," to begin with.

"No need. I can manage these, and my trunk is light." My neck warmed at the mention of my nearly empty trunk.

"I imagine the pullman will unload it, but I'll help you afterwards," Everett said in spite of my protest. "The conductor and the porter will be busy with the passengers who get off only to stretch their legs, getting everyone back on again before the train leaves."

"You mean none of the people getting off will stay in Larned?" I glanced at the window and through the spot I'd cleared. Passengers collected on the platform in a huddle, while others—likely Larned citizens, in clothing as brown as the town—stood off to the side. They were like oil and water, the East unable to blend with the West. Larned would never be more than a small dot on the map if things stayed that way.

"That's right, ma'am. None will stay. So again, about your husband's…" Whatever Everett's friend started to say, Everett cut short by a look. The slighter man stiffened as Everett did, a flash of silver at his wrist…at both wrists where he and Everett stood close.

I studied the man who'd given me this seat and his smaller well-dressed companion. They stood too near each other, the tall and strong next to the less tall and stout. The dark coat and hat next to the black and finely tailored suit. Weathered attentiveness next to smooth detachment.

I swallowed. One had to be a lawman. Likely the one with the observant eye…probably keen enough to spot a liar. "Please, take your seat." I swung my arm at the empty space, knowing now why they needed only one. "And thank you again. I'll be on my way."

"We'll see you settled first, ma'am." Everett twisted to let me pass, a shift which moved his partner with him.

"You really don't need to trouble yourself... selves."

"I've never seen a woman travel light." A movement and an invisible clink followed the smaller man's remark. "I meant that as a tribute, ma'am, to whatever brief work you've come to try and finish. Rudy's my name, by the way. Rudy Walters. At your service."

I focused on what I could see of his face instead of where silver might gleam. "I'm pleased to meet you, and I do travel light because my purpose is purely business, so if you'll both excuse me." I brushed past them, waving over my shoulder as I hurried toward the car's doorway.

"I told you that you should let her be," Everett's companion muttered as I hurried away. "Not sure why you singled her out to begin with. Her tears? Crying's normal at a train station. Unless she's someone special..."

Special? I'd never seen or heard of Everett McCloud before now. The man was just plain nosy, the way he'd stood off to the side and watched me and others board the train.

"Any woman who travels alone bears helping." Everett sounded curt, whereas when he'd spotted my red nose and watery eyes, his mannerisms had been nothing but gentle.

I slowed. I paused behind a brief entanglement of children and parents blocking the doorway and glanced back. Mr. McCloud might be nosy, but he had a heart. Maybe he had been watching for someone special just as I was headed for someone special, each of us too embarrassed to admit the truth of our situations. When his someone didn't board, he'd interfered with me instead. Meddlesome...though Everett did carry some of the characteristics I'd envisioned in Jim. I studied him—attentive, quietly kind, tall and comfortable in rugged attire, weathered skin, and brown hair above even darker brown eyes. The same way Jim had described himself. Plus everything I'd imagined.

No photographs of any type, please. Is that all right?

If only I'd argued that, I wouldn't be in Kansas in search of a man who might look like every other man out here, including Mr. McCloud.

Just words, that is how we will truly get to know one another.

I pondered the image Jim had built with his words. The one Mama called my open door—something similar to the man who now gazed back at me.

The family finally moved forward, and I hurried behind them to the car's door, where they disembarked and I paused. I gazed at the two cultures below—the sharper styles and colors of the East, and Larned's sparser earthy tones—buffeted by blowing dust on the platform. Jim had said brown. And he'd said wind. He'd also said, *Don't come. I can't marry you.* Well, I was coming anyway, and brown, wind, a nosy Everett, or his fresh prisoner wouldn't stand in my way.

Chapter 3

"The conductor tells me you will get off here instead of down the line?" The porter stretched his hand up to take mine.

"He did?"

"He did. And I'll unload your trunk…if you're sure."

I gazed down at the same look the conductor had given me. I was sure of only one thing—I had to get on the next train. "Yes, please unload my trunk. And how do I change my ticket?" I followed the porter's nod to a barred window on the outer wall of the depot. A shiny head gleamed from the inside. A man of age, his head like a warm beacon, a promise of diligence and a sunnier tomorrow. "Thank you. This should be simple enough."

The porter snorted as he glanced at the beacon bent over his tasks. "Just call him Mr. Weston when you talk to him."

I studied Mr. Weston, his efficiency, the line of people in front of his bobbing head. Strange, wide-brimmed bonnets slapped shut on Larned's women's faces between him and me, while durable-looking skirts and jackets flapped wildly in the wind.

I knotted my fingers around my bags' handles and cut through styles and fabrics foreign to me, singular designs without frills, vogues I'd never seen but had come west to be a part of. This wasn't a culture in the way I thought of St. Louis. This seemed more an environment, buildings and people fitted to what the land and weather dealt them in order to survive—square and rectangular wooden structures which housed sturdy people clad in heavy fabrics. All except for one...

I glanced as I passed one man who stood tall amongst Larned's few, his outfit a bold and expensive black—an almost wealthy sort of St. Louis black—which cut a slender hole through the drab of the plains. I looked from what he wore to his face, handsome in spite of its disgruntled twist of good features beneath the brim of the high hat he clapped to the top of his head. Gold flashed as the wind whipped his jacket, a lightning of buttons and chains in a storm of black clothing, dark eyes, and even darker hair.

He bordered on the sort of man and finery I'd grown up around, whereas the woman he frowned down upon depicted Larned—plain, faded clothing, wisps of blonde hair in a frantic escape beneath her extraordinarily large bonnet. Maybe these two were the bridge, the blend...albeit a seemingly unhappy blend...of West and almost East.

"Ma'am, I assume someone is to meet you here?"

"Certainly not. I mean, yes. Of course." I tried not to redden as the porter set my trunk at my feet. "Why do you ask?"

"Well, your change of plans..." He wiped his brow.

I glanced at the train's cars and counted the darkened windows to the one I regretted clearing a peephole through, in case someone else happened to be there wondering the same thing.

"The change couldn't be helped. I must be flexible as I tend to my late husband's business affairs." I extracted my coin purse and laid a few cents in his hand. The porter went his way, he and the conductor creating a duet as they called passengers to the next destination west. I looked at my train as it prepared to leave me behind, then at Mr. Weston, who stared through his bars across the platform while his fingers thrummed with nothing to do. I squeezed my coin purse, now a few cents lighter, and dropped it back into its bag. Changing my ticket wouldn't cost extra, especially for a train that should be right behind this one.

"I told you he wouldn't be here." A man spoke from behind me as I secured my hat and skirt against the wind and headed toward the ticket window. "You've wasted your time and mine." The man spoke again. "The train is ready to leave. We've seen everyone, and we need to go." He sounded impatient.

I glanced back and spotted the same man as before, the one in black, quite tall and extraordinarily handsome as he bent over the slight and worried woman who fixed her stare on my train with a demand it give up one more passenger.

"He'll come." She set her lips in a line, an unsteady line from what I could see. "He promised."

I paused and glanced at the train. I'd been in too much of a hurry...a fury more like it...to have noticed another man. A man who'd made a promise...and then didn't keep it. Who hadn't finished what he'd started...but left her with the hope that he would. I was watching for such a man, one she and I both needed, one we could trust, when Tall-and-Sturdy appeared in the train's doorway, Rudy squeezed at his side. Everett's boots hit the wooden platform. Drat.

What I needed at the moment was a local businessman, someone I could pretend I'd planned to meet, so Everett would get back on the train. Voices swirled with the wind as I searched around the depot, hearing the woman's whimper, the tall man's insistence, then Jim's warm attentiveness in Everett's footsteps as he neared.

I want you to be all right. I want you to be happy, safe, and taken care of. It's what a man does for his wife.

The train blew a warning, yet Everett continued toward me…he and Rudy…in a march to Jim's words.

I want you to be all right.

"We need to go, Miss Sanders. Your brother clearly wasn't on this train…just like he wasn't on any of the others we've stood here and watched. If he'd found gold, he'd have been back by now and caught up on his payments, though even at that… Well, you know the predicament the town is in. In any case, he's either had a stroke of bad luck…or something else has happened. I hope not, but this long without a word… I'm sorry. His default is more than the bank can carry and far more than you've been able to meet in his absence. There's paperwork to sign. Possibly a blessing your brother isn't here for the final dissolution of his restaurant." The tall man spoke, and the woman beside him gasped. I gasped with her at the loss of her brother, my fiancé, our footing under a dishonest uncle or burdens of paperwork which left us baffled and overwhelmed about a business which wasn't even our own.

"Phillip wouldn't do that." Her voice wavered. "He wouldn't just leave me this way, and I refuse to believe something happened to him. There's one more train. Surely he's…"

One more train…possibly headed west. I had no idea where her brother might have gone to search for gold, but he could be on his way here. Then I would board his train and go. While Everett came faster. Drat.

"Excuse me." I whirled to the handsome face above the pinched and worried one. "Excuse me," I said again, loud enough other heads began to turn. "I believe it is you I'm looking for. I'm here to complete a business arrangement initiated by Mr. Phillip Sanders for his restaurant. I'm Mrs. Penelope Strong."

They hadn't expected a woman. The tall man expected no one, while the modest woman at his side expected her brother. Time was of the essence, but that man's impatience and her dire need lit all too familiar flames inside of me that I could dowse while I rid myself of Mr. McCloud at the same time. I left my trunk and kicked against billowing skirts until I stood in front of dark eyes that looked down at me, and sallow blue ones which looked up.

"Again, I'm Mrs. Penelope Strong." I offered the woman my hand. "I'm here on behalf of Mr. Phillip Sanders and my late husband…" I stopped. My fictitious husband needed a first name. Drat. Living husbands had better be a lot less trouble than dead ones. "Alex. Mr. Alex Strong."

"I beg your pardon, Mrs. Strong." The tall man stretched taller. I stretched with him, my St. Louis style in the face of his almost East. "I'd say there's been a mistake."

Footsteps stopped behind me, boots I prayed belonged to Everett and not to Phillip. His sister nodded at whoever stood at my back, her attention on me instead of them. Not her brother, thank God.

"There's been no mistake." I looked at the tall, handsome man who would likely be as happy as I would for me to be on my way. "I have business with Phillip's sister, if you'll excuse us."

"If you have business which pertains to their restaurant, then your business is with me. I'm Nicholas Brandt, their banker. And I doubt very much that you or anyone else is able to cover the amount their restaurant owes in back payments."

Cover back payments? I knotted the handles of my bags and considered the small amount of money I carried. Mama had insisted I should bring more—more clothing and more money—wages I had earned in Papa's store but had spent to stay two steps ahead of her conniving brother and his attorney without her knowledge. I'd brought a bit more than enough to get to Jim, the man who'd said he wanted me to be all right. He would take care of me once I got there. I glanced at Phillip's sister as I twisted the handles tighter. Her desperate hope that her help had finally come hinged on me.

The shuffle of two sets of boots—Everett's and Rudy's, evidently—trapped me between the lie that got me here in the first place and whatever truth I'd have to make it to get me out.

I squared myself in front of Nicholas Brandt, his imposing height, the hand which capped his hat, the gold which flashed with every flap of his jacket. He dressed the way a gentleman would, wore money and power that possibly needed to be shared.

I turned to the small woman at Nicholas's side. "Your brother contacted my husband before Alex passed. Phillip believed the mine he currently worked would make good, but he knew payments were due on the restaurant that couldn't wait, so he sought for an investor and eventually connected with Alex."

"A good mine? And where would that be?" Nicholas blustered over the gasp of, "Phil's all right," which gushed from Phillip's sister.

"Your brother claimed to be fine, last I heard," I lied to the face that begged to hear it. My mouth dried. My goodness. Uncle Roy was the liar in my family, not me. He behaved like a scallywag, I didn't. I loosened my fingers from around my bags' handles. I could spare a little money. I could make a payment on Miss Sanders' restaurant if she needed it, before I boarded the next train west.

"I presume these are your late husband's business partners." Everett stepped forward, a lawman far too close to the near fraud I contemplated.

"Yes." I cleared the croak from my throat. "This is one of his...my...partners." I indicated Miss Sanders. Her grateful gaze beamed up at me as if I were a god. "And that is her banker." I tipped my head Nicholas's direction, a more speculative than adoring expression on his face.

"We've met." Everett nodded at Mr. Brandt, who gave him a cursory dip of the head in return, then at Miss Sanders. "Ma'am."

Her face colored, a rosy flush compared to Mr. Brandt's deepening bronze. She fidgeted, causing a handkerchief wound around her extraordinarily long fingers to come loose and flutter toward the ground. "Oops."

Wrinkled white caught a draft which swept it downward. We all did nothing but watch until a hand snatched it out of the air.

"Hate to see a lovely lady without aid," Rudy said as he smoothed the rescued handkerchief on his thigh, then handed it to her. He did it so well, so efficiently with only one hand, that the silver chain which bound his other to Everett never showed. "Rudy Walters is the name, ma'am," he said with far more warmth and attention than I would have imagined from him.

"Thank you." She took the handkerchief. "I'm Lizzy Sanders, and I really do thank you." Her color rose more, a blush which brought out attractiveness her pale worry had hidden. Lizzy had to be close to my age, another woman in need of an open door, a man other than her brother. Not the likes of the prisoner chained to Everett, though. He shouldn't be her open door, and I'd make sure she didn't open hers to him.

"Oops." I let go of one of my bags, sent it to the ground with an imperceptible flip aimed toward Rudy, but not close enough he could snatch it easily. He bent to where it hit the platform, stretched enough that silver flashed between him and Everett. I stared at the chain. Stared with an exaggerated gawk Lizzy couldn't miss.

"Can't dust it off for you, Mrs. Strong. It's a bit bulky." Rudy handed my bag to me with his free hand, then raised the one handcuffed to Everett's wrist. "Protective custody."

I glanced from Rudy to Everett. Protective custody had to be different from being escorted as a criminal. Maybe I'd misinterpreted his earlier detachment.

"You're a marshal…" I said to Everett. "And you're…"

"Probably not the evidence the law hopes," Rudy said.

"I presume you'll make sure Mrs. Strong is well taken care of, Mr. Brandt." Everett spoke the same moment the train's whistle blew. The station's platform lay nearly empty. I wanted to join those passengers. I wanted to slap money in Lizzy's hand and say my late husband had other urgent business down the line. Mr. Weston's shiny head bent over paperwork his hands sorted, every reason to hold this train in town on its way to a drawer.

"Well, quite honestly, Marshal," Mr. Brandt spouted behind me, "I've never heard of a Mister…" My fake husband's name became lost beneath the locomotive's belch of steam.

I should finish what the banker had started to say, admit I was a fraud before any money exchanged hands and I ended up handcuffed to Everett's other wrist. I could apologize and dart for the train. My heart built up steam along with the engine. I eyed my trunk in the middle of the platform as someone closed the doors where the baggage belonged.

I cast a desperate glance behind me, caught the serious faces of the banker and the marshal, the sparkle which brightened Lizzy's. Drat. "I want to thank you before you go," I muttered to Everett and Rudy as I swallowed the truth which would dowse Lizzy's light. "You were kind to lend me your seat on the train, and the sacrifice is much appreciated. I hope no one has taken it while you've been detained."

Everett didn't look at the train.

He looked at me, and I at him. I felt the gaze that

lingered the way it had in St. Louis, a look which said what Jim had written with the voice I'd come to believe would be my husband's—*I want you to be all right.*

I heard the sentiment again as Everett bid Lizzy goodbye and parted with a look at Mr. Brandt. I watched him go, Everett and the mismatched shadow at his side, until they boarded the train. My train. The one I'd chosen to take me to my husband.

Chapter 4

Tiny print crowded the contract Phillip had with the bank, letters and words crammed far too close together. Pages of financial gibberish which had consumed too much of the five hours I had before the last westbound train arrived...and went. Along with my ticket the uncooperative Mr. Weston had barely let me exchange. The next train after that one wouldn't be here for two days, and I refused to wrangle another ticket from that man. My head throbbed from the near shouts Mr. Weston and I had exchanged, and the too teeny print framed by the too shiny sheen of Mr. Brandt's desk.

Miss Sanders' banker settled back in his chair, his handsome features relaxed into the same expression my uncle's banker and attorney used to wear—an expectation that the paperwork had been too much for me. The corner of Mr. Brandt's mouth twitched upward as he waited for me to shove the contract back across his polished desktop and declare I couldn't make sense of it. But I could. I'd deciphered longer documents under worse lighting when my St. Louis attorney allowed me to take my uncle's attorney's verbose concoctions home to read late into the night after Mama had gone to bed.

I glanced at Mr. Brandt's barely concealed smirk. He couldn't possibly know my Jim. One moment of not being naïve and uninformed shouldn't get back to him. "What the bank has done to Mr. Sanders and his sister is unethical. Surely you knew that." I laid a hand on the top page of repetitious words, incalculable numbers, and hidden dollar signs.

Miss Sanders straightened at my side while Mr. Brandt glanced to his open office door, which faced the bank's ornate lobby.

"It is not unethical, Mrs. Strong." He leaned close and spoke low. "I don't do unethical. This is the sort of financing necessary for a business at risk."

"It's the sort of financing that creates risk, Mr. Brandt, and I won't offer assistance on anything which employs such tactics. Draw up new paperwork, something reasonable, so I can help Phillip Sanders as my late husband intended." The office grew quiet. So did the lobby behind Miss Sanders and me.

"I can't create new paperwork without Phillip's approval, or proof that you are who you claim to be," Mr. Brandt finally said. "I told you as much at the station." He had indeed told me as much, with a bluster of pomp and surety the moment the train's doors closed behind Everett, the man who had told Mr. Brandt to take care of me.

"And as I said before, I consider my late husband's money plenty of proof of who I am and why I'm here. Unless Larned happens to be a town frequently victimized by widows who try to lend aid to struggling businesses."

He frowned. More of a scowl his good looks and finery didn't hide. Bankers understood money. I'd learned that the hard way in St. Louis. And saw it again when I'd waved my fictitious husband's fictitious money under Mr. Brandt's nose at the depot. Enough to get me here so I could legitimize my lie...sort of...and leave town. I stole a glance around his office, ignored a cluster of framed oils and certificates, until I spotted a clock. Three more hours; then I would go.

"I need Phillip's signature." He sat straight in his chair, his fingertips poised as if to thrum. "Do you have anything besides your late husband's money to prove Mr. Sanders approves of this?"

"Of course I do." A warm mist formed around my collar.

Mr. Brandt frowned even more. "Can I see it?"

"Everything is locked up in a bank back home. I assumed you had copies. That's why I treated your requests for proof so blithely. Have you lost them?"

"Lost them?" Mr. Brandt sputtered. "I assure you, Mrs. Strong, the bank loses nothing."

"Except customers, apparently. Especially ones ready to pay." I grabbed at the excuse I needed, the chance for a delay, and rose to my feet, happy to skip back to the station and wait for my train. "I'm sorry we'll be forced to postpone this transaction while we wait for my late husband's bank to forward papers to me," I said. "Of course I won't stay in Larned while we do. I have other businesses in line for Mr. Strong's support. When I receive the documents, assuming I have sufficient funds left over, I'll return to help...this restaurant..." I glanced down at Miss Sanders. A real widow on her real late husband's business would know the name of the establishment they supported. "I'm sorry, I've forgotten the name of your restaurant in all the confusion."

"Eat Here."

I had to smile at a woman clearly as clever as I was and mouthed a private thanks for the levity she offered such a strained moment. "I mean the real name."

"It's called Eat Here."

My jaw nearly dropped. Miss Sanders hadn't made a jest. "Of course. How could I forget..." If there had been a real Mr. Strong and contract with Phillip, I would have insisted it include a name change for the restaurant. I turned to Mr. Brandt. "As I started to say, I'll return to Larned if I have any of the investment funds left over to help Eat Here. In the meantime, I assume you'll write up an agreement of delay to give Miss Sanders a reprieve—a no-interest reprieve—from more payments, since your bank's negligence caused this problem."

I'd left my trunk at the station under the supervision of Mr. Weston, who'd basically robbed me of a full day's storage fee to do nothing more than let it sit outside his window for five hours. I'd demand a refund since it would have been there only a fraction of a day. No wonder the man needed bars between him and the public.

"See here, Mrs. Strong..." Nicholas Brandt rose. "This is the first our bank has heard of an agreement between Phillip and your late husband, so we can't be expected to have the paperwork. And we can't afford to be hasty or careless about funding, here in the West, since we don't have the backing needed to take risks. Not to mention, things here likely take more time than you're accustomed to. Much different than where you're from. Which, by the way, would be..."

Everett knew where I'd boarded the train. If I said anything other than St. Louis, I'd be exposed as a liar if

Everett ever returned to Larned and spoke to this man about me. But to tell the truth would make it easy for Mr. Brandt to discover no bank in St. Louis had Phillip's fictitious paperwork or had ever heard of the Strongs.

I glanced at Miss Sanders, at the light I'd given birth to that waxed desperate in her eyes. A light built on a lie which would make Mama faint and Papa turn in his grave. The truth would be death to that light, especially if it came from someone else. "I'm from the East, and you're right. Finances move at an easy speed in a system large cities understand. However, my husband still practiced caution. He believed in diversity and housed his investments at more than one institution in cities scattered far from each other and far from here. So I will need time to contact each bank to see which one has the Sanders' paperwork."

"Your late husband sounds to have been savvy." Nicholas Brandt's expression changed, a fixed study of me in the place of his glower. "Like everyone else out here, I come from a family of homesteaders. A primitive lifestyle there seems no easy way out of. That's why I chose banking."

I heard slight admiration in what he spoke, and saw curiosity in his study of me, how I stood and what I wore. He took in everything I had and what I'd claimed Alex Strong had been. Mr. Brandt appreciated savvy. Savvy that would take the homesteader out of his gait and ancestry, and money from somewhere to put it somewhere else.

"So the health of Larned depends on your bank, then." I took a slower look at his well decorated office while recalling the lavish décor of the bank's lobby.

Then thought of what we'd passed on our way here— the strand of paintless buildings which lined the town's one street of businesses, its few houses, single church, and small school. "And I assume it's your intention to use your institution to boost this town?"

"Precisely." Mr. Brandt nodded.

"Then it seems to me a clean contract is the way to begin. Such as for Miss Sanders."

One brow arched on Mr. Brandt's face while the other dove low. I'd seen this look before on my uncle and his banker. If Nicholas Brandt did refuse me and my suggestion, I could go catch my train. Which would leave poor Miss Sanders in the same predicament as when I first saw her. Drat.

"Alex always said a clean contract is the way to solid business. He'd also likely say since you have very few connections with other banks out here, your institution's health depends on Larned as much as it depends on you. If all of the money is in your pocket...or theirs...then it's like trying to get rich when you work for someone else. It's lopsided, and the town as a whole can't benefit. My late husband would applaud any intent on your part to avoid that, Mr. Brandt."

Miss Sanders' banker bent and scraped the contract from in front of me. He shuffled and reshuffled its pages. "I appreciate your husband's opinion, Mrs. Strong." He straightened the sheets and tapped them on his desk. "But as I said, we're isolated and slow here. All of the West is, which calls for unique strategies evidently foreign to your husband...and you." The contract quieted in his hands. "That said, forgive us our ignorance of what Phillip intended to do, and for not having his paperwork."

"Forgiven. I'm glad at least we both agree Larned can change and grow." I said it like a pat on his back.

"We do agree on that." Mr. Brandt straightened and gestured toward my seat. "Please, you've traveled long to be here, and you have much more of it to do. Sit. I'll speak to someone and see if interim paperwork is in any way possible. As close to the speed you're accustomed to as I can."

The only speed that mattered to me was getting to the station on time. I settled into my chair and glanced at Miss Sanders to see if she understood, as her banker whisked from his office. The baffled and lost expression I'd seen at the depot surfaced. She had to understand. It was imperative she grasped the terms of whatever new agreement Mr. Brandt drew up, at least until her brother returned. "Miss Sanders…"

"Please call me Lizzy." She looked at me. "It's short for Elizabeth."

Elizabeth…my middle name. Louise Elizabeth Archer gazed at Elizabeth Sanders, at the baffled look common to women who were washed here and there by waves someone else caused. I wanted to assure her I understood. Save her time and money she didn't have by sharing everything I'd learned before I left. "Tell me about yourself, Lizzy," I said instead…to Elizabeth.

"There's not a lot to say." She fidgeted. I followed her hands, the knots she twisted her long fingers into. "My family has been around here for years, but my parents are gone now. Both died and left the restaurant to me, my three sisters, and Phillip. My sisters were all married by then and had lives and families of their own. None of them wanted anything to do with Eat Here. But

Phillip did."

"And you?"

She gazed around Mr. Brandt's office, passed over the hat and coat rack, the extra padded chair alongside a small table in the corner, furnishings she'd likely seen too many times lately. "Phil couldn't seem to make it work, but he tried. Our parents struggled, but he struggled more. Money came harder instead of easier. He finally asked me if I could help." She looked down at her fingers. "I came up with enough to hold onto Eat Here and keep it open while he went in search of gold."

Lizzy was like me—a bride wedded to her family business. "Your brother meant right..." Some sort of right. Not enough that the thought of a well deserved smack for leaving his sister this way didn't sound more right. I tapped a finger on Mr. Brandt's desk. "Phillip ever mine before?"

Lizzy shook her head.

I couldn't smack him because he knew nothing about mines before he went. I knew nothing about restaurants, other than how to eat in one. "Has he contacted you since he left?"

"Once, early on. Seems he's been better at contacting you...I mean, your late husband." Her face brightened. "That's a way of contacting me, isn't it, Mrs. Strong?"

"Please, call me Penelope." I bit my lip as she brightened more. I should have kept the formality between us. The distance would make the truth about me and her brother easier to bear when I left. Drat, drat, and drat.

Footsteps clicked as Mr. Brandt re-entered and stepped around his desk. He sat and slid new paperwork to me, pen and ink along with it. "The bank's original contract with Phillip for a risky business wasn't wrong, but in faith that you will provide proof of his permission, we've agreed to a small revision in the interim. This paperwork outlines the default payments you will catch up when confirmation is received from Phillip."

Payments I will catch up? I stared at the new paperwork, swallowed at the large dollar amount at the bottom. I squeezed the bags on my lap. Managing to outsmart, out plan, and outthink Mr. Brandt enough for me to catch my train could cost me money. I glanced at Lizzy. I could sign this, hand Mr. Brandt a little money, and leave with the promise my deceased husband's bank would contact me when paperwork that didn't even exist had been located. She smiled at the new contract, a woman who needed a wedding more than she needed my fake signature.

"I will read this first," I said to Mr. Brandt. "And if everything is acceptable, I will sign it, then be on my way." I could share some of my wedding gift for Jim with Lizzy, a portion of the little money I'd left behind in my account, the rest of it gone to my attorney to make sure Papa's business remained safe while I headed west.

Mr. Brandt smiled, handsomeness restored to his face. "You won't be able to sign it here, Mrs. Strong. This new agreement requires a thorough inspection of Eat Here by you. You will see a number of items that must meet with your approval or at least be acknowledged for the condition they're in. After that you can sign if you are still willing. Then I and the bank president will sign as well."

"The president?"

"Unconventional paperwork." Mr. Brandt nodded at the pages in front of me. "As you noted before, we're new at this. Most businesses in Larned haven't had this second chance. And since we have no outside support and are finding our own position tenuous, if this doesn't work, we won't allow this for other businesses. We just couldn't afford to."

My goodness. The whole town lay in my hands. Hands that couldn't hold Mr. Brandt's paperwork steady if I picked it up. "I have a train to catch…"

"You can go, of course. You're a busy and heavily taxed woman, so we would understand if you did. Of course, the original contract would stand, in that case. Otherwise an inspection of Eat Here is mandatory to sign this new form. It protects your assets and us…and will take longer than you probably imagine. After that the bank president"—Mr. Brandt fished his fob from his vest pocket—"who I'm afraid has gone now, will sign the agreement. Sometime late tomorrow when he gets back into town."

Chapter 5

"This is it, Mrs. Str...I mean, Penelope." Lizzy blushed at the use of my first name. "This is Eat Here."

Two days. The next train wouldn't arrive for two days. What could I possibly do with myself until then? I followed Lizzy's proud wave at her brother's restaurant as warm wind shoved against us, the town's main street a wooden funnel which added power to its heated blast. I leaned into a post and gazed at the two-story building I had agreed to inspect, squeezing my newest train ticket. Larned's gruff Mr. Weston had tried to charge me for it, the bald miser sending me off with a promise there'd be no more generosity. At least in two days I'd see the last of him.

"It used to say 'Eat Here' above the door, but it's barely visible now." Lizzy pointed at bare boards buffed to a near sheen by dirt and wind.

I squinted at them, searched for flecks of color, remnants of paint lost in the grooves. "Well, that can be remedied." With a new name to go along with new paint. I'd leave several suggestions behind. The door beneath the blank sign looked the same—bare wood— flanked at each side by two large front windows where several glows shone from within, faint round circles of light which twinkled through the glass.

"Well, you didn't tell me Eat Here was a fine dining establishment. I can see your candles from out here. Tasteful. I'm pleased to see that." I drank in the elegance which reminded me of home.

"We don't use candles." Lizzy frowned. "We have regular lamps."

I squinted at the fuzzy glows. "You need brighter ones then. Or maybe more of them."

"We have plenty. You just can't see them very well because there's so much grease on the windows."

"Grease? Why ever would you grease the windows? Because of the dust and wind? To keep dirt from contaminating the food?"

"Oh, we don't grease them. They're like that because Cook fries everything. He even adds a dollop of lard to the coffee."

I dropped my bags to the boardwalk and clapped both hands over my mouth. "Lard?" I asked between my fingers. "In coffee?" I squinted at the fragmented light that shone in distorted webs through the greasy film.

"You'll get used to it. Let's go in. There's a room above the restaurant you can stay in." Lizzy stepped to the door.

"Stay in?" I gazed up to the single window above the door.

"It's only right the new boss...almost owner...of Eat Here has that room. Come on in. Everyone will want to meet you."

"I'm not the boss and certainly not the owner. I just..." Lard-laden air hit my lungs as the door swung wide. I stumbled off the boardwalk and into the street, staggering backward as I peered into the haze at propped-up tables and crooked chairs.

Lizzy tilted her head to the side as she eyed me

from the doorway. "You look ill. Are you all right?"

"I'm fine," I lied. Again. "Just a little caught by surprise, that's all."

"By surprise? Because of Eat Here? Didn't my brother describe it to you...I mean, to your late husband?"

Drat. I looked again at what I could see through the door. "I'm sure he did. Forgive me. All this travel...and confusion..."

Lizzy smiled as she held the door. "Of course. Come in and relax. Meet Cook and Tina. Les might be here too."

"I'd love to, but I'll have my things taken to an inn, if it's all the same to you." I tipped my head toward my dropped bags and the trunk Mr. Weston had charged me to deliver, all of them far too close to the cloud of fat which rolled out the restaurant door. "It wouldn't be right to inconvenience your staff with a stranger living in the building. Maybe they could meet me out here before I go and get settled."

"Nonsense, the inn isn't doing well, just like every other business in town, and it's not open most of the time. But even if it was, you should stay upstairs since you're a part of us now. It needs to be cleaned up a little, but it's nice."

I pondered her interpretation of the word nice and the way the West defined other words like brown and wind. "Maybe they could meet me right inside the door. We could leave it open while we talk."

"We can't leave the front door open. Flies love it in there. Cook says they're his best customers. They don't complain, and it has nothing to do with the pistol he carries."

43

I gaped. Mama would faint at my unladylike behavior...if my lies didn't do her in first. I glanced through the dark doorway, to the sea of grease which waited inside. Being caught up on its payments wouldn't be enough for Eat Here. This restaurant needed to be civilized, not to mention scrubbed and repaired, and its armed cook dismissed. And I needed to get on the next train and find the man meant to be my real husband before my deceased one emptied my pocketbook.

Lizzy leaned through the door and shouted into the greasy dark. A boy no bigger than a stick appeared, too thin to be a customer since lard seemed to be Eat Here's main fare. Lizzy pointed to my trunk. With a grin no bigger than his arms and legs, he bent and dragged it into the building. I gasped as my few possessions—my wedding gown, Jim's album of letters, everything I had of him—disappeared through the restaurant's door and skidded across a wooden floor.

"That was Les," Lizzy said.

"The name suits him."

"Come on in. You can go up and see your room. I'll be up in a second after I tell Tina and Cook who you are and that we're to meet."

I set a toe inside, checked the floor with my boot, and drew it back when it nearly slipped out from under me.

"I can help you until you get used to the slick floor." Lizzy smiled. "I think our shoes gather a cake of street dust with this grease. The combination keeps us steady on our feet."

"That's all right. You go on. I'll be fine." I braced myself in the doorway once she disappeared inside, pressed both hands at its sides as I slid in, and scooted to a table. With a grip on each piece of furniture as I passed, I skated from rickety table to rickety chair until I found the shiny steps. Even the banister had a luster, making it useless as I crawled up the stairs to a small landing in front of another plain door. With one hand around the door's knob, I hoisted myself up and opened it to dim light and a stuffy room. I squinted, then screeched as a grin and a set of eyes manifested.

"Got yer trunk up here for ya."

I hammered my chest until I caught my breath as smudges and brown hair became visible. "Thank you, Les."

The trunk came into view within the four walls, along with a small table next to a cot, a wall shelf, and the single window I'd seen from the outside. Sunlight cast a pasty glow through its caked glass. The room made me want to cry. My St. Louis bedroom had been nothing like this...four windows so clean the glass seemed invisible. Jim said he had built his home with windows on every wall so light could shine in and make every room warm and cozy. And clean. I scraped a toe across the floorboards. Just as slick as below. Even the quilt on the bed looked stiff and had an unusual luster for fabric. Les dangled nearby, a gangly stretch of smile and dance in his eyes. I fished in one of my bags for a coin. "Thank you again."

He scampered off, lithe and adept on the oil. Southwestern Kansas wouldn't be this bad...surely.

"Penelope?" Lizzy stood in my doorway, she and another young woman who could have been her sister. "This is Tina Cole. She works here a lot to make up for Phil being gone."

Tina's dress looked plain in the dim light, or maybe faded...or maybe just covered with lard like everything else. Her hair was light brown, but loose and unkempt the same way Lizzy kept hers. Her face bore a simple expression...though inexplicably happy.

"I'm pleased to meet you, Tina."

"I'm happy to meet you too, ma'am. I hope you like living here."

"Oh, I don't intend to..."

A curse bellowed from below, a vile vulgarity which vibrated the floor.

"That's Cook," Lizzy explained to my horrified gape as Tina giggled.

"Your cook speaks that way? Thank God no customers were downstairs. I'd hate for them to be exposed to that."

"Oh, they're used to it."

"You may think they are, but I'd venture they want nothing to do with such...such...outbursts. The restaurant was empty, after all. Or are you closed? I didn't notice a sign with your hours out front."

"We don't have set hours. People generally show up around dawn, and we close at night when the last one leaves. We do the same thing every day."

"You what? Surely you don't mean every day. What about Sunday?"

"Sunday's the same."

"Sunday's for church. It's supposed to be a day of..." Repentance. For lies, for a lack of trust that God would open doors as Mama claimed, instead of forcing them open yourself. "You need to set some hours. And you should be closed on Sundays. For church."

"There's only that one church I pointed out to

you." Lizzy waved toward the window. "It's a Presbyterian church, and no new preacher's come yet. Local folks take turns preaching, but most don't like to, so Mr. Simpson has taken over. He says the same thing every Sunday, so folks stopped going. Most everyone comes to Eat Here or just stays home."

I imagined the downstairs, where people would gather, and thought of the vile oath I'd just heard. "That won't do. And no matter what day it is, never is it acceptable for people to hear"—I waved an arm toward the doorway—"the sort of ruckus we just heard. No, you need to put a stop to that, Lizzy. That won't do at all."

"That ruckus is just Cook's way." Tina blushed. She glowed when she said it, a patina that had nothing to do with a building full of grease. I winced at a twinkle which should be in no respectable woman's eyes for the likes of what I'd just heard from below. I may have behaved like a desperate spinster back home and flaunted Jim and his letters, but at least Jim had the essence of a decent man. Decent enough to not rail obscenities in front of women and a child.

"I think it's time to meet the cook," I said. Eat Here—maybe especially Tina—seemed in dire need of standards. Not to mention set hours. And a good scrubbing. My two empty days were beginning to look pretty full. "Put a Closed sign in the front window and ask your cook to meet us in the dining area. We'll sit close to the door and leave it open just a little."

"We don't have a Closed sign."

"No Closed sign? Because you don't have set hours?"

"No," Tina said, "because most people around here

can't read."

I stared at her. Then at Lizzy. "Can you two read?"

"Oh, we can read, but we're amongst the few. Lizzy taught me. She can read all sorts of things. She can even—"

"My mother taught me," Lizzy interrupted Tina's praise. "And as for closing, we just turn out the lights. Then when we're open, we turn them on again."

A major railway and the move of civilization westward hadn't done a thing for Larned. "Get the cook, shut off all but one light, and lock the front door. We'll meet in front of a window."

"Oh, we don't..."

I raised a hand. "You don't have a lock..." I couldn't sleep in a place with no lock. "Lizzy, I have two assignments for you today. One, make Open and Closed signs. And put pictures below the words. And second, you need a lock for the door. Two locks if you have two doors. Make that three. One on this room...in case you ever need it in the future."

"I can ask Ben Holt at the mercantile for a lock, but I've never seen one there." Lizzy frowned at Tina.

"Most people carry a gun or have a dog," Tina said. "We have Cook." She blushed again, utterly unacceptable for the likes of what I expected to encounter downstairs. From the sound of the brash sizzling and the slam of iron against iron, I'd likely need a pistol myself when I told him he had to go. Naïve and uninformed would have to wait.

Chapter 6

"What's your cook's name?" I asked Lizzy from the top of the slick stairs she and Tina had just scurried down.

She cupped a hand at the side of her mouth as she looked where the kitchen must be, the direction Tina had disappeared with far too much enthusiasm. "Cook's his name," she whispered. "Phil hired him before he left, and he's not missed a day since."

Whatever agreement Phillip and the cook had made was about to be modified. I'd managed Uncle Roy. I could handle this man.

"Here he comes." Lizzy dropped her hand and straightened as a man better named Crook than Cook stepped to the bottom of the stairs. Tina followed behind his scrawny dishevelment, undaunted by his grizzled form.

"I don't know who you are," he groused up the steps at me, "but we ain't havin' no fool meetin'."

"From the lack of customers in here, I'd say you need one." I set a hand on the gummy rail and scooted a toe to the edge of the slippery landing. Three sets of eyes stared up at me...four as Les manifested again in the dim light behind them. "I'll be right there. Go ahead. Choose a sturdy table close to the window...by the door, preferably." If sturdy anything existed in here.

They didn't budge. I flapped a hand to shoo them.

"Oh, for Pete's sake." Cook spat on the floor. Goodness! Another hazard to avoid. Not to mention another sign to make, with a sketch of no spitting, since this buzzard likely couldn't read.

I grabbed the rail as Cook led them away, slid a foot to the first step, and bungled my way down. Giving the bubbly spittle a wide berth, I skated across the room to the door, cracked it open, and propped it that way with a chair. Then I shuffled to their table, which was not near enough to the thin slice of fresh air.

"Thank you all for meeting with me."

"This ain't no meetin'. Just say yer piece, then go." Crook...Cook...stood and flipped his chair backward, then straddled it. This sort of man belonged chained to Everett's wrist, though the layers of grease on his skin and clothing would likely allow him to slip right through any restraints. Rangy and of an indeterminable age, he glared by means of two black dots between wiry strands of hair and an overgrowth of whiskers that matched the dim hue of the dining area.

"I am Mrs. Penelope Strong," I addressed the others—Les barely visible, Lizzy's hopeful anticipation, and Tina's blush next to Cook. "And it's due to correspondence between Mr. Phillip Sanders and my late husband, Mr. Alex Strong, that I'm here to fulfill their investment wishes of..."

"Just say it in English." Cook stood to reposition. A flash of silver caught my eye, a gleam from the butt of a pistol his apron hitched over.

"Mr. Cook, you should..."

"Just Cook."

"To call yourself just Cook sounds..."

"Allegorical. I know. Just talk English for the

womenfolk and the boy. And hurry up about it. We got things to do."

I stared at a creature who understood the concept of allegorical when the rest of the town couldn't read the word Closed.

"I will refer to you as Mr. Cook." I ignored his snort, but the heated glare he gave me made Miller, as in the bug—fragile, flitting, here and gone quickly, or squashed—seem a more appropriate allegorical last name for me than Strong. I turned to the two women. The two Misses. Miss wouldn't be an address of honor to them. Not at their...our...age and stage of life. "I'll call you by your first names. And Les..." I gazed at the boy. "Mr. Les."

The boy wriggled and grinned, shouldered next to Mr. Cook, a pound of pride on his thin face.

"We're used to Miss Sanders and Miss Cole, if you prefer that," Lizzy said. "That's what Amber called us."

"Amber? Who's Amber? You have another employee?" I glanced around the dim room, listened and waited for another person to glide across the floor.

"Amber Wingate. Mr. Brandt appointed her manager of Eat Here when we missed the first payment after Phil left. She's his fiancée."

Manager? Fiancée? "Well, her services won't be needed once the new contract is signed. It designates Lizzy as the manager."

Lizzy blanched, the same way she had at the bank when the new contract attached "Manager" to her name.

"New contract? And what's this hot air about investin'?"

"It's not hot air." My neck warmed. "Due to a

financial commitment my late husband made with Phillip Sanders, the bank has written a new and better contract for Eat Here. One that should alleviate the debt once Eat Here passes my inspection…and some paperwork is found."

"Inspection? We ain't changin' nothin' for no inspection. And what paperwork?"

"Paperwork Mr. Brandt wants. Don't worry, I plan to take care of it." I wanted to fan my face. "In any case, apparently Amber wasn't very successful, or Mr. Brandt wouldn't have been so ready to close the doors on Eat Here," I added for Lizzy's sake.

"Miss Wingate succeeded." Cook landed all four legs of his chair on the floor.

"Nicholas Brandt would likely want her and everyone else to think she did a good job," I corrected him.

"Believe whatever you want, Mrs. Strong, but a good job don't always mean good out here."

Good…another altered meaning to add to brown and wind, and Lizzy's definition of nice.

I turned to Lizzy as I ignored Tina's admiration of Cook. "Have Amber speak with me if she comes in. She likely won't, now that you're to take over, but no need to make her feel badly since the truth is she clearly didn't do well."

"She did well as some call well." Cook didn't snort this time, but I wanted to.

"We can discuss this later if you want, Mr. Cook. All word wrangling aside, Eat Here will be under new management and rules." I paused at Lizzy's look of desperation, her glance toward the same door I couldn't wait to exit. "Lizzy no doubt has ideas about how Eat

Here is to be run." I looked at her, her face vacant of ideas. I'd been in her shoes. Louise Elizabeth Archer had suffered Elizabeth Sanders' terror at decisions which needed to be made for people who relied on her. "For starters, I imagine Lizzy will appoint each of you as a leader over your area. Such as Mr. Cook over the kitchen, Tina over table settings…"

A gasp interrupted me. Then a tentative nod as a look of gratitude settled on Lizzy's face. I smiled at what Cook studied through a narrowed eye. She could manage this. I would make sure she could before I left.

"Lizzy will decide what's best for each of your areas so you will know how to manage them in harmony with the others," I continued. "In the meantime, hours will be set, and rules will be written up." I eyed the grizzled glare across from me. "And a new menu with more palatable offerings will be developed. I'll take responsibility for that."

Cook's chair clattered to the floor. Silver flashed at eye level as he stood, then dropped forward on two knuckled fists which forced the table my way. I pushed back below its surface to hold it up.

"Eat Here will open at six a.m. and close at seven p.m. every day except Sunday. You will be closed that day." I looked at everyone except him.

"You can say we'll be closed, but we ain't. Things here will stay just as they are." The table strained against my hands as Cook leaned harder.

"Sunday is for church. There will be a sign in the window and a lock on the door."

Silence overtook the room, a quiet Cook could destroy with a single gunshot. I saw myself in his eyes, my body dragged out the door and left where no one would care. Jim would never know I'd come for him but been killed at gunpoint before I got there. Mama'd live in utter poverty when Uncle Roy claimed Papa's store. These four would open my trunk and find Louise Archer instead of Penelope Strong, Louise's unused wedding gown, letters which spoke of commitment, plus a telegram that denied it and left Louise jilted.

I glanced toward the door and spotted gray globes in a line outside the opaque windows. Phantoms with hands cupped at each side of their heads pressed against glass they tried to see through. They wanted in, and I wanted out. The same place Cook wanted me.

"Listen," I said to Lizzy more than any of them. She, most of all, had to survive after I left. I tipped my head toward Larned's faces on the other side of the windows. "They will adjust to your new schedule." I started to add, "And your new menu," but the hot breath across the table threatened I'd be shot if I did. "You need—and so do they—order. Cleanliness. A plan. Tell them you will be closed for two days." I would give Lizzy more than a mere bank inspection, a checkmark for every broken or filthy item I saw. She needed help. This restaurant needed fixed and cleaned, her staff enlightened and reduced by one. "Two days. We'll work hard and fast to give Eat Here a fresh start."

"We ain't doin' none of that." Cook snorted and straightened.

"This restaurant will be pristine," I said, glad for air without his fumes. "Everything will be scrubbed, even the room upstairs. Every speck of grease will be gone and every stick of furniture repaired before you open your doors again." The allegorical name of Miller returned, a mere flutter before the fiery orbs that dared me to look at them. "And, Mr. Cook, the fare will change." I faced the heated glare. "No more frying everything. The new menu will have selections which are tastier and healthier. You will be surprised, and the townsfolks amazed, at how much flavor food can have when it's cooked properly."

Cook's fists hit the table. I clutched my chest and mentally searched for bullet holes, while visions of Jim as I'd imagined him flashed in my mind. Kind images, like Everett had been, but less nosy.

"Might as well close down for good with all this nonsense you're dumpin' on us, Mrs. Strong." Cook leaned close.

There were no holes, no pain or blood. I rose to my feet to engage my foe. Lizzy's foe, actually, the way he cooked and swore. "I understand you've been paid to do something here, but unless you have it in writing by Phillip Sanders himself that you were hired to drown everything in fat, that practice will cease. If the new conditions don't suit you, Mr. Cook, you may release yourself from that commitment, no hard feelings."

"But we need him, ma'am. That's what Phil said before he left."

I turned from the face I hoped would go, to Lizzy's. I saw fear again. Maybe of Cook. It couldn't possibly be worry over the loss of his culinary skills and the dollop of grease he dumped into the coffee. Loss crept across Tina's face, and disbelief on Les's. Goodness, all of them, including Phillip, were truly ignorant of what a good man...or cook...should be. They needed enlightened. And Cook, in spite of his couple of large words, needed outsmarted.

"You can stay." I leaned toward him. "But your

menu won't. There are better ways to fix food than the high heat you've used. And for what little oil you will use from now on, a lid will be employed when you do. It's the least you can do for Lizzy and her brother."

Cook didn't snort...or draw his enormous pistol. He turned to Lizzy, the one he'd been paid extra to be here for. Then to Tina, who would shortly know why she should refuse contact with a man of this sort. And lastly to Les who would soon understand what made a real hero. Cook nodded at the three of them. "I'm a man of promises, and I made some—long before you set foot in here—that I aim to keep." He lifted a hand and spit into it. The hand came my way, a puddle of spittle bubbled in the center of his crusty palm. "Just as yer husband apparently did, Mrs. Strong. I got my ideas and you got yers, but we're in this together. For Lizzy. So shake."

Chapter 7

My hand burned. It felt scalded. I unwound then rewound my handkerchief across the palm I'd scrubbed raw. Drat Cook and his saliva-sealed pact.

I leaned close to my room's opened window to breathe something besides oily air. Soft voices and the gentle clop of horses' hooves on the street evidence of Larned's indifference to the indignity I'd suffered. Two days.

I marched to the cot, snatched at the greasy bedding with my good hand, scraped it to the floor, and kicked it toward the door. Drat that old coot. I didn't need his spittle to help me keep a commitment. My commitment to Jim and my mother proved my character.

I dropped onto a mattress that didn't give. Drat this delay and the loss of precious time. Maybe I could find another way out of town, satisfy the bank with a completed inventory and a little money to pacify them while they waited for paperwork which didn't exist…but Lizzy and her brother's restaurant needed so much more.

I rose and walked across the room to my trunk where Jim's voice, the album of his letters, his chronicle of our courtship lay. I undid its leather straps and metal clasps, then lifted the lid to a cloud of white, a soft sheen of fabric muted by a layer of fine lace. My wedding gown, maybe too much for Jim if his territory lacked refinement the way this one did, but perfect for the celebration of the wonderful future we would have and what it would mean to Mama. I ran my finger across the lacy bodice and what showed of the skirt. Tiny beads and buttons marked a trail to the album below it, the book's cloth cover and thick pages. I drew it from beneath the gown and closed the trunk's lid, carried the album to the cot, and sat with it on my lap.

"Jim." His name sounded different than when I said it in St. Louis. The lilt it carried there dropped like a stone here. Because of the grease-laden atmosphere, most likely. I said it again, listening for his voice in return, the one which always spoke with his letters, his rich baritone promise to the woman he'd asked to become his wife.

I traced the edges of the simply adorned cover, tan with a dark brown vine entwined around an empty rectangle in its center—the spot for our wedding photograph. A real picture instead of the one drawn by my imagination—me beside Jim, he the way his words had made him look and painted him in my mind. His clothing would be simple but neat. Something like what Everett had worn instead of what Rudy Walters or Nicholas Brandt did, good but not too good, well made but not fine. I'd be next to him, draped in the elegance of my gown, a union of West and East, husband and wife. Mama would be thrilled when her promise of my open door finally came to be.

The album crackled as I drew back its front cover. The first page had my and Jim's given names, a space for his...our...last name, lines left blank for our wedding date and the name of the preacher. The next pages were our courtship, every one of his letters and what I could recall of mine, the path he'd carved for a wife.

I'm almost established. Have survived most of the required five years for homesteading, built a sturdy home, and worked the land. Farming has been tough. Most settlers run cattle along with planting crops. With a little ingenuity I rigged a system to bring water from Crooked Creek to my fields. I've been successful, but less so in the drier years. Shared my idea with a few other men, a local banker finally buying the plan from me, which gave me a little extra cash for this last year of obligation. Almost enough I can own this land free and clear and pay back what I borrowed to help. It's what I'm doing to make me and my house ready. A simple home large enough for a family, a place I hope a woman would like to settle someday.

I ran a finger over where my image of Jim had begun, that letter, not even written to me but to my friend's husband. My friend had shown it to me when she suggested I write him, hinted without saying it that if I stayed wed to my father's business too long, I'd never be wed to a man. She was right. I turned the page to what I'd written. As much as I could recall of my first letter to him, my introduction and explanation that his friend's wife had shown me his letter and her insistence I write. I blushed at what I'd said. I'd been too forward, maybe. Too brassy to write a man before he'd written me, then too smart about Papa's business afterward. Maybe he'd been too polite to say he thought that…until he'd said, *Don't come. I can't marry you.*

I clapped a hand over my letter, Jim's first to me on the facing page. Maybe he'd meant, "No, thank you." Something I'd been too blind to see.

Dear Miss Archer…

A shy man had responded to me. I saw it in his handwriting, the way his words crept onto the page, while what he'd written to his friend marched boldly. I looked at his graceful introduction and timid thanks for my letter.

A woman's words can soften the day. I've built and become accustomed to straight and firm, but your perspective takes the edge off. I welcome your thoughts and thank you for your views.

A tear splattered on the page. It distorted his words and smeared them into unnatural shapes. I stared at the man I'd come west to find…a fiancé…a husband…my first promise, my open door.

"Ma'am?"

I slammed the cover on Jim and his words.

"Ma'am?" Lizzy called and knocked.

The door swung open, and a plethora of color and flowery scent flooded in.

"Mrs. Strong, I'm Amber Wingate."

Mr. Brandt's fiancée, his now unappointed manager, stood between me and Lizzy, a palette of hues which shamed the rest of my room.

I slid the album beneath my cot and rose. "You were the manager Mr. Brandt appointed." I saw pretty as she approached, a head shorter than me; I looked down on beauty and youth beneath the too-vibrant color. "I'm happy to meet you. And I'm glad you're here, because I wanted to talk with you since apparently Mr. Brandt didn't."

"Nicholas and I discuss everything. I'm his fiancée, after all. He suggested I come here and meet you." She eyed me up and down, a study that ended in a tiny frown, a near squint in the poor lighting. "I want you to know that I took my role as manager here seriously. I did the best that can be done for Eat Here, and thought it fair to warn you that an investment will never effect the change truly needed here."

I looked away from too much red hair piled too high, to the relief Lizzy's simpler style and subdued color offered my eyes. Lizzy seemed almost transparent as she studied her hands behind Amber's back. Mama had taught me that eyes were the windows to the soul. Lizzy's seemed starved, an emptiness at least partly due to her missing brother. But the eyes next to her... I forced myself to look into the green of Amber's and saw a soul which teemed with determination.

"Generally a job done well is a job well done, Miss Wingate, as long as you put forth your best. And for the overall good." Which somehow escaped Cook.

The green ebbed. "I'm not here to evaluate me, Mrs. Strong, and I don't need a platitude to make excuses for the excellent work I did in a nearly hopeless situation. Besides, being from the East, I'd think you'd more likely have their attitude that whatever you do, do it well. That's what really matters."

"Some tout that." Some like Uncle Roy and his attorney. "I suppose a loose use of the word 'good' would be to define it relative to one's personal objective, but a more accurate measure would include its effect on others. Wouldn't you say you've done your best when what you've done benefits all? In this case Eat Here?"

"Nicholas said you weren't a woman to be trifled with."

"He what?"

"You need to know that I spent a year being schooled in the most modern business tactics. I assume you didn't go to school...or if you did, it must have been years ago, judging by your archaic business tactics. And your age." She turned to Lizzy. "Miss Sanders, Nicholas tells me nothing has been finalized yet, so you could still put your trust in my more modern methods to try to salvage this restaurant. After all, I'm well educated...and younger."

Younger? Anyone, even Cook, could look younger with that much powder and paste on their face. "Lizzy will assume the duties as Eat Here's manager from now on. She won't need your help."

The tart turned. "If Lizzy refuses my proffered expertise, I'll be assigned to one of the town's other struggling businesses Nicholas does his best to keep afloat. Which means when you realize you need my help—and you will since I employed methods likely foreign to you, and things Miss Sanders wouldn't understand—I won't be available."

Amber deserved a good slap. One she probably wouldn't feel through all that goo on her face. I leaned around Lizzy's ex-manager, whom I intended to show the door. "Do you have any last questions for Miss Wingate, Lizzy, before she leaves and you take over?"

Lizzy glanced from me to Amber. "Well..." Lizzy's brow knitted. "I have one."

"Of course." Amber dipped her head in a curt nod. "Very sensible of you under the circumstances."

"The most recent fee charged to Eat Here...could that be removed, since you won't be manager?"

"Fee? What fee?" I stepped around the hair and

color so I could face both women.

"The fee for my services, of course."

"Fee for your services?" I gaped. I'd never gaped in my life until I ended up here. "The town's businesses pay you...pay the bank...to help them with what they already owe?"

"Again, your ways are outdated, Mrs. Strong, and you clearly aren't familiar with the West. But you, Lizzy, you know Larned lives on the brink of failure. That's why Nicholas has to keep the bank strong. It's the backbone of an area subjected to sparse populations, primitive conditions, and weather extremes. If it weren't for the bank..." Amber shook her head. "I daresay businesses like Eat Here would already be gone."

I stared at the woman who claimed to have knowledge far superior to that acquired by my supposedly advanced years. A woman who flaunted the East while profiting in a West she deemed hopeless. I might be here on a lie, but the premise behind my subterfuge *could* be the truth. "Miss Wingate, Phillip Sanders has put his restaurant in a position to no longer need the bank or its extra services. And if his idea is successful, other businesses in town could do the same." There had to be genuine investors out there somewhere enterprising enough to sink money into Larned businesses for a small profit.

Amber stiffened, drew in a deep breath at what I'd learned from years of Uncle Roy's challenges and Papa's sound business skills, all of which Lizzy needed to absorb in two days. "Those extra fees weren't wrong," Amber finally blurted. "They were to help Lizzy and the whole town by helping the bank."

"A truly strong economy shouldn't leave the bulk of the money in one pocket, especially in a town which struggles," I blurted back, praying none of this would ever reach Jim.

Amber tipped her head back. "Again, a case of your lack of understanding. Lizzy should know a contract like you suggest will lead to the doom of her brother's restaurant."

Lizzy's eyes widened.

"It won't, Lizzy. How can money cause Eat Here to close?" I laid a hand on Lizzy's arm so I wouldn't clench it on Amber's throat.

Amber tossed her nose farther into the air. "Money hasn't helped so far."

"That's because it's all in your…I mean, the bank's pocket."

"At the ready for when she and Phillip need it."

"At a cost." I dropped my hand from Lizzy's arm and balled my fingers around the spit-laden handkerchief.

"And there isn't a cost to the money you have offered her?" Amber's eyes narrowed.

My face warmed. Amber had me. If there had been money, of course there would have been a fee. But money had nothing to do with how I ended up here and the mess Lizzy and I both needed a way out of. Fast. "There is more to my late husband's agreement with Phillip than just money. It's a complete plan, and thanks to your fiancé, an even more thorough one than what the two of them had agreed upon."

"Thanks to Nicholas?"

"Yes, because of his bank's mandatory inventory I've seen firsthand some of the problems Eat Here has.

I intend to remedy those before I go. Right, Lizzy?"

Lizzy nodded, her face flushed with pink discomfort while mine heated to barely curtailed rage. "We've begun to clean everything, Miss Wingate." Lizzy hedged. "And fix the furniture. And change the menu."

Amber emitted a fairly ladylike spout. "Clean it up? Fix things?" A dizzying blur of red swiveled back and forth between Lizzy and me. "But why? Why would you bother?"

Uncle Roy had asked similar questions about ideas I had, and turned my answers into his own cunning roadmap he didn't use for good. At least not good as I defined it. I studied the red-and-green flurry in front of me, the raised brows which waited for my answer for a town that had meant nothing more to me than a tiny dot on a map between where I came from and where I wanted to be. "Larned doesn't have to stay this size. It shouldn't. People should want to remain here rather than just pass through. You have a chance to turn Larned into a home for people who venture west. And the seed to start that growth is Eat Here—Larned's oasis."

Now Amber gaped. "Eat Here an oasis? No. You can't do that."

"Yes, I can. Well, Lizzy can. With this simple watering hole, actually a worthy watering hole when she finishes with it. Passengers from innumerable trains will come to Eat Here for refreshment and be pleasantly surprised by what they find."

Lizzy shook her head.

"You have trains, you have Eat Here, and I imagine you have other places where tired passengers could visit and shop, as well."

She shook her head again.

"No other good stores or cafés?"

"Not that many trains stop here," Lizzy said at the same time Amber spouted, "Impossible."

"At least not as many trains as…" Lizzy continued.

"Nicholas is looking into that." Amber swiped her arm through the air and Lizzy's explanation.

"You have some trains, though. And Lizzy pointed out other stores in town, places that surely have something to offer." I paused for another shake of the head or the wave of a hand. "Then the problem really is the trains…"

"They're not the problem." Amber shook her head again. "I told you where the main problem lies, and you ignored me. It's you and your ideas. You will lead Lizzy to ruin."

Trains were the problem if Larned suffered a lack. Not just for them, but for me. I had a ticket which promised me a ride west on one in two days. I couldn't risk a shortage. "Trains are the very reason Eat Here would become an oasis and the town would grow." I listened for the sound of a locomotive. There hadn't been another train all afternoon. That could affect me for a number of days…but it would affect Lizzy forever.

"More trains here would only amplify what Larned lacks, Mrs. Strong. You can't turn a town into a showboat with nothing to show."

"The East wasn't born civilized," I said to green eyes which glared red. "Civilization there was earned, grown, and developed, and the West can do likewise. Lizzy is about to turn Eat Here into the most civilized restaurant on the route west."

Red hair and color swiveled in a vehement "no" as I listened for evidence that several trains would come for Lizzy's sake, and one for mine. Amber gathered her skirts. "I must be going. But I promise you, Lizzy, if you believe everything Mrs. Strong says, you will have done worse than cost your brother his business because of missed payments." The swirl of the color which had filled my room left in a blur, the expensive scent that had accompanied it replaced by grease-laden air.

"Are you really planning all of that?" Lizzy asked as my eyes readjusted to the gray of the room.

"Yes." I certainly was now. I nodded to the woman I'd shaken a handful of spit for. "Is it true there is a lack of trains?"

"Yes. Not many that stop."

"Then, Lizzy, things are about to change."

Chapter 8

Gray globes lined Eat Here's windows in the early dawn. Round faces in a row, just as they'd been yesterday during my meeting with Lizzy and her staff, hands cupped at the sides of each as townsfolk tried to peer through opaque glass. Apparently grease was addictive.

"Those front windows will be the last thing cleaned," I said to Lizzy, Tina, and Les, the three of them armed with cleaning supplies I'd bought the afternoon before from Ben Holt of Holt's Mercantile. "Everyone out there will tire of trying to peek in and go about their business eventually." I nodded at silhouettes that didn't budge.

"Not likely," Cook groused as he came up behind the other three. "But you will." He marched to the kitchen, where he and I had wasted too much of what little time I had, engaged in a predawn battle of skillets as I'd introduced him to the new menu.

"Leave that back door locked," I called after him. Tina had been right about there being no locks for sale in town. "Keep that little board I nailed to the jamb flipped across the door's edge so no one can open it."

"No man west of wherever you're from lives long if he don't leave himself a way out," Cook shouted from the back.

"A way out is one thing. A way in is another." I

marched toward the kitchen. I never bellowed in Papa's store. How uncouth, how unladylike, and not a practice I intended to lower myself to for my two days here. "I won't have anyone slip in, or you hand greasy somethings out. Things will change here. I promised Lizzy they would," I said to the grizzled face that blocked the doorway between me and the kitchen.

"Change? The only reason you're gittin' away with your highfalutin nonsense is 'cause you hit what's hurtin'. Hurtin' them outside that window, partly 'cause they're likely hungry for my cookin'. And hurtin' us inside here. Especially her." He jerked his head toward the dining area behind me, toward Lizzy, and for the first time, lowered his voice to a less barbaric growl. "She asks you about her brother. His name bought you some rights here." Cook crowded me in the doorway. "All I'm sayin' is you better be dealin' in truth, not tradin' pains to get yerself out of a fix…Mrs. Strong. 'Cause I promise you, yer fix ain't big enough for what it might cost."

My hands began to tremble. I'd been up all night. Surely the tremor came from hours spent writing recipes as I guessed at ingredients in dishes I'd eaten in fine dining establishments in St. Louis. "I have reasons for everything I do." I clutched my hands. "And Lizzy is part of those reasons. A large part." I listened for a train, any train which would get me out of town and away from eyes that shot bullets through me and everything I said.

"Penelope?" Lizzy stood behind me with two white boards, black lettering and a picture on each. "I wanted to show you what I made last night." She held them up for me to see—Open, with an open door, in one hand,

and Closed, with a door shut, in the other. An excited blush colored her face. "I can't wait until we can use them."

I looked from what she'd done to the excitement on her face that she'd done it. "I can't either. They're wonderful."

I meant it. I touched one sign and then the other. I had done them good, no matter what the naysayer behind me claimed. I had brought good to Lizzy, just like I had to Ben Holt, who'd prospered not only by a bit of my money I handed him for nearly every cleaning supply his store had, but also by the savvy he'd heard I had and dragged from me about how a business can rise up out of trouble.

Lizzy glanced over her shoulder toward the dining area. "We started scrubbing in there. When it's all done and people start to come back, they will be…"

"Disappointed," Cook spat. "I'm sorry to say it, Lizzy, but once they git in, they'll leave. Have you seen some of the things she wants me to cook?" He waved an arm behind him at the pages of recipes I'd sweated over. "No one around here ever heard of coddled or soft boiled unless they're talkin' about someone's head." Like the one he rattled back and forth, a festoon of hair that could actually benefit from a little of his grease.

I rounded on the man whose pistol would likely kill whatever customers his food didn't. "You can't continue to fry everything, or this restaurant will stay exactly as it is—a failure with more flies than customers."

"Fine for you and your fancy ways. You're hightailin' it out of here and leavin' me behind to face these folks with a plate of somethin' that has *au jus* tacked onto the end. There ain't no picture for that, and I'll be laughed right out of town tryin' to explain it to 'em. Slivered and diced don't mean nothin' to these folks. They're here for hunks of meat or dough done crisp in fat, and they'll leave when there ain't none."

A gag lodged in my throat. I slapped my chest and hammered at the clog. "Well, don't think my 'hightailin' it out of here' means you can revert back to your old ways when I do. Ben Holt promised me he would never sell lard, fat, or grease to you again." Barely promised, as he added a gun to my order after I claimed Cook would adjust. "My menu will appeal to people who don't live here, those who are from the East. And the people here will come to appreciate it. If you're too embarrassed to face them, I'll do it for you. I'll cook for a grand opening preview tomorrow evening, and I'll introduce them to the new food." I could do this. I knew how to cook for a family of three. I knew what food should taste like.

"A grand opening preview?" Lizzy's face lit up, and her signs waved in anticipation.

"Yes, a sneak preview. It will be good for Eat Here and good for Larned. It will give your local customers their first taste of what travelers on the trains will recognize and appreciate."

"Fine with me that you cook." Cook stripped off his apron, his gun a sharp gleam in the morning light. "I'll stand out front when folks come in." His apron hit a table.

"You'll do no such thing. I won't have you out there warning everyone away just because I won't let you poison them. You'll either cook, and do it my way, or you can stay home. And not return unless you can cooperate."

Lizzy's brows raised as "Open" and "Closed" lowered.

"I'll remind you, Mr. Cook, that you and I shook hands. We made a pact for Lizzy's sake, and since everything done before didn't work, she has to try something new."

Cook looked from me to her. What we could see of his mouth leveled into a hard line as his beard jutted forward. He swiped his apron from the table. "I'll stay. I promised Phil. But she'll likely not have a customer left after tomorrow night, and it'll be all your fault, Mrs. Strong."

"One more thing, Mr. Cook," I said instead of the *Oh, good God* he deserved. "We're a civilized establishment now. Your pistol will be put away during open hours."

"We? We're a civilized establishment? Since when did you shift from 'you' to 'we'?"

I nearly gaped…again. Louise Elizabeth had just shared more than a name with Elizabeth Sanders. "Merely semantics," I blustered.

"Semantics?" Cook grinned. "Yer semantics say a lot more than a hint of saffron." He tightened his apron and hooked the dingy white cloth around the butt of his pistol. "Go on, Lizzy. Go help Tina and Les scrub yer restaurant. I'm feelin' the need to sear something." Cook eyed me as he latched onto a pan. "And I'll fry again if after two days this searin' and steamin' don't work. But you won't be here to know that, Mrs. Strong. Unless you got yourself a new 'we.' "

"I know we'll never be your real 'we,' Penelope." Lizzy held her signs close. "But I thank you and your husband for what you're trying to do for us here. Phil would thank you too."

Chapter 9

Phil would thank me to leave, if he thanked me for anything. He couldn't be a reasonable man. No sane person would hire the likes of Cook and leave him and his gun behind with the right to stay. I stared at the pan of rolls I'd barely had the energy to make. Surely Lizzy wouldn't let her cook shoot a widow. But Phillip might, unless my plan here worked.

"What's that God-awful smell?"

I turned from one of the spices I'd brought to share with Jim. "That's cinnamon."

Cook glared from the kitchen doorway, more bent, more grizzled, and evidently more surly after a long night of scrubbing his kitchen. "Is cinnamon another one of yer fancy cleaners? It'll drive folks away, if it is."

"Cinnamon is a spice, as you likely know. Or maybe you don't, since it doesn't take well to hot grease. Not quite as aromatic when it's mutilated."

"People don't eat aroma. They cain't chew it."

"Well, they can chew the delicious cinnamon rolls you're about to learn to bake this morning." I waved a tired arm over flour, cinnamon, sugar, and the other ingredients I'd laid out on the spotless table next to the equally spotless oven. "Aroma is far more than just a taste. It's a conversation."

"Conversation. Pshaw. Nothing says more than a

warnin' shot, though that stench you got there might accomplish the same thing." He coughed. "And it's my kitchen you're ruinin', and I…" An ugly round of wheezes seized him. Furrows bunched in crumpled welts across his forehead as he doubled over.

I opened the package of cinnamon wider. The old coot. I turned my back to his commotion and listened hard for that gentler voice, the one which lay shut in my trunk upstairs, the one I'd hear close and personal… soon. Very soon.

I'm an okay cook, but nothing to brag about. I do believe in eating well and hearty, making sure it tastes good as it goes down.

Jim's voice spoke over Cook's rasps, the apron he wrenched from the hook, shook out, wadded, and shook again.

I like the way my house smells afterward… savory…even my clothing a reminder of a meal worth waiting for.

Cook hammered his chest and dislodged a gag which raised one in me. I clapped a hand to my chest and leaned against the table. The hard work showed on all of us. Tina's smile had been dimmer this morning, and Les looked even less when he'd dragged through the front door. To set the "Open" sign in the window would be a blessed relief this evening for our sample meal to show off the newly scrubbed restaurant.

Jim's voice quieted as tired but happy ones rose in the dining area. Tina, Lizzy, and Les worked to polish silverware and place it on sturdy tables surrounded by freshly repaired chairs. The clink of metal against wood marked a beat to the words *contract*, *new*, and *signed*. They had new hope and new promise, neither of which

I'd seen on Mr. Brandt's face when Lizzy and I handed the signed document to him late yesterday.

"Would you stop all of your nonsense." I gave my chest a final slap and whirled at a fresh round of Cook's gags. "Cinnamon is a very popular spice and never hurt a soul."

"It might this time, if yer complicated schemes don't destroy the whole town first."

"They're not schemes, they're plans. And they're not complicated, they're civilized. And they will be good for Larned."

"Call 'em what you want. We both know one of us is right and the other is wrong." He planted his feet and I planted mine.

"You'll thank me someday," we said at the same time.

"Cinnamon…" Lizzy and Tina appeared side by side in the doorway, all tired grins. "How divine!"

"Tell Mr. Cook that."

"What's cookin'?" Les poked his head between the two.

"Cooking," I corrected him. "What's cooking."

"Yeah, what is it?" Les ran his tongue over his lips.

"Somethin' civilized," Cook snarled.

"Phil would like this." Lizzy drew in a deep breath. "I'm glad he had the foresight to find someone like Penelope's late husband. I can't wait for Phil to read the new contract we have with the bank."

"Read it?" My goodness. Phillip could come home before I got out of town.

"Oh, then everything will be perfect." Lizzy clasped her hands and smiled.

Perfectly awful. I wrung my hands.

"Anyway," Lizzy continued, "I had Les surround each table with four chairs, and Tina is arranging tablecloths and dinnerware. New menus are stacked at the side table, along with pitchers and extra plates. I thought I'd help in here. Those two know what else to do in the dining room to get ready for tonight." Lizzy had done it. She'd begun to manage, whether she knew it or not.

I looked at Elizabeth Sanders, who looked back at me, the starved soul within those blue eyes a little hardier. Phillip would surely be pleased. I opened my mouth to reward her with all the relish she deserved.

"Miss Sanders?"

I closed my mouth.

"Miss Sanders," Mr. Brandt called again from the dining room.

Cook's hand went to his pistol.

"Don't you dare." I smacked his hand away as Mr. Brandt asked for Lizzy again. "He's probably just curious about our changes now that he has the contract," I said as Lizzy turned toward the kitchen door.

"Of course he is." Cook adjusted the pistol in its holster.

Lizzy's banker called once more, his voice closer.

"How'd he git through your locked fortress?" Cook glared at me.

Les reddened.

"Must have been my fault." Tina stepped forward. "I may have left the door unlocked after I…I took some rags out to dry."

"It's no matter." Lizzy glanced at us. "Penelope is likely right. He wants to see what we've done before our preview tonight, and he should." She gave a nod to Les. "I'll go see."

Les hurried to Lizzy's side. I watched him and Tina disappear with her through the kitchen doorway, the three of them so harried and small.

"Lizzy needs my help." I fumbled and undid my apron, then tossed it to the side. "Probably better I'm the one to ask him what he wants." I eyed the nearest pan as I straightened clothing I'd worn far too long. Goodness. I'd need something fresh to wear when I reached Dodge City.

"We don't ask nothin' out here unless we're speakin' to a lady." Cook hiked his apron higher around his gun.

I nodded toward his pistol. "Exactly what do you plan to do? Shoot him because he wants to check on the restaurant?"

Cook jerked his head toward the skillet I'd eyed. "Were you intendin' to braise him?"

"Of course not." I turned my back to the pan. "I just..." Behaved ridiculously. I knew how to handle Nicholas Brandt. The same way I'd managed Uncle Roy. "There's a civilized way to handle situations. And people."

"Civilized ain't gonna accomplish nothin'. In fact, it'll ruin everythin'." Cook stepped in front of me.

"Weapons certainly aren't the answer." I shouldn't sneer, but I did.

"Trust me. You gotta be holdin' onto something when you go out there." Cook eyed me the way I'd expect a rattlesnake to. "And what you're holdin' onto, Mrs. Strong, ain't gonna help because it ain't this restaurant. Or the young woman out there that banker'll tussle for it. That's where yer side of the pact and yer 'we' falls apart." Cook wheeled from the kitchen.

He was right...my "we" was somewhere southwest of here. And somehow Cook sensed where my grasp really lay. The voices in the dining room grew, but the one in my head grew louder. Cook knew way more than he should. I fumbled for my apron. Maybe it was time for the truth. Privately to Lizzy, so I wouldn't be shot. She would understand the woes of a jilted spinster and the plight of a business in jeopardy. She would understand what I really held onto. My thoughts quieted as someone shouted, "Now wait just a minute."

A gunshot exploded. Lizzy screamed. I latched onto a pan and ran.

Chapter 10

The sound of Cook's gunshot wouldn't stop, an endless resonance as I followed his scrawny form with a bulleted glare he ignored in his march between Eat Here's front windows and the table where I sat with Tina and Lizzy. Les shadowed him, a thin rail which kept pace behind the self-appointed sentry we should be guarded from rather than by. Cook's black silhouette vanished as his stomp crossed between the closed door and us. The door which should have been Lizzy's open one tonight. An opportunity Cook's foolishness had likely ruined now that he'd sent Lizzy's banker off in a terrified scurry.

"Nothing Mr. Brandt said could have been so horrible it warranted…" I waved Cook off as I hissed to Lizzy, his reckless action equally devastating to me as I left her and her brother behind with nothing but rubble. "What caused him"—that scrawny imbecile—"to shoot?"

Lizzy glanced down at her lap, at her long fingers which clasped and unclasped each other. "Mr. Brandt said the bank president won't sign the contract until you show him the papers Phillip and your late husband agreed on. Mr. Brandt tried, but he hasn't been able to pinpoint anything about your husband or find a bank that knows…knew…him. He's forbidden everyone in town to seek help from outside investors. Especially from you."

I dropped back against my seat. Goodness. Everyone could know the truth in a matter of days...hours even. Lizzy would die when she learned I was a fraud, especially from someone else. The minute the bank or Mr. Brandt proved, or just concluded, no such person as Alex Strong—or Penelope—existed, I'd be jailed or run out of town with no defense or chance to explain. Lizzy would be crushed. And so would Mama...not to mention Jim.

I laid a hand over where my heart hammered. That could have happened right here. Today. Mr. Brandt's suspicions could have exposed me before I did my very best for Lizzy, bared my soul to her, then left on this evening's train. She and I had both been spared... thanks to Cook, and what I'd wrongly judged as pure hotheaded, senseless foolishness.

"So that's why Cook shot at Mr. Brandt. He fired his pistol because Mr. Brandt said those things." My ire waned and indebtedness rose. Cook looked less like a banty rooster as he paced between me and the faces lined outside the restaurant's windows...again. I'd been too hasty to judge him.

"Not exactly, Penelope. Cook shot after I told Mr. Brandt not to worry about that contract." Lizzy balled her fingers together. "Right after I told Mr. Brandt I'd find another bank. One that believed in me, and trusted you. That's when Cook fired his pistol...but not at Mr. Brandt."

So Cook hadn't... I heard again the shot and Lizzy's scream, thought back to the commotion I'd seen when I ran into the dining room with my pan. There had been no blood, no one who grabbed at their chest and dropped to the floor. A perusal of the dining room and its walls, the tables and their settings, had proven everything to be undamaged. Everything except the enraged Mr. Brandt, who'd stormed from the restaurant. How dare Cook fire a pointless shot who knew where, and leave everyone, especially me, in jeopardy! "Cook shouldn't have done that. He had no good reason, and God only knows what you will suffer now, Lizzy, the way Mr. Brandt charged out of here. Cook's ill-timed and poorly aimed shot didn't even…"

"Cook never misses." Tina's eyes shone as she watched his back-and-forth stomp.

My goodness, Cupid's arrow could be as misguided as Cook's bullet. "Really, Tina, you shouldn't…"

"Trust Cook? But I do, Penelope. He could have put a careless hole through anything, including Mr. Brandt. Any other man might have, but Cook knows what he's doing." Tina beamed as she followed Cook's black silhouette, Les right behind him, while Larned's townspeople continued to peer through windows I regretted scrubbing so clean.

I patted Tina's knee. "Real trust takes time." And a good man who actually deserves it. "You probably haven't known Cook all that long now, have you?"

"It feels like forever. And it will never be long enough." The shine I saw in Tina's eyes glowed brighter with every step her hero took.

I squeezed her leg and shook my head as I let go. "No matter what Cook shot at, Mr. Brandt will be infuriated and surely come back."

"Likely he will, but not the way he would have." Cook paused and faced our way. "And for sure, not some shadow." Cook pivoted and resumed his march.

"Some shadow?" I called, or rather spat, after him. "Shadows don't operate independently. That's ridiculous. I have no idea what you mean."

"A shadow," Cook barked over his shoulder. "Looks like someone and moves like someone, ain't them, but leads to 'em. Yer nonsense'll likely keep out what no lock of yers could, Mrs. Strong. Of course what those locks keep in can sometimes be worse."

I rose to my feet, sandwiched Cook between my glare and the stares of curious townsfolk. I knew he referred to me, another errant shot on his part. "You make no sense. Shooting at nothing again."

"I never shoot at nothin'. Or without aimin'. I always hit exactly what I intend to." He stopped again, Les with him.

Cook had missed. He'd only riled Mr. Brandt, and now me, and ruined everything I'd tried to accomplish the last two days. "Clearly you're wrong. And your carelessness could cost Lizzy her opening."

"I said I never miss, and I guarantee she and everyone else will be better for it."

"Look around. Where'd your bullet go?" My voice sounded rangy in the empty dining room, but I didn't care. "Not a single hole, no sunlight peeping through anywhere."

"Mrs. Strong, I know you think yer nebulous aroma of cinnamon is a conversation folks out here will understand."

Nebulous? No man could be obdurate and clever at the same time. I gave the unlikely enigma a little snort.

"A bullet's the only conversation that matters in the West, Mrs. Strong. My bullet said exactly what I meant for it to. Better than yer cinnamon ever will."

"Must I remind you again that where I come from conversations are civil, not brash? And like it or not, the place I'm from is headed west." I narrowed my gaze and did what no lady ever should. I raised my finger and pointed at him. "What you've just done, Mr. Cook, will cause Lizzy far more harm than it will good."

Cook shook his head. "That won't be the case," he said with the same calm and surety a person would who promised the sky wouldn't fall. "Just the opposite, in fact."

"You couldn't be more wrong. Now if you'll excuse me…" I hurried across the clean floor and up the stairs. Whoever heard of a gunshot as a conversation?

I shut the door to my room and threw my back against it. I would go. I would be safer at the train depot than here where one of Cook's stray conversations might hit me. Most of the food had been prepared. Lizzy didn't need me this evening if Mr. Brandt didn't squelch her grand opening. Or any evening from now on, especially if tonight turned out to be a success. The dining room was ready also, except for some stray bullet's hole they'd eventually find and plug.

I snatched the dress I planned to wear from the cot, a brush and a comb from the shelf, and nudged my trunk from the foot of the bed with a toe. I would write Lizzy from Crooked Creek, tell her the truth, and send what money I could spare to help her out. She had grown and changed in two days. She could do everything without me. She should make enough money with her pre-opening to decide whether to stick to the menu I'd planned or not.

Light beamed through a small hole in the floor where my trunk had been, a pinpoint from the dining room below. I tossed my belongings to the cot and dropped to my knees next to the hole, a rough splintering the size I'd guess a bullet to be. I glanced up to the ceiling to see where Cook's poorly aimed conversation had gone. Not there.

"Blast him." I yanked my trunk open, shoved my belongings to the side, pawed past my gown or anything else where Cook's bullet might have lodged. My finger stung—a sharp pain jabbed it beneath Jim's album. I spotted another splintery hole, a splay of wood and metal that exploded up through the trunk's bottom. Drat that Cook. He would pay for everything he'd ruined. Flipping Jim's album over, I saw Cook's one word had pierced Jim's many.

I felt a scream. It sounded like Lizzy's had at the very same gunshot. I opened the album's cover and hurried through pages until I spotted the gray slug and the words it had broken through.

There have been good times and hard ones. I'm thankful for both. Forced me to sturdy up who I am and what's important. I took gambles and risks that kept me awake at night until I realized I'd done everything I'd done out of love. I slept better after that, knowing I'd invested myself, taken uncomfortable chances, sunk roots deep that would hold even if nothing else did. Because those roots were made of love.

Love. I sat back. Jim's word felt like a bullet. I ran a finger around it and the hole where deep red should be. I closed the book on Jim's and Cook's conversations. I felt the sentiment, felt the wound, and for the first time, I bled.

Chapter 11

I smoothed a tablecloth over a table I thought I'd never see again, this white and the white of all the other covered tables soft glows beneath Eat Here's gas lights. I drifted between the puddles of luminescence to the front window, where I stood and gazed at my reflection. My face looked tired, and my eyes sagged from an afternoon spent reading and rereading Jim's words in my room. Words about the roots he'd sunk, the roots of love he eventually ripped out.

Don't come. I can't marry you.

I hadn't understood love or that Jim spoke of it until today. I didn't notice how in doing something, he had done much more than just prepare for a wife. I shifted my gaze from my face to the room behind me, the sturdy furniture, clean surroundings, slight elegance I'd devised as a way to get out of town. A means to an end for me...and Mama...but for Lizzy too. I could see now that everything he said had created the same desire in me—for so much more than the simple need to bear someone's last name. I wanted love, and to love now, like he must have earlier. I wanted with my heart what had only been calculated in my mind before, and I knew it the moment my jilted spinster's heart bled where Cook's bullet had gouged a hole—a hole which could only be filled with love.

I bought a chair. It's a rocker. My neighbor made

it, I asked him to build one for you. I told him to make it as much like mine as he could, and he did. They look nice sitting next to each other.

Additions such as those had cost Jim, just as others he'd spoken of had, frills and niceties which added a blush to the awkward homesteading bachelor's descriptions. He'd spent the money willingly, sunk roots, and suffered the discomfort of a man who wanted to fit a woman into his world. My goodness, I had warmed so much to such a man as well as his ways. I studied again the readied dining room behind me. How desirable a man who would do these things, for me, had become.

I paid a woman in my church to mend my clothes. Holes don't matter much to my cattle, but they might to...

"You..."

The smooth tenor of Jim's voice vanished. The words which I'd hoped would bid me to marry after all, turned raspy.

"You stayed..."

The brown hair and gentle demeanor I'd imagined as Jim's became wiry and wary in the window's glass.

"Yes, I did stay. But not because someone shot a hole through my luggage." I turned.

Cook, neatened somewhat by the clasp of a bolero which showed above the bib of a clean apron, looked less likely to fire the gun he'd hooked his apron over. "I made promises," he said matter-of-factly, a skirt around an admission.

Important promises he kept fervently with whatever sort of heart beat behind those whiskers and his normally grease-stained shirt. But in the process

Cook had blown a hole through the middle of mine, exposing my desire for far more than a rote promise. "You have all the social graces of a viper."

"And you look awful. I made coffee. Go git yerself some."

"With…or without?" I didn't move.

"Without lard. Now git on."

I still didn't move. He didn't either. "It hurt," I said.

"I know."

I walked around him to the side table where Lizzy and Tina fussed over whatever probably didn't need fussed over one more time before customers arrived.

"Everything looks ready," I said with a tentative smile, a shamed admission they'd prepared for the opening without me all afternoon.

They looked like Cook and me as they straightened and turned, neatened but tired in equally tired clothing. Lizzy's face flushed with the infancy of responsibility, the fear of being on her own with something far bigger than she or Phillip had likely imagined. The same flush and fear which had darkened my face the week Papa died and Uncle Roy stepped in where he shouldn't be.

"I know I didn't help much this afternoon," I confessed to Lizzy. "But can I interrupt your last-minute preparations and speak with you alone for a moment before we get busy?" Louise Elizabeth, the new Louise Elizabeth, had a heart to share with Elizabeth Sanders before that heart went to find its beloved.

She swiped her hands down the front of her apron and smiled. "*We* can," she said. It felt like a caress instead of a dart. She followed me to the small laundry room, scrubbed but still damp and lined with tubs, far too close to the kitchen, in my opinion.

"I have a confession to make. I have to before…before I go this evening," I said in a rush when we were alone. "I'm not what you think I am. I'm a bit lost, actually. And I'm not…"

"Of course you're a bit lost." Lizzy stilled my fidgeting hands. "You're uprooted."

"Uprooted? Did Cook say that?"

"You mean Mr. Cook?" She gave me another smile as my face warmed. "He and I talk all the time, but never about roots. Unless it's edible ones he wants to fry."

"Thank God those conversations should be over, though I admit potatoes and onions can be fried and not ruin a reasonable person's digestion." I shuddered anyway. "But that's not what we need to talk about. I want to apologize, Lizzy. I haven't been…"

"There's no need." Lizzy tightened her hold on my hands. "I understand. Larned isn't your home, and Eat Here isn't your restaurant. It's just…we were…a job that you took on for someone else. And, Penelope, you did this job well. Very well, and I thank you."

"No. Lizzy, it's far more than that…"

"Come," she interrupted. "Cook made the coffee especially for you. He said you were going to need it."

For my train and stagecoach rides? For the terror of finally meeting the one who'd broken our engagement and, as it turned out, my heart? Cook may have fired the shot which showed me that, but no matter what he claimed or Tina believed about his marksmanship…he couldn't possibly know.

"Lizzy, I…"

"Cook said it strengthens the heart." Maybe he did know. Lizzy took my hand and led me to the dining area where Tina and Cook stood close together, cups of coffee gripped in their hands. Even Les stood alongside them with his own steaming cup. No wonder the boy stayed so small.

Lizzy poured a cup for me and then one for her. For the first time since I'd come to Eat Here, the five of us stood still. Quiet and together, we shared drinks instead of mops and brooms or barbs. The restaurant smelled clean. It smelled good with the aroma of coffee and food Cook had evidently managed while I bled in my room.

"Everything looks and smells wonderful," I said, my words watered with tears. My packed trunk waited upstairs, ready to go. Everyone expected me to go, even Mr. Weston with his warning that tickets weren't sold to be exchanged. Foul man. And Mr. Brandt—God only knew what he expected after Cook's shot, but he did expect paperwork and a certain amount of money from me.

Lizzy thought she had everything she expected, but before I left, I would make sure I told her the whole truth. Explain the desperation of the old Louise Archer, and the heart of the one recently shot full of holes by Cook. I took another sip of greaseless coffee and waited with the others for Lizzy's open door I'd help make for her. Then I'd go open mine.

****

At five o'clock, Larned began to stream through Eat Here's door, the exact time Lizzy had posted for the pre-opening to begin. Two and a half hours before my train would arrive, more people than I ever imagined lived in this area entered Lizzy's restaurant.

"Well, Mrs. Strong," Cook said through a mustache that glistened with coffee. "We're about to see what my spit did for your grip."

I opened my mouth. Then closed it at the strange change of attitude in the still-armed man.

"Cook ain't so bad, ma'am." Tina patted my arm as Cook headed to the kitchen, Les close behind him.

"He's..." I watched him go. "He's...well, he's slightly unkempt."

"Only on the outside." Tina muffled a snicker. "I'd best get more coffee and extra water pitchers." She hurried to the kitchen.

This made two promises I had to keep before I left. I'd confess the whole truth to Lizzy, and I'd have that talk with Tina about the characteristics of a good man.

"I can't believe all these people are coming in," Lizzy whispered at my side. Her front door swung wide to happy voices full of excitement, eager noses which inhaled new aromas, and glad chatter that wanted to sit.

"I can seat people and get drinks while you take orders," I said to Lizzy's awe. I'd kept the menu simple, only a few selections for this pre-opening, a sample of meals to come, if Cook followed my plan. "Or the other way around—you're the boss."

Tina rushed back into the dining area, the aroma of coffee thick behind her. Exclamations over the room with its pristine, white tablecloths, the wonderful odor of good food minus grease, turned to urgent requests for tables.

"You help them get seated and take care of drinks." Lizzy laid a hand on my arm before I could dart away. "Penelope, I'm grateful to Phil for this. And both of us should be thankful to your late husband. But you're the one who really did it all. Just you. Phil and I will never be able to thank you enough."

I said nothing. There was nothing I could say to the sincere gratitude my confession would shortly destroy. I grabbed menus and hurried to the door as Tina breezed around Les on her way back to the kitchen, the boy's thin arms loaded with a tray of silverware rolled in napkins. We were going to need more. Lizzy would need more of everything.

I hurried, as Jim's voice chased along with me.

We learn to make do out here, become a part of a sparse land as it becomes a part of us. I grew unaccustomed to outside help, forged my own path through the farm and my home. So what you said about the way I'd arranged my house, Louise, opened my eyes. In my scanty description of my even scantier furnishings, you took my complaint of my inability to sleep and moved my bed across the room from where I had it. I now sleep soundly away from the rest of the house, in a windowed corner which I've curtained off. Thank you. Your new eyes are appreciated and welcome...needed.

He'd thanked me, shared what my eyes had envisioned and his had seen.

"Let me show you to a table," I said to yet another couple I didn't recognize.

Thank you. Your new eyes are appreciated and welcome...needed.

I hurried to do for Lizzy what I'd done for Jim, even for my parents—make do without letting it look like it as I arranged customers and rearranged tables to make everyone comfortable. Dozens thanked me, and thanked me again when I returned to their tables with drinks.

Thank you...

Don't come...

"We almost didn't come."

My hurry and Jim's voice stopped. "Didn't come" brought me to a halt. I turned to a woman with too much color beneath hair piled too high and the man beside her in a hat far too tall. "Well, Lizzy will be glad that you did come," I lied to Amber and Nicholas, who kept his eye on the kitchen doorway. "Can I take your hat, Mr. Brandt?" And your hair, Miss Wingate?

"No, just show us to a table, please. That one over there would be fine." Mr. Brandt indicated the farthest from the kitchen, one where he could keep his back to a wall.

"Certainly," I said. Mr. Brandt would be relieved to know Cook had shot at me and not him...if I would tell him. But Nicholas should still be smart, and so should I, and both stay out of Cook's range. "Can I bring you some coffee?" I asked as they settled into their seats.

I make the best coffee around, my own secret recipe everyone here would like to know. But I've shared how I make it with no one. Until now. I'm sharing it with you in this letter. And soon, we'll share it together.

Lizzy appeared at Nicholas and Amber's table as I served their drinks. I saw the missing paperwork on Nicholas's face. I saw the long look down Amber's nose at the manager who had taken her place. I saw the hesitation in both of them at the food Lizzy later delivered, something Cook might have poisoned if he'd known it went to them.

I rushed and smiled, greeted faces I'd never see again, as I kept Lizzy in view. Elizabeth Sanders was about to meet Louise Elizabeth. In another forty-five minutes, according to a watch a man pulled out. I hurried faster, smiled more, and did the best I could for Elizabeth Sanders before she heard the truth and sent me away.

"Have room for me and my friend, Mrs. Strong?"

I stopped at the same voice which had stopped me in St. Louis. The one I'd lied to, the one that had helped me get off the train in Larned…because he wanted me to be all right.

I crinkled the menus in my hands. "Mr. McCloud." I faced a different sort of tall than Nicholas Brandt's. A strong but gentle tall, in sturdy and far less pretentious clothing.

Everett smiled. He removed his hat, his smile clearer as he looked down at me. "It's good to see you, Mrs. Strong."

He meant it. Heat, which already coursed through me from my dash between tables, my juggle of Nicholas and Amber, my friendly greetings, and the ear I kept on Cook and the eye on the time, blazed hotter. "Thank you. I mean, it's good to see you as well. Again."

He raised his head and scanned the clean, busy, and aromatic atmosphere, his smile growing. "I'd heard things had changed here. Your husband would have been proud."

"My what? Oh, my husband." I fanned myself with the menus. "Yes, this is exactly what Alex would have wanted, God rest his soul."

"I imagine Miss Sanders feels indebted to you."

Everett nodded across the dining room at Lizzy, her face flushed, but not as scarlet as mine felt. "She'll probably hate to see you go." He paused. "Will that be soon?" He worked the brim of his hat through his fingers.

Go...I glanced around for someone's watch, listened above the happy diners for a train. "Yes, I'm afraid so." I spotted one and saw seven o'clock.

I looked for Lizzy again, saw her straighten from a customer. A bigger smile replaced her tired one when Everett waved a hand and tipped his head her way. She mouthed a welcome. With their amiability and the enthusiasm of the crowd, she should be fine. She had friends, and what I had accomplished would leave her better off than she'd been before. Eat Here had a clean start. If they kept it spotless and Cook behaved himself, it could only gain. It would become an oasis far beyond what my lies had predicted. Lizzy strained to her toes, and indicated a table Les had just cleared.

I held up two fingers, two diners, while my mind focused on seven...seven o'clock. Thirty more minutes. "You said a table for you and a friend, didn't you?" I glanced behind Everett and around where he stood.

"Yes, I did. He's on his way. He's...well, he needed to rest up. Just got in from south of here. Southwest, actually, about twenty miles from Dodge City, and...let's just say things have been rough for him. He's at the inn, but he'll be here shortly. That table Miss Sanders is pointing at will suit us fine."

Chapter 12

I sailed even faster around Eat Here's dining area, listening for my train while I watched the door. Everett's friend lived in southwestern Kansas, the same as Jim. The man was tired. He'd suffered rough times.

"This way, please," I said to a couple who'd just entered. I led them to a table the exhausted Les had just cleaned and staggered away from. "Is this suitable?" I waved my arm over the fresh cloth Les had laid and the sparkling dinnerware Tina added to it. The two smiled, commented as to the pleasant and rich aroma of sauces and meat well-seasoned, then took their seats. I glanced at the door as I handed menus to them. If Everett's friend was him…my Jim…I would know. At the very least his clothing would be patched and mended like he'd said in his letters, his hair brown, his eyes kind.

Have you a sound for my voice as well? Did it begin shortly after we first wrote? That's why I said no pictures of any sort, no drawings, only words. I wanted to be sure. I wanted each of us to recognize in our soul what belonged there and what didn't. A face doesn't last a lifetime. My brown hair will get lighter…maybe even disappear. My weathered skin will thin, my eyes become watery, my strong stature frailer. But my heart, that should remain, and that you will know.

I would recognize him. Even more now that Cook's bullet had exposed my heart and the place carved inside it that wanted to love…my Jim.

"Would you like coffee?" I asked the couple who smiled up at me. "Or would you prefer something else to drink?"

The door opened, and Ben Holt stepped through, a woman with him I assumed to be his wife, another couple close behind. Ben caught my glance, buried a nod and what might have been a wave as he removed his hat. He'd been discouraged, just like the other businessmen in the room, by Mr. Brandt's edict against outside investors, me in particular. The man behind Ben studied me. Another warned businessman, no doubt, come to see for himself what I'd done here.

"Coffee, please," the man I'd just seated said. "For both of us."

"Of course. I'll be right back." I stole a glance at the watch he pulled from his pocket. Seven fifteen. My train had to be near. But Everett's friend should be as well. The door opened to new happy voices, more families, but no other sound and no one else.

"Coffee?" I paused at Everett's table on my way. I smoothed the tablecloth where his friend would sit, the pot in my other hand.

"If it's good." Everett smiled and tapped the water glass I'd given him earlier, the kindness I recalled from when we'd first met still there but weary.

The wail of a train rose in the distance. My train, surely, a thin whistle from the east, which would take me west. But some part of the West had come here to Larned in the form of Everett's friend. "There's no more grease in it, if that's what you mean by, 'if it's good.' I assume since you're familiar with Larned, you've been here before." I listened to the whistle and the speed with which it drew closer, its urgent call for me to hurry.

Everett's smile turned to a soft chuckle before the weariness overcame it again. "You're right about that. I have had coffee here before. Before you." He paused, his gaze rested on me. "But I meant if your coffee's anywhere near as good as his." Everett nodded at the empty spot where my hand rested on the tablecloth. "He should be here shortly. But his is the best coffee I've ever had."

I make the best coffee around...I've shared how I make it with no one. Until now. I'm going to share it with you...

"It's not like his," I blurted. Everett's weariness piqued with a tiny frown. "I mean…"

The door opened, and a man nearly equal to Everett in height and size stepped in, the train's announcement loud behind him. Wheels squealed and raked over metal the same way they had when I'd first arrived. It slowed as the man scanned the dining area and fidgeted with the hat he'd removed. Everett waved, and the man spotted him, a distant smile which did little for the desolation on his face. Brown hair and weathered skin came our way.

"This coffee is good…but not the best," I stammered. I'd practiced Jim's coffee in St. Louis until I perfected it. I knew how his tasted, the secret method he'd shared which I had kept between us for when he and I drank it together. Everett's friend approached, his step tired, his strength weighed by an invisible load. I took the cup I'd set near his plate and filled it, a dark stream of aroma slopping over its side. "I'm sorry." I stared at the brown which marred the white of the tablecloth. I sopped it with a napkin, both cloths now the color of his hair. "I'll have Les bring a new tablecloth. Lizzy will get your food order." I backed away as the man stopped beside the table, so like Everett, so like…

"There you are." Everett stood and shook his friend's hand. I watched brownish, disheveled strands of hair jar with the shake as I backed away. I noted a strong build, a strength somehow lost in his clothing. Sturdy clothing, a well-worn jacket and trousers without visible patches or tears. The two sat as Lizzy came to take their order. She set a finger on the stain and glanced around the dining area for Les.

Other customers called for me, people who wanted refills, or new arrivals eager for a table. A tired belch of steam exploded outdoors as the train reached the station, and I rushed to do as each diner bade. My hurry staggered, impeded by the wide circles I made around Everett and his friend while I watched yet didn't as they leaned into their quiet conversation until Lizzy brought their food. Then they straightened and ate.

"Mrs. Strong." Mr. Brandt raised an arm and his voice. He caught everyone's attention along with mine—the outside investor Larned should avoid. I was the daughter of a hardware store owner, for goodness' sake, not an investor at all, a truth far too tempting to shout as conversations quieted and people watched me thread my way to his and Amber's table.

"Is there something else I can get for you?" I said 'else' congenially, a polite way to indicate he'd emptied and cleaned his plate while Amber had appropriately not finished hers, signs of a couple who'd enjoyed what they'd come for and now should go.

"No, nothing else." Mr. Brandt wiped his mouth with his napkin and set it neatly beside his sparkling plate. "I wish to speak with you, though, before we pay and leave."

"Your meal was satisfactory, I assume?"

"Adequate." Amber dabbed at her mouth then stuffed her napkin beside her plate. Her voice sounded loud in the hushed dining room, an alert which joined the rumble of the resting train. My train which would refresh and go.

"My fiancée tells me you have the notion Eat Here can be Larned's oasis." Mr. Brandt kept his voice low, not as loud as Amber's, a tactic which caused the town's businessmen to strain our way.

"Miss Wingate must have forgotten an important part of what I said. Every business in town can become part of that oasis, every store or service can offer something to travelers who would otherwise pass through. Every business should profit."

Ben Holt and the man with him leaned forward in their seats. Other men did the same. As did Everett. But not his friend. Everett straightened while his friend continued to eat.

"It comes down to this, Mrs. Strong." Mr. Brandt spoke again, drawing everyone's attention back to him. Everyone's except Everett's, his weariness gone, his kindness sharp, he focused on me. The way he had before.

I want you to be all right.

"Comes down to what, Mr. Brandt?" I asked.

He waited for the locomotive as it began to build up steam. I waited with him, a surge of power which gathered itself. I could still catch it. That couldn't possibly be Jim bent over his plate instead of turned my direction, because I wasn't all right.

"You've nothing to back your ambitious notions," Mr. Brandt spoke over the train's slow surge and the steam that built in me. "Different ideas, some cleaning, all to little avail without proper documentation to secure new long-term funding."

"You need to realize, Mr. Brandt..." Lizzy appeared at my side and looked down at her banker instead of up, this time. "We will no longer need long-term funding or your bank if all goes as planned. We will settle what we owe you, but as for any future assistance, we'll find another bank if we need one. One of Alex Strong's, since he did business with several. But most likely Penelope's plan and investment will save us from ever needing a loan again."

Mr. Brandt stiffened, and so did I.

"As you implied before, Miss Sanders." Mr. Brandt spoke the way he looked...brittle. "And at that point I thought your current contract remained unsigned by our president. Turns out he did sign it. He laid it on my desk after he reconsidered his position while I was here...being shot at. You are in a binding contract with us now, one which leaves us as much at risk as it does you. Therefore its conditions are tenuous. It will be cemented if and when Phillip's and Mr. Strong's first paperwork arrives. At that point we determine the strength of Eat Here and the degree of risk based on Mr. Strong's history, and which of our two contracts holds. I'm certain no bank will touch you until matters here are resolved."

Another burst of steam and a long whistle filled the silence. My trunk was ready. Everett sat halfway between me and the steps, his chair twisted my way. His friend had finished his meal, turned partially in his seat, and crossed his legs. The man could have been Jim. He looked like what I'd imagined. He came from the right part of Kansas, where things had been rough...

"We need your brother's paperwork with the late Mr. Strong, Miss Sanders. Until then, your restaurant hangs on the thread of whatever Mrs. Strong has claimed, promised, or done here. Hardly anything solid enough to warrant your confidence." Mr. Brandt stood. Another chair behind us raked backward. Mr. Brandt towered over Lizzy, then bent to hold Amber's chair so she could rise as well.

Metal clanked outside. A succession of wheels clattered as cars jolted into motion. My train budged from its rest. If it left, I'd be engaged in another ticket battle with Mr. Weston tomorrow.

I took hold of Lizzy's thin arm and held on, a tremor inside her sleeve as she held onto what I'd done and promised. I thought of the two men behind me, one the reason I ended up here, the other the reason I'd stay if he was Jim.

The clanks increased as the locomotive edged toward the west. I held tight to the woman beside me.

"Everything all right?"

I want you to be all right.

Everett towered behind Lizzy and me. "Mr. Brandt." Everett nodded at Lizzy's...and now my...banker. "I understood you intended to take care of Mrs. Strong."

"Of course I did. Am. I have and I will. But I'm also responsible to a bank. And a town. And my..."

"It's all right," I said to Everett. "What Mr. Brandt

means is that everything we've done here meets with his bank's approval, apparently. The president wouldn't have signed, otherwise. Which means Lizzy owes nothing in the interim while we wait for Phillip's and my late husband's paperwork. Based on my estimate of tonight's income, by the time the first payment comes due, she will be more than ready to make it. Especially since by then we…and any business in town which does the same…" I said a little louder, "…will have extra monies from travelers."

"Is that right?" Everett asked Nicholas Brandt.

"Only theoretically…"

"All right, then." Everett tipped his head and set his hat on it. "You and your fiancée must be ready to pay. Have a good evening, Mr. Brandt. Ma'am."

Amber wheeled toward the door. Nicholas unrolled several bills from a wad he should have been ashamed of and dropped them onto the table.

"And this is for you." Everett handed Lizzy more than enough to cover his and his friend's food. "My compliments to everyone here for a fine, fine meal. And especially fine to see you again, Mrs. Strong."

The train's whistle faded as Everett returned to his table, where Lizzy followed him with a smile. I watched the marshal and his friend and noted the extra bill Everett handed Lizzy as they turned to leave.

"Mrs. Strong, there is one more point the bank wants to make," Mr. Brandt spoke just as I spotted it— the tiny well-sewn tear in the elbow of Everett's friend's jacket, the stitching so precise the fix lay nearly invisible. The slight mismatch of the nap gave away the mended hole in the Southwestern Kansas man's sleeve. "As long as this restaurant is in the position to wait and the contract on hold, the bank maintains the say of how business will be conducted. And to protect our interests, we won't have a trigger-happy employee on the premises. It's up to you, Mrs. Strong, to make sure the cook is gone."

Gone.

Like the man who might be my Jim as he and Everett disappeared through Eat Here's door.

Chapter 13

"This is the inn." Lizzy flipped a hand at the front of a building, bare just like all of the others along Larned's main street. She dropped her hand back to her side and turned toward me. "I know you missed your train last night…for me. I can't thank you enough. A sacrifice like that proves what Mr. Brandt doubts—you mean everything you say."

"What? No…well most…"

"I don't need that paperwork to prove anything. I see in you what my brother saw in your late husband."

"Well, I doubt he saw…"

Lizzy grabbed my hand. "You've worked so hard, Penelope, and you deserve what you've come to this inn for." She glanced at the building. "I only ask that you don't."

"But I…how did you…" I reached for the steps' rail as the ground seemed to reach up for me.

"I realize nothing here is like what you're used to, and the little room I gave you isn't much, but do you think it could do until you go?"

"My room? Is that what you're talking about?" I held tight to the rail while I fanned my face. "My room is fine, Lizzy. I'm quite happy with it." Well, content might be more accurate. Sort of satisfied.

"Then you'll stay at Eat Here instead of…" She shrugged a shoulder toward the inn.

"Of course I will. I'm here because…" Because of Jim. But also because of her. Because whatever I found out about Jim… "I have a question for someone…for whoever runs this inn." For the man who stayed in it, actually, to see for myself if he was my Jim, to recognize the sense of him, hear his name in his voice. To pry open my door and marry him for the right reason, for love instead of duty. So I could tell Lizzy I did mean everything I said—but not all of it had been the truth.

"The Cringers," she gushed. Lizzy was nearly giddy. "They're hardly ever there, but they might be."

"I'll only be a minute." I pried my hand from hers, from her relieved giggle as she let go.

The inn looked empty, as empty on the inside as it was bare on the out, though I prayed at least one body was there. The windows were dark, the front door closed beneath a blank sign that I wondered if at one time had said Sleep Here. My heart beat louder than the door's squeal as I pulled it my way. Desperation mingled with protest, a disjointed cacophony in my chest as I stepped into the dark cave of an entryway. Shutting the door behind me, I let my eyes adjust to the gloom and the empty counter across from me, a bank of numbered cubbies behind it with keys in each. The ceiling vaulted upward, and a spiral of stairs wound its way toward the top. This cavern of a building should have brimmed with life, but it felt and smelled stagnant—no perfumes, no oils, only dust.

"Hello?" My voice traveled upward. "Is anyone here?" My echo faded as I counted the cubbies, seven rooms and seven keys. I bolted forward. I would check them all. Surely he'd still be here.

Floor to floor and door to door I ran in ways Mama would chastise me for, and called in a voice which would make her faint as I knocked at each. My hellos, my requests for anyone, especially a Jim, went unanswered at every one.

"Penelope?" The front door squealed again, and Lizzy's gentler voice rose from below to the top floor, where I stood with my forehead against the last unanswered door.

I'd found nothing, no one. Where could he be? Surely not far. I walked to the rail and peered over it. "I'll be right down."

I began my descent, glanced one last time at each door as I did. Everett's friend had been tired to the point of near collapse. Whatever had been rough in southwestern Kansas weighed on him, understandably kept his attention there instead of here, leaving Everett to see if everything…if I…had been all right.

I couldn't ask Everett outright about the man, but if they were still here in town… One close look, one sound of the man's voice, and I would know.

"Is there a marshal's office?" I asked Lizzy at the same moment she said, "Before you go, could you tell me a little about your life before you came here, and your husband?"

The two of us stepped from the inn into the Kansas wind.

"My husband?"

"Mr. Strong…" Lizzy laughed.

"Oh, yes. Alex. I'm sorry. I suppose I'm tired." I made my way to the wooden walkway, and she followed.

"Aren't we all." Lizzy marched alongside me,

certainly as tired as I felt, though the blue of her eyes seemed bluer.

"You should have stayed behind and rested this morning, Lizzy." Like I'd insisted, so she wouldn't see what I was up to.

"I couldn't have rested even though Cook said he has things under control." She continued alongside me at a brisk pace.

Drat Cook. She might have stayed if he hadn't ushered her out the door with me and kept Tina behind to do who knows what. To clean, he'd said. To get ready for the official opening at noon. I shuddered at what he might really be doing.

"He'd better be in the kitchen with both hands on pans, cooking what I said, the way I said." Another shudder passed through me.

Lizzy laughed. "We can go back if you want, but as for your question, there is an office for a deputy. We don't have one, though. Everett takes care of the whole territory. He's always on the move, which made me surprised to see him last night. I wonder how he found out about the pre-opening."

"He probably didn't know about it. Just lucky that he needed a meal as he passed through." He and his friend.

"No. He knew. He told me he knew all about what we've done and the reopening, but he didn't say how he found out. Certainly interesting that he came, don't you think?" She tilted her head as she smiled at me, too much of a tilt and too much of a smile.

"Maybe his friend knew about it. Did you know the man with Everett?"

Lizzy shook her head. "He looked a little familiar,

but when Phil ran the restaurant I didn't work there." The wind caught the enormous brim of her bonnet and covered her face. She left it that way. "Anyway," she said from within a hat that hid a lot, "I imagine Everett and that man are both gone. But we can stop by the deputy office to see." She lifted the brim and peered at me from within a hat I decided to buy.

There had been a train. Early in the morning one had passed through. I'd listened from the cot where I'd lain awake all night. Everett likely traveled by horseback, since he toured the territory, but not his friend. Surely no one could sit on a horse from somewhere in the southwest to here. "They're probably gone, like you said."

"We can ask Clement," Lizzy offered through the funnel of her hat. "He runs the stagecoach lines. He knows a lot about comings and goings...and he's much easier to talk to than Mr. Weston when it comes to passengers or tickets."

I frowned in the direction of the train depot, the scene of another spectacle I would make of myself and preferred Lizzy didn't see. "I do need to..." I indicated the ticket booth where Mr. Weston's shiny head bobbed over whatever occupied him on the other side of the window. There were no trains, no passengers in sight. No Everett, and no friend. Nothing to distract the man I intended to demand an open ticket from which wouldn't pin me to a specific day or time. "I'll just be a minute."

"Of course. And again, I'm sorry, Penelope. I know you have other places you need to be and other people to help besides me." Lizzy nibbled her lower lip.

I placed a hand on her arm. "It's not time for me to go yet. There is too much unfinished business here."

Like Cook's position, a pending contract to secure to keep Mr. Brandt away, an oasis to build, and a town to educate, if they'd listen. All wrapped neatly up in time for me to leave either for or with the fiancé I intended to find. Maybe today. I eyed the ticket booth across the platform.

"Good luck," Lizzy whispered. "Just make sure you call him Mr. Weston." Lizzy stayed safely behind as I marched to the booth's window.

"Mrs. Strong." Mr. Weston looked up from whatever papers he'd been involved with and gazed through the bars at me. "Here to purchase another ticket, I presume?"

"I'm here to do no such thing. I have a ticket, as you'll recall."

"Had. You had a ticket," he said through the barred window. "I believe that train left over twelve hours ago."

"I missed it due to circumstances beyond my control."

He shook his head as a series of tsks ratcheted from between his lips. "I've been a ticket master too long to believe circumstances have control over us. I've heard every excuse imaginable for a missed train, blame always put upon someone or something other than the one who chose to miss it. If you think back, Mrs. Strong, to seven o'clock yesterday and the thirty minutes or so after it, you'll likely realize you made a choice. And it wasn't to be here for a train." His bald head glimmered, a light which shone on my reasons— on Lizzy, on Everett's friend—on the heat which raged across my face because Mr. Weston questioned my reliability.

"I made a choice for the sake of someone else." I slapped a hand on the window's ledge. Lizzy turned, and I lowered my voice. "Now you can make a choice for me."

"I made a choice for you, Mrs. Strong. I gave you a ticket for the seven-thirty train yesterday evening. That was your open door, and you chose to miss it. Consider that door closed."

One closed door was enough. I glared at his smug look and the papers he'd sorted, looking through bars my arms would easily fit through.

"So, Mrs. Strong, are you ready to purchase another ticket?"

I eyed the man who blocked any quick and easy way out of town, but saw Uncle Roy instead, his attorney, and the problems they'd caused Mama and me. "No. But I'll be back." I would do what I'd learned in St. Louis—outsmart, outthink, and out plan my enemy. Mr. Weston had a first name, and someone in town would know it.

"Where's this Clement?" I barked, and Lizzy pointed toward another building farther down the street.

"I take it your talk with Mr. Weston didn't go well." Lizzy huffed to keep up as I marched in the direction of the stagecoach office.

"Let's just say I didn't go there for a lesson on how to make good choices." I kicked at the wind and the skirt it bound around my legs.

"I'm glad Phil didn't take the train when he went west for the gold," she said. "Several of the men did. But God only knows if he'd ever have gotten a ticket back home if every depot has someone like Mr. Weston in charge."

"Several men went?" I stopped. "You mean Larned had its own little gold rush out of town?"

Lizzy nodded, her bonnet flapping open and shut as my tiny hat left every bit of my frustration exposed. "Because of the posters…"

"Posters? What posters?"

"They were all over town, advertisements for men willing to work new veins for good pay and part of the gold."

"So you know the places Phillip could be?" The horror of it struck me all over again. It shouldn't be that difficult for Lizzy to figure out where her brother had gone…and even worse, when he would come back.

"I know where he first went. I wrote him and he wrote back, but that was so long ago. I sent another letter but have heard nothing since. I keep hoping he'll answer. Or just come home."

My goodness. I definitely needed an open ticket out of here. "Does Larned have a postal office?" I prayed she'd say no, and yes. If Phillip didn't come, a letter could…but I certainly needed to figure out a way to get one to Mama so she wouldn't come either.

"It's the same place as the stagecoach office." Lizzy tilted her head the direction we were headed. "Clement manages both."

Drat. "Maybe we should get back to the restaurant."

"The stage office is where Phil first saw the posters."

Drat again. I needed to meet this person, not just because of Phillip but also because of Mama. Things I couldn't do with Lizzy along. "We really should get back. Or at least you should, since you're in charge."

"Come on. I'll show you Clement's building first. And I'll introduce you to him, though you've met him."

"I have?"

"He came to the opening last night. You gave him a table, but you might not have noticed him. Especially in all the rush." Lizzy set a new pace, a smart clip I dragged behind until she stopped at the dull and paint-free building. "This is it." She opened the door and held it for me. A clerk across the room looked up as we entered, and rose to his feet behind a worn desk. Lizzy was right. I had seated him at Eat Here the night before, simple good looks which sat alone while he ate.

"Mister…" I extended a hand across a neat desktop to a man focused solely on Lizzy. "Mister…"

"Mr. Jones. Please call me Clement." He took my hand. He was older than Lizzy…and me…but not by much. Slender, a full head of hazel-colored hair which matched his eyes, straight strands smoothed to the side above a forehead etched with tiny creases.

"I'm happy to meet you, Clement. I'm Mrs. Penelope Strong. I'm in town to help…"

"Her." He let go of my hand.

"Her brother's restaurant," I said.

'Her' remained on his face as he gave a slight nod. "I went last night to the opening. Quite a crowd. Most of I arned attended, for sure."

"Maybe not as many as there would have been, since Lizzy just told me several men went in search of gold."

"They did."

I waited for him to say more. Apparently Clement was a man of few words. No wonder he sat alone last night. "They did that because…" I waited again, then indicated his office, the walls neatly lined with schedules, advertisements, even Wanted Posters. "Because of some posters," I said to help him.

"That…yes," Clement agreed. I gave Lizzy a look, one she answered with a hidden smile and a tiny shrug, then she drifted away to check the walls for posters Clement had been no help with.

"She wants to find her brother," I whispered to Clement once she reached the farthest side of the room. "Hear from him, at least." I let the suggestion dangle for a man hopelessly incapable of taking hints.

Clement's gaze followed Lizzy as she studied the items posted on his walls. "I'm not sure where Phillip is." His voice, also low, drew me closer to his desk. "There's been no word, no new letters, and several veins of gold were advertised. Men dispersed in different directions, and it's hard to say if they stayed where they started or moved around. Or worse…"

Or worse? I wanted to gasp at what worse would do to Lizzy. Mr. Brandt had hinted at such, the day he and Lizzy stood and watched my train for Phillip. "Do you have any of the posters still?" I leaned into Clement's desk. Phillip had to be found, preferably by me.

"Mr. Brandt took them all back."

"Mr. Brandt?" I straightened.

"He had them hung to begin with." Clement tapped on his desk. "You handled him well last night, by the way."

"It helped having a marshal behind me."

"Marshals can be a deterrent, but they're most effective when something tangible's been stolen," Clement mused. "Outright stolen. Not when

114

something's been eased out of fingers that are forced to let go." The tapping stopped. Clement splayed his fingers and pressed them to the desk's top.

"Eased out of fingers? Like…" I waited again for Clement to finish his thought and my sentence. "Eased out like Lizzy's brother? Her…"

"Song."

"Her song?"

Clement nodded. "She let it go. But in reality, it's been stolen."

The smile I've carried inside has surfaced now. Your words brought it to my face. Where it stays. You've written a song in my heart I can finally hear.

Lizzy'd had a song? Like Jim had? Like I found out so late that I had as well. Something in the heart which sang. Lizzy perused the last wall, her back still to us, wisps of blonde hair dangling from her bonnet. She'd lost her brother and her song. She'd done nothing but lose. Just like I had.

"Lizzy told me Larned lacks its own deputy," I said.

Clement nodded. "We do need one. Everett intends to place them all over the territory, including here."

A deputy. Everett's friend. Of course. Suddenly I understood. His friend wasn't Jim, but a man in search of a position. The brown hair, the mended jacket, the weariness, the rough something he'd been through, everything that had spoken of Jim…had spoken of a lawman instead. Everett's friend hadn't suffered through the sort of rough I'd imagined, the heartache I'd guessed, but from other more professional reasons. A profession he might have proven himself a better candidate for if he'd paid more attention to the ruckus than to his food. "So that man with Everett last night was…"

"No." Clement shook his head. "He's the marshal's friend from southwest of here. Not a deputy. He has land down there somewhere."

"Land? To farm or raise cattle on?" Or both? I gripped the desk.

"Not sure, but seen him here before. Never seen him look so glum, though. Something took the heart and soul out of that fellow, and he didn't look any better when he boarded the early stage for up north this morning. Maybe what or whoever's up there will make him feel better by the time he gets back. He and the marshal plan to meet up here again shortly."

My goodness. Should I stay or go? The man had so many of Jim's characteristics, from his build, the color of his hair, to the tiny mend in his sleeve. He'd been here before and would be back. "So he's…"

"Not the one."

"Not the one?"

"Nope." Clement shook his head. "Everett McCloud is."

"What?"

"If he'd take Larned as his and assign deputies everywhere else, there'd be fewer losses of the type Lizzy suffered."

"Oh. I see." Like last night, the way Lizzy let go of her smile at Mr. Brandt's words, then the way Everett restored it. "You've been helpful, Clement." Sort of. "But I have one more small favor to ask. I need to send a letter…"

"No need to be embarrassed asking me for help. Lots of folks around here can't read or write."

I stiffened. "I can both read and write." My voice sounded piqued and Lizzy glanced over her shoulder. "I mean I need help with the sending." I lowered my voice. "It can't be from here. From Dodge City would be better. Business matters…" My face warmed.

"I see." Clement's brows furrowed as Lizzy finished her study of Clement's walls and returned to my side. She shook her head. No posters. No brother. No song beneath the trust which looked at me. She stood alone without Everett, without an active deputy. But she stood with me, and once I wrote Mama I'd have more time for her…and Jim.

"I'll return soon to discuss my letters," I said to Clement to squelch any questions Lizzy didn't need to hear. I turned to her. "And I think it's time we went to the bank, Lizzy." To its ornate door, its gleaming windows, and money no one else had. Posters and possibly the whereabouts of a brother I had to find so I could contact him. Especially before he contacted his sister…or came home…and demolished everything I'd started for her, including the trust I wanted her to keep even after she knew the truth. "Thank you, Clement, and I'm glad to have met you."

"You as well." Clement's frown deepened as he bowed slightly.

"But before we go…" I raised a finger. "You wouldn't happen to know Mr. Weston's first name, would you?"

The frown vanished. Clement reddened and fidgeted with nothing on his desk. "It's Julius. But he's not fond of it."

Julius. *Et tu.* "Thank you. And good day."

Lizzy and I exited and hurried back down the

walkway toward the bank.

"You know you'll never get a ticket out of here if you use Mr. Weston's first name, don't you?" A grin lit Lizzy's face as we rushed.

"When I *choose* to get my ticket, Mr. Weston will *choose* to do things my way." I smiled. "Did you bring last night's money with you, Lizzy?"

"I did."

"I suggest we don't keep it at the bank after all," I announced. "Do you trust Cook?"

She nodded. Vigorously. And I had to agree with her. Drat.

"I suggest we appoint Cook guardian of all funds," I said as we neared the bank. "I think that should squelch any arguments Mr. Brandt may raise about Eat Here." And who works there. "I plan to say a few things to Mr. Brandt that I want you to just agree with," I said to Lizzy. "I'll explain later."

Lizzy nodded.

You've written a song in my heart I can finally hear.

I would help Lizzy find her song and get it back, while I waited for the one who might be my song to come back. I had work to do and a letter to write to Mama, a slight delay I prayed she'd trust while I went in search of everyone's songs…even Mama's.

Chapter 14

Cook hunched over my back as I bent to reach into the oven. "You need to move." Hot air and cinnamon wafted past my face and hopefully into his. "I said you need to move." I inched backward in an unladylike shuffle, a hot pan of freshly baked rolls in my hands, and a dozen questions mulling around in my head.

"I see you've concocted more of that aroma stuff," Cook groused, his voice muffled, probably by a hand clapped over his nose and mouth.

"If you don't step back, I'll expect you to marry me after this." I shuddered as he snorted through fingers I wouldn't put anywhere near my mouth.

"Might be that where you're from a man proposes to a woman's hind end, but out here we prefer to ask to her face." He paused. "Say, that wouldn't be how Mr. Strong…"

"Of course not. No one proposes that way. Now will you move?"

Cook inched back. "Might be advantageous, proposin' that way, I suppose."

"Advantageous?"

"Behoovin'?"

"Oh, for Heaven's sake." I let the pan clatter to the table alongside the one already there to cool and flapped my towel over both to fan cinnamon Cook's way. "Neither word is appropriate when discussing the solemnity of marriage." Especially from an overly whiskered mouth.

"Proposin' or bein' proposed to before you set eyes on the other could be advantageous in some situations. It happens, you know. Especially out here where…"

"I said move." I grabbed the last pan of raised cinnamon rolls and leaned down to the hot oven, slid the pan in, and slammed the door. My face burned. "We've no time to discuss marriage proposals. We have meatloaf to make for today's noon meal, and we need to get started."

"Never heard of such a thing," Cook muttered through the fingers he frowned over.

"Probably because it isn't fried."

"So yer husband met you before you married? Face-to-face?"

Not yet. Or maybe he had, the other night at Eat Here's pre-opening. And would again when he and Everett returned to Larned. "What happened between Mr. Strong and me is none of your business, God rest his soul. You and I have more important concerns to focus on now."

His eyes narrowed. "Important? What is it you're up to?"

"Up to? Why, nothing."

"I doubt that."

"Well there is one thing you might be able to help me with. Clement said something about Lizzy's song."

The eyes that had been slits widened.

"He said it hadn't been stolen, but almost. And not that a deputy could have prevented it, but that there isn't one here." I fidgeted with a nearby towel. "The town apparently needs one, and I thought maybe the man with Everett the other night could…"

"He cain't because he ain't, and it's enough you're messin' with Lizzy's restaurant. Don't go interferin' with her song. Or the law, for Pete's sake."

I planted floury fists on my hips. "I'm not the interfering type, and Larned and Lizzy's song legitimately concern me."

"The only thing needs to concern you is the meat hunks you wanna make." Cook narrowed an eye. "Which makes me wonder, why is it yer still here? Ain't you done enough already?"

"Meat loaves, and I'd thank you to credit my ability to take care of problems, as it deserves."

"The only problem around here is you. And meat hunks or meat loaves, no matter what you call 'em, folks ain't gonna go for 'em."

"Of course people will like them. Meatloaf is popular where I'm from. The meat is chopped and ground, then mixed with onion and spices, and slowly baked. It is savory and aromatic, and will work just like these cinnamon rolls."

"Ain't gonna be nothin' aromatic about meat you start cookin' before the sun's even up. We'll be servin' rawhide come noon."

"I said *slowly* baked so its odor, along with that of these rolls, will spread. You might have noticed that new cheesecloth-covered door I had hung out front last night. It lets the aroma that's in here pass through to the street. Fragrance seeps out, and hungry diners come in. All part of my ability to help solve others' problems, not be one."

"Pshaw. I saw that door and I intend to take it down. The only thing that contraption's gonna do is let folks slip in without me knowin'. I cain't see through that cheese stuff to tell who's comin', and I cain't hear 'em without the big door squeakin' when they open it."

"You won't touch that door. And I've ordered screen, so your first problem will be solved."

"You what?"

"I said I…"

"I know what you said. Are you sure yer husband actually met you before the weddin'?"

That's why I said no pictures, no drawings, only words… A face doesn't last a lifetime. My brown hair will get lighter…maybe even disappear. My weathered skin will thin, my eyes become watery, my strong stature frailer. But my heart, that should remain, and that you will know.

"All this fuss about my marriage is a waste of our time." I locked my arms across my chest. Then dropped them. "Unless you're thinking about marriage…" Now I wanted to clap a hand over my mouth. Surely not. Poor Tina. I had to warn her. If a sight-unseen proposal churned in Cook's thoughts, then the object of his affection couldn't be her. But if somehow he did hinge his intentions on Tina… I shuddered. That would be worse.

"I take marryin' serious and consider a proposal as bindin' as a ceremony. A man should think on it before he asks. Changin' yer mind is like takin' a bullet back once you shoot. You cain't. So you gotta be sure when you raise that gun or pop the question."

I felt the bullet. It landed in the mush which beat inside my chest. I felt the hit, heard the chaos, crossed my arms again so Cook couldn't hear what he seemed to have an uncanny ear for. "Let's get back to the meatloaf…"

"That ain't no way to treat a lady, changin' yer mind. I wouldn't do somethin' like that, so yes'm, I do think on things."

"Enough of this talk." My voice ranged beyond proper. "And I don't know why everything has to be about guns and bullets out here."

"You mean instead of bein' about aromas and holey doors?"

"Those are strategies, and just as viable as weapons as your firearms are. They're part of a plan."

"Mrs. Strong, out here a bullet's far more effective for accomplishin' somethin' than a pile of meat."

"It's a loaf of meat. And your weapon hurts people, whereas mine is to be smart."

"How's a bunch of odor gonna outsmart the bank who's holdin' both of Lizzy's contracts?"

"Well it's a twofold plan, if you must know. The first part is to draw customers, local and traveling, to increase Lizzy's income. The second is to delay the contract so Lizzy has time to make more than enough money to pay everything off at once. Then she can wash her hands of the bank for good."

"Delay? You mean that paperwork that's on its way from back east?"

"No. Yes. Sort of. It just so happens the original paperwork between Phillip and my late husband is unattainable right now. I informed Mr. Brandt when Lizzy and I stopped there yesterday that the bank which first drafted it has been sold. I hadn't realized that until the other night when I went through all of Alex's papers."

"You just now went through yer late husband's

papers?"

"Well…it took me a while to get to it. I'm a distraught widow."

"And Brandt didn't balk at that?"

"Of course not. I *am* a distraught widow. But I promised him I'd write the new bank and ask the whereabouts of the original documents. It will just take longer than expected."

"I smell somethin', and it ain't savory or aromatic." Cook yanked at his apron, wrestled his way out of it, and slapped it on the table. "Brandt might be toleratin' this delay…which I doubt he is…but I don't like it. There are more holes in yer strategy than there are in that cheesy door you put up, and ain't none of it gonna do Lizzy or this town a bit of good in the end. I need air. I need to think. Bake yer own meat hunks."

"Loaves."

"Call 'em whatever you like." Cook aimed a finger at me. "Since you've been in Larned, every business is under new rules and restrictions by the bank. Every contract has been tightened to a stranglehold because of the one you finagled for Lizzy. Folks are gonna get scrawny eatin' what's on your new menu here, and then when winter comes they won't be able to hold up. What you're doin' ain't smart and it ain't good for Lizzy or the town. Those supposed smarts of yers ain't doin' nobody a bit of good. I'd say it's time for you to be movin' on." Cook wheeled, a blur of fury and hair as he yanked the back door open and slammed it behind him. The lock I'd had made splintered, and pieces of wood clattered across the floor.

I did all of that? Harmed so many just so I could find one?

"I know how to chop up and grind meat, ma'am."

Les's quiet offer hung in the air as I bent and gathered what remained of my lock, collecting its broken pieces before I turned to the whisper behind me. "You can?" I asked the less which proved once again to be more.

"Yes, ma'am. I can." Les bobbed his head.

"That would be wonderful. Thank you."

"Cook ain't so bad." Tina stepped into the kitchen and around Les, then me. She opened the oven and saved the rolls, which had browned too much, her movements smoothly stilted as she set the tray on the counter.

How long had they been in or near the kitchen? How much of what Cook said had they heard? How much of it did they agree with? How much did I need to face?

"I'll ice these rolls and get them out to the diners." Tina reached for the thin glaze I'd made. Maybe she hadn't heard Cook, especially his marriage ideals. "Your door idea's working, Penelope." Tina nodded toward the dining room as she finished icing the rolls. "It's filling up in there. Everyone wants to try one of these."

"Really? I mean...well, Cook thought..." I stared at the door he had slammed. "He said..."

"We need him." Tina grasped onto the tray. "And we need you too." She darted from the kitchen with a pan of my plan. She had just extended grace to me, but devotion to Cook.

"You ready to show me how to start the meat heaps?" Les asked from beside me.

"Loaves." I looked at the boy, at his uneasy blush,

a boy whose every move and word attested to a lack of fine teaching and being raised right. He needed so much. "And, yes, let's get started."

My hands moved mechanically as I arranged the meat, the cleavers, and the grinder Les dragged from somewhere. I spoke with the same rhythm as my hands, an emotionless beat of words and broken phrases, remnants of a ridiculous plan. Cook had been right. Maybe I wasn't so smart…especially out here. I should go on to Crooked Creek and look or wait there for my Jim…unobtrusively and naïvely…if he happened to be Everett's friend.

The back door banged open as whiskers and grumbles exploded through it. I looked away. I wouldn't give Cook the chance to see on my face how right he'd been.

"One thing I can teach you, Les, is the definition of a true gentleman." I splayed my hands on the counter.

Cook grumbled something unintelligible as he stomped across the floor.

"Lesson one, no gentleman ever leaves or enters an establishment with brutish force. Doors are to be…"

"Scoot." Cook shoved between Les and me as he fought to get the apron he had shrugged into over his pistol. "Git on. Me and the boy can do this. You got better things to do."

Better things like pack and leave, apologize to everyone on my way out of town. I would, but not because this coot said I should.

"I will not 'git on.' Les and I happen to be in the middle of your job, and we intend to finish it, so 'git' yourself."

"Mrs. Strong, you ain't listenin'. As usual. I said

you need to git."

Les drank in everything, his eyes wider than his scrawny frame. I stepped between him and Cook and spoke so the boy couldn't hear. "Maybe I have made a mess of some things for the town, and maybe for Lizzy as well. Honestly, I just... Oh, never mind. You'd never understand. I will fix my mistakes and start with Mr. Brandt. I'll talk to him..."

"No, you won't." Cook spoke loud enough anyone could hear.

"I will so." My volume rose.

"No, you won't talk to that ba..." Cook glanced at Les. "Banker. You need to talk to them instead." Cook yanked his head toward the back door.

"Them?"

"Like I said, you got better things to do, 'cause there's things you apparently do better. Holt, Griffen from the leather shop, Miller the blacksmith, and a few others want to hear more about what all you've done for Lizzy and that oasis you yap about. Guess your strategy's aromatic, at least." Cook latched onto a cleaver. "I told 'em they could meet here tonight after we close, if that's all right with you."

"They're out there now?"

"Yep. Waitin' to see if you'll agree to meetin' with 'em."

"They need me..." Eat Here needed me.

I need you.

"Surprisin' to me as well."

"Of course I'll meet with them." I fumbled with my apron. "We can have regular meetings. This will benefit Lizzy, especially if the whole town works together to welcome travelers. Pretty soon our rolls will be in stores, and some of their goods will be here. There'll be trinkets and gifts all over town, which travelers will be eager to buy." I spoke fast as I strained and struggled to untie the strings in back.

"Slow down just a goldarned minute." Cook whacked the cleaver into the countertop's wood. I jumped. Les jumped as well. "Stand still and stop squirmin'." Cook came around behind me. I stood still for hands I hadn't wanted anywhere near me, as Cook worked to undo the knot I'd created.

"Lizzy sold her song," he said near my ear.

I didn't move.

"And that man, the one you asked about with McCloud..." Cook spoke even closer. "Only a woman could put that look on a man's face."

Chapter 15

"The stage will be here any minute," I called into the kitchen. And he could be on it. Clement had said Everett's friend would be back. This could be his stagecoach. This could be the man Cook had said looked the way he did because of a woman. And if it was my Jim, I'd let him know that I was the woman who'd hurt him somehow, though I didn't know how. And that my heart had broken for him as well. He'd be relieved. So would I. And because my plan for Lizzy and Larned was well on its way, Jim and I could…

"If you're announcin' the stage to insinuate I ain't ready for 'em, you're wrong, though I don't agree with none of this." Cook planted himself above trays of cookies, which lined the kitchen's counter, one hand not far from his pistol, the other wielding a spatula.

"I'm not insinuating anything. I'm just…" Excited about Jim, but relieved Cook stood over rows of golden cookies instead of another tray of charcoaled lumps like the hundreds we'd buried outside of town as I'd taught him how to bake my latest strategy to bring business Lizzy's way. "I'm pleased everything looks so inviting and smells so delectable. Except…" I tipped my head toward his gun.

"You'll thank me for it someday."

"Much more likely I'll thank you for baking the…"

"The what?" His face pinched, a dare to say the

word that sissified his name.

"The trays of sweet cakelike mounds with nuts and spices."

"You mean the waste of good flour and sugar."

"It's no waste. And we need as many as you can bake."

"Because you're expectin' trouble? These oughta do the job. Probably can kill most anythin' with 'em."

I swiped a tray from the counter. "Keep baking. We need several batches for tomorrow's stage as well, and enough for the afternoon train. Clement and Mr. Weston"—Julius—"will have their passengers either dropped off or sent here for refreshments, and we need to be ready."

Cook spat. It sizzled on the hot stovetop. "Don't sound smart to me to offer free eatin's to the stage drivers and train engineers. Not to mention the meal Weston finagled for lettin' you hang up a sign. The pittance Lizzy's gonna make over these...these things...won't cover the food those vultures will wolf down."

"You've sat in on my meetings with the local businessmen. You should understand what investment means by now. You're just irritated because you don't like the word *cookies*." I nodded at the spittle which had sizzled itself to a white dust. "And clean that up. We can't behave like barbarians here. We have to act and think like the people who will come through, cultured people who don't think of every surface as their spittoon. Sophisticated people who are used to fine dining and enjoyable shopping, and we will have it for them. Larned will feel like home to them. They'll tell their families and friends, and the town will grow."

"Fancy folks or not, you might as well understand I'll likely shoot anyone that calls me Cookie."

"Likely." I marched the tray to the dining room.

"Set it here." Tina patted a tabletop, white linen with an arc of pitchers of tea and lemonade in a half moon, room for the tray in the center.

I set it in place, then stood alongside her and admired everything—the elegance of the dining area, the aroma, the clean shine which had replaced the slippery sheen. The genteel atmosphere instead of the obstinate one in the kitchen Phillip had too hastily hired before he left.

"This should work just fine," I said, pleased.

"I hope so…"

"What do you mean, you hope so?" I followed Tina's pinched brow to the customers, mostly regulars who bent over their tables but stole glances at us and our cookie display.

"They just need a little encouragement. You know how slow some people are about change." Like the hoodlum in the back. "I'll take care of this." I snatched a napkin, stacked two cookies on top of it, and carried it to the nearest table. "Cookies to go along with your coffee? On the house, compliments of Eat Here as we try them out."

They looked down at their table and their hands and half-eaten breakfasts, sideways glances everywhere except the kitchen. Drat Cook. "These are cookeeeez," I pronounced clearly. "Nothing to do with…" They withdrew more, as if the aberration of Cook's name promised a bullet hole with it. "Fine." I marched to the next table, and the next, their stubborn refusals sending me on. "Very well," I said to the last group.

I mustered a barely civilized march to the kitchen. "People refuse to eat these," I railed the moment I cleared the kitchen doorway. "Have you done something to make them afraid?" I waved the napkin at Cook.

"You mean besides cook without lard like they're used to? Let you scare 'em to death with white tablecloths they're terrified to git dirty?" Cook slapped a towel next to a tray of cookies.

I glanced around for a towel to slap over his. "I'm referring to what you might have done, not me. Our customers are afraid to eat the cookies."

"They ain't eatin' 'em?" Cook's brows raised.

"That's what I said. How dare you stand in the way of Lizzy and progress."

Cook's brows lowered, and he stared beyond me at the doorway to the dining room. "It ain't me." He lifted his towel and wrapped it around his hand. "Hmmm. And after all you did to the contrary, that I thought surely ruined everythin'… Well I'd say you got bigger problems than me, Mrs. Strong." He unwound and laid his towel aside. "Yer strategizin' musta caught the ear of someone equally strategizin'. Word spreads faster than a bullet amongst towns like this."

"That's ridiculous. And besides, no one is more strategizing than I am."

"Yer meetin's with the townsfolks did it, I'd say. But who…" He tugged his beard then snapped his fingers. "Someone who's got his hand in every single one of those folks' pockets. If he says don't eat…"

"You mean Mr. Brandt? He wouldn't say a thing like that."

"Are they eatin'? It ain't me that's keepin' 'em

from eatin' them…" Cook brandished his arm over the trays. "Them things, so somebody else is."

That would be foolish. Mr. Brandt may be unschooled, but he took his position seriously. "No good banker would cut his own throat by keeping a chokehold on the businesses he supports."

"Good bankers ain't always good men." Cook waved his arm over "them things" again. "If you weren't so busy doin' all the talkin' at yer meetin's, you might have learned a thing or two yourself. Like how Larned and towns like it were supposed to have grown with the railroad comin' through. Everybody got the word to git ready for it. Businesses stocked up without the funds to do it. That's where the bank stepped in. Loanin' funds, then callin' 'em back in. Claimed they'd lent too much and had to recover funds."

"And that's why Phillip went off to the mines."

"He did. I came to town lookin' for work right after signs sprang up yakkin' about successful strikes. Quite a few went, some turnin' their businesses or land over to the bank and takin' their families with 'em. Eat Here's the only restaurant in town, so Brandt offered to let Phillip borrow a little extra to keep it goin'."

"Because Larned would eventually grow."

"But it ain't. I warned him."

"You warned him growth takes time? That maybe the push to be ready came too soon?"

Cook snorted.

"Stop making that ridiculous noise. It's possible the bank made an error in judgment and even more erroneously decided the gold mines were a way to fix the problem. Lizzy told me about those posters. I tried to find one."

"You thinkin' about leavin' and pannin' for gold?" Cook's eyes lit up.

"Of course not. Did Phillip borrow the extra money before he left?"

"Some. He had to git some for the horse and wagon Brandt 'rented' him. But Lizzy came up with the rest."

Tina breezed into the kitchen and latched onto one of the cooled trays. "The stage just stopped out front. Got to get more of this good smell out there." She disappeared, with an inexplicable smile in spite of the terse silence in the kitchen. Cook's moods, glares, sour expressions, and phrases like, "Git out of my way," didn't set the same kind of fire in her that they did in me.

"You're saying there's another smell mingling with our aroma," I said more to myself than him.

Cook nodded. "Yep, somethin' surely does stink. But more important than that, yer aim just improved, Mrs. Strong."

"My what?" My goodness. Had I turned into a ruffian like him and just shot a bullet I didn't even know about through something I didn't understand? Mama would be horrified.

"Yer aim. You've been sharin' all yer fancy eastern lessons with us. Now it's time for you to latch onto some of the learnin' I've been tryin' to give you about the West. So listen...again. If somethin' foul's afoot, but you ain't sure who or what it is, you look for shadows. And you watch 'em. They're the spittin' image of the one that casts 'em, and they're the trail right to his feet."

"Shadows?" What a ridiculous and convoluted way to root out wrong. "I'm sorry. This makes no sense to me, no matter how much it does to you. And let both of us be clear on this—I'll never carry or shoot a gun of any sort."

"It would behoove you to learn how."

"I have no intention of learning how, ever. Words and being smart are weapons enough for me."

"Well, you certainly got a knack for slingin' words. And since you're so good at it, how about comin' up with a new word for these things I been bakin'?"

"Honestly, if you'd just go by your real name, the word cookies wouldn't be a problem for you."

"Real name?" Cook shook his head. "Lesson number two on survivin' the West. Real names end up on tombstones. Trust me."

I sputtered. "How absurd. Why, if I died today it would have nothing to do with my…" My name. My fake name. I felt myself blanch.

"I need another tray. The stagecoach folks love these, Penelope. You should come out and say hi to them. Some are asking for you." Tina breezed in and out again.

Everett's friend could be one of them. He could be my Jim, Jim Baylis, at last.

"We will call these Kansas Confections," I said. "No one will have told our regulars not to eat a Kansas Confection."

Cook grinned. "Look at you, Mrs. Strong. Ycr aim's gittin' better and better, and you ain't against usin' fake names at all. Somehow, I ain't surprised."

"Keep baking." I marched, skin on fire, to the dining area with my tray. How did that old coot do that? How could his aim be so accurate when he didn't even shoot? I set the tray on our side table, kept my back to the diners as I fanned my face and then checked my hair for loose strands. He could be here. He could be in this restaurant at this very moment. I patted hairpins and tucked them tighter.

"Well, things have certainly improved here. Who should I compliment for the change, Mrs. Strong?"

My hands stopped. I'd heard that voice before. I dropped my arms to my sides and turned. "Mr. Walters?" Rudy Walters, not a voice I'd ever expected to hear again.

"I thought maybe I'd stepped into the wrong place. Especially when I saw you." Rudy patted his jacket, his clothing every bit as fine as when I'd first met him…minus the handcuff. He was a man unbound as he looked from me to Eat Here. A new freedom marked the way he stood, the easy closeness, almost possessiveness, he displayed with his surroundings.

"I never thought I'd see you again either." I nearly clapped a hand over my mouth. What a careless thing to say to a man previously chained to a marshal. "I mean…"

"Shall we just concede we are both surprised?" Rudy gave me an unruffled smile. "Pleasantly surprised, I might add."

"Mr. Walters, I hardly think that is…"

Rudy raised a hand. "I merely meant I'm surprised but pleased to find you here. In fact, it's because of something you said that I've returned to Larned."

"Something I said?" I thought back to that day, raced through what boiled down to strained good manners interlaced with a few lies.

"Opportunity," Rudy said. "You remarked your husband had found investment opportunities here."

Oh. That lie. "Well, only one investment. This one." I tossed a wave across the room.

Rudy followed it, perused the dining area with a steady but casual study which stopped on Lizzy.

"So the little lady whose handkerchief I retrieved that day needed even more help. I see a table over there." He nodded her direction. "If the food has improved as much as the atmosphere, I'm anxious to see everything this investment offers."

I wasn't about to let an ex-prisoner or witness exercise his new-found freedom here. "There's no more offer…"

Rudy smoothed his jacket, then started the direction of the table.

Drat that I'd blathered falsehoods about investments and my fake husband. I latched onto a menu and followed him, set his menu and a roll of dinnerware on the white cloth so that his back stayed to everyone…especially Lizzy.

He took his seat with the grace of a perfect gentleman. He even opened the menu with finesse. "I must say, I did think your business here was to be brief, Mrs. Strong." Rudy glanced up. "That tells me things here have gone terribly well, or terribly wrong."

I stole a glance at his wrist. No redness, no sign of struggle. He could be free for all of the right reasons, possibly a good man who had needed protection more than us, a man merely ready to return to his prior life. "I discovered more needed done here than I thought. That is all."

"Or your husband thought."

"Pardon?"

"Your late husband. Complications he hadn't

foreseen. Or had time to."

"Oh. Yes." I prayed the heat on my face looked like unfinished grief.

"Then I credit you for being a good wife, Mrs. Strong. Your husband did well to find a woman like you. One who is clever and honors his memory by finishing what he started. And pretty as well." He turned his head to focus on the menu.

My goodness. Mr. Walters had been fresh when he'd been chained, and now that he'd been loosed he was even fresher yet. "That boy over there will take your order as soon as you decide what you want." I nodded toward Les. My good manners would likely fray at any more of Mr. Walters' impertinence. "I'll send him right over."

"No need to bother the lad," Rudy said. "I know exactly what I want."

Drat. "Very well. Proceed."

Rudy did proceed. Minute details the length of a book spilled out before he handed me the menu. Rudy Walters' order would cause Cook to spout like a geyser.

"Coffee also," Rudy said before I walked away. "Black, three quarters of a cup, no sugar but still a spoon with it, not in it." I staggered to certain doom.

I went for paper we kept at our side table, small scraps along with ink and a pen. I scribbled Rudy's long list of not just what but specifically how his lunch should be, as Lizzy stared, brows raised. "This is for Rudy Walters, that man over there." I paused and pointed with the pen. "You might remember him. He was chained to Everett when I arrived in town." I paused for emphasis, watched her nod, gauged the too-casual expression on her face. "As you can see from his order, he's pretty finicky. It's possible he's just glad to be free, but... Never mind. In any case, he wants coffee as well, black, three quarters of a cup, no sugar, but a spoon with it. Not in it. I don't want you to take it to him, but could you get it ready while I throw his elaborate order through the kitchen door to Cook and then run?"

We both looked at Rudy, his back comfortably to us, then at each other.

"Good luck." Lizzy glanced toward the kitchen then began to piece together Rudy's exact coffee order.

"Remember, don't take it to him. I will, after I risk life and limb with Cook." I carried Rudy's voluminous list to the kitchen, slid it across the table near the oven, and ran.

"Is this for those blasted drivers and that snob, Weston?" Cook shouted before I cleared the doorway. "Free don't include elaborate and frilly."

"No." I glanced over my shoulder. "It's not for them. But even if it had been, we're here to serve. This is for a paying customer, so please do your best."

"Just one customer?" Cook snatched up Rudy's order. Furrowed brows leveled as he stared at the paper. "I think I need to meet this person."

"Need I remind you that your job is to do as the customer requests, not discuss it with him?" I said from a safe distance.

"Well I might have a suggestion or two fer this one." Cook marched around me, paused in the doorway, and scanned the dining room. I crowded behind him, praying he'd ignore the one head which thankfully had its back to us.

"That's him, ain't it." Cook gazed long and hard at

Rudy.

"That 'him' is Mr. Walters. He's mannerly and finely dressed. He isn't some..." I paused. I could be wrong. Mr. Walters seemed a bit of a conundrum... "Is he a scoundrel?" I whispered.

"Like I told you not even an hour ago, you look for shadows."

Shadows. Goodness. "You go on back to the kitchen, and I'll ask Mr. Walters politely if he can make any concessions on his order."

Cook caught my arm as I stepped around him. "You'll just make a mess of things."

"I will not. I never..."

"You will. You always do. But I never do." Cook marched to Rudy's table, his pistol a bulge beneath his apron I prayed none of the travelers would notice.

Lizzy scurried to my side, her eyes bright as Cook propped himself straight-armed on Rudy's table.

"Cook says he's checking for shadows, or some nonsense like that." My head spun as I watched the two of them, praying there'd be no shooting. "Rudy's a bit forward, but his manners are refined."

Cook straightened as Rudy looked up at him.

"Rudy told me they released him after he gave testimony," Lizzy whispered.

"He told you what?" I asked. "You didn't even wait his table. When did he say that?"

"On my way here this morning I saw him out early on the street. I didn't say anything about it because I thought it didn't matter."

Early before the sun came up...before a shadow could be cast.

A faint color rose around Lizzy's neck. "He said he

learned something while bound to Mr. McCloud. It arrested him in a way that slowed him down and made him see life with the marshal's eye."

My goodness. Well, that couldn't be bad, except for unwarranted nosiness. We watched Cook and Rudy.

"Rudy said he might be able to find Phil. Do you think he could?" Lizzy whispered.

My goodness. Rudy had offered her the same treasure Cook suggested I had by using Phillip's name.

Cook turned and walked our way. "Keep yer eyes open," he muttered to Lizzy. "And yer mouth closed," he said to me as he marched past us to the kitchen.

"Well, I have several things to say, but not to Mr. Walters."

Rudy twisted our direction and raised a hand, his thumb and forefinger pinched as if he held a cup...or wanted to.

"I'll take it to him," Lizzy said.

"No, I will. No overly whiskered..."

"I have to, Penelope. For Phil."

She went to the side table and finished Rudy's drink the way he wanted it. I did as Cook said and kept my eyes on Rudy, who never took his off Lizzy as she approached. She set the cup in front of him, her face changing to red with whatever he said.

"Order up," Cook shouted.

I hurried to the kitchen, to a plate of such precision, such detailed perfection, I couldn't believe Cook had done it. "Why, this is a work of art."

He rattled pans at the stove, marched to his shelves, and returned two bottles to the rows of unlabeled spices he'd refused to mark or let me organize.

I took a whiff of Rudy's food and raised a brow.

"You wouldn't, would you?"

"I told you, shadows are trails. You need the shadow so you can trace it to the feet of the real culprit. You keep the shadow as long as you need it, then you git rid of both. Now git out there with his ridiculous order, and git Lizzy away from his table."

Chapter 16

I set the second letter I'd written to Mama beside me on my cot, pondered my most recent list of reasons why she shouldn't yet come, fabrications about crops and cattle I knew nothing about, and obligations which must be met before a wedding could take place. I set one hand on it and the other on my album of Jim's words on my lap, the bond between Mama's wish, my heart, and Jim's proposal. "Forgive the lies," I whispered to both of them. "It's all for the best."

The lack of a name or address other than my mother's on her letter shouted yet another lie. This one to Clement, who had argued when he saw the first one, even when I explained any letters I sent to the Archer family in St. Louis had to be mailed from Dodge City for business reasons. Hopefully Clement's affinity for Lizzy would keep him cooperative.

I opened Jim's album to hear again the voice my heart said to wait here for.

I've known you all along. Even in the alone times as I've worked this homestead, I've been readying it at the sound of your voice. You spoke to me before you ever wrote a word, and I recognized you at your very first letter.

I spread my hands over his letter, one of his last, then glanced around my room, the strange place I'd ended up. A place between me and my open door…unless Jim happened to be Everett's friend.

From what Jim said, he should recognize me, and I him, because we each had already known the other deep inside, though at the time he wrote this I saw no deeper than the rote ceremony to become his wife. But now my heart cried with the desire to cherish and be cherished by a man who stood tall, weathered, kind, and determined to make sure I was all right.

I turned the page to other letters and re-read his descriptions of himself, words which had built the vision of a strong husband with hair that matched mine, rugged from outdoor work, and a warm heart which brought gentleness to his face.

The Good Book says you can't give your heart to two at the same time. I certainly can't. I see that now. That must be why two become one. What they share makes something stronger, a joined heart with twice the room to receive and twice the capacity to give.

How had I missed this man's heart? I'd been such a fool, an old young fool, allowing twenty-eight years of age to be so terrifying I'd even missed my own heart inside.

Tell me about yourself, how you see yourself, how you see your future.

I shuddered. I'd told him too much, most likely. What man really wanted to hear some near-spinster's desperation to move from her past to her future which she laced with business strategies. Drat. I likely seemed scattered, a silly ninny and too clever at the same time.

Don't come. I can't marry you.

I looked away from his final telegram and flipped back to his letters, accounts and descriptions of the man who'd penned our lives together. A simple photograph couldn't have accomplished what Jim's words had, but it would have at least helped me recognize him, not left me baffled whether Everett's friend was him for sure. Drat again. I needed him to return soon. I needed to study him. More than anything, I needed to ask his name.

"Penelope?"

I shut the album and slid it along with Mama's letter under my cot. "Yes?"

"It's me. Lizzy." Her face, which had been so pale and afraid the day we'd met, peered around my room's door with color and conviction in its features. "Are you busy?"

I rose and stepped away from my lies to my mother and Jim's voice which continued to speak, his words and mine meant to build truthful sentences together, phrases which shouldn't have fallen apart. "Has the afternoon stage arrived?"

"Not yet, but it should be here any minute." Lizzy eased into my room and left the door slightly ajar. "Tina will let us know. I just wondered if you had a few minutes."

Lizzy never asked for a few minutes, only one at a time. Short pauses as we'd come to know one another, shared thoughts and brief smiles which entwined Elizabeth Sanders to Louise Elizabeth. Lizzy crossed the room toward Penelope Strong, but Louise Elizabeth waited for her.

"There's so much more I want to do here," I said the same time Lizzy said, "You've done enough here, Penelope."

We both frowned.

"There is more, though, things you and your

workers need," I said, as she said, "No."

"Yes, there is," I insisted. Not just her faded dress which needed replaced, or the stray wisps of straw-colored hair that suffered from a lack of combs. There were things that couldn't be seen, like her lost song I still didn't understand.

"No, Penelope," Lizzy said. "The temporary contract, the clean restaurant, the new menu, and now the cookies. Eat Here is doing so much better, thanks to you, and it would be wrong for me to keep you here any longer. You can't miss the chance to do what you really set out to do...fulfill Alex's desire. And because of your goodness to me, you live from a trunk when you should be just living."

I studied my sister in more than just name. We were two women stuck in temporary existences on our way from something left behind to something ahead. The sounds of happy diners sifted up from below. A sound I had helped create, an open door she had desperately needed to stabilize Eat Here, and one she could eventually escape through when Phillip returned. An open door that could lead to mine as well. "Alex would have stayed just as I have, Lizzy. I've learned that every investment requires enough commitment to see it through. And every commitment requires an investment."

She fumbled for a handkerchief. "That's just it, Penelope. Your husband's first commitment was to you. He wanted to make sure you were all right." Lizzy dabbed her eyes. "He never would have expected you to carry this much load yourself."

"He would understand. Alex happened to be a wonderful man." If my fictitious husband resembled the voice which said, *I want you to be all right*, then he would have been wonderful. "Phillip would feel the same about you being left here under such a load." At least he should.

"Phil would. He never intended for..." Lizzy's eyes erupted like fountains. I ran for one of my handkerchiefs and handed it to her. "It isn't like Phil to be so long without a word. He would write. He would come home. He felt so sorry about...he said he'd hurry to fix...things." Her face disappeared in sobs behind her and my hankies. "Do you think it's possible, Penelope?" Red eyes peered above a soaked wad of white. "Do you think Phil could be..."

"I think Phillip could be just fine, if that's what you mean. Gold mines would be scattered here, there, and yonder. Give him time. I'm certain you'll hear something soon."

Her arms wrapped around me and gripped me tight as she sobbed into my shoulder. She would never do this again if her brother returned. She'd regret this when Phillip told her he'd never heard of Alex or Penelope Strong. "Lizzy, when it's time for me to go, you'll be the first to know." And the first to hear the truth. I took her by the shoulders and held her at arm's length. And the time for that part was now. "There's something I have to say before..."

"Stage is here," Tina called up the stairs.

"Oh." Lizzy dabbed at her face. "I'm sorry. I don't know why I broke down so. All this talk about Phil... I guess I couldn't stand the thought of being here without him if you went too." She hiccupped and blew her nose into the soaked handkerchiefs. "I'm so selfish. I know I said you should go, but I truly don't want you to."

I went for another handkerchief and brought it to her, taking the soiled ones. "When I do go someday, Lizzy, I'm afraid you'll be glad I did."

"No, Penelope, never."

"Stage!" Cook's shout from the bottom of the stairs shook my room, a roar which surely terrified our customers.

"He won't pull his gun, will he?" I glanced toward the door.

"We'd better get down there." Lizzy swiped at her face, rubbed her cheeks, then took hold of my arm. "And never, Penelope. I'll never be glad to see you go."

****

Lizzy would be glad to see me go if I didn't tell her the truth before she found out some other way. I hustled Kansas Confections from table to table, hurried customers in and out so Lizzy and I could talk. She and Tina hustled along with me while Les ran clean and dirty tableware back and forth. The three of them worked, but I raced. Any swing of Eat Here's door could be Phillip.

"Coffee?" I smoothed the tablecloth with a free hand, the pot in my other, my attention on the door as it opened again.

"If it's as good as his."

"Mr. McCloud?" I looked from the door to the weary kindness seated at the table, the smile pointed up at me.

"His is excellent, but yours is close. So please fill both cups," Everett said with a comfortable grin. He nodded toward a man across the table. I looked from Everett to the man who made the best coffee...his friend. They had returned, at last, just as Clement said.

This could be Jim, the man who had shown me my heart. I studied the face that didn't look up. Everett's friend bent over his empty cup and rotated it with a finger. No, this couldn't possibly be my Jim. He would sense me. He would recognize me from our letters. Drat…he would recognize Louise Archer the moment he tasted this coffee. I withdrew the pot. I'd made his brew. I'd switched to it ever since Clement said this man planned to come back. I intended it to be a surprise, an eye opener for him to undo his *Don't come. I can't marry you.* But if his eye opener came in front of Everett, Lizzy, and all of Larned… Drat. The eye opener would be theirs. They'd be appalled when he called me Louise, and this man would never marry me.

Everett inched his cup my way. "I have to say, that coffee does smell good."

"It's cold," I blurted. "I'm sorry. This pot is nearly empty as well. I need to get some more. I need to brew some." I exhausted my lies. I couldn't have Everett's sullen friend who'd been undone by some woman…possibly me…say Louise Archer out loud. I couldn't have him and Lizzy both discover I was a liar without the chance to explain first.

"I'll take what little is left, if you don't mind." Everett smiled.

Drat again. I dribbled a thin stream into Everett's cup, barely a sip that I prayed would cool to the cold I'd claimed it to be. "That's all I have. I'll be right back. After I make fresh." After I made my own brew, not Jim's. I took a step backward as Everett raised his cup to his mouth. "It's different from what you had before," I said to his frown after he swallowed the tiny sip. "Not what you remember." I backed farther away. "I've been experimenting and came up with something new."

Everett set his cup down and eyed it. "We need to go." He rose to his feet, his chair rocking backward as he did. "We don't have time to wait."

His friend glanced up from the empty cup he still rotated. "We're going?" He stood. "Thank you, ma'am." He raked his fingers through coarse and disheveled brown strands before he covered them with his hat.

"Her name is Mrs. Strong." Everett dropped money onto the table. The face which had always been kind and attentive remained buried beneath the shadow of his hat. I clutched the pot close, felt its heat and fullness as Everett turned away. He walked through the door, his friend—the one with the mended tear in his sleeve, who made the best coffee, and who would recognize me if he was Jim—close behind.

Chapter 17

Eat Here's door flew open and stayed that way as a steady stream of weary travelers poured in, late arrivals from a delayed stagecoach, dusty and in search of our promised oasis. Sweaty exhaustion blended with Eat Here's scent of coffee and cinnamon as tables filled. My neck ached as I sifted through their faces and those of our regular customers, all of whom I seated and served, one eye on the door in hopes that he…Everett's friend…or Everett, had at last returned.

The door opened, then slammed definitively, a tall and sinewy man in front of it. Young and rough, steeped in a bare ruggedness he didn't try to hide, he panned the dining area until his gaze found me. Long legs started my way, an immeasurable stride which made nothing of the circuitous course around the tables.

"Mrs. Strong?" He towered over where I stood.

I clutched a coffeepot and nodded.

"I'm Deputy Joshua Cravens." He gave me a quick but thorough study, then tipped his hat. "I've been assigned to Larned. You were on the list of people Everett suggested I introduce myself to."

"List?" Everett? Gone? And relegating me to a list? I glanced at the door Everett's kindness had come through more than once. His tired smile actually gone just like Clement had said it would someday. But now? So suddenly? "Would you like some coffee?" The pot jiggled as I studied the stranger who took Everett's place.

"Yes, ma'am." Joshua sat. "That coffee smells mighty good." He grinned up at me. "Someone told me it was."

Everett would have told him that. "Two cups?" I asked. Maybe Everett really did have to leave after his sip, days ago, but had come back to help his new deputy get started. Maybe his kindness would return, less weary from now on with Joshua here. "I mean, do you expect anyone else?" I glanced at the door, at the trickle of newcomers who entered, no dark hat, no gentle smile, no comfortable strides my way. And no friend.

"Just me, ma'am." Joshua nudged the empty cup. "And maybe a menu?"

"Of course." I poured an unsteady stream of my brew into his cup as the door opened again. I glanced up as Rudy Walters stepped inside and scanned the busy restaurant while the door closed behind him. He paused, then made his own way toward an empty table.

"That'll do," the deputy said.

I looked where Joshua nodded. Coffee teemed over the brim of his cup and its saucer's edges, a brown circle which darkened the white tablecloth. "Oh my." I set the pot to the side, grabbed napkins, and tried to sop up the growing ring. "I'm so sorry…"

Rudy paused near Lizzy as I daubed, and said something. Hopefully just something finicky about what he wanted on his plate.

"Don't worry." Joshua laid a hand on my wrist. "Go on and wait on others. You've left me plenty of coffee to keep me satisfied until you bring a menu."

I caught his grin as I let go of the soaked napkins. "I'll be right back," I said as he took a sip from his over-full cup.

"Everett sure knows his coffee." Joshua returned the cup to the pool in the saucer. Everett had liked mine and praised Jim's, a recipe I refused to use again until the man drinking it knew who I was…first.

"Everett," I hedged. "He won't be…"

"Won't be coming back? Not often. He actually hired me weeks ago, then changed his mind. Said he might consider settling here instead of farther west like he always intended. Next thing I knew he sent a telegram, told me I had the job in Larned right away. Guess he decided to make somewhere else his permanent home after all."

Lizzy rushed to the table where Rudy had gone to sit, a cup three quarters full of coffee but no spoon alongside it on a saucer. I frowned. First at Everett's change of plans, then at Rudy's change of order. Lizzy bent close when she reached him, listened as he spoke while color drained from her cheeks.

"Everett won't be here…" I looked from Lizzy to Joshua. "Well, welcome, Deputy Joshua. I'm sure Everett chose well when he chose you."

"Everett does have a knack for choosing well." He eyed me and then his cup. "This coffee, I mean. It's the best I've ever had."

"It's not my best. But I'm glad you like it."

Joshua took another drink, gave a satisfied nod at the black liquid, and settled back in his chair. Long legs stretched in front of him as he studied the room.

"Kansas Concoctions." Cook burst into the dining area with a shout, a tray in one hand and a spatula in the other. The tray clattered on the side table. Every head turned, every brow raised, surely every eye spotted the butt of his pistol that jutted from his apron. The gasp which issued from the civilized sector told me they had.

Drat. "Confections," I said to Joshua. "He means Kansas Confections. Excuse me." I marched in Cook's direction, a steady but civilized step which quickened when the spatula thudded next to the tray. "Cook," I hissed. He turned, his surly glare stopping before it reached me. He leveled a gaze on Rudy, and Lizzy next to him. "Cook," I hissed even louder. He set out Mr. Walters' direction. I switched my course and saw Deputy Joshua come to his feet. Now three sets of footsteps marched through the hush which fell over Eat Here. Travelers I had worked so hard to make comfortable stopped eating and talking, everyone's attention on the Wild West show which promised to ruin everything. Drat Cook.

Joshua's long legs maneuvered between tables with an impressive deftness my skirt made impossible. Small yelps erupted around the room as he, Cook, and I gained speed. Chairs raked out of our way, frantic footsteps raced to the opposite wall as we converged on Rudy and Lizzy.

"If you're here for another one of your Bible-length orders, I thought it best if you told it straight to me." Cook's voice reached Rudy's table first.

"There a problem here?" Joshua stopped alongside Cook.

Rudy glanced up at the deputy's badge. "Not with me, unless it's wrong to offer Miss Sanders help in her search for her brother." He turned to Cook. "But I'll take another cup of coffee. Why don't you get me one?"

Silver flashed as Cook's gun spun out of his holster, a circular exhibition that brought gasps before he shoved it back in. "I can handle that."

Chairs tipped, and people scattered. The cheesecloth-covered door banged repeatedly as customers fled.

"Keep that gun in your holster." Deputy Joshua aimed a finger at Cook.

"I've never seen a hash slinger who could sling a gun that way." Rudy eyed Cook.

"Don't want you to forget it." Cook's pistol spun in the air again, a blur of silver in a flash around his finger.

Drat that man. "Give me that." I snatched the gun from Cook's hand and nearly dropped the unwieldy weapon as I shoved it into my apron's front pocket. "It'll be safe with me." I nodded at the four of them.

"Safer with me." Deputy Joshua extended his hand, palm up. He tucked the gun I laid in it under an arm.

Drat Cook and all the trouble he caused me. My face burned. Mama'd be so horrified.

"You're Miss Sanders, I take it," Joshua said to Lizzy, the lack of color I'd seen earlier on her face worse as her skin bleached white as the tablecloths...except for the one with the enormous coffee ring on it.

I grasped Lizzy's arm and held tight. "It's okay. Everett hired Deputy Joshua to work here in Larned."

She turned wide eyes my way instead of to the deputy. "Everett's gone? But he... Oh, Penelope, I'm so sorry." She laid a hand over mine, her skin cool to my warmth.

"It's all right. There's no reason to be sorry." I thought of Everett's kindness, which had vexed me. The way he had made sure I was all right. And his frown as he'd left after his sip of Jim's coffee. "It's all right, really." Everett's kindness and his friend were both gone. Maybe neither would return. "It's all right," I said again. I held tight to the only reason I had left to remain in this town.

"So, Miss Sanders, is there a problem here?" Joshua asked Lizzy.

Rudy stood. "Miss Sanders' brother is missing, sir. I've come to offer her aid."

"Bah." Cook spat. Spittle hit the floor in the circle made by our feet. Disgust rounded the dining room, and Eat Here's door opened and closed a few times more. As soon as this fiasco ended, I would scrub every inch of Lizzy's floor with Cook's whiskers.

"There's no call for vulgarity, especially in front of the ladies." Rudy bent, and with his own white handkerchief he cleared Cook's saliva from the floor.

I stared. Lizzy stared. What few customers we hopefully had left must have stared as well, for not a sound came from behind us.

Rudy straightened and folded the damp handkerchief. "The least I could do." He tucked it into his pocket, whereas I would have burned it right there on the floor.

"Might be the least you'd do, but it ain't the least you intend." Cook's face contorted as another wad of spit formed.

"Cook!" I shouted as another voice called from across the room.

"Is Mr. Walters here, by chance?" Mr. Brandt

stepped through the front door and scanned what customers remained plastered along the walls. He motioned to Amber, who appeared behind him, to stay by the door, which surprisingly she did, as he spotted us and came our way.

"He was just leavin'. Maybe the two of you can do yer yakkin' outside," Cook grumbled as Eat Here's door slammed twice more. This wasn't the story I intended Eastern travelers to take back home.

Mr. Brandt stopped alongside Rudy and clapped a hand on his shoulder. "I would do my talking with Mr. Walters outside, but I have good news." He fixed a smile on Lizzy. "Not just for him, but for you too, Miss Sanders. The whole town in fact. Thanks to Rudy's financial savvy, he just turned a moderate amount of cash into riches."

"He what?" Cook and I asked as exclamations traveled around the room, fewer than would have, had Cook kept his gun holstered, his saliva contained, and his mouth closed to begin with.

Mr. Brandt grabbed Rudy's hand and shook it. "If you would come to the bank, we can settle your account...your now huge account. You're a wealthy man."

Lizzy's customers' earlier fright turned to a buzz of excitement, exclamations of praise which Amber fanned with her own version of untold opportunities in the West. She whisked from person to person, escorted the once stunned voyeurs back to tables. She offered comfort and hope to Lizzy's customers, who thanked her as they settled into chairs.

Mr. Brandt nodded approval as she, instead of Tina or Les, who stood paralyzed at the side table, served coffee and Kansas Confections for free.

"Lizzy don't got nothin' to do with either of you, so best you three be goin'." Cook waved a hand toward Mr. Brandt, Amber, and Rudy.

"But she does." Mr. Brandt ignored Cook's rancor. "Rudy's success opens a door to me as his banker, a share of his profits which I want to share with her."

"Phooey." Cook crossed his arms, and judgment circulated the room. I glanced at Eastern frowns which surrounded Amber's look of shock.

"Miss Sanders…" Mr. Brandt ignored Cook again. "What you've done with Eat Here is commendable, but the results likely come to a pittance compared to what I have to offer you. Amber and I would like to hold a gala engagement party here. Everyone will be invited. It will be an enormous celebration we never could have afforded until now, thanks to Mr. Walters."

"What?" I trumpeted as Cook spat another, "Bah."

"This will mean a lot of income for you." Mr. Brandt ignored both of us this time. "I will pay for your services and the plans we hope you'll help make, since we're getting a late start. My fiancée will be in charge, but because my time is taken with the bank, I hope you will assist her. Along with Mr. Walters, who has proven himself savvy."

Sounds of approval came from Mr. Brandt's audience at Rudy's nod and the eye-batting clasp of his fiancée's hands. The perfect show had been staged, the Wild West tamed by striking it rich in a virgin land full of supposed opportunity.

I needed to find Jim. Mama needed the long-awaited news I was finally walking through her promised open door. But Lizzy needed me more. "I have savvy." I stepped forward. "You said as much yourself, Mr. Brandt. I will be the person who assists Lizzy and Amber. Mr. Walters will surely be a busy man from now on. I'm the right person to help."

Mr. Brandt turned my way. "Mrs. Strong, you are indeed an amalgamation of talents. You've proven yourself to be far more than just some successful man's widow, I'd say. But since this party will do as much for Eat Here as you can by delivering to me your late husband's paperwork, I suggest you do just that. Then you can go as you intended."

Cook aimed his trigger finger Mr. Brandt's direction. "You ain't arrangin' no party here without Lizzy's say. And if she does agree to this crazy notion, it's Lizzy that will choose her help, not you. And as for Mrs. Strong, her ways might call for some head-scratchin', but she's got more of what this place needs than any folks you ain't gonna plant here."

My jaw dropped. Cook deserved a hug. I wanted to wrap my hands around that trigger finger and plant a kiss on its tip. I eyed his bush of hair and whiskers, the kitschy clothing I'd kept a distance from. He glanced my direction, and I smiled. A grateful expression he looked right through as he nodded at Lizzy.

A silent conversation passed between the two, then Lizzy said, "Eat Here welcomes Penelope's help for as long as she wishes. And we will be happy to host a celebration for Larned's townspeople, and do our best to make your party a success."

"I offer my help as well, Miss Sanders." Rudy dipped into a slight bow.

"I said we don't want no outside help. Hers is outside enough." Cook shrugged a shoulder my direction.

I glared at Cook. "Now you listen to me, you old…"

Joshua raised his free arm. "All of you, listen. You apparently have a party to plan, and it will be done without guns or name calling. Therefore I suggest discussions about this party be held in a neutral place. Not here and not at the bank."

"They can use my office," someone offered across the room.

We all turned.

"Thank you, Clement," Joshua said. "Your office will suit just fine. I recommend you be there for the meetings. Mr. Brandt and his fiancée are to be there, along with Miss Sanders and…" Joshua studied those of us who worked at Eat Here.

"Mrs. Strong," Cook interjected, which stunned me.

"And Mrs. Strong. As long as she's here," Joshua finished. "Clement will be the deciding voice if there's a deadlock in the plans. Is that clear to all of you?"

Quiet agreements and Cook's grunt circled our group.

"Okay, then. Arrange a time to meet at the stage office and let me know." Joshua scanned the group and ended with Cook. "I believe this is yours." He handed Cook his pistol. "I suggest it not be part of your uniform here. Now, good day, ma'am," Joshua said to me and then Lizzy. He handed me a few coins for the coffee he never got to drink, nodded at the others, and left Eat Here.

Mr. Brandt clapped a hand on Rudy's shoulder again. "Miss Sanders, you were wise to agree to our party and the benefits it will bring you. We look forward to working with you. For everyone else…" Mr. Brandt gazed at customers across the room as he added, "the door is open if you are interested in what this brilliant man did. Follow us to the bank, and we can show you." He smiled. Amber smiled as she hurried to his side. The two of them joined hands and steered Rudy out the door. Chairs scooted away from tables as Lizzy's customers raced to follow.

"No one paid," I gasped as remnants of Amber's coffee and half eaten Kansas Confections were left behind.

"Git on," Cook said from beside me.

We'd been out-savvied. I couldn't believe it.

"I think I know what that Walters fellow did. Git on. Go follow 'em. Take yer words and go shoot. It's what you're good at. Go blow holes through everythin' he done, because if I go, there won't be nothin' left."

Chapter 18

The door to the bank swung wide before I even laid a hand on it. A face I'd seen a time or two at the restaurant greeted me, a young man whose name I didn't know. He bowed as if we were old friends, then flung his arm to the side to usher me in. "Paperwork's that way, ma'am."

"Paperwork? What paperwork?" I clutched my bag close as I veered in the direction he indicated, where a cluster of Larned's townspeople idled in the main lobby amidst complete strangers, paperwork in everyone's hands. "What is happening here?" I turned back to the young man, who bowed again. "Just answer my question."

"Finance papers, ma'am." He reddened as he straightened. "That's why you're here, isn't it? Everyone else is, now that they've heard about Mr. Walters' instant wealth."

I scanned the crowd and spotted men who had attended my meetings. They at least should know better than to trust a promise of instant wealth. I'd taught every single one of them that easy money was just that, and it flowed just as easily both directions. "Is Mr. Brandt in his office?"

"Yes, but you need to…"

I shoved through a mixture of annoyance and humiliation as paperwork yanked out of my way.

"Quick and easy is just that, you know," I remarked loudly to those who barely stepped aside as I marched to Mr. Brandt's office. "It leaves your hands just as speedily as it came to them."

I stormed toward the familiar feel of one of Uncle Roy's "by hook or by crook" schemes. Every face turned from me to an uneasy glance at the papers gripped in their hands. Grasping Mr. Brandt's office door handle, I swung it wide and left it that way as I stepped alongside Ben Holt and his wife, seated so that their chairs faced Nicholas Brandt across his too-shiny desk, while Mr. Rudy Walters sat comfortably to the side.

"Mrs. Strong?" Mr. Brandt looked up, his handsome brows pinched at the interruption, then raised in surprise. "You want to try your hand at money-making opportunities before you leave town? I wouldn't have thought it, but have a seat in the lobby, and I'll…"

"Your lobby is quite crowded." I indicated the faces bunched close to his door.

Mr. Brandt's surprise settled into a smile. "Wonderful, isn't it? Like discovering gold. Mr. Walters has generously agreed to share his insight with everyone here. Proven business tactics as opposed to…well, the general information you offer."

"I teach foundational tools. And in a single session with everyone present. Why would you share with each one individually? And why the paperwork? Don't some of these people have a train or stage to catch? Or a business to run?" I set a hand on the back of Ben Holt's chair. "If Mr. Walters has a successful tactic, it seems to me that could be taught more efficiently in a group.

Individual decisions can come later."

"It's personal." Rudy rose to his feet. "Like what I offered Miss Sanders. Personal concern and individual attention."

Cook had sent me here to shoot—at a man willing to share, and who'd snatched Lizzy's handkerchief out of the air while the rest of us watched it drop. A man who paid attention to personal details, the same way he ordered his food.

"Yes," Mr. Brandt added, "Mr. Walters does things well. So, Mrs. Strong, if you're interested in some of his tailored advice, I suggest you take a seat out there." He nodded toward the lobby.

Rudy seemed sincere for a man who'd been chained to a marshal. More reliable than unreliable as a witness. I studied the refined black outfits Mr. Brandt and Rudy wore, the dark hair, the proper mannerisms. Two men so alike…either could be the shadow of the other. Something Cook claimed to see.

"I'm not here for advice. I'm here on normal bank business. A deposit of Eat Here's earnings." I raised my bag, not a cent inside. I rattled my few personal belongings and prayed they looked and sounded like a bulky deposit to a town and strangers who needed to be careful. "I have the equivalent of a payment and a half based on Eat Here's original contract. Every penny made free and clear." I spoke loud enough everyone in the lobby could hear. "Done without a loan. Made with a little ingenuity and elbow grease. We never spent above our means or borrowed to get ahead. We never risked what we had because of a rumor of easy cash." I lowered my bag. "I believe you referred to Eat Here's income as a pittance, Mr. Brandt."

"I see this business has nothing to do with me." Rudy bowed and started toward the door. "Congratulations on your hard work, Mrs. Strong. Now, if you'll excuse me, I'll leave you to settle your affairs." He threaded past me and into the lobby, where he disappeared through rustled paperwork and shuffling feet. He did it with finesse. A man freed, no longer chained, maybe a shadow to no one.

"Mrs. Strong, what's the meaning of this?" Mr. Brandt came to his feet with less grace than Rudy had. "You don't have an account in which to deposit money. You decided to keep your cash with…with that…" He waved an arm. "That ruffian you call a cook."

I couldn't argue that. Ruffian fit Cook better than his allegorical name. "We do keep our earnings with Cook. The bulk of it will stay with him, but we've decided to diversify." I positioned my bag in view of the lobby. "We want to keep our income in more than one place for security, in case one of our holders fails…which happens. I have a payment and a half, but not a cent for that interest you said you forgot to figure into the new contract. No one in their right mind would agree to undocumented fees."

The bank's front door slammed. Mr. Brandt hurried around his desk. "Alvin," he called, the bowing assistant suddenly visible through the crowd, which edged away. "See if you can find Mr. Walters. And, folks, Mrs. Strong's business has nothing to do with what I and Mr. Walters have to offer you. Please form a line, and I will get to each of you while Mrs. Strong waits her turn."

"My turn? But I have a deposit. I would think that would take precedence over speculation. Unless you're collecting a fee from everyone here. Surely you wouldn't do that."

"Your deposit does not take precedence. What it will take is valuable time. And what we collect is none of your concern unless you wish to partake of our offer of strategies to manipulate opportunities."

"Manipulate? That word isn't very flattering for a bank." I glanced down at the Holts. "Have you signed anything?"

Ben stared at his lap while his wife shook her head.

"Mrs. Strong. You've disrupted the Holts' and Mr. Walters' tight schedules. Please. Kindly step out of my office so I can help these people until Rudy returns." Perspiration beaded across Mr. Brandt's handsome brow. "Everyone else…" He smiled and waved at the diminished throng outside his door. "I apologize for this disruption. My assistant will return with Mr. Walters shortly, but in the meantime, we'll continue, and I'll get to each of you as quickly as I can."

Mr. Brandt extended an arm toward the lobby to usher me out. I followed it but paused alongside him in his doorway. "Back home, whenever I…I mean, Mr. Strong…considered a banker, he would introduce me to him, let us get acquainted, and then ask if I would marry the man."

"Mrs. Strong. Whatever are you talking about?" Mr. Brandt sputtered. "A potential customer consider marriage to a banker? We only offer financial services, not love relationships."

"Alex believed any contract with a bank to be an important union, one signed only by partners well suited to each other. Both should benefit, both should give something, and both should have at the core a deep trust and trustworthiness."

The bank's door opened and closed again. And again. The same way Eat Here's had earlier. I glanced at the emptier lobby and thinner crowd. "I know you take your position seriously here in Larned, Mr. Brandt. I thought you…and they…might be interested in what we look for in a good banker in the East."

"Well, thanks to your nonsense, Mrs. Strong, no one in town will recognize a good banker or what he can do for them. And not one of them will become a penny richer. You'll be to blame when they are forced to come to me for a loan. Or have to fold their business because they missed this opportunity. Or in the case of those here for a visit but who will no longer consider a move out here, the stagnant condition of Larned will be your fault as well." Mr. Brandt looked at those who still lingered, paperwork pressed to their chests as they backed away.

I had shot words the way Cook said, with ruin as the result. A dead town and dead businesses resulted from my spray of words. I had aimed for men and women who wouldn't behave like a pack of animals and leave unpaid tabs to follow vague promises over the edge of a cliff.

"I think a town meeting would have been better," I muttered. The last few people backed away. "Like the ones I hold. Tell everyone at once. Let them think about the costs and benefits, and learn."

"I'm very familiar with the classes you offer, Mrs. Strong. You, who have no real financial training. I have to confess that what I've heard makes me question Mr. Strong and my first impression of his financial savvy." Mr. Brandt stared down at me with an expression I had seen on Uncle Roy's face. Not to mention his attorney's and banker's.

"My meetings cover the basics, Mr. Brandt, simple tools even the uneducated can manage. I've covered contracts, loans, reasonable interest, and how businesses can work together. Each one is full of Mr. Strong's hard-learned lessons in his years of business."

"Well, then, I hope your meetings do someone some good, since what you've done here has cost Lizzy."

"I'm here to make a deposit for her. How does that cost her?"

"Think, Mrs. Strong. By casting doubt on Mr. Walters and me, you just cost both of us and the town guaranteed revenue. Because of you, Amber and I will cancel our party. You have not only blocked Lizzy and everyone else from a source of income, you have cut amiable ties to this bank and her banker as well. Out west, Mrs. Strong, that is cutting your own throat."

I'm at the end of my homestead time, the last year granted me to live here so I can own it. The last two have been hard, this territory throwing everything it could in my path. Many have been broken by the elements and the land, gone into debt to salvage what Mother Nature destroyed. I have done a little of the same, holding on through a small loan as a last resort because there is one thing more I want. In the heart. Not just in the soil. I'm doing a little more than most so my heart and my home will be ready to share. It's a risk, but worth it. I believe you understand.

Jim's voice, his words, his wish which had culminated in *Marry me* had in the end sewn him and everyone else in knots with western money.

Would you be willing to come here, live in my world, and be my wife on this land that's nearly mine? You may visit first before you answer, come taste Crooked Creek's land before you decide. Meet me and see me, even before that final payment is made. Let who I've tried to show you through words, show you in real life.

Would I have done to Jim what I'd done to Lizzy? Cut his throat with my Eastern ways, my financial savvy which came from being buffeted by Uncle Roy's wrongs? The Holts stood and squeezed between Mr. Brandt and me, a flight from one or both of us.

"Good day, Mrs. Strong."

I stepped through the door Mr. Brandt closed behind me, crossed the empty lobby, went out the bank's ornate entryway, and into the street. I gazed west through plain wooden buildings toward the door I'd come to pry open. Closed by a man who'd had his encounters with western bankers as well. Hopefully with better results than I'd had. The way Rudy would have if I hadn't interfered. Another person I owed an apology to before I went.

A train whistled as it built up steam to take bank and restaurant customers, potential borrowers or residents, away from Larned. It was time. I should go as well. My reason to stay here for Everett or his friend no longer existed. I had only Lizzy, and I'd just closed her open door.

"Mrs. Strong?"

"Deputy Joshua?" I prayed the man who'd replaced Everett would blame the flush of my cheeks and the wetness in my eyes on the sun. Drat the small hat I still wore.

"There's been a complaint."

I laughed. A bitter derision, then asked, "Just one?"

"Well, two, actually."

"What?"

"I managed to reach a compromise on one. Sort of. The first complaint is about Cook. His gun. You need to have a talk with him."

"I've had several talks with him, all of them falling on deaf ears." Deaf ears would be a blessing compared to the boxing I intended to give whoever's had complained.

"That surprises me since the other complaint, the one I mostly squelched, claims your voice has quite an impact."

"My voice?" The only person who ever complained about my voice was Cook. He'd get an earful of it when I got back to Eat Here.

"The person who registered the complaint insists you be denied access to the bank in the future."

"The bank? Denied access?"

"The request is that you conduct financial business elsewhere. And quietly. No more audiences."

"That's ludicrous. I'm glad you were able to thwart such a ridiculous mandate."

"I didn't completely block it, ma'am. I reached an agreement with the accusing party. Any business that pertains to contracts Miss Sanders has, and involve you, can be processed at the bank as long as a representative is with you and speaks for you." Joshua glanced down the street, his ruddy face looking ruddier.

"A representative? How did he manage such fast work?" I glared at the bank. "I'm barely out the door and already Nicholas Brandt has found a way to complain."

"Mr. Brandt didn't do it." The ruddiness on Joshua's face grew even darker. "Mr. Walters filed the complaints against you."

I felt the hole someone else's words shot through me, while mine had barely nicked the shadows.

Chapter 19

Drat Rudy. And drat his complaint that slammed another door on me. Pretty soon neither Louise Archer nor Penelope Strong would have any place to go.

"Amber dropped in to say our first meeting about her and Nicholas's engagement party is tomorrow morning," Lizzy said as I stormed through Eat Here's door.

My face burned, likely scarlet after my stomp up and down the main street to calm my rage. Perspiration plastered my clothing to me. "Well, she's mistaken." I marched toward the stairs, blistering inside over Rudy and his ridiculous complaints, and now Mr. Brandt, who failed to inform his fiancée—though they discussed everything, according to her—he'd canceled the engagement party.

"Amber said Nicholas changed his mind," Lizzy added as I hurried past.

"He what?" I stopped at the foot of the stairs. Goodness. Amber had likely divulged the party had been cancelled because of me, and that I'd been banned from the bank, and Cook barred from carrying his gun. I wrangled my fervor to something more contrite. "I mean, he what?"

Tina and Les hustled from table to table, ears wide open, no doubt, thanks to my initial screech. Regular customers who had come back, likely for information about our earlier Wild West show, studied their hands, their coffee cups, anything but me.

"She told me…well, us…that you'd upset him." Now Lizzy looked at her hands.

"You done good, Mrs. Strong. It's called target practice." Cook stepped from the kitchen, wiping his hands on a towel. "You'll get the hang of it. But sometimes a stray bullet is as effective as a well-aimed one. It's the blast that does it. Sends vermin out into the light where you can see 'em." He grinned and flipped the towel over his shoulder. I'd never seen Cook grin the way he did now, or the gaps where teeth should have been.

I shuddered and glanced around the restaurant. Lizzy's customers didn't need this much information. "Come with me." I waved Cook's grin and Lizzy's embarrassment to follow as I marched to the kitchen. "I went to the bank armed with words," I said as I turned and faced them. "Not bullets, as you implied. If you recall, you're the one who said to do what I did best." I yanked my chin upward.

"And you did it well, Mrs. Strong." He beamed, exposing even more gaps. I wondered if Tina had ever had a good look at his grin.

"I doubt I did anything well," I retorted. "Mr. Brandt…"

"Agreed to let Amber have the party of her dreams after all," Lizzy finished with something far more noble than what could have been said. "As long as you are minimally involved, that is." Now Lizzy grinned. "Maybe you should have upset him a bit more, Penelope. Then you wouldn't have to interact with either of them at all."

My face heated hotter than the oven I stood next to.

"Naw. She did it just right. This way we can keep our friends close and our enemies closer." Cook snatched the towel from one shoulder and flapped it over his other.

"You know adages?" I turned my hot face toward him.

"Cook knows everything." Tina smiled. She had joined our group, Les close behind her.

I stepped between the nearly toothless man whose answer for everything boiled down to a bullet, and the woman who wrongly idolized him. "Lizzy, I might have made a slight mess of things. Maybe a little." Or terribly. I stole glances at the four of them and searched for indications Amber had revealed my ban from the bank and Cook's from his gun.

"Whatever you done, ain't no matter. Much as I hate havin' that banker around, or throwin' a party that honors the likes of him, better he's within sight than outside it."

"You mean within your sights." I would be Cook's target once I told him Joshua ruled he could no longer carry a gun in Eat Here…and that Rudy had requested it.

"I mean just what I said. You nicked one of 'em with somethin' you babbled, and thanks to that redhead Brandt hinges his future on, he couldn't go off somewhere, reload, and fire back. If he's gonna bleed out, it's gonna be right here where we can see it."

I shuddered. Such an ugly analogy. And such a slight to me. "I don't babble."

Cook grinned, a nearly toothless smile I glanced away from before I babbled something else. I focused on the fading sunlight, its soft glow through Eat Here's solitary kitchen window. How could an old coot like him hit his mark every time while I sprayed the air with everything in my arsenal and accomplished nothing? I needed a plan to leave town. Lizzy needed a plan which would defend her from Mr. Brandt and his redhead once I was gone. The two Elizabeths needed a plan.

"Lizzy, you have to be smart. You have to be ready for any problems which might arise. For your sake and the whole town's, since we will include everyone in this celebration. I'll set up a meeting with the local businesses and get them involved. We will share the wealth and strengthen Larned." *Then* I'd tell her the truth and go find my Jim.

"Oh. Speaking of the party and wealth." Lizzy fished an envelope from her apron pocket. "Mr. Brandt sent this with Amber." She handed it to me. "It's a contract for the party, but there is also a form which states we owe the interest he'd forgotten to add to our new contract the bank's still waiting to enforce."

"What?" Drat me and my babbling. I kept my back to Cook.

"Amber said he'd calm down a bit more if we at least offered to cover that."

"I hope you didn't give her any money or promises." I studied his interest paperwork.

"I didn't." Lizzy shook her head. "But I did have to agree to one of their terms in the party contract." She nodded at the thicker stack of papers.

"Such as…" I shook out the book-length document concocted to cover a one-evening event. *Bah.* For once Cook had the right word.

"According to their contract, Amber will supervise

all plans. She's to have free reign over the arrangements and everything she wants." Lizzy fidgeted. "I had to agree to that part. Since the party is supposed to be in three weeks, Amber claimed preparations would go faster if she led them since she knows what she wants."

Three weeks... Now even spitting like Cook made sense. I stared at the first page, a detailed list of decorations I hadn't seen the like of since St. Louis. Keep your friends close and your enemies closer. Goodness. Cook made more and more sense. Eat Here was bound to see the best and the worst of Lizzy's banker as Amber tried to drag the impossible out of it and Larned.

"Amber said they need a large space with servers and a kitchen, so they'd pay well for the use of Eat Here." Lizzy fidgeted more. "She said we can thank you for all of this, Penelope."

"What? Well, I...of course I may have been hasty in a few things I..."

"She said you made this place quite suitable with our help, and that with some embellishments, it will be even better."

"She what?" The heat which crept up my neck, stopped. Amber had rightly assessed Eat Here and my hand in it...my unintended step into Lizzy's life. I glanced at Lizzy, my sister in name and song. I might have nearly stepped into Jim's as well. Nearly. If I resumed my trip westward, leaving my suitable accomplishments behind...I'd also be leaving behind a ruffled banker, the finance problems I'd caused the town, and Rudy's complaints. Maybe I needed to arm Lizzy with what Cook said I did best. "Lizzy, we must give Amber and her fiancé the appropriate paperwork from your end."

"My end?" Lizzy frowned.

"You will have your own contract for outside affairs. Any gathering other than business as usual will affect your standard earnings, your workers, the building, your supplies, travelers, guests, and your regular customers."

"That's so much…"

"So much paperwork?" I waved Mr. Brandt's lengthy contract. "We'll have yours drawn up before tomorrow's meeting."

"Include fees in it," Tina blurted. She blushed as we all turned. "I think there should be a fee to secure the building and our services before the planning ever gets started."

I saw then what I had never seen. The glint of admiration…maybe love…in Cook's beady eyes as he sidled next to her.

"You are so right, Tina." I wanted to applaud her timid pride. "Thanks to you, we will calculate a deposit fee which covers the cost of closure, a cleaning portion, and a hazard fee in case there is damage. Not just to the building, but to a person. And as for this particular party, Nicholas will have to pay the salaries of whatever staff it requires, the cost of the food and drinks, the purchase price of decorations, any shipment fees, and a little extra for us to prepare everything."

"I don't think Mr. Brandt will pay all of that." Lizzy shook her head.

"He will if his engagement is worth it to him." I waved his bulky contract in the air again. "This and what we will add to it should suit a man who says he wants more for the town. I'll draw up the contract, but you, Lizzy, will sign it. Now you have a plan." Hers was set. Mine would be, as soon as I wrangled another ticket out of Julius Weston.

****

I glanced at Joshua as he came to his feet behind the lone desk in his deputy's office, another building as plain on the inside as on the out. Morning sunlight filled the room and baked already dry motes of dust, nothing to stop it other than a single jail cell and the chairs clustered around where he stood. "We meet with Amber and Mr. Brandt this morning at Clement's stagecoach office. Ten thirty, if you can be there."

Joshua gnawed one side of his lower lip. "I hadn't planned to be part of these."

"I realize the time is inconvenient." For everyone except Amber. I nodded toward Lizzy beside me, the straps of her bag knotted around her fingers. "But Lizzy and I thought that since this is the first meeting, it might be wise to have a lawman there. Amber has quite a list of wants that her fiancé has turned into a contract." I fished it and Eat Here's out of my bag. "We have one as well."

"Good God." Joshua whistled.

"I expect Mr. Brandt will be just as shocked when I show him Lizzy's. And likely groan when he sees our terms." He'd better get used to groaning if he married Amber. I stuffed the contracts back into my bag.

"I'll be there," Joshua agreed. "Looks like you might need me."

"We appreciate it. And by the way, Mr. Walters dropped by Eat Here to confirm the meeting time." Or to check Cook for a pistol, or because I wasn't allowed at the bank.

"He's no part of these meetings." Joshua lifted his holster off a wall hook and fitted it low around his hips. "Mr. Brandt's to plan his own party. If he wants Walters to do the grunt work, then he…" Joshua paused his buckling. "Unless you want Rudy to help as a go-between since you can't…"

"Can't do everything at once?" I raised a warning brow to stop Joshua before he spouted what Lizzy still didn't know about Rudy's complaints against me and Cook. "We're plenty busy, but I suppose Mr. Walters' intention is congenial enough. Of course the first time I saw him he was chained to Everett."

"Handcuffed." Joshua focused on his buckle.

"Whatever it's called. In any case, maybe you could monitor Mr. Walters' activity." Until I found a reason to have Rudy banned from Eat Here the way he'd had me banned from the bank.

"I could stop by to make sure any help he offers is in line. I have plenty to do, but I should be able to handle an occasional visit to Eat Here. In case a fight breaks out…or someone wields a gun…" He gave me a look I prayed Lizzy didn't notice.

"I'm sure that won't be the case." As soon as I told Cook.

"Well, I can handle fights and guns." Joshua slapped a hand over his holster's tightened buckle. "But don't expect any help from me if squabbles sprout up about the romantic parts of this party. Matters of the heart aren't my jurisdiction. You could probably twist Everett's arm into interfering if personal issues popped up. He's doing something like that right now, in fact."

"Right now?" My voice came out so loud, even I jumped.

"Southwest of Dodge City. Went there for a wedding that troubled him."

"His own?" It had to be. That would be why Everett decided to settle out there. But no, it couldn't be. Everett had never mentioned being engaged. But he should be. His gentle demeanor created a kindness that could wed. He could be the sort of man some woman would want to come home to her...

Joshua laughed. "No, it isn't Everett getting married. Someone else, some friend of his is. Or was. Maybe didn't." Joshua shook his head and shrugged. "Whichever way it turned out, Everett paced a lot before he went."

Everett's friend... He didn't look like a man wanting to wed. He lacked the warmth, the readiness, the passion which had been in Jim's letters. Maybe Everett saw that as well. Maybe Everett had gone to prevent a broken heart.

"We should go." I looked past Lizzy and toward the west, where I needed to go. "We should hurry to get ready for the meeting." I needed to hurry. I needed to go west yesterday. I needed to go where Everett had gone and do what Everett was doing. Just in case my Jim had decided to marry...someone else.

****

Amber tapped the first page of their contract while Nicholas sat at her side and pored through Eat Here's. Clement, with a new list of delays to be mailed to Mama from Dodge City in his pocket, stood behind Lizzy and me on our side of his office table, closer to Lizzy's chair than mine.

"I want music." Amber looked from Lizzy to me. "I've chosen the tunes, some from operas, some from famous orchestras. I don't want any folk or war songs. Only waltzes and sophisticated melodies."

"That's absurd," I sputtered. "There are no orchestras in Larned."

"I'm aware of that." Amber gave me a glare. "And of course Eat Here is too dinky to hold one even if such an ensemble could be found. You, Mrs. Strong, since you're from the East, should understand what it would take to achieve the sound I want." Amber tapped her newest list, its top page music and composers.

I glanced at the selections around her finger. Lizzy did as well, as she leaned close and studied titles and names she'd likely never heard of.

"Well, who around here can sing?" I asked Amber. "And what instruments are available? Violins? Music boxes? A piano?"

"No piano." Amber spoke definitively as Lizzy slunk back in her chair. "I want other instruments. If it's impossible to find the appropriate ones, a Victorian music box will do. And I have no idea who in the area can sing. It is up to you to find the best. The music has to be perfect."

"I…" I couldn't think of a single song I'd heard since I'd come here other than whatever Tina hummed as she worked.

"We will manage it," Clement cut in. I glanced behind Lizzy. He stood with his arms crossed. Maybe he knew someone in town with a banjo.

"Good." Amber drew her papers her way. "I also want candles on every table and a red rug beside mine where we can stand to greet guests. Beside *our* table, I mean." The glimmer of excitement in Amber's eyes roared past sparkle and turned to a blaze.

"Since you've set the party date for three weeks from now, there's not much time to order, gather, and prepare all of this on top of the first list you gave us with your contract," I said.

This was nonsense. A real wedding somewhere out west needed my attention.

Unless Everett had successfully intervened…

Don't come. I can't marry you.

"What Lizzy can't find in Larned, she'll have to send for, and there isn't enough time for that," I added.

"Nicholas said to get what I want." Amber tapped their contract again, then the new pages she had added. She looked at her fiancé, his head bent in a frown over the last page of what I had drafted for Lizzy, the final line a dollar amount. "He told me not to hold back. This is my…I mean, our…party to celebrate our upcoming marriage. And I've done everything I could to make it easy for you. I have my list of music and specifics for the decorations. I've even designed the cake and the other hors d'oeuvres. I wrote down the recipes. I did all of that. All you have to do is put it together."

Mr. Brandt finished reading Eat Here's contract and straightened the pages. He pinned the neatened stack to the table with a frown and his palm.

Amber's newest list slid our way. "The top page is the music. The second is the food, the next are the recipes. And the last is the extra décor we need. It's all organized and simple to understand." She pointed to the pile.

I drew them the rest of the way to Lizzy and me. Names of compositions and composers flowed from the top to the bottom of the first page, few if any Larned would likely have heard of. Clement cleared his throat behind us…behind Lizzy…as she ran her finger down the list and paused at every title.

"It's okay, Lizzy. Don't worry yourself about the details," I whispered. Clement had clearly made a promise he couldn't keep. He stood there as Lizzy finished her slow perusal. She leaned back in her seat, then flipped the page to recipes Cook would never have heard of and would likely refuse to make.

"A woman becoming a bride is a momentous event." Mr. Brandt slapped Eat Here's contract with his hand. Lizzy and I jumped. Clement drew back. Amber turned to Nicholas, her profile toward his, a moment of beauty beneath too much color gazing at handsome beneath too much smile. "Anything for you," he said. "A momentous celebration for a momentous occasion."

"Then the occasion should reflect that," Clement said. "But no more. The celebration, though momentous, shouldn't outshine the bride. Miss Wingate, or any worthy woman, should not be diminished beneath food and frills."

Mr. Brandt shifted a less adoring look to the mediator I found suddenly admirable. "We'll cut no corners for my fiancée," Nicholas said. "This is for and about her. Place whatever orders you need to within the hour. Expedite everything. Pay extra if you must."

"Eat Here pay?" I tapped our contract beneath his hand. "You pay, you mean. It's in this agreement. An agreement we'll have to alter now that your fiancée has sprung several more pages of her momentous occasion on us."

"An agreement I haven't signed to begin with. It's well written, but all to your benefit. As you said before, Mrs. Strong, a banker and his customer must benefit each other."

Warmth crept into my face. Drat. Between Mr. Brandt and Joshua—who so far had stood back and said nothing—my fiasco at the bank could be exposed. "We will uphold our end to your benefit." I withdrew my hand.

"I will cover any of the fees I find reasonable, as well as initial costs for the items my intended wants. I assure you, it will be more than generous. And if the event goes above that, then Eat Here will be reimbursed for all approved costs after the party, when we pay you the balance for your services and the use of the restaurant."

"Well, that's ridiculous." I stood, which caused Joshua to budge. I returned to my seat. "I mean, a deposit won't cover last-minute changes." And I couldn't imagine Amber without hundreds more of them.

"We'll draft a third agreement which ties both of these together, if you wish. In it you can increase our deposit, which I will gladly pay. This is for my bride. It's what a husband does."

A husband doesn't wire, *Don't come. I can't marry you.* I stared at my ring finger where a husband should have placed his promise by now. "Draft the agreement while Lizzy and I do a quick estimate of costs. We'll call it an addendum."

He nodded, grasped Amber's ring hand, and held it fondly on the tabletop.

"And as long as we're adjusting the terms, there's one more I want made firm," I said, not looking at their love knot.

Mr. Brandt's smile waned. "And what would that

be?""

"The final balance that's to be paid the night of the party—it will be paid. Even if the party isn't held. Eat Here will be reimbursed for everything, no matter what."

Mr. Brandt squeezed Amber's hand. "Of course the party will be held. And of course we'll pay. We'll have a thorough agreement of terms and expenses, and a healthy deposit of my earnest promise. My bride will get everything she wants." Mr. Brandt stood, drew Amber to her feet alongside him. "I trust I'll hear from you shortly about estimated expenses. In the meantime, I'll have your addendum drafted." He took Amber's arm. "My dear…"

We watched them go. The handsome and happy couple closed Clement's office door behind them.

"Money doesn't buy happiness," Clement said after they were gone. "But it can rob you of it." He held the back of Lizzy's chair as he looked at Joshua. "Thank you for being here, Deputy."

"I'll keep an eye on things." Joshua tipped his head to Clement, then to us. "Good day, ladies."

The room became even quieter with only the three of us.

Lizzy studied Amber's list, shuffled to the page of music, and set it on top. "We have work to do," she said.

Clement stretched over her and took the papers. "Eat Here is yours," he said to Lizzy as he sifted out and handed her the list of decorations. "And the kitchen seems your…domain." He handed me the menu and recipes. "I'll go through the rest."

"But…" Lizzy and I both said as she eyed the

pages Clement kept, and I the list of duties he'd handed me.

"I know how to handle this," he said. "Trust me."

Chapter 20

Lizzy frowned at the delicate ivory blouse, the tiny rows of lace which ran along the pleats down its front. Her head tilted to the side in the dim light of my room as she held it at arm's length. "You really think so? What do you think, Tina?" Lizzy twisted so the two of them could see, her head next to Tina's as they eyed the simple attire which outshone what they usually wore for work.

"Well, *I* really think so," I answered instead of Tina. I took the blouse and set it on my cot with the others I'd had made. A rush order well worth every cent it cost me to add to my plan to outthink Lizzy's banker before I left. "They are to be worn with these. Every day." I unwrapped a stack of deep burgundy skirts, the latest styles in St. Louis, and arranged them near the blouses. I lifted one and held it by the belted waist. Soft exclamations escaped from Lizzy and Tina.

"I want you both to try on the sizes I estimated for you, in case we have to make alterations."

Tina latched onto the blouse and skirt I handed her. "What about Cook?"

I held back a snort. "It will take Cook a while to come to grips with a change like this at the restaurant, and Les will likely mimic whatever Cook does. They can keep wearing what they usually do for now, but when it comes to the engagement party, they'll wear similar colors."

Tina blushed. "I meant, do you think Cook will notice?" She held the blouse and skirt against her, gazed down at the newness and the color, and blushed more as she glanced up. "I sort of hoped..." She glowed like a bride who tried on a gown with the hope her chosen would see what she wanted him to. He already had, and I knew it, even without her new clothing. He'd more than noticed, the day we'd plotted and planned Amber's party. Cook's affection for Tina had glimmered in his eyes.

"He has, Tina. And he approves, no matter what you wear."

Tina's eyes watered, her smile bowed upward to catch the joy which trickled down her cheeks. "Thank you, Penelope."

Tina and Cook. A connection which ignored whiskers, foul manners, and simple adornment. A bond that had been quietly made without words—either my curt warnings or sentences which flowed like Jim's. "Cook will be happy with this new outfit on you, Tina. Though I imagine he'll fill anything I ask him to wear with bullet holes."

Tina giggled and Lizzy laughed. All three of us burst into a united gaiety as Tina swirled with the outfit Cook would approve of.

"You will begin to wear these right away," I said again as I wiped happy tears from my face. "But for Amber's party, there will be special outfits. That's when Cook and Les will have to wear theirs."

"What about you?" Tina frowned. "Are there outfits for you as well?"

This wasn't the time for blatant honesty about

Louise Archer or my plan to wrangle a train ticket out of Larned's arrogant ticket master for shortly before the engagement party. I intended to solidify a foolproof celebration as my last gift to Lizzy before the bitter truth and my departure. I pointed to the longest skirt and blouse.

"But there's only one for you." Tina frowned at the clothing on the cot. "And two for each for us." Their smiles vanished, taking all the light of gaiety which had been in the room with them. Tina laid her outfit next to mine. "It won't be the same here," she muttered alongside Lizzy.

"It won't, but it will," Lizzy said more to me. "Nothing will ever be the same, because from now on everything will be better. It will be different without you, Penelope, but it will always have your presence, your touch...and your love."

An embrace I didn't deserve wrapped around me, my arms rising to join theirs. Six arms and three hearts entwined in a way I'd never known. Two unexpected friends held onto me with a fervor I returned. I'd always relish their warmth and unmerited trust. I'd take it with me. It would likely be retracted once they knew the truth. And if it happened that no Jim had a part in Louise's future, there would always be these two women in Penelope's past.

I raised my head from our lengthy hug. Begrudgingly we let go and wiped our eyes and faces. I pointed toward the outfits on my cot. "When people ask...or criticize"—like her banker and his fiancée likely would—"let them know we aren't being uppity with these nice uniforms. Eat Here is Larned's open door. Travelers from the East will look for refreshment before anything else, and relish the little taste of home you will give them. Familiar is important. Attire like this will make them feel comfortable. These skirts and blouses are the East. They're elegance. Elegance which will make Eat Here and eventually all of Larned shine." I looked at my two friends, their simple and understated miens. "You are the ones. You can do this."

Tina stared at the clothing on my bed. She shook her head, but said with a squeak, "Thank you, Penelope."

"It's you who should be thanked. You and Lizzy. And if you're settled with all of this, there's more." I knelt and stretched beneath my cot, latched onto the handles of two pails, and scooted both out to the open. "Paint." I looked up at their frowns. "Guess what colors?"

They glanced at the skirts and blouses then back to the pails. "You will paint Eat Here the same colors," Lizzy said.

"Well, Les will. And hopefully Cook. The walls will be the same ivory as your shirts, the trim in burgundy. And this." I stretched again under my bed and came out with a smaller can. "Dark gray for accent."

"You're so wise, Penelope," Lizzy said. "So good and so smart. I'll never be able to thank you enough for all you've done. Neither will Phil."

Phil. Her smile would vanish completely if he returned before I left. I rose to my feet. "Well I..."

"Ma'am?" Les poked his head in my door. "Miss Amber said to give this to you and Miss Lizzy."

I accepted, then unfolded the paper Les handed me. "My goodness." I brought it alongside Lizzy. "Maybe good and smart won't be enough."

"She wants all of this?" Lizzy took Amber's latest list of requirements for her party. "But we already turned in our estimate. Mr. Brandt gave us a deposit."

"She may want all of this, but that doesn't mean she'll get it." Eat Here was no place for a fountain of sherry. And Cook could scramble or fry anything, but I doubted he would steam a lobster we had no chance of getting anyway. And heart-shaped mints? The original decorations were outrageous enough, but these additions were impossible. "Is she still here?" I demanded from Les, who backed from my doorway.

"No, ma'am," he said, nearly out of sight. "She's done gone. She said her or Mr. Brandt would come back, though."

"She's not 'done gone,' " I corrected Les. "And you mean 'she or Mr. Brandt,' not 'her or Mr. Brandt.' A steak can be considered done, but a…"

Les disappeared from view. Drat. I hadn't been able to spare Tina from Cook's inexplicable allure, but I needed to at least save this boy from grammar Cook likely knew better than to use.

"Never mind," I called after him. "You did well to bring this to us. You and I will talk about grammar later. In the meantime, I hope Amber and Nicholas plan to come back to explain how they expect to pay for all of this." I took the list from Lizzy's hand.

"No, ma'am." One of Les's eyes peered around the doorway. "That ain't why Miss Amber said they were comin', but they did send other help. Maybe to do that explainin' part."

"Other help?" I leaned so I could see more of the boy as a bellow came from below.

"Let me guess what you want," Cook roared from downstairs.

We raced through my door, Lizzy, Tina, and I, behind Les to the landing, where the four of us stretched over the railing to stare below.

"I'm here to help." Rudy stood not far from the bottom of the stairs, the lapels of his black suit clasped decisively in his fingers as he faced Cook. "It's an offering of generosity by Mr. Brandt."

"Brandt don't give nothin' without a price tag attached." Cook slapped a towel against the palm of his hand, then looped his apron around the butt of his pistol. I still hadn't told him Joshua had banned it from Eat Here. But Rudy might.

Drat. "I'll take care of this," I said to the three who gaped alongside me.

"No, I will." Lizzy caught me by the sleeve. "Better me than you."

"Not in this case. I think Mr. Walters is best left to me." Before he called Joshua in, and Cook and I were dragged off to jail for not following orders. "Cook," I essentially barked over the railing.

"Not now," Cook barked back.

"Mrs. Strong." Rudy glanced up, tipped his head in a rather amiable nod for someone who had filed a complaint against me. "And Miss Sanders." His expression softened. "I've come to help. I understand you've been given new party requirements."

"We have," I answered for Lizzy and waved Amber's latest additions as Lizzy let go of my sleeve and started down the steps. I hurried after her, Tina and Les's footsteps close behind mine. Another Wild West show in the making. "We call them requests rather than requirements."

"May I see them?" Rudy asked as Lizzy and I reached the floor. I handed the new list to him and waited for the appropriate shock at Amber's nonsense. And a humble retraction of Rudy's complaint when he realized the troubles I faced.

"This would make quite the affair." Rudy perused the impossible, unsuitably unruffled.

"Quite the affair? You mean quite the disaster, don't you?"

Rudy ignored me. "Could you and I discuss this privately?" he asked Lizzy. "For expediency, of course. Fewer people, less discussion. Then you can present our thoughts to the others. Of course if you prefer someone be with you as we meet, I understand." His smile and his slight bow were the epitome of congeniality as Lizzy hedged, then considered the three of us—her armed cook, his timid admirer, me with the hand I wanted to wave so she'd choose me pinned down, and of course...

"Les," she said. "The others have things to do for our customers." For the two or three tables of quiet coffee drinkers we should charge extra for the entertainment.

Les shot a look at Cook before he turned and followed Lizzy. Cook's nod fixed an expression on the boy's face I believed would get Les into trouble.

"What did your nod mean?" I hissed at Cook as Lizzy led Rudy and Les to the farthest table.

"It meant everythin' Brandt ever did only made things harder for Lizzy and Phil."

"Well, Les wouldn't know that or what to do about it."

Cook watched Rudy hold a chair for Lizzy as she sat. "Les knows a trick or two. I've been teachin' him."

I clapped a hand over my chest as I eyed Les. He had the build of a stick and no apron. He surely couldn't hide a pistol that likely weighed more than he did. "God help that boy."

Rudy indicated a seat for Les and made sure he was comfortable. I studied Mr. Walters' fine manners, the exceptional calm, which reminded me of St. Louis…except for the fact that his wrist had at one time been shackled to a marshal and he'd dared to ban me from Lizzy's bank.

"Les'll be fine. What you really mean is God help Lizzy," Cook muttered. "Mark my words, you'll be hearin' marriage suggested between Rudy and Lizzy, a marriage of financial convenience that would be convenient for everyone but her."

Now I clutched my throat. "But Eat Here is doing well. Amber's engagement party should only make it more secure. If money is the bait for such a marriage, Lizzy doesn't need it." I waited for Cook to agree. "Lizzy knows better than to marry for money. And besides, we have a plan to outthink, outsmart, out…"

"Out shoot." Cook patted his pistol. "You keep forgettin' where you are, Mrs. Strong. This ain't the East."

"And it never will be as long as people out here think a gun can settle everything." I smacked his hand away from his pistol. "There won't be any of that."

"There wouldn't if that blasted door of yers didn't let riff-raff sneak in," Cook grumbled.

"I'll have you know that door has—"

"Let in as many flies and vermin as payin'

customers," Cook cut me off.

I couldn't argue that as I watched across the room where Lizzy and Rudy bent their heads over Amber's insanity, Les pitched back in his chair, his gaze steady on Mr. Walters. Either God or I would have to help that boy.

Rudy glanced our way, then rose, Lizzy and Les doing the same. His tiny frown met my larger one as he started across the room, the other two behind him.

"I have made some suggestions," Rudy said as he latched onto his lapels.

"Which we may or may not take into consideration at our meeting tomorrow morning," I said. "And by we, I mean me, Lizzy, Clement, Amber, and Mr. Brandt. No extras other than Joshua, who I suggest be included again."

Rudy shook his head. "I'm afraid Joshua won't be there. Everett sent him on a matter to another town."

"Everett?" I clapped a hand over my chest again. "He's back? I mean, the marshal is…"

"He *was* back. From his friend's wedding… supposedly," Rudy finished for me. "Probably Jim's."

"Jim's?" I clamped tighter to my chest. Everett had a friend who resembled my Jim. Now he had a friend named Jim. What if one… What if both… "Are you sure?"

"Yes, I'm sure. You might recall the marshal and I were together for a short time. Enough time to learn Everett had a friend who planned to wed. You also know Joshua and I have had business together recently." A slight glint shone in Rudy's eye. "You learn a lot when you're near someone. And listen. Especially with your eyes."

Cook stepped between Rudy and my distress. "I think I've heard all I need to hear. Or see. All talkin' will be done at the stagecoach office. This whole shindig ain't about nothin' but money anyway, and the one with the money ain't here."

Rudy turned and faced Cook. "Money? This is an engagement party. Love is, of course, essential."

"Oh, for Pete's sake." Cook flapped his towel toward Rudy's face. "We're talkin' arrangement more than engagement. There ain't no love in that."

Rudy didn't blink or move. "Some folks don't see love until it's gone. When it hurts. A pained emptiness you can only pray goes away."

"And if whatever might cause that hurt don't go away first, it's time to do somethin' about it." Cook flapped his towel again, and to my horror, Les raised an arm and mimicked him.

"You might do well to consider what I said." Rudy still didn't budge.

Glass hit the floor and shattered. We turned toward Tina and her gasp. Her eyes were wide and apologetic with a tiny glow of admiration as she focused on Cook before she bent to clean up whatever had broken.

Lizzy ran to help her, wisely taking Les along. She left him with Tina as she made excuses to her few customers and escorted them out the door. She closed the large inner door between our show and the few who argued missing it, then returned and bent with Tina and Les over the glass.

Rudy's words about love being gone cycled through my head as I watched them along with Cook, who cocked his head, his eye, and his ear on the three…but especially on Tina.

I want you to be all right.

Cook monitored his friends and the girl who would scurry over the floor for Mr. Brandt's arrangement, while Rudy monitored Cook.

"We will talk at tomorrow's meeting," I nearly shouted to disrupt everyone. "The original four of us. Deputy Joshua gave us rules we will stick to."

"If you plan to follow rules, follow all of them." Rudy turned toward me.

Cook frowned. "What rules?"

Drat. "I'll explain later."

"I'll explain now." Rudy pointed at Cook's gun. "That pistol for one. In order to protect innocent people, the deputy has decreed you are not to carry it in this restaurant. You're to leave it with Mrs. Strong."

"Phooey. Innocent people are safe. I ain't never killed nothin' I didn't intend to. And it ain't like the Good Lord didn't make more than one gun."

"And likely you have more than one," Rudy said.

"Likely." Cook wheeled and marched toward the kitchen, Tina, her apron corners gathered in a fist to carry the broken glass, close behind him.

Rudy watched, then studied the doorway they disappeared through and could be heard on the other side of, Cook's grouse and Tina's soothing tone.

"We'll meet tomorrow," I said louder than necessary. Rudy continued to stare at the door. "No more impromptu meetings here and no more new lists except at our regular meetings." I increased my volume more.

Rudy finally spared a brief glance my direction, then eyed the kitchen one last time. "Good day, Mrs. Strong."

Chapter 21

I've built a home worthy of and ready for two with my hands. And you and I have built two lives worthy of and ready to become one with our words in our letters. Miss Archer, we've done everything except meet. Please come. Please consider me. And please say yes that you will marry me.

The rest of the words in one of Jim's last letters wavered along with the album I held on my lap, my eyes glassy and my hands unsteady. Surely this man wouldn't marry another. Surely he still had a heart…for me, like I did for him.

Don't come. I can't marry you.

I twisted on my cot and stared at the door to my room. Could the voice which had courted me by letters and let me go by wire say, "I do," to someone else? Surely not. The West spread far and wide enough to hold hundreds of Jims. The one Everett knew could be any of them, not necessarily mine. I could ask Everett, if he'd just return. Which he rarely would now that he'd appointed Joshua. I looked down at the opened trunk near my feet, where my wedding gown lay, folds of white with tiny lace and buttons, creases where creases would never have been if it had been worn.

"Jim…" I set my collection of his words atop the gown and closed the lid. My Jim wouldn't marry another. He wanted me and he wanted me to be all right. "Soon," I promised as I stood to go downstairs. As soon as I kept a promise to the other Elizabeth.

I feel so at home with you. Funny, since we've not actually met...yet we have. In words, the way that matters, in tales that have made me laugh, in stories which helped me understand you.

Jim's voice spoke with every step down to the dining area, to the blur of beauty which met me, Lizzy and Tina on a run from table to table in their new outfits, which matched Eat Here's fresh paint. The simple lines and elegant hues of what they wore brought color to their cheeks. Color which had blossomed with Cook's initial gape when he first laid eyes on them, his whistle and smile which Les wrongly imitated. I ran my hands down the front of my outfit, identical to theirs though Cook had snorted and remarked I'd be harder to 'git a bead on' against the walls or next to Lizzy and Tina. The old coot.

"Stagecoach will be delayed this morning," Tina said as she hurried to serve the large number of our regulars. She nodded toward the door, now covered with screen. "He told us." She rushed off, coffeepot and water pitcher in her hands.

I glanced to Eat Here's door, where Clement's silhouette shrank in a frame of outdoor sunlight, his shy pose intent on Lizzy across the room. The way he stood, the way he worked his hat in his hands, spoke. *I feel so at home with you.*

"Good," Cook barked from the kitchen. "I'm not makin' any more of those blasted Kansas Concoctions, even if we run out before the stage gets here. And I won't be botherin' with the drivers' free breakfasts, either."

"Excuse me. Or excuse him," I said to a nearby customer who frowned toward Cook's outburst beyond the kitchen door. I marched to the back where Cook wielded a spatula in a cloud of cinnamon and steam. "You will too make more Kansas Confections," I ordered him. "And if the stage comes at midday, we will feed the drivers a free lunch instead."

"I'm plenty busy back here with yer good will and aroma advertisin', without yankin' my day around for late strangers and freeloadin' drivers."

"I'm aware of how busy you are. You might recall that was our goal."

"Your goal." Cook slapped his spatula on the stove. "I had another. Which is all twisted up and dang near ruint by yers."

"Whatever yours was, mine is better. Do I have to drag you out to the dining room by your whiskers to remind you that busy is good? Advertising did it, aroma along with the new signs painted in restaurant colors that we posted at the train station." For a ridiculous fee, thanks to the greedy Mr. Weston. "We are doing well, which means Lizzy is. So bake more Kansas Confections. Now."

I turned and cleared the door to the dining room before a hot spatula could be tossed at my back. Tina whirled past as she wove from one customer to the next, while Lizzy stood at the side where we kept spare pots of coffee and trays of Kansas Confections... cookies, drat Cook. Lizzy had a pot in one hand and a plate in her other, Clement in front of her. *I feel so at home with you...* Whatever Clement said, Lizzy listened, the pot and plate lowering as the color on her cheeks rose. The hat, which had become nothing but a blur in his hands, stopped. He gave Lizzy a little bow and hurried away.

"I think he's sweet on her."

I glanced to my side, where Tina stood, a wisp of hair loose, which she brushed back over her forehead as she watched Clement thread his way toward the screen door.

"Lizzy could do worse." I emphasized the word "worse" and resisted the urge to tip my head toward the kitchen at an unseemly ruckus which made Tina blush and grin.

"You know how sometimes a tune can get stuck in your head?" Tina looked at me. "Lizzy's got one stuck in hers. Clement probably sounds just like it, but she doesn't know that."

"You mean her song? Clement said she lost it."

"It's in her head still. She just doesn't have a way to get it out because she thinks she'll never get it back."

Lizzy watched Clement as he slipped through Eat Here's door. I thought of the list of music and composers Amber had given us that Lizzy had pored through. The list Clement had taken from her and not returned. How could he sound like something she knew and wanted? Even more, how could she not recognize a tune which meant so much to her? I shook my head. How did Tina and Cook ever communicate with his one-word bullet conversations and her many-word convoluted ones?

"Can you take over serving drinks?" Tina asked. She raised the pot and pitcher she held.

I nodded and took them.

"I have so many orders. We've never been this full before, and without the stage even here yet. That see-through door sure became an open door for us." She grinned, then waved an arm toward the kitchen. Toward Cook, with a gleam in her eye which said they sang and heard the same tune. I shuddered.

"You go on. Take the orders to Cook, and I'll manage the drinks." I started toward the nearest table as Tina darted away, Jim's words in my mind, his imaginary voice which I so longed to become real...soon. His tune played in my head with every glass of water I poured and cup of coffee I filled. *You feel like home to me...* The tune would sing relief for both of us when Jim saw I'd come in spite of his wire and in spite of some other Jim out here who'd possibly married. His voice continued on, his song in the customers' thanks and requests for help. *Please... Say yes... Say you'll marry me. Please.*

"Please."

I glanced down. Everett looked up from the chair next to the table I paused by. "I was saying, no coffee. Just water. Please." He covered the empty cup with a hand and nudged the glass my way. *Please.* His voice blended with Jim's, Everett's real overshadowing Jim's imaginary.

I set the coffeepot down with a thump and snatched the water glass to fill it.

"What you've done is nice."

Water slopped over the sides and ran down my hand. I clunked the glass next to the coffeepot. I listened for *Please*, the right *Please*.

"Thank you." Everett scanned the room, our outfits, the paint, the elegance of the tables, until his tour ended...with me. "Very nice. I believe Alex would have been proud."

"Alex? Oh. Yes, God rest his soul. Mr. Strong would be very pleased. Our ideas were pretty much the same." A warm mist formed around my collar.

"It looks remarkably better in here. You've done well for them. And him."

"I only did what was right." Mostly. My skin began to heat. "But as for you, Mr. McCloud, I'm surprised to see you here." I latched onto the coffeepot, poised it above the cup still covered by his hand. "I thought with Joshua here, you wouldn't be." Wouldn't be back. Would be with Jim. Wouldn't refuse the one drink which possibly reminded him of his friend. I positioned the pot even closer to his cup.

"Just water, please, if it's all right." He removed his hand from the mug.

Please say yes.

"Yes," I said. Heat raged from my neck to my face. I'd look like a lit candle in a matter of seconds. "I mean, yes, of course it's all right. I'm just…well, I'm surprised you're… I heard you'd been away to a…" Wedding? Jim Baylis's? Did he marry, or did Everett do something to change his mind, like Joshua thought? Flames engulfed my head.

Everett leaned forward, bent over his water glass, and studied it. "Yes, I was gone, but I came back." One long finger traced the glass's rim. "Been some changes. Might be more."

"Changes?" The coffeepot's handle slipped. I set it on the table and placed the water pitcher beside it. My goodness. Everett evidently had to come back because of me, because of the two rules Joshua had made that I hadn't complied with. I glanced at the kitchen where the still-armed Cook ranted. Hopefully he and his gun would stay back there like I'd told him to. "It's not Joshua's fault, especially if you're here because of Mr. Walters and his…"

Everett looked up. "Has Mr. Walters bothered you?"

"Bothered me?" Besides my ban from the bank, the edict to restrain Cook, and his involvement with Amber's party? To mention those would be akin to a confession I'd broken some rules. Everett had been chained to Rudy long enough to witness Rudy's good manners, fine clothing, and willingness to help. Drat. "It's my fault, all of it, and the biggest and worst consequence is that Cook might shoot Rudy." Heat spread to my toes. "I should have…I realize the gun…" Drat again.

Everett settled back in his chair. "Which one of them are you more worried for, Mrs. Strong?"

"Them?" Clearly he didn't hear me. They weren't the problem. However, I paused and pondered a future with either or both of my nemeses shot.

"Mrs. Strong, it's been my experience as a lawman that most shootings stem from some hurt, and most heroic ones from a hatred of hurt or a defense against it…often with a vengeance. That doesn't excuse the perpetrator, or the hero if he exercises revenge in his own way. I don't suggest you embrace someone like Mr. Walters. That would be akin to taking in a starved cougar and insisting he diet. But I also don't recommend he be shot when he visits Eat Here."

Everett tapped his water glass. "I understand you've been told to inform Cook that any gun he tries to carry beneath that apron he's to hand over to you."

Would the fire in my face never stop? I ground

both cheeks with the heels of my palms. "Has anyone stopped to consider the ramifications of that if someone really does need to be shot and I'm the one with the gun?"

"The kind of hurt you have, Mrs. Strong, wants to heal. Not kill. Killing for you would be a matter of discretion, not passion."

Discretion. I hardly felt discretion when I read, *Don't come. I can't marry you.* Or when I boarded the train, and Everett first saw me. "I would never kill someone."

"I would hope not, ma'am. Or that you'd be put in a position to. But as far as your cook is concerned, everything you've done here is packaging over whatever he's fiercely devoted to…which isn't altogether clear yet."

"You think my plan here is shallow?"

"Ma'am, I'd never think of you as shallow. You have my word on that."

I'd never think of you as shallow.

Jim had said those very words. I listened for his voice over Everett's, inhaled the aroma of coffee Everett refused.

"Call upon your discretion when it comes to your cook…and anyone else who crosses Eat Here's threshold. And send for me."

"For you? Not for your deputy?"

"There might be some changes, as I said."

Eat Here's door flung open as a stream of weary travelers pushed through, late arrivals from the slow stagecoach, dusty and in search of a promised oasis.

"Just arrived," Les shouted in his soprano boy's voice, then tried the announcement again with a failed attempt to sound like Cook.

Everett glanced toward the door at the exhausted passengers. "I don't mean to detain you," he said. "Or upset anything…"

I studied his profile, the taut kindness, eyes that counted, watched travelers the same way he had watched me in St. Louis. The same way he looked at me now as he turned. "Penelope…"

Please…

I heard it again but saw it on Everett's face this time. "Either Lizzy or Tina will take your order." I snatched up the pot and pitcher and darted away. Jim's word…Everett's voice. I couldn't seem to make my way to Jim, but somehow he kept coming to me.

Chapter 22

I turned from what I thought I wouldn't, and hadn't intended, to be here to see—Amber's candles arranged on one of Eat Here's tables, all one hundred of them she had requested for her party, each seven inches in height. Exactly. "I'll never count or measure another stick of wax in my life. Most brides-to-be wouldn't care if there were one hundred or one hundred and ten candles, or if they were all different sizes. How ridiculous."

Lizzy rolled the sewing tape around her fingers. "You're right. A bride-to-be shouldn't care. Unless the ceremony is all she has." She focused on her fingers, wound the tape slowly and bound them together. "Amber's already done exactly what we just did."

"She what?" I winced at the unladylike screech in my voice.

"She stopped by last night and counted and measured the candles just to be sure we were ready for their party tonight. She did it quietly so you wouldn't hear her. Probably because she wanted to tell us to get eight more and she knew you would ask for cash to do it." Lizzy scooted one candle aside with her free hand. "She said this one's bent a little. And in addition to the eight extra she wanted, she said to get five more."

I closed my eyes. And my mouth. Of course I would have demanded money up front, but Lizzy wouldn't have. Goodness, I had let Lizzy down again.

Left her with Amber's reedy voice while I sequestered myself upstairs with that much nicer one I planned to hear soon. Jim's. Not Everett's. I'd had to silence his first.

We'll have a small wedding, if that's all right. I have neighbors who will come, all of them excited to meet you and help you settle in. Small and simple. That is the sort of wedding I want. Small and simple, but full.

My need for assurance that Jim's gentle tenor remained with me as I remained here had apparently deafened me to the garish one poor Lizzy had been subjected to. His...our...wedding which seemed like less, would have been...hopefully still somehow would be...so much more. Full, but not of candles, music sufficient even if a folk tune, food not so exotic no one would recognize it.

My neighbor will bake a cake. I make the best coffee around, as you know since I've told you my secret. And another friend with the heaviest producing cow in the area will make ice cream. The only extravagance is that my friend...my very best friend...is coming. He intends to travel here, just for me, to meet you, to witness what is to be a celebration, not an event.

Jim had a friend, someone who wanted to meet me enough to travel and celebrate with us, be involved in what and who Jim cherished. Jim had such a friend...but so did I. I glanced at Lizzy. She had a friend as well—me. "I'm so sorry I didn't hear Amber and come down. Really, I am." I studied my friend and her profile as she studied her long fingers bound by the tape.

She glanced up with a slight frown. "I'm the one who should be sorry. Here you are still in Larned. I know you need to go. I see it in your distraction, yet you continue to stay. You're a wonderful friend, and I'll never be able to thank you enough, Penelope."

"I…" I wouldn't go. Not when Elizabeth Sanders needed the hard-learned lessons of Louise Elizabeth. Mama should be pacified with my chain of written excuses for the delay. Even my attorney should have received one by now, Clement raising another brow when I asked that his stage drivers also carry that one to Dodge City to send…for business reasons.

"It's okay." Lizzy smiled a tired but sincere smile. "I didn't want to bother you myself, but for a different reason. I can tell weddings upset you, and not just the annoyance Amber creates. I understand you have a hole where love should be. Or had been." She loosened the tape and splayed her fingers. "We just have to get through this…this…"

"This event." I used Jim's word for what no wedding should be, and which ours wouldn't, a word which made Lizzy's face light up.

"Amber's event." She smiled. Briefly. "It's sad, isn't it? I mean, when we recover from her event, we'll go on to other things. But she…" Lizzy shrugged. "What will Amber do?"

Amber certainly wouldn't throw herself into others' needs. Unless she ended up in a predicament like mine. My face warmed. "Well, she can't come here. She will not use Eat Here to create some new outlet for herself." My face heated even more that I had done that very thing. Unintentionally, though. Goodness. I had gone from "How did I end up here" to "Everybody stand back while I fix this." I fanned my face with a hand. "Well, never mind what Amber will do with herself." I picked up and waved the candle Amber deemed inadequate. "The immediate problem is what she will do now, since there isn't a new candle left to buy at Holt's store. Thirteen more will be impossible no matter how much money Mr. Brandt offers. She'll just have to settle for this."

"I have a straighter one at home. It used to be Phil's. I'll take this one and Amber can have mine…his."

"You'll do no such thing. I'll go to the bank and ask Mr. Brandt for candle money. If he gives it to me without a lot of argument, we'll send Les to the next town to…" Drat. I was banned from the bank. Something Lizzy still didn't know. "Never mind. Forget that idea. We'll send Les around town to ask for candles we can use. Buy. We'll tell everyone the Brandts will pay them back."

"Quite honestly, I've already bought and borrowed used candles and extra holders around town and pinched the black tips from their wicks so Amber wouldn't know," Lizzy confessed. "I went so far as to tell her they made those candles with the wax running down the sides that way on purpose."

"Well, Lizzy Sanders. You remind me more and more of myself…I mean, someone." I fidgeted with the candles we'd counted. Could lying be contagious? Had I infected Lizzy? Surely not. She and I were two honorable women pushed to the extreme. "You exercised business savvy, Lizzy. And those candles did come to you that way, so you didn't lie. Much. I'll send Les around one more time for whatever candles people can spare, and we'll melt them together and make them slightly thinner if they're too short. And next time

Amber sneaks into the restaurant to make more demands, just call me downstairs. No need for you to put up with her on your own, or the two of them if he comes as well."

"He didn't come, if you mean Mr. Brandt." Lizzy shook her head. "But Mr. Walters did."

"He what?"

Lizzy rewound the tape, the tips of her fingers turning red. "He helped." She peeled the tape off and stuffed it into her apron pocket. "He didn't say much."

"Which was…" I braced for the worst and steeled for the word *banned*.

"He said love is felt the most when it's lost."

"Why would he say that again? Or at all?" Surely Rudy wouldn't know about Lizzy's song or Jim's voice. The sounds she and I chased and that chased us.

"He said it like a fact. Something important."

Important? How could lost love be important at an engagement celebration? Lizzy and I glanced around the empty dining room, closed all day to prepare for Amber's event. Tina and Les scurried from table to table as they set up decorations…mostly the candles we'd counted…for the party.

"Well, thank God we'll be done with Mr. Walters and his maxims soon."

****

The five of us stood in a circle in the kitchen, unfamiliar aromas of food we'd never cooked before in a swirl around us. No cinnamon, no grease, Amber's menu choices were a conflict of pungent and sweet, roasted and sautéed.

"It's too much, don't you think?" Lizzy ran her hands down the front of the special outfit I'd had made for her to wear for Amber's party.

"No, it's lovely." Tina smoothed her new skirt and blouse as she admired the extra elegance I'd had added to Lizzy's. "I love those tiny rows of maroon lace on your blouse. And your skirt, I've never seen gold thread." Tina ran a finger along the pleats of Lizzy's skirt, then stood back and admired the belt stitched the same way. "It matches the shiny fastener in the front. It's just beautiful." Tina clasped her hands and smiled, her outfit identical to mine, a little more than our regular uniforms, but less than what Lizzy wore.

"You're the matron of Eat Here," I said to Lizzy. "And you're to look it. And the rest of us are to look…" I swept an arm to Cook and Les, the two of them scratching at cream shirts and gray pants with maroon trim. "Look grand. Unless one or two of us wrinkles or tears our clothing." I glared until Cook and Les stopped raking their fingers over the new fabric. "That's better. And I have soft maroon aprons for each of us." I went to a package I'd kept to the side and drew out sensible but elegant aprons for us three women, a long and thin one for Les, and a snug one Cook couldn't possibly conceal a pistol under.

"Pink?" Cook roared.

"Soft maroon. Now put this on." I handed his to him. "And cinch it tight." I handed the others their aprons as voices came from the dining room. "My goodness, this is it," I said as we each tied our aprons in place. "Anything you want to say before we start, Matron of Eat Here?" I looked at Lizzy, at her wide eyes as Amber's voice rang above the others. Rudy's and Mr. Brandt's hovered in a low conversation as Amber's grated the atmosphere with a verbal checklist of everything we were to have done.

"Thank you," Lizzy said to the four of us. "Thank you for all you have suffered. And all you've done." Her gaze ended with me. Elizabeth Sanders thanked Louise Elizabeth with a quiet gratitude I prayed could forgive when I told her no such person as Penelope Strong existed after tonight's affair, right before I left Larned…for good.

"Where is everyone?" Amber shrilled from the dining area. "I need all of you out here to get this room ready. I need these candles lit. And where are the musicians?"

"Let the last of the suffering begin," Cook grumbled.

Lizzy, Tina, Les, and I rushed through the kitchen doorway to Amber and Nicholas at the head of the room, side by side on their red rug. Her outfit stopped us. It spoke of royalty, while her fiancé's suit outdid any I'd seen in St. Louis. Stately in design and posture, Nicholas smiled down at Amber, who lacked only a tiara to crown her facial tints, enormous red hair, and flowing green gown.

"Well?" She pointed around the room, enough fire in her tone to light the candles from where she stood.

"We're ready," I lied. We weren't, other than the food and the decorations. But no candle should be lit this early in my opinion—which clearly didn't matter— and no musical instrument or singer could be seen.

"I expected a harpsichord, at the very least." Amber's foot tapped beneath her gown.

"A harpsichord?" A harmonica, maybe. I glanced around the room for Clement, for the answer to Amber's rage.

"I knew this would happen." Amber turned to Rudy, who stood behind her and Nicholas. "Would you please take care of this?" The bladed edge that had been her voice to us melted like butter. "Thank you."

Early guests began to enter as Rudy exited. Tina and Les rushed from table to table and lit candles as the unexpected arrivals threaded their way to the engaged couple.

Nicholas played the perfect host as he bowed to each person as if early was proper. Amber's scowl vanished, radiant beauty and warm greetings took its place as their guests filed past.

"They will hurt each other forever," Lizzy whispered at my side.

"If you mean Nicholas and Amber, and because of that thing Rudy Walters said about love..."

"He's right. Love hurts when it's lost. But in their case neither one will know about that because neither really cares."

"That's horrible..." And astute. I watched the couple whose layers of finery at least tied them together. "They surely have some morsel of love." Beneath all that fluff.

"Not for each other."

I studied Larned's resident royalty. Rudy had been positioned close enough behind to guard them from hurt, but surely close enough to know no love existed there to begin with.

"I don't understand Rudy's obsession about love," I whispered to Lizzy as I choked on a thick cloud of burning wax. "Especially if you're right that there isn't any. Something I can certainly imagine."

"I don't know if Rudy meant them." Lizzy nodded

toward Amber and Nicholas, who greeted yet another early arrival, someone else apparently unable to read their invitation properly.

"Whatever he meant, all I can say is I'll be glad when this whole affair is over and the three of them are out of your restaurant." Though I'd be out of her restaurant as well.

Fingers snapped, a repeated click which pointed to tables where guests began to sit. Amber's arm and finger aimed around the room.

"For Pete's sake," I muttered as Tina broke into a run across the dining area. She caught herself and slowed to the more elegant step Amber had taught her...us...as she hurried water glasses and goblets to tables. Les responded as well and darted to the kitchen for Amber's outlandish hors d'oeuvres.

The big event had begun. Slightly early. But not early enough for Amber, who raised a hand and signaled to Lizzy as Rudy re-entered Eat Here, his arms full of contraptions which had no resemblance to instruments or singers.

"Be careful," I whispered as Lizzy started Amber's direction, then stopped as Amber shifted her wave to the side and directed Lizzy where Rudy headed to the far wall. Lizzy inched forward until she joined Rudy as he set Amber's contraptions on a table. Lizzy gathered its lit candles and moved them to other locations while Rudy set up and wound a tiny but elegant machine, then arranged an enormous horn next to it which sent tinny strains of unidentifiable plinks throughout the room.

Cook manifested in the kitchen doorway. Tina and Les pressed alongside him, three frowns focused the direction of the metallic tone. Rudy adjusted the horn and delivered even more volume to the annoying racket.

"Save that cat fight for when there's enough people here we cain't hear it," Cook shouted across the room. "We cain't hear ourselves talk, tryin' to get this goldarned shindig set up."

I checked Cook's apron. No bulge...no gun. No reason for me to have to take it or hold it for him.

"Cook's right," a man called from Eat Here's front door.

I turned with every other person as the door closed behind Clement. Finally, the party's mediator I wanted to dress down for his negligence regarding the music. He looked exceptionally nice, handsome even, as he strode to a point halfway across the floor. "Let the staff get the final touches ready while the real music is set up."

Rudy let go of the enormous horn and faced our mediator.

"We will respect the bride." Clement drew himself up taller than Rudy, the hues of his suit subtle against the sharp black Rudy and Nicholas wore, his hair smoothed more than usual and more than theirs. "But we will also respect the woman whose work honors the bride." He looked at Lizzy. "This night would never have happened without either of these two women." He extended an arm which paid homage to Amber and then to Lizzy, where it lingered.

"And so in light of what the bride-to-be wants..." Clement bowed in deference to Amber and her unabated fury, which caused her cheeks to match her hair. "And what the hostess can best offer..." Clement extended his arm toward the door.

The door opened. Two men backed through as Clement hurried to help, the three wedging something enormous through the thankfully broad space.

Lizzy gasped as a piano appeared, gasped through the incessant pings of the music box and the hands she clapped over her mouth. Tears found their way over her long fingers, glistening streaks like silver as the piano began its trek across the floor.

"I said no piano. We won't pay for that." Amber abandoned her rug and marched to the men. "This isn't what I requested. We didn't agree to this." She looked back at Nicholas. "I said music. I said which type and which tunes."

Lizzy fell into the wake of the piano. Clement and the men brought it to the side not far from the table and the box which issued grating sounds he walked over and stopped. Lizzy circled the large instrument and the stool another man carried and set in front of it. With one finger she traced the dark wood as Amber babbled behind her.

Clement stepped between Lizzy and Amber. "You won't need to pay for this," he said to the bride-to-be's flaming red. "The music from it is yours, the exact compositions you requested. But the piano, and the heart which will turn it into a song, belong to Eat Here."

And to him. I could see it from where I stood. Clement wanted that heart. The one which cried when he handed Lizzy a stack of music carried in by yet another man. Clement wanted that heart to be happy…and all right. This piano would release Lizzy's lost song. The tune which sounded like him.

Chapter 23

Amber trooped to her music box and stepped around Rudy to restart the machine. In less than a moment, the air filled with a new rash of clanks and pings which caused the flames above the candles to vibrate.

I marched to the boxed orchestra. "Not only can we not hear each other, your guests can't hear anything either," I shouted to Amber over the racket, one arm in an arc across the room where hands cupped ears.

"Mrs. Strong is right." Nicholas appeared at his fiancée's side and touched her arm. "Not everyone has your youthful ears, my dear." He lifted a brow toward me.

I eyed his handsome and somewhat youthful ears that needed to be boxed.

"Come." Nicholas took Amber by the elbow. "This is your party. Come and enjoy yourself. It's almost time for our toast."

"But I can't without my music," she whined, her high pitch a perfect blend with the cat fight Cook had so rightly deemed her music. "We paid for it—we paid for everything to be perfect and my way."

Nicholas led her and her complaints away, pules her tin racket harmonized with all the way to their carpet.

"You haven't paid yet," I whispered as soon as

they resumed their places.

"You wouldn't be suggesting Mr. Brandt won't keep his agreement to pay for this party, would you?"

Drat. I'd forgotten about Rudy. I lifted the enormous horn between his face and mine. "Excuse me while I save the older ears." I fidgeted with the box until its racket stopped. People rubbed their ears at the sudden quiet. I wanted to tug at the ringing in my own as I set the horn back down. "As for your question, Mr. Walters, Mr. Brandt's agreement with me or Lizzy is just that. It's between us."

Lines which marked the features in his stolid expression darkened, then eased. "An appropriate answer." Rudy nodded. "Mrs. Strong." He walked away in an easy exchange of pleasantries with guests as he returned to his place behind Mr. Brandt and Amber. Once he faced the room again with his hands clasped in front of him, I turned to the table and gripped it. Of course my answer was appropriate. Drat that Mr. Brandt.

A hum of voices grew in the room, a soft sound which mellowed the sharp sound still in my ears. Easy conversations, chairs drawn around tables, the clink of glass and silverware. I kept my hold on the table's edge and breathed. Inhaled the expensive event and food Cook had managed to fix under great duress. Lizzy would be paid, Lizzy would be paid...

"There's a difference between wedding and marriage."

I stopped my chant and glanced to the left, to Everett who had approached the table without being heard. I tugged at my supposedly old ears one more time. "A difference between wedding and marriage?

What do you mean by that?"

"I'd think you'd know."

I frowned at a face which didn't frown back. Everett was watching again, watching me. Again. "Oh. You mean my marriage. Of course. I'm just surprised you'd say something like that."

"Because I've never been married? I've witnessed friends take that step." His gaze drifted to the heavily decorated room with its ocean of fire from Amber's one hundred and thirteen candles. "Weddings are made up of the things fancied, but marriage is reality. And honeymoons…if the couple can afford one…are the bridges between the two that get the couple from one to the other." He looked at me again. "If all goes as planned."

We'll stay here after the ceremony, if that is all right with you. This homestead, your new home, will be christened by our step across the bridge from wedding to marriage.

I held tighter to the table. Everett and my Jim both said bridge. It must be a Western term.

Everett grinned. "That's a honeymoon I wouldn't want to be on."

"What?" I would have clapped one hand over my chest and the other over my mouth if I didn't need the table to stabilize me.

"Those two." Everett nodded toward the royalty on their red rug, their hands holding the champagne glasses we'd paid an enormous amount for. "Love isn't in every union." He reined his usual kindness close as he studied them. "You might know that already. Though I'd not wish the personal experience of it on you."

I couldn't say yes or shake my head no, the personal experience of 'what if Jim had decided he didn't love me' a swirl of horror. What if his words had reached out for love but had returned to him empty, with my misguided drive simply to be someone's wife?

I stared at the white cloth where I supported myself as a new sound rose across the room, a swirl of something peaceable which battled the questions that tortured my mind. A melody like the voice I'd interpreted as love, but this one made of chords instead of words. Laughter and talk died down as I turned with everyone to the sound.

Everett's hand touched my back, and I let go of the table. We listened together, his warm fingertips small guides which directed me to the source—the piano and a voice which ascended with its song. Lizzy's notes and Clement's harmony changed the atmosphere. I rested against the five round touches at my back. Jim, and everything that should have been of him, streamed down my cheeks.

We stood silent, all of the room rapt until the music created by Lizzy's long fingers and Clement's fine voice, eventually subsided. Guests applauded and begged for more. Lizzy had played Amber's music, a choice she'd made which Lizzy apparently recognized. And knew. Couples formed as Lizzy complied with a smile. My friend's fingers spanned the keys, while Everett's spanned my back.

"Shall we dance?" he asked as Clement began to sing again. Other couples swept across the floor, the candle flames swaying with their movement. Everett pressed firmer. I closed my eyes and squeezed back the what-should-have-been which continued to flow down my face. "Here," he said.

I opened my eyes to a handkerchief. I took it and dabbed at my face as he led me into the midst of the other couples. One hand behind me, and his other wrapped around mine, he waltzed me into the slow swirl of Lizzy's and Clement's love song. Everett held me close as his kindness glided me around the floor, his handkerchief, which made sure I was all right, squeezed tight in my hand.

Lizzy's chords and Clement's solo flowed into other tunes and dances, bringing Tina—first with Les, then with Cook—onto the floor. Even Amber and Nicholas danced, though Rudy stayed in his spot and watched...listened his way.

I'd never heard a piano played so well. Everett spun me with a wordless ease through every measure. I caught sight of Lizzy as I twirled past, saw her hands, her grace, her gaze and Clement's together in their own musical waltz.

"I had no idea," I said as Everett guided us across the floor. "Lizzy never said a word about pianos or that she could play." I looked up at him. "Did you know? Do you know where she learned or how?"

"I only know she stopped," Everett said close to my hair. "She stopped when her piano went away."

"Went away?" I paused so abruptly we nearly stumbled.

"Sold to Mr. Brandt." Everett shot a brief glance at the engaged couple. "Phil needed money."

I thought of Amber's fuss, her insistence a piano not be played. "Is that it?" I nodded toward the instrument Lizzy seemed one with. "Is that the same one?"

"I don't think so." Everett studied the upright instrument. "I'd say this one is a gift." He smiled. "From someone who cares."

Clement sang to Lizzy's tune. I wanted to waltz toward them, pause, and give him a hug. Then waltz to Amber and yank her beehive of hair. How dare Amber hand Lizzy a list of music she would recognize and ache for. And how gallant of Clement to fulfill that list for Lizzy. He truly made sure Lizzy was all right.

"May I?" Deputy Joshua appeared at Everett's shoulder.

"Of course." Everett's hands tightened before he released me.

I took Joshua's outstretched hand and found myself pulled into a more powerful though less secure hold.

I want to know you're all right.

I looked for Everett as Joshua marched us through a waltz. I searched for kindness, for watchful eyes in an attentive expression.

"The candles are low." A sharp voice behind me brought a frown to Joshua's face. "Some are even out. You need to light the extras." Amber stepped where I could see her as Joshua halted. I looked around the room at the lowering glows, some candles burned out and dark. No one seemed to notice as couples huddled together even at those tables, wooed into the atmosphere the piano created.

"I think people are happy with the conditions," Joshua said. "Now, if you'll excuse us…"

"No, I requested candles at every table. Mrs. Strong, you're to make sure they're there. Not fritter away the good money we paid you by dancing."

"Money?" I let go of Joshua's hand while his other

stayed at my back. Couples danced farther away to hold onto the mood created by Lizzy's and Clement's tones and escape Amber's less attractive one. "You asked for a certain number of candles, one candle per table of a certain height. We did that. Exactly as you asked and exactly what your fiancé paid for. The few extras you requested, but didn't pay for, have already been put to use. As you can see, there are none left at the side table where we kept them. Honestly, you should be pleased the tapers are tapering. That means people are enjoying themselves and stayed longer than you anticipated."

"If I wanted one candle per table, then you had the responsibility to assure each table had one no matter how long people stayed." The thick powder on Amber's face creased with her frown.

"The list I gave Mr. Brandt for the deposit and fees said exactly how many candles you originally requested and we were to provide. We did, and we bought extras after the fact, as you requested, none of which you have paid for yet. To figure an extra candle for each table would have doubled our expense." I eyed Amber's color, which would stick to my hand if I slapped her.

"Maybe we could ask folks here if someone has a candle to donate." Joshua leaned in.

"We already did that," I said more harshly than I should. "We were forced to ask the town for candles when Amber added to what she wanted at the last minute."

"You what? These are used candles?" Amber's eyes grew wide. "I never approved of used anything for this party." She spun away, a blur of red and green which disrupted dancing couples as she charged toward her fiancé.

"I'll never…" I began.

"Never do a party like this again, or never do one for her again?" Joshua asked.

"Both." Even if I didn't have a ticket in my room for a train ride west of here tomorrow, I'd never host a party for Amber-Whoever-Dared-To-Marry-Her again.

I bit my lower lip at the thought of my ticket and stole a sideways glance at Joshua. Mr. Weston had threatened to file a complaint after I called him Julius—something the buzzard deserved after he refused an even trade for the ticket I hadn't used any of the previous times. I should file a complaint against that bald miser before I found myself waltzed right out of Eat Here's door and into a jail cell. How dare he charge half the full price and then hand me a ticket which only took me halfway to where I wanted to go.

I checked for complaints against me in Joshua's expression. This could be why he and Everett both danced with me, to keep hands and eyes on me before I escaped or offended someone else.

"Are you still a deputy in this town?" I asked, calculating who to avoid. "It wouldn't be you and Everett both, would it?"

"Wish I knew," Joshua mused.

The piano stopped. Joshua and I turned to where Clement sang on, *a capella*, stilted and unsteady without Lizzy's accompaniment. She staggered to her feet as Rudy wrapped his hand around her long fingers and led her across the floor. Clement watched as the distance between him and Lizzy grew.

"I have no idea what that Mr. Walters is up to." I started toward Lizzy, then jolted back, Joshua's fingers around my arm. Rudy maneuvered her to Amber and her fiancé.

"She needs my help," I hissed at the deputy who wasn't sure he was one.

Joshua's hold tightened. "Sometimes you got to stand back to see...look for who's who and what's what."

"You sound like Rudy Walters," I fairly spat. And Cook. Lizzy looked pale from where we stood, that's what was what. The same wan feeling mottled Clement's voice. Mr. Brandt smiled as he spoke to my friend. Then he laughed, an easy chortle which enhanced good looks I suspected shouldn't be trusted. Rudy bent his head near Lizzy's and said something that widened her eyes.

I wrenched at my arm, but Joshua held on. I looked for Everett. Surely he saw what was happening. I scanned the couples. He was nowhere. Clement's solo strained as Mr. Brandt unfolded a white sheet of paper and showed it to Lizzy.

I yanked forward, broke Joshua's grip, and marched toward the white. The paper vanished into Rudy's pocket after he took it from Mr. Brandt. He drew Lizzy aside as I trooped their way, Mr. Brandt sending the two of them off with a nod.

"We need yer help in the kitchen." Cook reached Lizzy and Rudy before I did, Tina one step behind him. His voice sounded more gravelly than usual. Like rocks...large rocks. "We're runnin' low on food and are short some ingredients. I want yer approval before I make substitutes." Those were words and questions Cook had never bothered to say or ask before and, from the poisonous expression he aimed at Rudy, likely never intended to again. Lizzy's head spun from a shake to a nod as I reached her and latched onto her free arm.

"Lizzy, I'll go with you. I understand the supplies we ordered, so together we can help Cook."

"You go too," Cook said to Tina. *I want you to be all right* in the gesture which encouraged her our way.

I took both their arms and hurried Lizzy and Tina toward the kitchen. "What was that paper I saw?" I whispered to Lizzy as we went.

"A revised contract," she whispered back with a glance over her shoulder. "Mr. Brandt said there'd been some changes. I had no idea what he meant. Everything looks perfect to me."

"Everything is perfect. You didn't agree to anything, did you?"

"I didn't have the chance. I wouldn't have anyway, but Rudy took it and told me not to worry about it."

I slowed and checked behind us where Rudy, the picture of refinement, stood in front of Cook. Whatever words were being exchanged, I doubted it had to do with spices.

Clement's solo began to resemble Amber's music box as we passed, his voice pitchy, little more than a scratchy wail. "Well, they won't be charged for that, even though they should, since it's their fault poor Clement is left alone," I said.

"I wish I could play the piano to help him out, but I can't." Tina glanced at Clement, then back at Cook, her eyes still dancing.

"Would you go ask someone to start that dreadful machine of Amber's again so poor Clement can rest?" I interrupted her admiration.

"Certainly." With a final, quick glance at Cook,

Tina hurried away. I led Lizzy into the warm kitchen as Clement's woe subsided, and the catlike plinks of a tinny orchestra started up again.

"Lizzy…"

A ruckus different from Amber's music interrupted me, a commotion at the kitchen doorway, where Rudy's finery appeared, his haberdashery at war with the neatened bulwark of Cook for position.

"Miss Sanders…" Rudy squeezed past Cook and stepped into the kitchen. "We have business together. I promised you my help."

"You got nothin' with her." Cook squared himself between Lizzy and Mr. Walters. "Only business you got is with me. And I'd say it's high time."

"Cook. Apt for what you've become." Rudy spoke it as a word, not a name. He made it sound like an insult, not even a title. "I have everything it takes to prosper Eat Here and Miss Sanders. You have…just an apron, Sa…"

"And this."

I saw a flash at Cook's other side. I heard a blast, watched Rudy double forward, then listened to a guttural sound as he dropped to the floor.

"Cook!" His name turned to a scream in my head as Rudy fell. Another scream rose behind me—Lizzy's.

"Stop gawkin'. Git out there and make excuses for the noise. That deputy cain't be far away." Cook leaned over the balled man, his pistol aimed at the body that didn't move.

"Is he dead?" I gawked anyway, frozen where I stood.

"Lizzy, you git out there. You know what to do." Cook waved her off with his free hand before he fished inside Rudy's jacket. White appeared, the contract held high where Rudy wouldn't reach it...even if he could. "Grab a leg," Cook ordered me, a fire far fiercer than any I'd ever seen in his eyes. I staggered back, latched onto the kitchen table, recoiled at the animal in Cook's gaze. "We gotta hide him under some laundry till this mob clears."

"What's going on?"

"What was that noise?"

"Everything all right?"

Voices and questions came from outside the kitchen doorway. None were Joshua's, but Lizzy responded to them all, a quick assurance we'd dropped a tub full of dishes and everything was indeed all right.

"Everyone knows. They heard you shoot." I stared at the man on the floor.

"They heard a noise. With all that racket and everythin' goin' on out there, they won't waste much time questionin' Lizzy. Now git a move on," Cook growled.

I snatched the paper from Cook's hand and stared at Rudy's ankles as I stuffed it into my apron's pocket. "This is so horrible..." I eyed Rudy's trouser legs. How long before cold would be felt through the fabric? I didn't want to know. I bunched his pants' leg in my fists and held on.

"You gotta grab his actual leg unless you wanna take him down to his under things."

I stared where Rudy's dress boot showed.

"Now."

I latched onto his leg above his boot and prayed his calf wouldn't feel cold.

"To the laundry room," Cook grunted. He grabbed

Rudy's other leg, and we backed across the floor together, dragging Rudy from the kitchen to the nearby wash area, guest questions and Lizzy's strangely calm assurances left farther and farther behind. Thank God Clement had tired. Amber's tinny music was the perfect cover for Cook's gunshot...and me...as we dragged Rudy past heaps of laundry to the far corner. I watched the floor behind Rudy's head for a trail of blood, then looked away, a morbid fascination I could neither stand nor resist.

"He's not bleeding," I whispered when my backend hit the laundry area's far wall. I dropped Rudy's leg with a horrid thump. "Rigor mortis has set in." I clapped a hand over my mouth.

"He ain't dead, and stiff don't happen that fast." Cook dropped the other leg with an equally horrid thump. "Grab some of those dirty towels and wet rags and cover him up. Got plenty of 'em, with this foolish fiasco we're holdin'."

"He's not dead?" I asked through my fingers.

"Git a hold of yerself. He's just wounded." He gave a furious rip to cloth, a violent shred that joined the wail of the music. A wail which grew louder. Lizzy must have set that magnifying horn even closer to the machine. Cook bent over Rudy's still form and bound strips of cloth he'd torn across Rudy's shoulder where a dark stain grew around a hole in his coat.

"He's just unconscious?"

"If he weren't, I really would have to kill him. God knows he deserves it. Are you gonna cover him up or just stand there bein' useless?"

I slid my hand from my mouth and bit back bile. I scooped damp towels and soiled tablecloths and dribbled them over Rudy's body. It had all happened so quickly. It was so uncalled for. I hadn't even seen the bulge of a gun beneath Cook's apron. Cook bound the wound tight and packed Rudy—and the laundry I'd dropped over him—into the corner. He set a four-legged tub in front of the limp man, then stood and checked his gun.

"You're worried about your pistol?"

Cook rubbed the butt of it with a towel. "No, ma'am. Worried about Lizzy right now." The gun went back where it had been, amazingly invisible beneath Cook's tight apron.

"So you are perfectly capable of hiding that gun, and all this time you've let it show just to annoy me?" My voice resembled Amber's tinny chords. "Not to mention, I told you that any shooting at all had to…"

"Mrs. Strong." Cook's voice hit a new low with harshness akin to a slap. I quieted in front of a glower that could shoot me next. "We gotta git down to business." He nodded toward my pocket where the paper lay. "That ain't just a contract. And the fella I took it from ain't no gentleman. And certainly no hero like he wanted Lizzy to think."

I tugged it out and stared stupidly at white which quivered. "You mean the fellow you shot."

"And that you just helped me hide."

My skin turned cold. As white, no doubt, as the paper. "I…I…" I forced my hands to work and the sheet to open. A contract…no, our contract…the agreement we'd reached for this party, but with lines drawn through candles, the musicians and instruments, some of the food Cook had made, and with miscellaneous comments penned in below. "Null and

Void" stretched across signatures and the balance Mr. Brandt agreed to reimburse. "This can't be." I heard the wail again, the screech I'd never known I was capable of.

"Come on." Cook took me by the arm. With him I peered out the laundry door, scooted to the kitchen, and peeked from there across the restaurant at what tables and candles and guests we could see…at Lizzy as she assured everyone that everything was all right. But it wasn't. I looked to the altered contract, toward the shot man not far away. I'd caused some of this, helped other parts of it, and had done nothing to prevent the rest. My goodness. Why had I lied to begin with? Why hadn't I admitted the truth and stayed on the train?

Lizzy's voice carried to where I stood. She checked drinks and asked if she could do anything for the guests. I staggered to the dining room, scoured couples and people for handsome and colorful to make things right for Lizzy. Mr. Brandt and Amber were nowhere to be seen. They were gone, an unpaid bill and a voided contract left behind.

Chapter 24

"Where'd they go?" I latched onto Clement's lapel.
"Amber and Nicholas, where did they go?" I listened
for Amber's voice over the twang of the music and the
conversations of her guests who didn't seem to notice
their faux hosts were gone. "The dirty scoundrels,
where'd they go?"

"They went out right before that ruckus in the
kitchen started. Joshua and Everett went behind them."

Everett? He'd been here all along? Standing back
with Joshua while everything went wrong? "Take care
of Lizzy. She will need it."

Clement would. His eyes promised me as he set
aside obvious questions about the ruckus I certainly
wouldn't answer. He hurried across the room in a way
quite unlike the meek stagecoach manager I'd first met.
He slowed at Lizzy's side, worked with her to soothe
and distract Amber's guests, the harmony to her song.

I slipped back to the kitchen. "The crowd's thinner,
and the marshals are gone. So are Amber and
Nicholas," I exhaled in one gush to Cook.

"Good," he grunted. "Come help me drag that
good-for-nothing friend of the banker out back."

"We don't really know if Rudy was up to no
good…"

Cook pointed to the voided contract I clutched
even tighter now that I knew Nicholas had run off

without paying.

"But Rudy told Lizzy he would take care of it. That could mean…" I needed Rudy to be bad, to justify Cook shooting him and me hiding him. But I also needed him to be good. Because of Lizzy. Drat. For once, I needed the truth.

"I never miss." Cook wagged a finger close to my face. "I always hit where I'm supposed to. I told you that. Now let's git to it." He didn't regret what he'd done. Nor would he apologize that he'd left a man he believed deserved it bleeding on the floor.

I began to tremble, a shake which started deep inside and wouldn't stop. My head wagged back and forth with the "no" I couldn't find the voice to say. Cook came close, eyes like hell's fire, powerful, dangerous, impatient…and on me.

"It may seem right, but it's wrong." I drew back from his fervor and finger, then followed him to the heap of soiled towels and helped peel away the dampness to a groan beneath. "He really is alive." I stared at the fine attire now dotted with orbs of food, the pale face, the tight mouth which had baffled me with words which were either very astute or misleading. Rudy Walters, finicky and neat in all that mattered to him, lay damp, smelly, and bloodied. "Do you think…"

"Take a leg," Cook growled.

"But he needs tended to." A cold moan whispered at my feet. I looked at the cool and damp, but felt the impatient heat beside me. "We need to do something."

"We are doin' somethin'. We're helpin' Lizzy and givin' him a chance he don't deserve because I need to know who the shadow ain't. Now grab on, like I said."

Shoving the contract into my apron pocket, I bent,

latched onto one leg while Cook grasped the other, and tugged backward, the two of us dragging a groaning Rudy from the laundry to the kitchen and out the back door into the dark.

"Now let go," Cook ordered.

Rudy's boots hit the dirt of the alleyway behind Eat Here, two thuds followed by a gasp and another groan.

We should call a doctor. We should drag him somewhere else. I stared into the dark where Rudy lay. "Will he live? Will he come back if he does? Will he come for Lizzy or us once he comes to?"

Cook stood somewhere in the blackness. I could feel his presence. Then I felt his hands and what they laid in mine. He closed my fingers around a wallet, stuffed fat and full. "Mr. Walters' contribution for the trouble he's caused. He's got more somewhere, and I aim to find it. He had a few deeds in his pocket, also. Some stake of land far west of here, and a train ticket to take him to Colorado Territory. I know what to do with the deeds."

My ears rang in the silence. Stolen money lay in my hand and a wounded man at my feet. A jilting fiancé to the west and a ticket in Cook's hand that could take me all the way there instead of halfway like the one the cheapskate Julius Weston had sold me.

"West of here." Cook's soft gravel spoke to my sins, my broken heart, and nudged at the closed door I'd come west to open. He knew things he shouldn't.

I shook my head, which Cook would use his uncanny animal sense to see in the dark.

"Very well." He also knew I wasn't headed just anywhere, not the vague places I'd claimed the fictitious Alex Strong had investments. He'd deduced I had a specific destination in mind. I heard Cook bend and Rudy gasp as he stuffed the ticket back inside Rudy's jacket.

"There's a code out here men live by." Cook grunted and cursed while Rudy gasped a curse back. Two more thuds hit the dirt. "That should keep him from comin' back. Unless he's even lower than I think he is." The aroma of leather, warm and dusty and tinged with sweat, wafted upward. "You strip a man of his boots, he's stripped of everythin'. No greater shame than bein' left barefoot. He'll be needin' that ticket more than...well, more than one of us."

Cook's footsteps crossed the dirt and scaled the few steps to the restaurant. Eat Here's kitchen door opened, and a fan of light spread to the barefoot lump on the ground.

"After you, Mrs. Strong."

"But..."

"I swear to you, I hit exactly what I want when I aim. My one word conversation to this lousy excuse for a man was a promise he heard and won't forget. It weren't meant to kill him, and it didn't. He's gonna live a long, long time. Just not the luxurious way he thought." Cook tossed Rudy's boots inside and extended a hand my way. "You can trust me, Mrs. Strong."

I glanced to the door, to the hand which waited to help me, the first honor that grizzled man had ever offered. He grinned, toothless spaces even blacker in the night. I took his hand. I needed it.

****

We sat in a row in the stagecoach office—Mr. Brandt, Amber, Lizzy, and I—as we watched Clement

236

across the table from us, his head bent over scattered contract pages Mr. Brandt contested, the banker's lines and slashes through Amber's demands he claimed we'd failed to meet at his party the night before. I pressed close to Lizzy, my chair and skirt squeezed against hers instead of some stranger's on a train on my way to Jim.

Mr. Brandt tapped immaculate fingertips on the tabletop. "I don't have all day to wait for you to agree with me that Miss Sanders and Mrs. Strong didn't follow our contract."

He hadn't said a word about Rudy when he and Amber entered. Maybe because of his big hurry. Or possibly he didn't know his friend had been wounded...yet.

I centered myself on my seat to keep Lizzy and Amber between me and the banker's eyes. His fingers thrummed louder, an impatient cadence which brought a stir from the door, a shuffle and rearrangement of Joshua's feet. Mr. Brandt's fingers stopped. So did terse noises which came from his throat. Nicholas should be glad those weren't Cook's boots at the door. He'd likely have me help drag Lizzy's impatient banker out by the legs.

I sank lower. What sort of woman had I become? I peered past Lizzy to see if Joshua had his eye on me. Surely someone knew what Cook and I had done. Maybe Everett. He could be with Rudy now, gathering evidence to hang Cook and me.

The door opened. I stiffened. It could be Everett. I stole another peek at the deputy. Ben and a few others of the town's business owners were outside looking in. Men and women Lizzy and I owed money to for goods or services they'd supplied above and beyond

Nicholas's initial deposit for Amber's outrageous party. More faces crowded behind them. Goodness. So many people had been affected by Nicholas's refusal to pay. Even for a used candle.

"This is a private meeting," Joshua said to the crowd.

"We're involved," Ben retorted. "We're owed money, and we need it. We trusted them." He nodded at Lizzy and me.

Mr. Brandt twisted in his seat and gave a casual scan of the townspeople who owed him far more than he owed them. "You trusted Miss Sanders and Mrs. Strong for reimbursement?" Mr. Brandt asked them, sounding surprised. "We trusted them also, and you see what's happened. They didn't follow our contract, so they likely didn't follow yours as well."

"We had no contracts," someone said from the back of the group.

Mr. Brandt's brows rose. "No contracts? Is that what Mrs. Strong taught when you met with her in the evenings?"

The townsfolk shrank back, those who'd felt betrayed by us now worried they'd betrayed Mr. Brandt. He shook his head at Lizzy and me. "You two have misled innocent people. That's not the right way to do business. Of course, violating a contract, when you actually have one, isn't either." He turned to the faces behind Joshua. "A word of advice as your banker. Deal directly with me from now on. Any events or projects should be managed through the bank for your protection. None of this would have happened if…"

"If you had done your part." I came to my feet. I glared over Lizzy's head and Amber's pile of hair.

"None of this would have happened if you…"

"I beg your pardon, Mrs. Strong. My only error was to trust you to uphold your end of our bargain. Now the whole town is affected by your and Miss Sanders' unwillingness to make good on promises. It may be ignorance on her part…to trust and believe what you told her. But as for you, Penelope, there is no ignorance. You know exactly what you are doing."

Nicholas's dark eyes glinted, but with questions. He wanted to know who I was, really was, and why I was here. Where all the proof for Alex Strong and his agreement with Phillip was.

Drat Amber's party. I should have drawn up fake paperwork for him before now and left town. What if Mr. Brandt decided to ask those questions in front of Lizzy and the townspeople I'd encouraged to trust me? His dark eyes were pensive, full of thoughts and plans to outsmart me faster than I could him.

"This was quite a scheme of yours." Lizzy rose between us. She looked down on her banker. "You arranged an impossible party, let Amber have her head about every unreasonable whim, and wrote it into a contract you promised to pay the balance of on the night of the party." She snatched the pages from Clement. "Then you began to mark it up like this." She waved the X'd out papers in Nicholas's face. "You nitpicked every detail, called each problem a violation, and even tried to catch me off guard with this at the party so I'd agree to it."

I wanted to hug Lizzy, wrap my arms around the wisp of a woman who'd swelled to a giant. I leaned around her instead, one hand of assurance on her back as I focused on Amber. "Doesn't your relationship and future matter more than this?" I pointed at the contract. "Weren't the exceptions we made so your party could go on seamlessly worth more than a certain number of candles or type of music?"

"No." Mr. Brandt squeezed Amber's hand. "My fiancée wanted a specific party, and I assured her she would get it. I trusted you to supply exactly what she specified so she could have what she wanted."

"Then you've missed the heart of a bride," Lizzy said to Nicholas before she turned to Amber. "You've missed it also."

"How would you know anything about the heart of a bride?" Amber let go of Nicholas's hand and gripped the table's edge until her fingertips blanched.

Lizzy didn't know. *Don't come. I can't marry you* said I didn't either.

"This meeting is done." Joshua broke the silent screams of two sister spinsters.

No one moved except him as the deputy strode to the end of our table. "We'll convene another time," Joshua said. "But for now, just Clement and I will meet."

Boots and shoes shuffled outside the door, slow scrapes which wanted to stay and recover the money that belonged to them. Money fisted in Mr. Brandt's pocket, though the townspeople's stares were at Lizzy and me.

"Mrs. Strong." Joshua turned to me. I checked the doorway for enough clearance for a quick getaway. "Go on back to the restaurant. Take Miss Sanders with you."

"Oh. Okay."

"And you, Mr. Brandt...and ma'am." Joshua nodded at Amber. "You two go on your way also. I'll meet with Clement, and if we can't resolve this, we'll put it before a judge."

A judge? Now I gripped the table with whitened fingertips. A judge would uncover that I was a fraud. Answer the question in Mr. Brandt's eyes in front of everyone. A judge would also discover that I'd assisted in a shooting. He'd decree me everything terrible the townsfolks thought...and even worse.

The train meant to take me halfway to my closed door on my half train ticket had come and gone. Whatever ticket of Rudy's had likely gone as well. Wherever Rudy went, whatever had happened to him...I didn't know. That's what I could say if a judge or anyone else asked. I truly didn't know. And if they asked the same about Cook, I'd have to lie...one more time...and deny he had stationed himself at the kitchen door all night and sent me off this morning with, "That ain't necessary, he's done gone somewhere," when I tried to slip out back with bandages and coffee.

One more lie to fix the little one which got me into this mess to begin with. A desperate and jilted woman had lied to her mother and a man on the train. Everett's kindness would vanish when he learned the truth. Mama would be so ashamed and crushed. She'd think more highly of Uncle Roy than me. And Jim, if I ever truly met him and he wasn't already married, would be glad he'd changed his mind. And Lizzy. I had to tell her the truth before someone else did.

Chapter 25

"I sent Lizzy home." I faced Tina, Cook, and Les in the kitchen. "I told her to rest while I let you know how the meeting with Nicholas and Amber went this morning." I glanced at the silver lump which bulged at Cook's hip, heard the shot all over again, smelled the stench of blood, damp laundry, sweaty boots, and bare feet.

Cook shook his head, a sharp wag that jolted me back. "I made sure."

I nodded stupidly. Cook assured me again Rudy had gone. Hopefully to wherever his ticket and bootless feet would take him. Tina stood next to Cook, a strangely apt fit even with his pistol between them. They belonged together. Thankfully, I hadn't had time to interfere with whatever sort of love Tina believed Cook capable of, and which somehow made her happy.

"So Clement and Joshua will review the contract," I continued over sounds from the dining area, people ready for more coffee, hushed voices, and new footsteps coming in. Hopefully friends and not voyeurs, vultures come to see if any scraps remained on our carcass. "Anyway, Mr. Brandt refuses to pay for the party." Yet. "Which leaves the whole town in his clutch, since they're waiting for us to pay them after he pays us."

"You don't need to worry none about that," Les

piped up.

Goodness. What else had Cook taught this poor boy besides horrible grammar? "What do you mean we don't have to worry, Les?"

"Those folks out there ain't payin' nothin' for what they're eatin'. Said we owe 'em money but exchangin' it for food will do. We oughta come out even." Les beamed, as if he'd managed some brilliant business transaction.

"Les, we can't afford…"

"To let any opportunity to do what's right slip through our fingers," Cook cut in. He stepped to the boy and clamped Les's shoulder in his fingers. "Sometimes what's right don't look like it, but it is. Ain't that so, Mrs. Strong?"

"I guess that's so…" I prayed it wasn't just another western aberration of a word. "Thank you, Les. Thanks to each of you for what you did to make last night a success." I looked at everyone except Cook. We'd iron out his definition of right in private. "A judge may be summoned to decide if what we did violated the contract as Mr. Brandt claims it did. In the meantime, I'm here to work while Lizzy rests. Then I have to go speak with her."

I listened for Jim's voice over the sound of my own. If I shared him and what he'd said with Lizzy, maybe she could understand how much the things he'd spoken of called to me. How much I'd longed for him. Like she had for her song. Then maybe the truth about me wouldn't sound so ugly.

Goodness. I sounded like Cook. I couldn't twist wrong into right, when in truth I lived a lie which had culminated in financial ruin and a near murder.

"I ain't ashamed of a thing we done," Cook spouted. "Nothin' wrong with any of it, and I'll be glad to stand before a judge and tell him."

Jail cells burst into my mind, prison time, a harsh duet of my sobs and Cook's rake of a tin cup across the bars. "Surely it won't come to having a judge decide what's right and wrong." Hopefully. "In the meantime, we have customers who need tended to." I cinched my apron tighter than a noose.

"Don't you worry none," Cook said without any spat.

I tightened my apron more. As soon as everyone cleared the room I'd let Cook know exactly why we should worry. Tina stopped alongside me on her way to the dining room, her demeanor calm, her hair less unkempt, her maroon and cream outfit like mine. The glow on her face showed fierce devotion, as fierce as the grizzled one behind her. Love came in strange packages.

Tina stretched to her toes to come close. "He's good at heart, so you can trust him. I know because he does me good." She dropped to the flat of her feet and trotted off, taking Les with her. Cook does her good. Spit, vinegar, grease, and bullets. He had done me good too, but it hurt.

"A western rule, Mrs. Strong," Cook said. "Don't say more than what needs sayin'. That'll hone yer aim you're developin'." He watched the doorway where Tina rushed on its other side from table to table.

"I'm developing no such thing."

"Just pick yer shots from now on." He grinned. "Anyway, I'm thinkin' we need a healin' party around here." Cook jutted his beard forward. "I asked Tina to marry me. And I'd like all of it done here. And arranged by you."

"Cook…" I clasped my hands together, listened for Jim in the rough voice which spoke of celebration and love, of healing and truth deeper than circumstances. Of trust and the encouragement to be trustworthy. All of the worry and fear I'd planned to discuss disappeared under Jim's soft tones, which spoke in Cook's gaze where Tina resided. I saw laughter there, the hurry which made her dance in her run. I saw Les as well, in those less-beady eyes, the stick of a boy who ran with her. Les would be theirs in a way, hers and Cook's, the combination the perfect mentor for the boy.

I wanted to hug the slight blush which darkened where no whiskers could hide it, cry against a shirt still likely tinged with grease. "You will have your celebration," I promised a man who for all his crudeness made the perfect insurance for Lizzy and now Tina. "I will take care of everything. It will be an honor." The kitchen had never been so quiet. No curses, no competition, no shouts, we both blushed as he looked one way and I looked the other. I loosened the ties a bit on my apron. "Now to get out there and serve free coffee, free drinks, and free whatever anyone thinks we owe them." I said to get out there, but I didn't. I stayed. "There's a right—your kind of right and now mine—in this. We can use Rudy's money to pay for your and Tina's celebration."

I turned at our mutual blush and stepped into the dining area to join Tina and Les while Cook remained in the kitchen and sang. Boisterously bellowed love songs filled Eat Here instead of his usual curses. Tina paused, then hurried on, her steps at least a foot off the floor.

"Mrs. Strong, I believe?" someone said behind me. "I'm sorry to disturb you, but I'm supposed to meet…"

I turned at the slight touch on my shoulder, the coffeepot nearly slipping from my hand. "To meet Everett," I said to his friend, who stood near. "You must be here to meet Everett."

I looked into the eyes of Everett's Jim as he nodded and blushed. I saw kindness there, faint kindness beneath a shadow. He could be, this might be…my Jim… I panicked. Everett had come back to town? Because of Rudy? And what I'd done? And now this Jim would see me dragged off to jail.

"Yes, ma'am." Jim's hat hung in his hands. "But not just me. Me and…" He beckoned toward a table where a woman sat. A woman of the West, yet more. One who belonged…but didn't.

"I'll get coffee." I staggered back, then rushed away with the pot I held, hurried from the scent of homestead, the dust of travel, the woman who… I flailed through coffeepots and trays at the side table and shoved the perfectly good one I'd had aside. Was he… What about her?

I braced my arms on the table. Could Everett be on his way to question and arrest me? I shook myself. I latched onto another perfectly good pot and staggered to the table where Jim and…that woman sat.

"There he is." Jim stood as I wavered the pot above their two cups. He and I looked where Everett filled Eat Here's doorway.

"I'll be right back." The pot clattered onto their table, and I went for a third cup. Then a water glass. I should have looked at her hand, her ring finger in particular. Drat. I should have looked at Everett and his expression, as well. His friend must surely be one of the other hundreds of Jims in the West. Surely Everett wouldn't handcuff me in front of him. I tucked a water glass under my arm and held a new cup and saucer close to quiet the rattle, then returned to his…Jim's…table where Everett stood behind one of the empty chairs.

"Fresh coffee," I said. The three of them watched steam coil like a snake from the unsteady black stream I started to pour. "Wait. I'll bring rolls." The pot hit the table next to the two empty and one nearly empty cup as I darted off. Drat. I patted my face with both hands. Were there handcuffs on Everett's belt? Surely most of the Jims out here were married. Except hopefully this one, who should at least visit me in prison.

"Rolls," I barked at Cook as I bolted through the kitchen door. His crooning stopped. "And more coffee." I grabbed a pot I didn't need from the stovetop. Coffee slopped everywhere, and splatters spewed like sparks as they hit the hot surface. "Sorry," I muttered to his frown as I dropped three rolls onto a tray. I latched onto the pot's handle as a weathered hand clasped my white-knuckled grip. "I'm sorry, Cook," I gushed to his hold on me. "I'm just so afraid."

"It's me, Penelope." Everett released my hand. "And I'm not surprised you're afraid."

I let go of the pot's handle and raked sweaty palms down the front of my apron.

"Well, that's a little more afraid than I would have thought for you. I understand you've had some tangles while I was gone, but you look a lot more unsettled than I expected."

"I didn't mean to," I babbled in another gush. "We didn't mean to." I pressed my palms to both sides of my face as Cook wedged himself between Everett and me.

"Can I help you, Marshal?" Cook blocked Everett from me...or maybe me from Everett. I scrubbed at my cheeks behind him, heat and guilt burning my face.

"I hear things haven't settled down much since the party," Everett said. He peered around Cook.

"You got that right." Cook repositioned and blocked Everett again. "Criminal, that's what it is. All that work done essentially for free."

"That's what I heard." Everett settled back.

"It's...it's been..." Cook tugged at his beard.

I dropped my hands to my sides and stepped into the open. "A challenge." I stared at the coffeepot, shiny and silver like Cook's pistol when he'd fired it at Rudy. I clapped my hands over my warm cheeks again.

"Joshua told me the money for the party is tied up for now. And that it might go before a judge."

I began to tremble. This was horrible, almost as horrible as there being a Jim from southwest of here in Eat Here with a woman. Cook threw his arm around my shoulders and held me tight.

"No call for a judge," Cook said. "We'll be fine. We got us a good head here on this woman's shoulders, and she's got ways of comin' up with cash no one else would think of. Ain't that right, Mrs. Strong?" Cook's whiskers raked my scorched face, his toothless grin too close, the slight scent of cooking overpowered by odors which made a man a man. Rudy's money. That's what he meant. Money we stole from the man he shot...money I'd intended to plan a party with. Mama would just die. And she may, in a poorhouse, thanks to the messes I'd made.

I nodded stupidly, adding another crime to my list of offenses.

"She can use that head to solve this contract problem as well. I got faith in her." Cook squeezed the wind out of me. Probably so I couldn't speak.

"I believe you about Mrs. Strong's capabilities." Everett studied me. "And I hope you're right that Eat Here will stay solvent, and this contract discrepancy can be resolved without a judge. Joshua is handling most of it here, while I'm doing what I can in the background." Everett glanced at the kitchen doorway. "Speaking of which, I wondered if Miss Sanders happened to be around."

I shook my head and squirmed out of Cook's chokehold. "I sent her home to rest."

"I've been looking for her brother."

"You've what?" Cook and I yelped together.

"I need to find him." Everett's kindness seemed worn. But not so worn he'd miss a lie if I decided to tell one to steer him away from finding Phillip before I left town. Cook could pass a bullet through anything I said that he didn't agree with anyway.

"I can ask her if she's heard anything about him. But if she had, we'd have been the first to know." Drat. Lizzy would want to talk to Everett about her brother. "You go sit with your...go sit. I'll bring these rolls and a fresh pot of coffee. If you want it this time." Or I could risk everything and brew a quick pot of the recipe that would cause his Jim to say "Louise Archer," so I'd know for certain this Jim was mine...maybe soon enough he still could be.

Everett glanced at the doorway. "I'll have water,

thank you, but my friend will want…" Everett hedged. "And I don't know what… I don't know her. Not to speak of, anyway." He turned back to me. "Just tea for all three of us."

"Tea?" Cook rattled his head as I gasped in relief. "Mrs. Strong's coffee's plenty good for coffee without a skin of grease floatin' on its top." Cook pointed at the pot. "On the house. Them rolls on that tray too. Go sit and talk to yer friend. We'll warm everythin' up and have 'em right out."

Everett shook his head. "No coffee."

"You git on, and we'll take care of it." Cook shooed Everett with a far too boisterous chuckle.

Everett took a step back, and Cook shooed him again.

"Tea and water will be fine, thank you. And thank you too, Miss…" He paused. "I mean, Mrs. Strong." Everett hurried to the dining area.

Miss. He'd called me Miss. I latched onto the table.

"I see you need remindin' how to handle yerself out here." Cook's whiskers jutted my direction. "Don't say more than…"

The way Everett said Miss felt like one of Cook's bullets. I edged from the table, from Cook, the pot of coffee Everett didn't want, and the tray. I wheeled to the back door and shot through it.

Larned's wind hit as I barreled down the steps and into the alleyway. It whipped my skirts and tangled them around my legs. I kicked, cursed my choppy stride, fought to make my baby steps longer and faster. My war raged against swirling dust, cumbersome skirts, and blowing dirt as I plowed behind Larned's stores. Family-owned businesses I'd compromised. I should have stayed on the train, admitted to Everett that I'd lied, so Jim…maybe my Jim…wouldn't be here with someone else. And Lizzy's life could have gone on uninterrupted by the likes of me.

I pushed hard with the wind, strong strides forward until my boot snagged the hem of my skirt. I staggered with a nasty rip until I tumbled face first onto the ground. Dirt muffled my scream as the hard ground burned my chin and palms. My face throbbed; my skin turned to fire. I inhaled grit that turned to mud in my mouth. I lifted my head and spit the way I'd seen Cook do it, a metallic paste shooting from my mouth. Bloody mud hit the ground. I spit more, the way no lady ever should, then forced myself to all fours.

I stared at the muddy and bloody ground, rolled to my haunches, dropped my face into sore and bleeding hands, and sobbed. Goo, red goo, collected on my palms where my nose and lips bled. My clothes were ruined. Everything was. Ruined by and for me.

I couldn't go back to Eat Here. Not this way. Not with Everett, Jim, and that woman inside. I couldn't go west this way either, especially if no one there wanted me. I scraped tears and blood from my face and flung it the direction Cook and I had dragged and left the wounded Mr. Walters without his boots. Justice. A ruined woman's equivalent of being bootless.

I staggered to my feet, caught my heel in the same rip, and tore my skirt even more. Grabbing the shredded hem, I yanked, a satisfying rip which resulted in a strip big enough to wipe my face. I balled the tear-soaked scrap beneath my bloody nose, and hurried, head down and skirt up, to Lizzy's.

"Clement?" I asked in surprise to his roar of, "My

251

God, what happened to you?" He grabbed my raised arm, the one I had used to hammer on Lizzy's door, and yanked me inside.

"Clement?" I asked again through the bloodied ball of cloth. I glanced around the small house for Lizzy, spotted her by her shriek which found me first, the three of us in a triangle of gapes at each other.

"Penelope, what happened?" She tugged my skirt from my hand and let it drop into place where it belonged. Then she peeled the torn strip from beneath my nose, gasped, and pressed it back.

"It's not as bad as it looks," I assured her through the soaked material. Or maybe it was, their expressions saying my face was nothing short of terrifying. "I'm sure it looks worse than it feels." I waited for agreement that didn't come. "Why are you here?" I winced toward Clement.

"I...I..."

"Never mind that," Lizzy interrupted. "Come with me, Penelope, and let's doctor you up." Lizzy took my elbow and sat me in a small chair near her washstand. "Tip your head back."

I did, but I peeked down my cheeks to study Clement. "What are you..."

Lizzy shushed me as her blue eyes and wisps of hair bent over my tilted face. "This won't hurt." She took my hand, peeled it and the cloth aside, lifted the scrap of my hem like the tail of a red rat. "Can you hand me a wet cloth?" She turned to Clement.

I strained to watch the two of them, one of her hands at my forehead to hold it back and keep my nose in the air.

A damp rag covered my lips and nose, another

moved around my face and neck. My eyes ached from the strain of watching them, so I stared at the ceiling and listened instead. Like Rudy would—watch with my ears since I couldn't listen with my eyes. The white boards of Lizzy's ceiling began to warp as I concentrated on her and Clement's soft voices. Straight lines became wavy where grooves and paint blurred. A stream of warmth flowed from each eye onto the cool of my face.

"It hurts?" Lizzy whispered above me.

I nodded. It did. But not my face.

She let go of my forehead. "You can straighten now." She handed Clement a dirty cloth and set a hand on my shoulder. "Who did this to you?" Her small face leaned close.

I looked at her table, her stove, anything in her tiny house besides what really hurt deep inside. "I fell, that's all. I tripped and fell in the dirt." More warmth ran down my face. I had tripped. I had fallen. I'd tripped and fallen over everything and everyone, and swallowed nothing but dirt.

Lizzy handed me a hankie and stood next to Clement as I dabbed my face. I winced again. "Am I bruised?" I glanced at the two of them and saw the yes in their refusals to comment. "Goodness."

"I'd venture there are more bruises than are showing," Lizzy said.

I glanced down at Eat Here's ruined outfit. "Goodness," I said again.

"I think you need to rest more than I do," Lizzy added. "I'll go back to the restaurant. You stay here until you've calmed down and relaxed. Put on one of my blouses, if you want. I'm afraid my skirts will be too short for you, though."

I caught her grin and Clement's blush. My face heated at how I'd run the streets with my ragged skirt hiked up in my hand. "Goodness," I said stupidly again.

"I'll walk you to the restaurant, Liz." Clement's red face turned toward the door, where his hat hung alongside.

I needed to talk to her. She had to know the truth before Everett found Phillip.

"Was it busy there?" Lizzy asked as Clement donned his hat.

"I saw Everett," I said, then stopped. Lizzy stopped too. I caught the change in her expression after she caught the change in mine. "He wanted..." To talk about her brother. "He met..." Jim. And a woman. "His friend from down south."

"Jim Baylis." Clement said it. The name I didn't want to hear rang loud and clear in Lizzy's little house. "He came in on the stagecoach this morning with his new bride."

Chapter 26

My name is Jim Baylis…

I stared at Jim's first letter, pinched and lifted it above the fire, then let go. Jim's voice caught the updraft of heat, flipped to the side, and settled into the flames.

I live near Crooked Creek… His voice rose from the hot orange and red, then turned to black powdery fragments and danced away in the smoky wind. I watched him go, listened as words I'd trusted floated away. I stared at the fire I'd set outside of Larned, the only place Jim and I would ever be together.

I gathered more rocks and stacked them higher at every side against the constant wind. I'd done enough damage to the town; they didn't need one of my sparks to catch the prairie, cover the quarter mile to it faster than I could, and burn what was left.

Tell me about yourself. Not with a picture. I want words. I want to see you and your life through your words.

Jim's words wafted above the flames, then dropped into their hungry heat. Sparks shot upward, orange crackled and sprang to life at his promises' death. Everett's Jim…my Jim…didn't look like a man who painted pictures through words. He looked like a man who had run out of them.

I love my homestead…

Neither did he look like a man who thrived on his land. I turned to the next page in my...his...album, removed his letter, heard every word in his voice without looking at it.

I've done my part here. The land is essentially mine, though it's been a struggle. This last herd of cattle, this last bit of crop have to make a profit, then the strain and worry will let up. I'll be able to pay off what I borrowed and start my real life. With a family...

The description of his home caught and burned, the work he'd put into it and the land, the excitement of making everything ready, being ready, doing his best to make it the best for someone...else.

Would you...do you think you could...I'd be honored if you'd consider being my wife.

Pages went from the album to the fire, our plans, our excitement...my future. The open door Mama'd promised me and I'd promised back so we could both be safe on the other side of it. Everything danced in ashes across Larned's tufts of grass which dotted the plain. I leaned close to the fire, inhaled a great draught of the hot and smoky destruction, drank it in to clear out everything of Jim that might remain. Then...

Don't come. I can't marry you.

Jim's tiny telegram floated from my fingers to the greedy ones of the flames. His rejection lit up for a moment, then disappeared. Fast, a flash of light and sparks, and then nothing.

"Penelope Strong." I said the name to the nothing I had left. I could choose to be Mrs. Penelope Strong from now on, claim to be a woman who had once been loved. "Louise Archer." Or I could be her, return to St. Louis, lie that Jim had died before I could carry his name, and claim also that I'd once been loved. Would either lie secure Papa's business? Both identities lived the lie of being loved, but neither experienced the truth of how much I'd wanted to love in return.

I tossed the empty album into the flames, settled down on a rock, and watched the burning of the wedding I'd never have, and the woman I'd never have the chance to be.

****

If every head hadn't turned, or the boisterous piano hadn't insisted the bride be regaled, I wouldn't have looked. My jaw tensed at the church aisle too narrow to hold the wedding gown Amber wore as she entered. She nearly smothered her well-groomed and wealthy father, swallowed him in her gown's outrageous fluff. The man tried to escort the expensive plume toward Nicholas Brandt, his chest and head shoved against pews.

I couldn't face this. Not when two days ago the real Jim Baylis had left town with his bride, and my Jim Baylis went up in smoke. My stomach roiled at Amber's white as it squeezed between the two sections of pews. My gown had been much simpler. Tonight it would be ashes.

"She is beautiful." Lizzy whispered admission more than admiration. "I'd like to get my hands on that dress." She glanced at me and smiled.

"You'd wear it?" I whispered back. Lizzy planned to marry? She and Tina both? Well, they had come by love the proper way, whereas I had done everything wrong. Would they even invite the Brandts, since the couple had offered us invitations? Keep your friends close and your enemies closer. How could Cook be so right? Maybe Mr. Brandt felt the same way.

"No, I wouldn't wear it," Lizzy whispered. "I'd sell it. Maybe we could get back some of that money the two of them owe us."

Mama would be aghast at the snort I let out. Several around me were. I watched with Lizzy as one of her ways out of debt walked by. The other way, Rudy's stolen wallet, lay hidden beneath the mattress on my cot. Between that money and Amber's ridiculous gown, Cook could have his celebration and everyone else get out of the debt caused by the party Amber had thrown.

Mr. Brandt stood tall and straight, in black which seemed even darker than his usual black. A flash lit the room. The acrid scent of a photograph being taken overpowered the perfumed heat of flowers and fragrant washes in the packed church. Amber and her father paused at Nicholas's side, and the music waned. I jumped as a hand touched my arm.

"Mind if I sit with you?"

I turned and looked into the face that had given up a seat for me in St. Louis. Kind eyes which asked permission…for once.

"Of course." I squeezed closer to Lizzy, and Everett wedged in between me and the person at my other side. What if Everett had found Phillip? Or Rudy? I closed my eyes against that and the blinding wedding gown. I closed my ears to the bride being given away and the well wishes from her father. I sat as everyone sat, pressed between the best friend I'd ever had, whose brother I selfishly wished would stay far away, and one of the best men I'd ever known, who I prayed wouldn't handcuff me at the end of this ceremony.

I stared at my gloves while the preacher rambled on about the attributes of love, distracted myself with tomorrow's menu during the vows that love would never cease. Lizzy strained to peer to the other side of the church, where Clement sat. He'd been an usher, met us…her…at the church door and escorted us…her…to our pew while I followed.

"I now present to you Mr. and Mrs. Nicholas Brandt."

Music swelled, and we stood, a strong hand at my back. Everett kept it there as if he knew I needed to be steadied. Or worried I would bolt for the door at the sight of handcuffs. We watched the handsome couple hurry down the aisle toward the church door. White disappeared with the black. Just as my gown would do later—white turn to black.

"Mrs. Strong?"

I looked at Everett, at his smile, and the elbow bent my way.

"May I?"

I looked for Lizzy. She had already gone, in search of Clement, no doubt, as the crowd flowed toward the door. Plotting the torching of my wedding dress would have to wait. "Of course." I took his elbow.

"I have something for you," Everett said as we walked toward the door. He slid a hand inside his jacket, and I braced. He came out with an envelope.

"For me?" I stared at what he held, relieved I didn't see silver chains.

"Well, for you and Lizzy." He handed it to me. "From the good Mr. Brandt."

I opened the envelope and gaped at its inside. "This is…this looks like…"

"Not enough for all you've been through, but consider Eat Here partially paid."

"And the contract?" I held my breath.

"Signed, with a promise to pay you the rest. I have a copy of that for you as well."

"My goodness." I closed the envelope. This money could help Lizzy carry on…without me. She could replenish a few supplies and pay a bit of the debt owed the town. "Thank you." I glanced at the church door and listened to the revelry, Amber's voice pitchy above the rest. "I don't think I can thank them, though."

"I thanked him for you…in a way he won't expect more. I doubt he's told his bride. I wouldn't, if I was him." Everett grinned. "And besides Mr. Brandt's change of policy, I have something else for Lizzy." Everett looked around, glanced at each person left in the church. "This shouldn't tax her either."

"She must be outside already. But she might be busy. Or gone." I began to perspire. I could think of only one thing he could have to say to Lizzy with a smile like that.

"Let's go see." Everett extended his elbow again. "I have news of her brother."

I didn't budge. "Is he dead? Or is he alive?" I had to pack if he was alive, and leave town before he got here.

"Alive, last I knew. I didn't think you'd be as happy as Lizzy, but I thought you'd at least be a little excited. After all, he is the man responsible for your being here, since he enlisted your late husband." Everett did too deep a study of my face. "Am I right?"

"Lizzy will be thrilled. And I'm glad, especially for her." I couldn't stay here, not with Everett's look too intense, and Phillip too close. I couldn't go west, now that Jim had married. If I went east, I'd have to kill Jim…in a made-up story to Mama, my attorney, and my friends. I couldn't go to the next town north. Too many people knew me in the area. I refused to go farther north; I detested the cold. South? I nibbled my lip.

"I said, I'm sure Lizzy will be, and do you plan to stay for the reception?" Everett frowned down at me.

"What? Oh. I'm sorry, I didn't hear you."

His generally kind eyes turned even more astute. "So are you staying?"

"Not here. That's impossible. I mean, no, not here to congratulate the happy couple. I need to get back to Eat Here."

"I'd say most of the town is at this wedding. You could stay…if you would."

Please say you will. Please say yes.

I shook my head. "There are things I have to do." Plans I had to make, confessions to admit, a gown to burn. Money from Mr. Brandt dispersed to Eat Here and the people we owed, so Larned could get back on its feet. Rudy's money given to Cook to throw the wedding party he and Tina deserved.

"I'll walk you." Everett took my elbow and led me to the church door. He paused as we gazed down the few steps at Larned—people I'd nearly ruined, people I'd befriended even if they turned on me. People I liked, but one I loved like a sister. Lizzy stood with Clement, the two of them beneath a tree.

"You've made quite an impact here," Everett said. "More than you intended, and more than you know." Everett turned me his way. "Did the woman I met getting on the train in St. Louis have any idea what sort of door she was walking through?"

Chapter 27

I dropped to my cot, lifted the wedding gown, and clasped it to my heart one last time before I carried it outside of town to burn. Jim was my open door, not Larned. Everett surely thought me deranged the way I'd burst into tears at the church, shaken myself loose from his grasp, and run. But Larned could never have been any sort of door. Just like Jim hadn't been, either. I buried my face in my gown, inhaled what should have been, and sobbed.

"Penelope?" Lizzy's soft voice called outside my door. She tapped gently. "I have a letter that might be for you. Are you all right?"

"A letter for me?" I asked from the wet folds of my gown.

"I can't hear you. I have a letter. May I come in?"

I scrubbed my face with my wedding dress, tossed it into my trunk, and slammed the lid. I fanned my cheeks and smoothed my hair. "There must be some mistake," I called. There had to be a mistake. No one who would write to me knew I was here. I stood and swiped my eyes dry.

"It's from St. Louis."

I dropped my hands from my face. "St. Louis?"

"Yes. May I come in?"

I hurried across the room and opened the door, stared at the envelope Lizzy held.

I saw Mrs. Otis Archer in the upper corner and my real name above Dodge City. Mama. Her handwriting marked the letter, her billowy cursive which believed in and taught me about open doors…something she and Everett would agree about. They'd also both agree I deserved the sorry plight of spinsterhood once I confessed all I'd done to force my way through a closed door.

"One of the stage drivers gave it to Clement," Lizzy said. "The man said he picked it up in Dodge City because of the Archer name, though I can't imagine you know any Archer in Dodge City. Clement said it might be some business correspondence of yours, so he brought it to Amber's wedding to show you, but he forgot. Then you disappeared. Why did you leave so suddenly?"

"I had things to do." I couldn't take my eyes off Mama's name. Had she somehow heard about all I'd done?

"Clement said if it's not for you, he'll have the driver take it back. He muttered something about a loose connection to St. Louis."

"Oh, he's right. This is business correspondence I asked a driver to manage from Dodge City." Goodness. Someday I'd tell Lizzy the truth. Mama had evidently tried to answer the letters I'd asked her not to. My tales of fictitious delays, with made-up complications as to why Jim and I hadn't married yet but how wonderful it felt to be with him, must have piqued her longing. "I must thank that driver…for the Archers' sakes." Mama's letter could have been lost, or maybe in Dodge City long enough she could be on her way…there to find Jim Baylis…but she would discover his wife instead of his fiancée. "Would you excuse me, Lizzy?" I snatched it from her hand.

"Of course. Take your time. We still don't have customers to speak of, with the wedding reception going on. I have an errand to run anyway, but I'll be right back to help Cook and Tina." Lizzy smiled and backed away, then closed the door behind her. I rested my back against it until her footsteps disappeared down the stairs.

Whatever Mama had to say to the lies I'd told her lay in this envelope. I'd told her to wait for my next letter…which should have been written from Crooked Creek if things had gone correctly. Evidently Mama hadn't been pacified by my lies that things were going well and I would marry Jim soon. Maybe I could further lie and write that Jim had taken ill. No. She would board the first train west…if she hadn't already.

I ripped her envelope with the same ferocity my hem had torn the day I'd run from Jim and his new bride. With the rending of paper I tossed to the floor, Mama's pages were left quivering in my hands.

My dearest Louise,

"Oh, Mama." I staggered to the window, dropped to the sill, and laid her letter—book, more like it—on my lap. I rested my hands on the top page and held her words in place. "Mama…" I ran my palm over the familiar cursive and soaked it in.

I read Mama's congratulations for a safe and successful train trip, her plea for more details about Jim's and my plans, her praise of God for how my life had turned out and the open door He'd given me. Then she offered to send me…Jim and me…anything we wanted from St. Louis. She begged us to come, suggested I have a word with Uncle Roy, who seemed strangely out of sorts, and then offered to visit us soon.

I slapped both hands on the letter. I had to stop her. I had to stop the loving hand which had steered me well except for the open door misconception. "No, Mama. You can't come where Jim lives but I don't."

Tales she shared of my friends blurred as I read the rest of her letter, stories of our church, the business Uncle Roy was likely ruining more than running. The dresses I'd left behind, which were packed and ready to be sent, Mama certain Jim would appreciate seeing his pretty wife in something elegant now and then.

St. Louis flowed with every line, the sense of it seen through odd angles misshapen by my tears. My childhood home rose up, my friends and their families with it...distorted images of them while they had distorted images of me. I pressed the letter to my face, inhaled every word Mama wrote, and kept it there.

I'd successfully been a widow here...most of the time...Alex Strong sometimes slipped my mind. Could I be as successful in front of people who really knew me? I had to go somewhere soon, before Phillip was found. I had to be someone, even the fiancée of the deceased Jim Baylis. Forever a master with dead men since I was an utter failure with live ones.

I looked across the room at my trunk and the shelf above it where I kept paper and ink. I'd write Mama and promise she could come soon...after a harvest or something. Of course poor Jim would have to get sick and maybe die before then.

An explosion shook the floor and jarred my feet. My room rattled at every side. The air vibrated as everything around me quaked. I tried to stand with its resounding echo. Then a second blast equal to the first sent Mama's thousand words into the air. I staggered forward at a scream, stumbling over the slippery sheets of Mama's letter.

"Lizzy?" I grabbed my door and yanked it open to another scream, this one even louder, and to wails. The stairs disappeared beneath my feet, a blur of brown as I raced and tumbled to the restaurant floor, to a handful of wide-eyed people plastered against walls and windows as they stared at the kitchen door. "Lizzy?" She wasn't supposed to be here. How long had I been upstairs absorbed in Mama's letter and my lies?

Her scream came again, wordless sounds from the back. I turned toward them and then darted to Lizzy, who crouched on the kitchen floor, her back bent over another body, a skirted body, one of Eat Here's uniforms splayed across the boards.

"Tina?" Tina's name came up as a shudder, a horror which swirled deep within, something I felt rather than heard as Lizzy's cries filled the air. "Tina?" Her name sounded like air as my knees hit the floor next to my friends.

Lizzy's hands cupped Tina's sleeping face, no color in either, no expression, no light where Tina's happiness had been. Red marked above and below her, a growing splotch flooding the cream-colored blouse Tina wore and the floor she lay on.

"No, no, no," Lizzy wailed.

I tried to think, I tried to feel, a shuddering mummy in the center of chaos. The splotch of blood continued to grow on Tina's blouse and in a pool beneath her back. "Go get the doctor." I grasped Lizzy's hands, icier than mine, and peeled them from Tina's face. "Go, go fast. You have to."

Lizzy gulped, she sat back with a gasp, a wide-eyed look of horror at her friend. She scooted backward to the kitchen door, where she rolled to all fours and staggered to her feet. She went, her wails trailing her, fading as she crossed the restaurant, then vanished with the slam of the door.

"Tina." I touched the face Lizzy had held, felt the waning warmth. "Tina." I pressed fingers to her neck the way I'd seen it done in Papa's store when a customer had suddenly dropped to the floor. I felt for something, anything—a pulse was what I'd been told. I pressed hard until I found it. A tiny flutter. Weakening as it oozed onto the floor.

I turned at the sound of footsteps behind me. Les, a thin rail, shook above one of the few real ladies he'd known. "Go get towels, napkins, anything you can tear. Rip them into strips and hurry back to me." Rocking to my backside, I did the same. I tore my petticoats beneath the skirt I'd just had made to replace my other, into bandages...the way Cook had for Rudy and would have for Tina. If he were here...

I scanned the kitchen for Cook during Les's repeats of "Excuse me" as he worked through the audience in the kitchen doorway.

"Please stand aside," I called as the last strip of my underclothing came loose. "Make room for Les and the doctor." No one budged, no gravelly voice said it the way I couldn't. I bent over Tina and opened her blouse where the red grew. Skin flared outward. She must have been shot in the back. There must be a bullet somewhere. I clapped a hand over my mouth, over the bile which lurched up with the shudder.

"Where's Cook?" I shouted through my fingers to the spectators behind me.

"He went after the fellow that did this." Les dropped rags he'd torn at my side.

"Thank you, Les. Now please get those people away from the door."

He staggered backward, a hand over his mouth as he prodded Tina's audience away from the doorway.

"Hold on, Tina. This might hurt," I said to no response. I pushed wadded strips of fabric into the wound on her chest, stared at the larger puddle beneath her. "Should I move you?" I asked her nonresponsive face.

"No." Doc dropped beside me, Lizzy did the same across from us, her knees in Tina's blood. He whisked instruments from his bag as he listened to Tina's chest and frowned. "Boil some water," he said, his mouth taut.

I stood, gawked around the kitchen for kettles, while Lizzy bent over her friend. The stove felt warm, but not hot. I staggered through the back door, stared stupidly behind Eat Here, and looked for and at wood. Before I stepped down to the ground, I stopped, my foot suspended above dark splatters...blood in ugly dots on each board of the small stairs. Pea-sized black balls of dust made a jagged trail away. Someone else had been shot. I jumped to the ground, stumbled around the trail of blood, and went for wood.

"What happened?" Joshua's voice bellowed from inside, the same question that screamed in my mind as I bent and scooped an armload of wood. I ran back to the kitchen, where Joshua knelt next to Doc, his hands in perfect rhythm with the doctor's. I dropped wood into the stove and jabbed it with a poker to force tiny flames to kick up.

"I heard the shot," Lizzy wailed. "It sounded like a blast. I'd just come back to Eat Here. Then I heard Cook and another shot as I ran in. Will she be all right?"

I set the pot of water on the stovetop and listened for who, what, and most of all, would Tina be all right. I stood over Lizzy, her hunched and rocking form in the doctor's way.

"Cover that doorway." Doc jerked his head behind him as he looked at Lizzy. I touched her, helped her find her feet and fumble around for something to hang between Tina and Larned's gapes and sobs huddled in the dining room. We concocted a curtain of tablecloths and rags and hung it in the doorway.

Doc had stripped away Tina's blouse and undergarments when we finished, and probed at her chest around the wound.

"Should we leave?" I asked.

Doc shook his head. "Is the water ready?"

I glanced at the steam and nodded.

"This won't be the best of situations." Doc glanced up at me and then at Lizzy. "I'll do what I can. Hand me hot, wet rags when I ask."

Lizzy and I nodded. We were side by side, our hands locked together.

Joshua worked with Doc as if they'd always been a team, Lizzy and I remained transfixed, an occasional nod or shake of her head answered Joshua's questions. I heard her repeat what she'd said before, Cook's holler, his threat, the second gunshot that followed.

"There's blood," I interjected, surprised to hear my

own voice. "Out there." I pointed toward the back door.

"Get Les," Joshua barked. "We had him step to the other side of the curtain when Doc cut Tina's blouse away. Tell him Everett's at my office. Have Les bring him here. Pronto."

I weaved forward, my feet nailed to the floor. Lizzy caught me and held my hand as I forced my legs to move through the curtain to Les's white face amidst a throng of others just like his. I bent slightly, trembled as I lowered before the boy, grasped his shoulders, and asked him to run to Everett. He did. For Tina. I stayed bowed forward and watched him go.

"He asked for you."

"What?" I glanced up at the faces around me, their eyes too wide as I straightened and searched for who had spoken.

"That fellow, Mr. Walters. He caught me down the street and asked if you were here."

I stared at one of our regulars.

"I told him you likely were because you're most always here." He glanced at the hat he clasped in front of him, pink fingertips squeezed tight on the brim. "Guess you weren't."

"I was upstairs..." I said it to every eye which looked my way. Upstairs conjuring lies, constructing open doors for closed ones while Tina was here where I should have been. "Oh, no."

The door burst open. "Where's Deputy Joshua?" Everett thundered past, through the questioning eyes aimed toward me.

"He's...she's..." I raised a hand toward the curtain Everett plowed through. I glanced at my stained blouse, my new cream-colored blouse and maroon skirt just like Tina's. It should have been me. That should have been my blood. Les came and stood beside me, voices loud in the back, but not louder than the one in my head.

"Mr. Walters came here?" I asked the people around me.

"Not in here." Another man shrugged toward the empty tables. "Whoever did it came in back there." He nodded at the curtain. Toward the same place Cook had shot Rudy before, where I'd helped Cook drag him out and shame him. Rudy wouldn't have to ask if Cook was here. He always was. Even after a wedding which left Eat Here practically empty…and without customers as witnesses.

A new tremor began. I stared at Tina's blood on my outfit. Stains that would never come out.

"Sit, ma'am." A chair scraped across the wooden floor behind me, bumped into the back of my knees, and I sat. My audience edged away, quiet shuffles across the floorboards. They were right to. I had caused them nothing but trouble. And now I had…

"Ma'am." Everett spoke above me. I looked up, and he shook his head. Tina was gone.

Chapter 28

A rip split the air. Seams which held my wedding gown together tore apart. Buttons, once shiny and finely placed, hung by threads, their tiny loops left to dangle, while severed strings jutted like lifeless limbs from the fabric. Sections of white cloth and notions dotted my floor. I tore at the remnants, scratched at seams and buttons, tossed tiny rows of lace to my cot. I flung the last of it on top of its dismembered pieces and the scattered pages of Mama's letter.

It was my fault. Tina's death had been caused by my selfish obsession to get out of town to marry a man who married someone else.

"Don't come." I cried the words of someone who had fled, and who I should have fled from first. I shoved the debris to the floor and kicked it. If I had stayed in St. Louis, remained spinster Louise Archer, borne my own disgrace, found some clever way to keep Papa's store, I wouldn't have caused...this. I shot my foot through the fabric and notions again, watched it and Mama's words scatter across the room.

I stood in the middle of my storm and glanced at my room's door, listened to the silence below. The morgue I'd turned Eat Here into.

I marched over Louise Archer's ruins and to the top of the stairs to gaze down on the destruction Penelope Strong had caused. I listened to Lizzy's sobs, louder with each step I took down until I came to where Everett stood with his arms around her. I looked at them, turned, and left.

Larned's silence hurt my ears. Its empty streets crowded me. Its shock and grief squeezed and shoved at this foreign object which didn't belong. I hurried along the boardwalk, the clop of my boots a terrible announcement I was still here.

The wind swept me beyond Larned's streets and homes. It drove me to the open, into the barrenness, to the distant patch of dirt I'd blackened with Jim's letters.

"I'm sorry." My words whisked away with the wind. I was sorry—sorry I'd come here, sorry I'd stayed, sorry I'd set my sights on a man who hadn't set his sights on me. Sorry I'd lost sight of those who trusted me. Those who mattered. I kicked the dirt. Jim had told me not to come.

I returned to the only place I belonged—the rocks I'd piled to block the wind while I burned Jim's letters, the same spot I'd meant to destroy my gown. My stones were there but haphazardly strewn across the ground. A broken branch from one of the few trees in the area lay wilted and curled, dried leaves blackened with ash on both sides. I studied the ground, spotted brush marks where charred dirt and ashes had been swept. Someone had been here. Someone had tried to erase the damage I'd caused. Someone had tried to clean me off the land.

I re-gathered the rocks and stacked them close to where Jim's letters had burned. One more fire, then I would go.

****

Eat Here stood empty when I slipped inside for the pieces of my gown. I listened for Lizzy, listened for sobs, refused to hear the gunshots which echoed and re-echoed in my mind. I closed the door behind me, tiptoed to the stairs, paused, and glanced toward the curtain. "Tina," I whispered. I had to face her. I had to take back what I couldn't. I had to kneel where she'd last lay.

I stepped through what I'd hung to protect Tina's privacy and dropped to the darkened spot on the floor. With a finger I traced the deep maroon, deeper and richer than the color I'd clothed her with. The boards were still moist, a large wet circle darkening the wood in front of my skirt as I rested my hands on the cold which had absorbed the last of her warmth. Sobs rumbled deep within. I dropped forward, fell onto my folded arms, and gasped. Tina rose between the sobs, the scent of her lifeblood with the ancient grease of the man she'd loved.

"Rudy thought you were me," I confessed to the little left of her. "These ridiculous outfits made us all look the same when we weren't. You were so much better, you and Lizzy. You two should have had outfits of gold."

Tina said nothing, but her sweet presence remained. So much like Mama, happy and trusting, both certain there were open doors all around. I sobbed harder. They'd both suffered through my self-made doors, Mama alone now with the escapades of Uncle Roy, and Tina alone on a slab as she waited to be buried. And Cook...somewhere...alone without her.

"I'm so sorry." I breathed the words into her scent, mingled living breath with her absence to keep her sweet innocence alive. I stayed, face to the floor, until the essence of Tina faded, only blood and grease left behind.

I heaved up on both arms, straightened my legs, and stood. "Goodbye, Tina." I went back through the curtain to the stairs, to a dark splotch on the first step where I set my foot. I bent and studied the wood, glanced toward the curtain where more spots darkened the floor. I set my other foot on the next step and paused to look and listen to the quiet upstairs. The second step was clean, and the third. I eased upward into the eerie emptiness at the top.

Rudy. I deserved whatever I got. With Tina gone, and Cook evidently gone as well, Rudy had come back to finish his revenge against our insult. I stared at the closed bedroom door I knew I'd left open.

As I pressed my ear to its wood, I spotted another dark spot soaked into the flooring at my feet. There were two shots when Tina was killed, and Cook hadn't come back. I twisted the knob. There would be one last shot.

A sliver of near darkness lined the edge of the door as it cracked open. I waited for movement or sound, a gun blast from the dim room. I nudged the door a little farther and glanced inside. "Who's there?" I opened the door wider, saw my bed, the quilt with a mountain of white on its top instead of scattered across the floor. "Lizzy?" I peered into the meager light of the room. I saw Mama's letter then, its pages held by a gnarly hand.

"Cook?"

He looked at me instead of through me. The fire in his eyes now like the blackened ground where I'd burned Jim's letters. Mama's letter quivered in his hand.

"I always thought so." The gravel in his voice had

turned to dust. He nodded at the shredded gown on my bed. "I thought you got splintered somehow. Before you even got here." He stared at the tattered gown until his hand with Mama's pages dropped to his side. "I called for her. I called my Tina to the kitchen at just the wrong moment," he said to my ruined dress. "You were upstairs, Lizzy off somewhere. Phil was supposedly alive, so it seemed the right time to set a date."

I saw the blood on his hands and his shirt, the hole through the center of a dark circle. "Cook..."

"Sam's the name."

I rushed to him, turned him toward the meager light from the window, and peered at the hole in his shirt too far below his shoulder. "You need to see Doc, Cook...I mean, Sam." I grabbed his arm, but he didn't budge.

"Walters came in the back door. I heard him say, 'Good,' and he shot. Through her. Then he said, 'Sam,' and shot me as I hollered and grabbed onto her to hold her up. I never even got my pistol up. Then he was gone."

I held his arm but stopped tugging.

"I left her with Lizzy, who must have just returned. I knew you were close and you'd get help for my Tina. I went after him. I promised her as I laid her on the floor, but I don't know as she heard me." He stared at Mama's letter. "Love hurts when it's gone."

"Joshua went after Rudy. He'll find him." I held tight to Cook's arm. Everett likely had also.

Cook shook his head. "No need. The deputy won't find him. And I ain't gonna let any law find me. So keep my name to yerself."

"But..."

"Justice has been served. There ain't no more Rudy Walters."

I stared at Mama's letter, the shredded gown Cook had gathered and laid on my bed. "It hasn't been served," I choked. "What happened to Tina and to you, whatever happened to Mr. Walters, all happened because of me. And this." I waved a hand over my wedding ruins. "I'll go with you, Cook...Sam... wherever you go. Of course if you want nothing to do with me, I understand."

He raised Mama's letter, her last page on top.

"I'm Louise Archer," I confessed, though it would never be enough. My lies remained. So did the ramifications of them.

"There's a Penelope Strong, too," Cook rattled over my tears. "And I need her to stay here and bury my intended. And help Miss Lizzy mourn. And defend Eat Here and the rest of the town. Like you've already been doin' yer way...and like I just did."

"I can't...no, I couldn't possibly..." Something cold and hard hit my hand, something which caught a gleam in the low light as I looked down at it. "Your gun?"

"One of many. This is the one I shoulda nailed Walters with the first time I wanted to. I sure shoulda when he came through the door earlier today. But I used it to make up for both of them mistakes."

The gun felt colder and heavier now that I knew what it had done. I wondered how many other times this gun had been the only law Cook lived by. "I couldn't possibly..."

Cook squeezed his rough and bloodied hand over mine that held his pistol. Then he raised Mama's letter, waved it between the two of us. "Penelope Strong can."

Mama's words warped, the pages which credited Louise Archer for becoming someone she never became. She became a liar, a spinster disguised as a once-loved widow, a heart which learned what it wanted but never found it, a woman with an allegorical name which didn't suit her. "I'm so sorry…"

"Me too," Cook said.

I wrapped my hand with the gun behind his back, clasped it in my other as I held onto him, Mama's tribute between us. He cried with me, his raspy gravel a bass to my soprano. His song and mine. We were in harmony, at last.

Chapter 29

"Have they found Mr. Walters yet?" Ben Holt mumbled his hesitant question to Everett in Eat Here's dining area. I heard dirt instead of his sad tone, my handful at the cemetery as I'd dropped it onto Tina's coffin. Lizzy's handful had been first, she, Everett, Les, and I the initial few in a long line, each person with a fist of earth to drop where Tina lay.

The unsteady stream of coffee I poured didn't erase the sound of dry ground on pine boards. But it gave away the shake of my hands as I tried to fill Ben's cup.

"Not yet." Everett shook his head at the wavering pool of black. He'd stayed close to me throughout Tina's funeral. With handcuffs ready, likely. His generally kind voice took on its own sound of gravel now, dry crumbs raining onto Tina's pine box. It should have been me and my box. Everyone knew it.

"Cook?" Ben spoke even more quietly, his mouth behind a coffee cup and steam.

I closed my eyes. They still burned from my scan of the horizon during Tina's service. My head bowed, I had searched invisibly for any sign of Cook. He surely watched from somewhere to say goodbye from a safe distance…or from Heaven, if he hadn't survived the hole in his chest.

"No, not him either."

I heard a gasp. It came from me. I opened my eyes

to Everett and Ben, and their surprise. "Excuse me." I patted my chest. "It's just so…" Hard. Impossible. The same thing I saw on these two men's faces, everyone's face in Eat Here as we tried to celebrate Tina's brief life when her death screamed so much louder.

"Cook must have gone after Rudy, if that's who shot her." Ben wallowed his thoughts aloud.

"Don't know," Everett said and stared again at his glass of water, his brows low, hiding questions and thoughts about at least two people who'd skirted the law.

I wanted to rub my calf, where Cook's gun lodged between it and my new boot, a more western style I'd traded my own for, with plenty of room for a pistol. *Watch the shadow…* Cook's voice reminded me, along with his weapon. Or shadows. He hadn't answered when I asked if he intended to go after others. He'd nodded at his pistol he'd laid in my hand, and staggered out the door.

I looked toward other tables. Everett could surely see on my face the things Cook had left me with. Guilt, responsibility, and a gun. Everett was a lawman. He missed nothing. He surely knew I'd lied, turned a town upside down, helped drag a shot hoodlum—who now lay dead somewhere—to the street, and shame him. No wonder Everett came to Larned more than he'd originally said he would. The phony Penelope Strong had cost Cook his heart, Tina her life, every business their stability, and Everett the life out west he'd intended for himself.

"You'd think Cook would have been at the ceremony." Ben wallowed some more. "Not like him to miss it. I surely do hope he's all right."

I'd raised my arm high when I stepped to the edge of Tina's grave. If Cook had been anywhere near, he would have seen and heard. Not my whispered apologies which could never be resolved, or my, "Goodbye, Tina," from me and him...from Sam...but the steady stream of dirt, more dirt than my fist could rightly hold, enough for Cook and me both as it sifted through my fingers.

"You'd think he would have been there." Everett tapped his water glass as he studied me. He didn't flinch, and I tried not to.

I pressed the warm pot to my stomach. I should have been serving champagne. This should have been the gay celebration Cook had wanted for him and Tina, Rudy's money splurged on them instead of still hidden beneath my mattress upstairs. People stood in clusters, a dozen such groups scattered throughout the dining area, huddles of shock and disbelief instead of grins of festivity. People glanced my way, expressions which surely wondered why it hadn't been me instead.

"He has to be all right." Lizzy appeared at Ben's and Everett's table, her wish a whimper which hadn't left since her friend had. Her best friend...her two best friends. "What happened? Why? How?" She stared at each of us the same way she had been since the day Tina died.

My skin felt cold. Because of our uniforms, because I'd humiliated the gunman, because I had interfered in these lives. I checked to see if Everett still watched me.

"Cook surely isn't far away." I laid a hand on Lizzy's arm as I tried to keep Cook's bloodied shirt from my expression, the hole through it and him, the dark halo which surrounded it. If I could hike up my skirt and show her Cook's gun, she'd likely feel worse instead of better.

"Does he even know? Does he know his beloved is gone?" Lizzy leaned her head against me, tears which hadn't stopped for Tina started now for Cook.

Everett watched with eyes that wouldn't miss what Lizzy's might. I turned my gun side away from him. "Let's go upstairs," I said to Lizzy. But I didn't move. We couldn't go upstairs. We had no Tina or Cook to take our places. Only Les, who cowered in a corner, his eyes vacant orbs with Cook and Tina gone.

"I'll take over. You go on." Amber, inappropriately colorful on a day of mourning, stepped to the table, her husband in his usual but now proper black beside her.

"Thank you. But we can manage." I nodded toward Les, his thin form wound into a ball, which made him even less than usual. I checked Lizzy, the lack of color in her face. "And then again," I said to Amber, "if you could just take care of the coffee and tea…"

"I know what to do." Amber swiveled away, a rainbow of color arcing over the dreary room. She did what we should, but couldn't, as she spread warm drinks and sentiments to every needy cup and heart.

"Any word on Mr. Walters?" Mr. Brandt jarred me from my study of his wife.

Only the coffeepot in my hands kept me from clapping both to my chest. I watched his face and Everett's as Lizzy continued to lean into my shoulder. I held her up and set the coffeepot on a nearby table as Everett muttered his same response as before.

I trembled enough to know Lizzy and I would both crumple to the floor. "Excuse us," I said with too much force. I steered Lizzy to the stairs, over the spots where Cook had bled and I'd scoured hard until their darkness blended with the wood. I glanced back for a glimmer of whether Mr. Brandt really cared about Rudy and why.

Amber's voice rose, her sing-song lilt strangely less offensive than her music box. She busied herself with offers of drinks and consolations, seemingly sincere "Too bad's," as Lizzy and I reached the top of the stairs. "Too bad a murder took place in the only restaurant in town." Amber tsked and wagged her head. "Such a shame."

I cursed. Probably because of Cook's gun in my boot. "Go on in and rest, Lizzy." I led her to my room's door. "I need to…" I glanced toward the stairs, the too-sweet consolations, the man who asked about Rudy, below us—aromas Cook had warned me about.

Chapter 30

"It's just temporary," Amber cooed. "Nicholas is so concerned about the town. It was his idea, and it's such a good one, don't you think?"

I didn't think it was a good idea, and neither was this what I thought would happen. Lizzy and I both knew that once Amber had her party and wedding she'd need something else to do. But not this, and not this way. I planted both fists on my hips and searched for a ladylike way to say of course I didn't think so. Cook's gun burned against my leg as Amber's blinding color burned my eyes.

"Larned needs a place to go, a place they can eat and recover. No one can do that here." Amber shook her head and tsked as she swung her arm around Eat Here's empty dining area. "So for their sakes, we opened that little café. There are no bad memories there, no unsolved crimes. And no missing cook."

"That's a ridiculous idea." I thumped my foot, lodging Cook's gun deeper in my boot where, thankfully, it would be harder to retrieve.

"Mrs. Strong, calm yourself. Clearly you haven't recovered. You look flushed. You're in no condition to tend to others' needs until you first address your own."

"Others' needs? Like yours and your husband's? Isn't that what you're really concerned about?"

"Now, see, this is exactly what I mean. This isn't

like you, Penelope. You're edgy." Amber patted my arm, the one that itched to hike my skirt up and burrow deep into my boot to frighten her out the door with what I hid in it. But then Joshua would come, and probably Everett too. They'd take Cook's gun before they took me away. I almost wished they would take Cook's gun. His aim was perfect. Mine would be a spray of shots with little hope for a lucky hit.

"You know I'm right, Penelope. Take some time to mend." Amber waved an arm across the room where Lizzy and I should be, our customers also, not to mention Tina. And Cook...Sam. "We have everything under control at Better Times. That's the name of our café. Isn't it perfectly refreshing? We've done everything we could to soothe the town. We offer cookies like you used to, just bigger. And to further help, we've incorporated something from each business. That way everyone has a part in the healing. You can rest and recover. Nicholas and I have everything under control."

Goodness. She'd stolen every single one of my ideas, even down to involving all of Larned. "You're wrong, Amber. Les and Lizzy and I will continue our business here. It will be therapeutic for us and our friends."

"Poor dear. I'm far more right than you think. Take Les, for example. He could never work here in his condition. He's barely capable of working at all. That's why I hired him. He's my youngest waiter in a whole new setting. I gave him a promotion from just clearing tables like you had him do, and it has helped him tremendously. He's getting better every minute."

Mama taught me ladies never swore or gaped. I

wanted to do both. How could Amber do what I hadn't? How could she have seen what I didn't? Maybe because she hadn't caused death and destruction amongst her friends…if she had any. She'd saved Les, my little friend, from the haunted vacancy we'd all felt and shared—while I'd left him cowering in a corner. She was right that I was wrong.

"I'm sorry…" It sounded like a whimper. Like everything else I'd done, my efforts to thwart Amber had failed.

"I'm sorry you're doing this to Tina's memory." Another voice shattered my apology.

Amber and I turned. Like a silent wraith Lizzy had come from behind me, fire in her previously pale cheeks, fists instead of the hands which had done nothing but wad damp handkerchiefs for days.

Lizzy stepped into the space between Amber and me. "Disrespecting the deceased, that's what you're doing. Using them to make a dime. You're the lowest form of woman there is, Amber Brandt. Even cathouse women give something to gain what they earn. You, however, give nothing. You have nothing. You take."

The color caked on Amber's face cracked. Tiny creases cut through the powdered paste as her mouth opened and closed. She staggered backward, the dainty parasol which had dangled from her arm exploded open as if she'd fired at us. "Well, I never." A blazing ring of color turned and ran out Eat Here's door.

I listened for tears in the wake of Amber's departure, expecting more from Lizzy as Amber disappeared. A gurgle erupted beside me, a cacophony of indistinguishable sounds roiled upward and out of Lizzy's mouth. The jumbled chaos became a giggle, then a laugh, then a round of gaiety which doubled her over and brought a different type of tears.

"Lizzy?" I laid a hand on her back. The vibration of her laughter created a tremor which rattled up my arm until a giggle of my own erupted. I clapped a hand over my mouth. I had no right to do something so wrong. I should never smile or laugh again.

Lizzy straightened and looked me. "Tina liked that," she said as she wiped her cheeks. "I felt her right there with me when I said that to Amber."

I gasped. I listened for Tina, looked for her while Lizzy cried clear tears, not ones clouded with grief. "Did Tina actually say something?" I whispered. Tina would know everything about me now. I listened for words like "liar," "spinster in disguise," "wrongly alive."

"Tina's all right. But we need to find Cook." Lizzy wiped her face again. Her eyes shone through the red.

I thought of Cook's guilt, his broken heart, that wound and the other he may or may not have healed from.

"Clement offered to go hunt for him. I didn't say anything, because I was too sad. Oh, my goodness. Grief can make a person so self-centered, can't it? How can any of you ever forgive me?" Lizzy clapped her hands over her cheeks, her blue eyes wide.

Forgive Lizzy? "You've done nothing wrong, Lizzy. Grief is natural. It's a part of the healing process, a wound to protect until it's gone." Different from self-centered blindness, which leads a person to lie, manipulate others, and set fires. "You've never done a selfish thing since I've known you. We'll honor Tina by setting things right here."

Lizzy grasped my arm and squeezed it. "First I will tell Clement to go find Cook and bring him back. Phooey on that hoodlum Cook is probably still after. Joshua can get Rudy. Cook needs to come here and heal with us."

"Well, I...he..."

Cook didn't want someone to find him. If they did, he wouldn't have the chance to heal with us. He'd be thrown in jail...or worse...for whatever happened to Rudy. "No, don't do that. Cook wouldn't want to be dragged back before he's..."

"You'll be okay here for a few minutes?" Lizzy glanced around the restaurant. She hadn't heard a thing I'd said. What she heard and thought came from the heart of Tina now. "I guess you will, since there's no one here."

Lizzy rushed out, leaving me to watch over her restaurant, which didn't need watched at all. I listened for the heart of Tina as I glanced at the tables all neatly set, chairs pushed up against them, and inhaled deep to find the faint aroma of grease which had said home to her. It was quiet. Just like Tina—too quiet. She and I both needed noise.

I stomped to the kitchen and set up a cacophony of racket the way Cook would. I clattered pans, slammed the coffeepot on the stove, and even cursed out loud. I bellowed, tried to sing, and slammed a tray of cold cookies next to a pot of lukewarm coffee. Then I raked both from the counter, marched them to the dining area, rounded to the side table, and plopped them down.

I swiped my hands across my apron. "Good for nothin' Kansas Concoctions," I bellowed. "A grand waste of time," I shouted to the empty room.

I felt a smile behind me. Tina? A chair scooted, and a coffee cup twisted on a tabletop. Heat scorched my neck and fried my face. "Mr. McCloud." I peered over my shoulder at the one-man audience to my raucous display. "I...I did a tribute... I'm sure you understand."

Everett might be kind, but he probably didn't understand. I caught the tautness of his jaw as he raised his cup my direction.

"You want coffee?" It had been so long. I grabbed the pot and hurried to his table, slopped lukewarm brown into his cup. I dropped a Kansas Concoction on a nearby plate. It slipped and skidded away. Everett's hand collided with mine as we both reached to rescue it.

"Thank you," he said as I dropped the retrieved cookie onto his plate.

"You're welcome." I glanced to the side, afraid to look into eyes which had watched me, made sure I was all right, danced with me, attended a wedding and a funeral with me. "Let me know if you need anything else." I backed to the side table, set the pot down, and dusted my hands.

Everett sipped, a pensive drink as he returned his cup to the table. He leaned back in his chair and stared at his cup.

"I'm sorry," I blurted across the room. "I thought...I just..." I waved a hand toward the kitchen, then around where I stood. I could never be sorry enough for everything, things he may or may not know.

"You were grieving," Everett finished for me. "Anger's a natural stage of grief."

"I'm not angry, I just..." But I was angry. I had been angry when I boarded that train, and I was more angry now. At Jim, at Mr. Brandt, at Rudy, at that weasel Julius Weston who'd refused to give me an open ticket ages ago so I could leave town whenever I wanted. Most of all, I was angry at myself.

"There's no right or wrong way to recover from a loss, Mrs. Strong. You should know that."

"You mean my father…"

He looked at me. "I meant your husband."

"Oh. Right." Drat. "You wouldn't know about Papa." I grabbed the coffeepot and crept to his table. "Looks like you need more."

"Please sit." Everett gestured toward the chair across from him.

"Oh, I can't. I have to…" I motioned toward the empty room. "I have to…" I drew out the chair and sat.

"There are stages of grief, and it's not unusual for them to be expressed in…well, in ways the person wouldn't normally behave."

I looked at my hands. I understood grief. I had suffered it alongside Mama, suffered the blow of it alone when I learned Everett's married friend, Jim, was mine. I'd even just coached Lizzy. But grief with guilt…

Everett rested his elbows on the table, laid his palms flat on the white cloth, his fingers splayed my way. "Broken hearts behave unpredictably. And it doesn't have to be a death that breaks a heart."

I stared hard at my hands, hands that intended good but ended up destroying…even losing…everything. "You've had a broken heart?" I glanced up beneath my brows.

"I've suffered loss. As a son, a friend, and a lawman. But I haven't gone through everything you've gone through. Yet." His fingers stretched longer. "Grief makes people do odd things," Everett repeated.

"I suppose."

"The degree of passion a person's heart is capable of is revealed in the degree of erratic behavior after a loss." He stood, came around the table, and drew me to my feet. Large hands held me by my upper arms. "You are such as those. You are a passionate woman, Miss…Mrs. Strong…a passionate and determined woman from St. Louis, who has been very hurt."

****

Beautiful chords wafted unimpeded in Eat Here's dining room. Lizzy's sorrowful selfishness done, her healed passion flowed freely through the piano Clement had given her. I envied and encouraged her beautiful sounds, her song, in the midst of chaos.

I moved through the aroma of beef stew and the breath of music. Somehow she'd survived, while I hadn't. I wanted to flow from table to table the way her tunes did. I'd tried every evening, since Clement had gone in search of Cook, while she played. I tended empty tables as her serenades began with a simple song then grew to complicated compilations. Lizzy had passion like Everett suggested I did. Hers swelled to healing beauty, while mine hammered an erratic tempo with my feet.

I straightened the silverware no one had touched, turned unused coffee cups upside down to keep dust from collecting in them. Lizzy'd played hymns the second night, trust for open doors which I accompanied with a dropped tray of sugar bowls.

She played long this evening, longer than usual. I lowered the heat on the stew neither one of us would eat and took a seat while she played love to a missing brother, an absent admirer, a deceased friend, and the man who had tried to be her insurance. She played to herself and me, country songs and state songs, folk songs and war songs, old classics which wove chords of lovely strands in her, while unbearable loss and accusations shouted in me.

Her aches flowed while mine congealed. I rested my forehead on my arms on top of the table and listened to the instrument. Jim's voice had gone. A somber emptiness replaced the tone he'd once had.

In the unaccompanied quiet of Lizzy's music a harmony came. A voice, a smooth baritone added words to Lizzy's chords. It began soft and far away, then grew clearer as it reached the door. Lizzy stopped, but the words sang on. I lifted my face to see Clement enter the restaurant and cross the room, bedraggled, his love song ending at her side.

My breath caught as Lizzy heaved to her feet. Both songs had ended, but the music continued. Lizzy wrapped herself in Clement's embrace, a marriage without the ceremony. No pomp, no expense, no arrangement to turn a spinster into a wife. Theirs was a melody I'd never sung but recognized, a tune even Jim's voice had never touched. I rose and walked to the door, past the large hand which held it open for me, and into the night on the other side.

Everett let go of the door, his dark coat and hat nearly invisible on the boarded walkway. The door shut without a sound, and in the quiet black, I felt him look at me.

"Cook?" My voice felt like a shout. Everett's fingers took my elbow and steered me away. I didn't want another death. I wanted life the way I'd heard it in Lizzy and Clement, felt it for a moment in my own heart. The way it should be, should have been for Tina and Cook. I didn't want to hear he'd been taken into custody, either. Everett held tight as I stumbled down the walk past closed businesses, water troughs, and Better Times' noisy din.

I glanced in the café's window as we passed, paused at the sight of Amber's trollops around the room, and Mr. Brandt on the butt end of a cigar as he dealt cards to local men who laid their money—soon to be his—in front of him. Les looked harried, a cravat too tight, a cummerbund—of all things—cinched around his skinny waist. "Excuse me." I wrenched my elbow from Everett. "I have business to…"

"You have business with me." He took my elbow again.

"But look at that." I waved my free hand toward the window, the jovial ruckus on the other side.

"I'd rather not."

"Such a din. Listen to that racket. Look at poor Les. And what's that high-pitched sound? Is that Amber's ridiculous music box, or does some cat have its tail caught in their door?" I thought of Eat Here, of Lizzy's lovely serenade, of Clement, an unlikely hero who harmonized and held her close. "How is it that…that man"—I waved an arm Mr. Brandt's direction—"manages to lift money out of everyone's pockets without them aware of it? He and his café are so vile, while what Lizzy has to offer is so…so…"

"I suggest another engagement party," Everett said beside me. I turned his way, his rugged features highlighted by the gaiety which oozed from Better

Times. His tiredness vanished in the crevices of his kind face which looked down at me. "And I recommend lots of grease."

"Cook…" I said it out loud this time, threw myself at Everett, and swallowed his broad chest with a hug.

"Like I said, you're passionate." He laughed above me and in my ear, where I heard his heart vibrate with what he felt. "Enough to torch the things that offend you and defend those that need it." He took me by the shoulders and held me where he could see the blazes I'd set and the one which crawled up my face. "I bet Mrs. Strong didn't behave that way in St. Louis, did she?"

"I…she…" Thank God for the dark.

"My guess is she may have been a slightly different person there…"

I squirmed.

"Sometimes it takes just the right spark to bring out the flame that was there all along." He let go of my shoulders. "The spark burns and stings for a moment. Nothing compared to the flame it sets. But that fire is something to behold."

Cook's pistol burned in my boot, like the lies I'd told burned in my soul. I glanced at the café I'd been ready to storm and the ears inside I'd intended to burn.

"From a distance…" He smiled down at me after a nod at the din I despised.

"I suppose discretion would be prudent."

Everett laughed. This laugh rang deep and strong, something new, something solid, part of a man I'd never been this close to before. His heart beat in that resonance, his kindness the song he hadn't sung yet…but wanted to. "Far better to burn than to smolder." His laughter mellowed to a slight smile.

"Misdirected blazes do require some cleanup afterward, maybe an apology or two. But better that than keeping all that fire penned up inside."

"I take it you've some experience with smoldering."

"Almost. But someone I know has." He looked down at me. "Most horrible burn I've ever encountered. But enough of that. Shall we go? Shall we direct your enthusiasm where it's needed?"

I took Everett's elbow, held it tight, and looked down the dark boardwalk ahead of us. "Is he…is Cook locked up? Is that where we're headed?"

"You expect Cook to be locked up?"

Drat. I shook my head. Harder than I should have. "No more than I'd expect me to be. Let's go." More uncontrolled burning, but on my face this time. Thank God again for the dark.

Chapter 31

"You're not as tough as you thought." I dropped into a chair beside Cook's bed. I wanted to touch his gray skin and clear the sallow from his eyes. He mustered a faint grizzled countenance, a thin and raspy harrumph. "I shouldn't have let you run off while you were wounded."

"You couldn't have stopped me," he gasped more than said. Gray speckled his brow in ways it hadn't days ago, age blending with infection and loss. The blood he had lost and the love he had lost as well. Cook was passionate, the same thing Everett said about me.

"Still got my gun?" Cook's eyes were closed.

I nodded, confident he had other eyes that saw. "In my boot," I whispered though no one else was near. Everett had left Cook and me alone, and Doc stayed in the other room. "But of course I would never use it."

One of his eyes opened. "Of course you'll use it. That's why you're the one I gave it to."

"I'm not the one to carry it." I swallowed. "I'm the one who should have been... I should be..." I stared at my lap, the knot I made in my skirt, the dark splotches which soaked the fabric around it.

Cook's hand, gray and wrinkled, slid from the tented blanket he lay under, and rested atop mine. "Not so."

"But it is so. Rudy asked for me before he came to

Eat Here." I withdrew my hands from his. "It happened because of those awful uniforms. He meant to shoot me. I'm so, so sorry, Cook." I choked. Sorry sounded feeble. "Rudy thought Tina was…"

"Tina." Cook took my hands again. "Walters said, 'Good,' when he saw her standin' next to me in the kitchen. He meant, 'Lost love hurts,' when he shot her." Cook's other eye opened. "I woulda killed him, but I grabbed her instead." The hand over mine trembled, a grip which couldn't wield a gun or aim perfectly…for once.

"But…" I stared at the stream which ran down the side of his face. "But he…"

Cook turned my way. "He was a shadow, Penelope…Louise…whatever. If I'd figured that out as fast as he figured I was Sam, Tina might still be with us. He's a scalawag from the war, takin' advantage of homesteaders off fightin', payin' a fee and lyin' he was them to get a quick title on their land. Walters stole deeds from soldiers where the railroad was headed, sellin' 'em slightly below top dollar to investors, sometimes bankers, who made a profit resellin' to cattlemen or the railroad itself. When he stole from my brother, I caught on. Been chasin' him and a couple like him ever since, gettin' revenge for the homesteaders."

"Why didn't you tell me?"

"You know how you tend to spray words?"

I reddened while he paled. "But why was Rudy in Larned?"

"It's called doublin' back out here. Cut back with yer dirty money to see what other strugglin' folks you can take advantage of. Like Eat Here or most any business in Larned."

I reddened more. "And that's why you fought all of the improvements I brought to Eat Here and the town."

Cook nodded. Barely. "They was my bait. Even Lizzy. But I guess you spoutin' about investments worked about as good as keepin' 'em poor and strugglin'."

"I've been…if I hadn't…what Rudy did to you and…"

"What Rudy did to me…and my Tina…was personal."

I stared at him as he stared at me. "But…"

His chest rose and dropped with a gurgle. "But now that Rudy is gone, and I'm hurt…" Cook's sallow eye checked the door. "You're out in the open. Use the gun."

"What? I can't. I didn't learn to fight this way in St. Louis. I used my head, never a gun." I grabbed his hand, mine trembling now. "I need you."

Black holes of eyes looked at me. "Keep my gun with you at all times."

I shook my head, shook all over as I held him tighter. "I will wire St. Louis for some medicine I know of to help you get well. The doctor here probably hasn't heard of it. My father's doctor told me about it, and it's just what you need."

"You wire St. Louis, and they'll know you're here. And not married." Cook focused on something invisible, yet palpable. "I'm sorry, Louise."

We were sorry for each other, for lost loves neither of us could ever talk to again. "The wire will be sent with Doc's name and refer to me only as someone he encountered in the Larned area. It will say I suggested this medicine for someone as I passed through, giving him the name of my old doctor for a local case of infection."

"Too risky." The black of Cook's eyes began to fade.

"It's a chance I'm willing take. Like I said, I need you." I needed, we all needed, that weathered hand which had held mine when he left the shadow in Eat Here's alleyway to help me up the steps.

"Louise Archer, you don't need anyone. You just thought you did." The heavy eyelids closed, and the man with the broken heart slept.

****

"I want to ask her tonight." Clement's hat twirled in his hands as we stood near the front door of the restaurant. His hair lay too neat, plastered excessively, ready for that moment when he hoped Lizzy would say yes. "I want the best for Lizzy. I want her to go back to who and what she'd started before Eat Here. She used to play piano for everyone and everything. Not just here in Larned, but all around. I want Eat Here to thrive so she can return to her song." His hat stopped. Clement leveled a gaze at me, the man who had mailed odd letters in odd ways when I insisted, and recovered Cook when no one else had. "I don't expect anything fancy, but I'd like to give her a nice wedding."

"Do it here," I said. A celebration like Everett had said, a party and a meal which should bring Larned back to Eat Here. A meal with grease. "We will have everything here. Just ask her." I squeezed Clement's hand. "She'll say yes. And we'll make sure your engagement and wedding are unforgettable."

He relaxed. Rigidity melted from his shoulders, and the hat returned to his head. "You were married.

You know what a wedding needs. A real wedding."

Don't come. I can't marry you. The voice which had married another returned. Without harmony, without laughter, without passion.

"I do," I said.

****

The bells rang as I entered the mercantile. Mr. Holt's worker looked up and approached me, Ben most likely foolishly handing his money over to the Brandts at Better Times.

"May I help you, Mrs. Strong?"

"I need a few things. Some I'm afraid we may have to order."

Mr. Holt's worker led me to the counter and smiled his way through my list of supplies for Lizzy's celebration, which included the lard Mr. Holt had informed me Cook could easily find when I refused to let him sell it to Cook.

"We have most of this." The clerk tapped his notes with the pen. "I'll order the rest. You want everything as soon as we can get it?"

"Soon. Yes. Thank you. And send me the total bill."

The tapping stopped, the smile with it. "I'm not supposed to…"

"You're not authorized to take an order on credit?"

"Not exactly…"

"Then what do you…" I had only a tiny bit of my own money left, and Eat Here had almost none, Mr. Brandt's partial payment he had yet to add to long gone during our evenings of preparing food no one came to eat, and Rudy Walters' contribution, revolting and untouchable, still under my mattress. This party for

Lizzy should revive her brother's restaurant, bring her old customers back so Eat Here could thrive again. I dropped my bag on the counter and riffled through its contents. "Here." I brought out Jim's ring, a glint of gold which shimmered unsteadily in my hand. "Use this for payment."

He stared at the ring like it would bite him.

"It's pure gold. It's more than enough. I'll expect change when we settle." I snatched my bag off the counter and set the ring in its place. "Let me know when everything has come in."

I marched out, through bells which shrieked my hurried exit. I sped past businesses I should have stopped at for more wedding supplies but knew they also wouldn't trust Eat Here to pay—because of the one who cast shadows.

Tinny music seeped into the street as Better Times came into view, and the smell of cinnamon filled the walkway the way it used to in front of Eat Here. People moved in and out of a door which chimed instead of squeaked. Voices spilled out with the music each time the door opened, and satisfied smiles lumbered away.

I marched to Better Times' window and stared through my reflection, which stared back at me. I gazed from table to table, scanned faces for Mr. Holt's, or any of the business owners I needed to free from Mr. Brandt's hold long enough to help me help Lizzy. I glanced from man to man, face to face, studied each, and then moved on until I stopped at a woman. A woman seated with two men.

She sat straight while Jim slouched and Everett leaned back. He listened to the woman, then to Jim, Everett's finger tapping the table's edge as he watched his friend. Then watched me as our eyes met through my reflection. I took a step back as he stood. He spoke to Jim and his bride and headed toward the door as I backed farther away. Jim and the woman turned and looked through the window as Everett came through Better Times' door.

"Louise."

I stopped mid pivot and let go of the skirt bunched in my fists. I reached for the nearest post, grabbed it and hung on, as Everett's hand grabbed above mine.

"You know," I whispered. Cook wouldn't have betrayed me. He'd shoot me before he'd harm me this way.

"I do," Everett said.

"And he…" I couldn't say Jim's name.

"Jim doesn't know."

"And…"

"And neither does Clara, his wife. I'm sorry." Everett was sorry. I'd never seen a hole through his kindness before, but I saw it now. Some deadly aim had hollowed him. "Grief does odd things to people."

"You mean them? Or me again?"

"Of course you. But also him. And me. Or him, because of me."

I knew that guilt. I'd felt it with every one of my lies. It poured out of Everett now, and took the kindness of his eyes with it.

"I knew too little before it was too late. When I figured things out…" He gazed through the window at the man I'd come west to marry. "That's why I'm here and we're in there." Everett nodded at the newlyweds.

Don't come. I can't marry you.

I gripped the post tighter, leaned into it, my face

against Everett's hand. Tears seeped between my skin and his.

"You might want to know…" he began.

"I don't." I pulled back. "I don't want to know a thing."

I let go of the post and ran, ran to Eat Here and up the stairs to my room, where the rip of satin satisfied me even more than before. I split more seams and ripped what lace remained. Tiny buttons skittered across the floor. I tore again at the gown I'd never wear, sectioned it to an unrecognizable heap. I screamed inside, shouted how vile, how unfair life turned out to be. How damaging closed doors were, how futile to trust any man, or fight for doors to open.

My tears sizzled with violent fury, the awful sound interrupted by music from downstairs. Lizzy's piano wafted upward and through my wall, tangled with my grief, and choked the futility I lived. I yanked a section of my gown's skirt from the floor, grabbed the hem, and tugged. Threads popped loose at a yelp from below. A laugh and then Lizzy squealed.

Another voice joined hers, a man's voice. The two of them ascended the stairs in a happy lilt. I bent and scooped satin rags, buttons, and lace from the cot and floor, tossed everything into the trunk, and slammed its lid.

"Penelope?"

I heard a tap at my door, another giggle, and Clement's urge to call my name again, but louder.

I kicked the last few buttons and strips of lace beneath the bed. "Yes?"

"Can we come in? Clement and I have something to tell you."

"Of course." I plastered a smile over my seething grief.

The door opened, and euphoria sailed in, two faces in utter bliss, two hands locked tight…forever.

"Are we bothering you?" Lizzy asked.

"Of course not."

"Are you sure?" Lizzy studied my face.

"Of course I'm sure." I waved them in.

Lizzy resumed her smile, and Clement did the same. "We have something to tell you."

"It must be good news. Heaven knows we could use some of that here."

"It is." They stood close, joined by hand, joined by the grin they shared with each other and me.

"We're getting married." Lizzy rose to her toes and let out a happy squeak. I could see what Lizzy must have looked like as a girl, the innocent gaiety which made her bounce now.

"Lizzy, that's wonderful." I stepped her way, grabbed her happy warmth, and squeezed. "We'll celebrate here." I smiled a teary smile.

"Are you sure you're all right?" Lizzy frowned at me.

"I'm fine. Really."

"Well, you rest. We won't bother you, and as usual there's no one downstairs. I'll put our Closed sign in the window."

How long ago had I asked her to make such a sign? It seemed like forever. Back when I still thought a door waited for me, one I could open, just not here. Hand in hand, they left. Hand in hand they closed my door. Hand in hand and voice in voice they descended the stairs. When they were gone, my hand touched the trunk at my feet.

"Goodbye, Jim." Goodbye to him and his Mrs. Baylis forever.

Chapter 32

"I can't do that for you." I heard the same words again, ones I'd heard all over town as the rope cinched around me and Eat Here, the only business which refused to celebrate better times with Better Times. "And this…" Ben held what would have been Jim's wedding band in his fingertips. "I can't accept this as payment, not even a down payment."

"So you've ordered nothing."

"I can't." Ben and I stared at the ring he held between us, a band of promise, twice now a band of rejection. "Your husband's?" he whispered.

I caught his disgust at the trade of something beloved. I snatched the band from Ben's fingers. "Very well. It seems the whole town has the same policy."

"It's not our policy, Mrs. Strong." Ben reddened. "It's the bank's. If they'd forgive my debt, I could forgive yours. I think that's in the Bible."

"I know the Bible." I steeled for a bolt of lightning.

"My debt isn't likely to be forgiven because the bank expects it to be paid. And until it is, they control my assets." Ben became himself again, suddenly a beaten comrade, poor like Eat Here. "I do have the medicine you ordered, though." Ben turned to the shelves behind his counter and retrieved a small package.

"It's for Doc," I said. "He will pay you."

The package came my way, and I snatched it.

"Good day, Ben."

****

"If you could kindly pay Ben for this." I plunked the package into Doc's hands, his face reddening. So he knew as well, the vendetta against Eat Here...against me. I marched to the back where Cook lay, his gray grayer, his eyes duller. "Your medicine just came." I dropped into the chair next to him, scooted it close, and studied the skeleton he'd become. "It will make you better." It had to.

"You still got that pistol?" His head rolled slightly to the side as he looked at me.

"You need it back?"

"No, you will. Just makin' sure."

I sat back. "I doubt that. Admittedly there are money troubles around town, but I think..." I glanced over my shoulder, checking for Doc nearby. "I think you took care of the only one who actually wielded a gun," I whispered.

"Money and passion bring out the worst in any man. And woman."

My face warmed. "Well, I think I've already done my worst."

"That doesn't make you any less passionate."

My goodness, did every man have to see through my widow's clothing?

"How're your funds? I got a little money." Cook coughed, his body barely able to heave forward. I stood and took him by the arm and tipped him upward, held on until the hacking stopped. "Hope that medicine of yours has something strong in it."

"Well, Doc needs to get in here and administer it."

I turned to the door but stopped as Cook's dry hand latched onto mine.

"Sit back down. He'll get here soon enough." He nodded to my seat, and I sat and watched him clear his throat and settle back into the pillow, gray against white. "What'd you do with Rudy's money?"

"Nothing. I kept it under my mattress for you and…" Tina.

"That's okay," Cook wheezed. He stared at the ceiling, and I stared at my hands. "Blood money woulda been all right for Tina's and my celebration. Until now."

Blood money. I shuddered. No wonder I hadn't been able to touch it. "Does that mean…"

Cook glanced to the side at me. "That money weren't meant to kill my beloved, but to ruin Lizzy and Eat Here. Do what you want with it, but don't use it to help Lizzy celebrate."

I shook my head. I wouldn't. I shuddered again at what filthy money lay hidden in my room.

"Lizzy talked their weddin' down when she and her man came and told me, and said she didn't need nothin' fancy, but that ain't what I saw in Clement's eyes. You and I could do that much for her, don't you agree?" Cook waited, and I nodded. Vigorously. "Do it then. Give Lizzy the weddin' she deserves with our—my—money…mine's in one of them spice jars I never let you touch. Then after that, Louise Archer, alias Penelope Strong, I want you to put that good head of yers to use in other ways. Eat Here needs salvaged, and Larned needs wrangled from the hands of a greedy banker, at least. You can do it. You got good aim."

Doc entered the room before I could protest or

blush or cry, a frown on his face as he studied the medicine I'd ordered. He carried it to a nearby table cluttered with vials and cotton, jars and medical supplies. I came to my feet and went to stand behind him, peering over his shoulder and watching what he concocted. "Make it strong," I whispered. He glanced over his shoulder at me. Cook needed to mend enough to wield a pistol so I wouldn't have to. "I just thought it would be good if…"

"I'll follow your doctor's recommendations."

I faded back to Cook's bedside. He winked when I glanced down. I patted his arm. "Rest and heal. We need you."

"Keep your boots on." Cook winked again, then closed his eyes.

****

"We're getting married at the Justice of the Peace's office." Lizzy scoured a tabletop which didn't need it.

"Not in Eat Here? Or the church, even?" I gaped the way Mama wouldn't tolerate. "Why?"

Lizzy bent harder into her scrubbing. "No need for anything special," she said without looking up.

"But the church, and a get-together here afterwards, that's not too special. That's normal."

"We talked it over, and Clement and I agree. Something quiet and private. Maybe you could witness for me. I think he intends to ask Everett to do it for him. I plan to wear my best dress, that soft gray with tiny flowers. I have a bonnet that doesn't clash with it."

"No flowers? What about a honeymoon? A reception?"

Lizzy flipped her rag and scrubbed more, bent over a sheen which couldn't possibly gleam any brighter. "I envision your wedding with Alex as wonderful." She paused and looked up. "I imagine it as perfect, with all the trimmings. I wish I'd known you then, so I could have been there. I would have stood and witnessed for you. I would have loved to see a real wedding, not the farce Amber had. One done well, tastefully, and full of love. Clement and I have that last part, and that's enough. Thank you, Penelope. You and Tina have been...or she was...the best friends I could ever have."

I barely squeaked an "Excuse me" as I stumbled to and up the stairs. Shutting the door to my room behind me, I stared at my trunk. I knew nothing about weddings, but I understood passion. I went to it and opened its lid to the white mess of shredded fabric and buttons that I thanked God I hadn't had time to burn. It was time to remind myself how to sew and mend like I'd meant to on the train ages ago...but this time as a friend instead of as a wife.

Chapter 33

"What's that?" Ben Holt stared at the poster in my hands.

"It's a game where everyone wins, but a few people will win more." I held the poster up. "Can I hang this in your store?" I'd asked every business in town except two. The bank and Better Times. Doing what Cook had told me to—save Eat Here and Larned...if Larned would cooperate.

"What do you win? And what's the cost? There's surely a cost."

"There's a difference between cost and investment. Something you should know." I gazed over my poster at him. I'd covered this in one of my classes. Ben lived it now, trapped in costs too steep to climb out of, since he evidently hadn't learned a thing. "Anyway, you win information on finances and business, on thriving communities. You win cash if you invest. And the cost to attend the class is a cup of coffee, a dollar for the one who invests to support it and to gain more."

Mr. Holt scratched his head and stared at my poster the same way he had Jim's wedding band. No one understood, but Nicholas Brandt would when my plan for classes leaked to him. "Come to Eat Here in the evening for one week, buy a cup of coffee each time, and get information on how to run a business and how a township can work together to thrive. If you invest a dollar to support one of those nights, you get your dollar back, plus ten percent of the amount taken in for the coffee and the extra large cookies we'll serve. So the more people who attend the class you invest in, the more you'll make. One person will win a half dollar and another a free meal at Eat Here."

"A dollar..."

My pocket held the four dollars I'd collected so far, one investor each for one class. Mr. Holt's would make five. Mr. Brandt would be my sixth. I counted on it. "Enrollment is limited by the number of seats in Eat Here, which is quite a few, and a lot of cups of coffee. Plus cookies."

Larned wasn't ignorant, just deceived. Each businessman I'd asked for a dollar did the math, ten percent of a cup of coffee for every seat in the restaurant. Plus information. Cookies waited at Eat Here where I told everyone to go sign up. Excellent coffee waited, also, and cinnamon rolls, and greasy gravy Cook had shown me how to make now that he was up and hobbling around. Hobbling freely, since no one had found Rudy—or his body—yet. Lizzy waited there with paper and pen to take their names. And Cook as well, feeble but armed.

"I'll invest a dollar." Mr. Holt dropped his hand from the stubble on his chin.

"You can give that dollar to me, but first sign this form. It's a contract, a promise of your return. A good contract." To outsmart the wiles of Mr. Brandt. "I will talk about truth in contracts in the first class...again. If you want to attend, run over to Eat Here and sign up. Have some coffee and a cookie when you do. Free."

Mr. Holt signed, and I left my last poster in his

store, where one of the Brandts would eventually see it.

****

"So you're holding classes." Everett toyed with his coffee cup. The table he'd chosen sat far from where Lizzy and Cook stationed themselves near the front door. Everett picked a place he could watch people as they shied into Eat Here's door, catch their apologetic grimaces and fear as Cook barked a brazen welcome.

"I am," I said. I sat, twirled my cup also, the one I'd been carrying around the dining area and around Everett. "For the cost of a cup of this…" I raised my cup of what was now Jim's brew with a slight modification of my own.

"That's mighty generous of you." He looked up. "Though we both know that coffee's the best…the very best."

My face felt as hot as the coffee should be.

"I mean you're a deliberate woman. And if you are being generous, there's a reason for it."

I nodded.

"It's also quite the talk around town."

"Everyone will get something." I took a drink.

"Who gets the most, may I ask?"

"I'll be honest with you." I set my cup down. "It's not about the most, it's about what's fair."

"In other words, the rich won't necessarily get richer." Everett eyed me as one side of his lawman's mouth inched up. "There are ways to rob a man without robbing him. And there are ways to restore justice without the law. And some who hold to that."

I looked away so Everett wouldn't see justice on my face—Cook's justice, his way of doing right, and his restoring gun in my boot.

"I may have to add another deputy in Larned, thanks to you." Everett leaned back in his chair. "Lots more going on, it seems. I even saw a bundle of your cookies for sale at the mercantile at a slightly reduced cost from Better Times', and travelers asking for more."

"It's the open-your-doors-to-travelers plan Lizzy and I initiated." The one Amber stole. I looked at the face which puzzled over me, the same look I'd seen in St. Louis. But this one pried deeper. "Every merchant in Larned is to give a little something to visitors so they'll associate this town with a pleasant memory." I twisted my cup. "I'd never been far from home until I left St. Louis." Boarded that train in a fury and raw devotion to Mama, blinded by rejection and tears, anger which didn't see what I saw now. "Anyway, I told the local businessmen that when I came here on that train, the two things I needed were refreshment and a welcome." And a ticket out. "Maybe you recall…"

Everett nodded. "I do."

My face warmed. "I never thanked you…"

"You thanked me to leave you alone, if I remember correctly." A full grin curled his mouth. "I'm sorry if I was too…"

"You were doing your job. Not just escorting a witness, but being concerned about a widow…a supposed widow…alone."

"I'm not always doing my job, Penelope. Nor am I always a lawman."

I glanced at his cup. Our quiet felt louder than the bustle of Eat Here as I looked up at a face which wasn't always a lawman. A face that had found me somehow when I'd boarded that train, watched me and watched out for me, paid attention from the beginning. "I thank you properly, then." For the non-lawman duties. Everett's sort of right.

"You are welcome…properly."

"And as for your job, I'm sorry for the extra work I've caused. But it's for a reason. To make Larned more appealing."

"I'm not complaining. Deputy Joshua has his hands full. And in case you haven't noticed, I've been here more."

I had noticed. I twisted my cup again.

"I understand what you've done…and why, as well as I can. I've never been engaged, but I've seen the tension that comes with it…in my friends. There's a sort of irrational fluster with getting married…a pre-wedding insanity that there aren't enough apologies for later."

I felt naked in front of a man and marshal who missed little. "No one else knows," I said. "Just you and Cook. Everyone else still thinks I'm the widowed Penelope Strong, but I will fix that. Right after these classes." Then I'd go, walk if I had to, since I'd likely not be able to force Julius Weston to give me a full train ticket, no matter how relieved he'd be to get me out of town.

"I'll be here for all of your classes. I'll pay. I'm more than happy to get a cup of your coffee." Everett lifted his cup. "Do I need to sign up?"

I shook my head in a way that said, "Thank you." Thank you for letting Louise continue to be Penelope as long as I needed and thank you for making sure Lizzy and I were all right. Everett, the lawman Everett, would be our insurance. He would be there because Cook was right. Something lay beneath the money problems in town, and I'd just pried the lid off it so we could reach in and grab back Lizzy's share. Money and passion were bringing out the worst in men...and at least one woman. "You're more than welcome to attend. I'll give you free coffee."

We sat and spoke without speaking, watched without watching guilty friends instead of each other, old customers who stuck their heads in Eat Here's door to see if they were welcome or would be shot by Cook, the man they'd once called a friend. Lizzy hurried to greet each one, her kind welcome prying the door from their grasp. Cook bellowed at them as monitor and protector of the place where his lover had died. I wondered if Rudy's body had actually been found, and whether Everett or Joshua had just let it lie and called it justice without the law.

I glanced at Everett's profile—the muted ruggedness, the kindness which observed keenly while seemingly at ease. He didn't flinch when the door opened and Mr. Brandt's voice carried across the room. I turned at the sound, at Amber with him, her coos bringing Cook to the edge of his seat.

"I heard about some classes to be offered here." Mr. Brandt stopped in front of Lizzy and removed his hat. I caught Everett's tiny glance my way, the lawman's search to affirm whether these were the rich that wouldn't get richer if my plan worked. I didn't squirm under the frisk of Everett's gaze. I focused on Mr. Brandt, his glance at tables where our old customers and his new ones stopped eating and drinking and gazed back.

Lizzy rose to her feet and straightened a stack of papers just as we'd rehearsed. "We're holding finance classes."

"I'm surprised you've decided to offer them, when you should have asked me to." He towered over her exactly as he had the first day I'd met them. I scooted to the edge of my seat.

Don't. Everett said it with a nearly invisible shake of his head.

Mr. Brandt saw only Lizzy, her upturned face and the pen she held out to him.

"We're registering people for the classes. If you want to attend, you can." Lizzy extended the pen farther.

"You intend to rob him, don't you?" Everett kept his voice low, his lips didn't even move.

"Is it robbery to take back what's yours to begin with?" I spoke just as low. I would use Mr. Brandt's money for Lizzy's wedding. It belonged to her and the town, cleaner than the filth Cook had taken from Rudy, which I'd turned over to Cook the first time he hobbled back into Eat Here. He'd said nothing when he took it, but he smelled of smoke the next time I saw him. I glanced at the keen but weakened man across the room, my passionate twin, his aim growing stronger.

"It's an exercise and a game, not just a class," Lizzy offered. "We need an exact tally of participants. For refreshments and the investors." She lowered the pen in the exact manner we'd planned, and I smiled.

Mr. Brandt watched the pen, his eyes off her and focused on what she withdrew. "Game?" He looked from her hand to her face. "It sounds like gambling, from what I've heard. Risky for a town of floundering businesses, don't you think?"

"Everyone wins," Lizzy said. My lips moved with

hers, with the lines she and I had practiced. "But our investors earn." She tapped the pen on the table now.

"I heard some sort of nonsense like that." Mr. Brandt frowned at the pen and then her, glanced Everett's and my direction and frowned even harder at us. "Sounds like a recipe to go under," he added. I saw the calculations as he gazed at me, felt the tally of ingredients that would make his prediction come true.

"It's spelled out right here." Lizzy slid a contract his way, one I'd written just for him. "Each investor has the power to gain a little or a lot, up to them. We have outlined the terms clearly and guarantee a return of their dollar."

Mr. Brandt broke his study of me and stared at the contract, saw the stack of five signed ones she'd slid it from beneath. "It's an absurd way to do business. Why, the bank would fold if I managed its money that way." He glanced at the customers, their eyes and ears glued to the one their pockets were glued to. "Not only will you risk your own business with this sort of silliness, you'll risk theirs as well." He turned to me and stared with a question, a probe to the East, a wonder again who I really was.

My legs strained, every muscle taut to stand and march across the room to confront the man and his bride, who twirled her lacy parasol at his side. I sat tight. This victory belonged to Lizzy. Her pocketbook would strengthen, and Mr. Brandt's would break. The last thing I would do for my friend. My very best friend.

"It's God's principle," Lizzy said. "Give and receive. We give by offering the community a chance to give and receive back. Eat Here will receive also."

Bankers and men of culture weren't supposed to snort, but Mr. Brandt did. Right before he looked away from me and turned to her. "Ludicrous" covered his face as he did, and disbelief...and then greed. The thing I'd hoped to see.

"Give to receive. It won't work, but I understand your plight. Do you need another investor?" pomposity asked as the banker straightened.

"Just one more," Lizzy said and nodded at the contract in front of him.

"I'll be your one more," he said. "I can buffer a loss more than most." He gazed over the roomful that stared at him. "Better the bank take a risk than these other businesses, which could end up in ruin."

"Then here is the contract you and I will sign." Lizzy slid it his way, the pen on top of it, the ink nearby. "All we need is a dollar for your investment, and your name on which class or classes you'd like to attend."

Mr. Brandt's brows raised and his mouth kicked up in a grin. "A dollar? That isn't much."

"That's it." Lizzy smiled back. "That's plenty for anyone."

"How about more than a dollar?" His gaze traveled around the restaurant. Had he wanted Eat Here all along? Cook was right about Rudy, but maybe what I saw in Mr. Brandt's calculations was that he intended to wrest it from Lizzy and Phillip, not help them salvage it. "How about fifty of them? Or a hundred?" He leveled his gaze on Lizzy.

"You realize that no matter how much you invest, your return is limited to seating and profit from the cost of a cup of coffee, possibly a cookie, and that's all."

Lizzy held firm.

Mr. Brandt shook his head. "No, for a hundred dollars I want more than a cup of coffee to be admission. I want it to be a meal. You serve the meal and charge for it. Drinks are free."

I glanced at Everett. Mr. Brandt seemed more daring than I'd thought. I'd expected greed to boost his investment to ten dollars, but not one hundred. His proposal would undo my plan to trick him out of money for Lizzy. I gripped the table's edge to stand, but stopped at Everett's invisible warning. Did every lawman in the West think it right to sit back while evil flourished?

"I don't think we…" Lizzy hedged.

"I will hand you a hundred dollars. With that you can feed the town. You'll make it back and more, since I promise to pack the house. I'll even add extra seating."

He certainly would pack the house. He already had, with every customer on point, at the edge of seats he'd just guaranteed they'd return to, all of them ready to dart out and spread the word. Drat, drat, drat.

"I suppose that would work…" Lizzy tapped a finger on the table.

"Done, then." A wallet the size of Larned appeared from inside Mr. Brandt's jacket, a bill extracted and laid on the table. He took the pen, dabbed it into the ink as he scanned the contract, then signed his name.

"And one of these forms also, if you're interested in the classes." Lizzy waved an amazingly steady arm across the six class rosters.

"Which night will you use my investment?" he asked.

"The last one. You're the last investor, so that's the order we've scheduled them."

"Then that's the class I will attend. Everyone will. You can count on it." He bent again and signed, straightened, tipped his hat Lizzy's way, and escorted a petulant Amber out, her last gaze at the bill in front of Lizzy.

Cook and Lizzy exchanged invisible nods as the door closed, chairs scooted back, and customers raced to spread the word. Everett didn't budge as Lizzy stacked the contracts and slid them into an envelope. I wanted to run across the room and hug her for the way she'd stuck with our plan even with Nicholas's unexpected hundred-dollar glitch. Hugs and gratitude could wait. Later she, Cook, and I would celebrate...then rethink our plan.

"I don't want to know," Everett said before he looked at me. "But there's something you may want to."

Lizzy faded into the background with her and Cook's slightly unsettled movements as they hid shaky gasps of relief from customers who streamed out the door.

"You're right," I whispered to Everett. I did want to know. The "I don't want to know" I'd spoken to him outside Better Times had dissipated. I needed to know how or why another woman had come to be with the man Louise Archer had intended to marry.

"I've known Jim a long time. He spoke of you often while the two of you corresponded. I had an image of you from what he said and read to me, and I have to say it didn't do justice to the woman I saw board that train in St. Louis. You were fire and ice. That passion you carry seared your heart on your sleeve." He looked down at his cup. "I confess I felt something the moment I spotted you, an unexpected flicker, before I could even remember why I'd made it a point to be on that train...which had nothing to do with the man handcuffed to me." Everett paused. His admission hung in the air. His own wrong to make a right. I stared wide-eyed at my cup until he resumed.

"Something in me responded to you before it struck me who you might be. I watched you, forgot all about my intention to find and scrutinize the woman my best friend wanted to marry before she made it that far. Rudy didn't budge when I stepped toward you, my own interest and desire all I could hear. The jolt back made me stop long enough to realize you might be Jim's. I set my own flicker aside and determined to do what I'd come to do for my friend...until I heard your name. When you said you were the widowed Mrs. Strong and headed to Larned, that flicker flared to a fire. It consumed me, a blaze I couldn't contain until I visited Jim and heard what had happened. He told me about the telegram he sent. On occasion I wondered if you, a very capable and determined woman from what I'd seen, happened to be the woman Jim had chosen." Everett tapped the table with a fingertip. "And still chose in spite of the wire he sent. And still does."

Still does. I focused on Lizzy as she helped Cook across the restaurant. Jim still does... But he was broken. I was broken. Just like the broken kindness which sat across from me.

"I became sure you were Louise Archer after that sip of Jim's coffee. And more sure as I witnessed your passion and the way it burned, albeit erratically, especially when you'd forget you had a late husband. That made my own flames all the more wrong because Jim's still smoldered. The two of you each wanted a person you'd never met, whereas I had met both of you." Everett stared a hole through his cup. "And you would have met, the two of you would have made that union happen…if a crooked banker hadn't stepped in."

I heard my gasp, saw that my two worlds hadn't been so far apart at all. What I'd suffered and saw happening here, Jim had suffered there. Everett saw it. He'd straddled both worlds, let his own heart smolder to give Jim's a chance to burn again. Everett never once tried to keep us apart. Jim did that.

"Jim made a couple of misjudgments. First in choosing land with a good water source in a dry area, then letting it be known. Then he got in debt. He had wanted to make sure you had a pleasant place to come to, you being from the East. He borrowed on a weak harvest to buy some furniture. He planned for everything except a greedy banker with a single daughter and an eye on good property, who then called in the loan early with a claim that the bank had suffered too many loans during a weak year."

"A daughter…" I sank in my seat. I could see her again, the too-nice clothing, the self-possessed look.

The lack of fire in Jim turned out to be smoldering; the voice which no longer burned in my imagination.

"Part of the deal he made so he would only lose a portion of what he had."

"A portion? Didn't he get to keep everything after he agreed to an arrangement like that?"

Everett shook his head. "He lost the best part. Jim lost you. Miss Archer, it will be a very fortunate man who turns your Miss to a Mrs. someday. My friend intended for that man to be him."

Chapter 34

I stared at men I didn't know, well groomed and serious, who filled the extra tables Mr. Brandt had brought into Eat Here for his night, the last class his exorbitant one hundred dollars supported.

"I don't like this," Lizzy whispered beside me, our hands busy with paper, pens, and ink to be handed out after the meal.

"I haven't liked any of it," I whispered back. Mr. Brandt's menu he'd insisted upon contained dishes even more outrageous than Amber's hors d'oeuvres at their engagement party, items impossible to come by in Larned, which forced us to order from far away and dip deeper into his hundred dollars we were to give back.

"I don't think we'll have enough room." Lizzy spoke close at my side. "They just keep coming."

She was right. Larned found itself shoved aside, a plain brown pool overcome by more dashing finery which took its place. "We can't let these newcomers push our friends aside."

"Friends." Lizzy gave me a smile. "You haven't said the word 'friend' for a while."

I glanced at Lizzy, the friend I staged all of this for. "You're more than a friend, Lizzy. You're like a sister." Two Elizabeths. "And Larned is like family. The kind which squabbles with you." I would be their Uncle Roy if this plan didn't work.

Lizzy nudged my hand. "There's a man across the room who keeps staring at you. Next to the door. He hasn't moved since he stepped inside."

I let my gaze travel that way, nonchalantly viewed the crowd until I spotted him.

"My God." I looked down. "I mean, my goodness, it's about time to begin." I wanted to look again to be sure, but I didn't dare. If I ignored him, maybe he would vanish.

"Penelope." A hand touched my shoulder, and I jumped. I looked up to Everett, who had sat through every class just as he promised, stayed and helped each night as we cleaned and cleared the dining area, smiled as we reveled in our success which had indeed brought customers creeping back through our doors under Cook's steady eye.

"It's…there's someone from…" I didn't look again at the man near the door, but Everett knew. His nod finished what I didn't want to say.

I watched Everett's face to see what I didn't dare look at. His focus ignored the attorney from St. Louis and stayed on me, leaving Mr. Snyder, my Uncle Roy's lawyer he employed to wedge me out of Papa's business, in the background. I wanted to grab Everett and shake out of him how that man had come to be in Larned and at my class. But I spotted my probable answer before I made a passionate fool of myself. Mr. Brandt. The darkened figure who wove throughout his guests…and cast shadows everywhere he went.

"Who is it?" Lizzy whispered.

The woman I'd claimed to be like a sister was about to find out she'd been lied to. Lizzy would hear about Louise Archer…but from a stranger instead of me if I couldn't outsmart him one more time. I needed a word far worse than drat. I had lied too much and for too long. And done a poor job of it, since at least three men in this town had found me out.

"I have deputies here," Everett said. "Three in suits, one in ordinary clothing."

Lizzy's eyes became enormous as she looked from Everett to me.

"We're watching him," Everett said. "Them, actually."

"What do we do? What is happening? Should we change our plans?" Lizzy's eyes were too wide.

"You serve the meal, mingle as you've already decided, and continue on with your plan." Everett's tone turned serious, but his expression remained calm. Goodness. He could put up a false front better than I could.

Lizzy paled, utterly incapable of lying as well as Everett and me.

"Now," Everett continued, "where is the money you're taking in for this?"

"Over there." I tipped my head toward the front door. "Cook brought Les back here to work for us again. Les collects the money as they come in. Then he will carry it to the kitchen and leave it with Cook."

"Because Cook is…" Everett looked down at me.

"Armed," I said with a face as red as my leg where Cook's other pistol rubbed.

"I meant because Cook is trustworthy." Everett raised a brow.

"Yes. That's what I meant too. Armed with goodwill."

"Well we can't jeopardize Cook," Everett said with

mirth in the eyes he turned toward the crowd. "I want you to intercept that money, Penelope, do it in an obvious way so everyone sees you, and then carry it up to your room and leave it there. It's easier to watch those stairs than the kitchen. Only one way up there, but two ways to Cook."

I nodded, unable to mimic the ease on Everett's face. I envisioned myself with more money than I'd ever handled, enough to ruin Mr. Brandt if our plan worked, but also enough to turn Eat Here over to his greedy hands if it didn't. Too much could go wrong. I'd have to yank Cook's gun from my boot and blaze my way through black jackets to protect Lizzy's money on my way up the stairs.

Everett put one hand on my shoulder and his other on Lizzy's, steadying us both with an expression which looked like good wishes. I nodded hard as he pointed to the nearby coffeepot, let go of us, and walked that way as if we'd chatted about nothing more serious than food and drinks. Lizzy and I watched Everett go, a congenial spread of welcomes and salutations as he threaded through the crowd. He reached the pot and filled a cup with his favorite drink. I watched the look of satisfaction as he eyed the crowd over the steam as he took a sip. He disappeared before I saw again that tiny assurance I needed, his dark clothing lost in the crowd.

"Cook is waving from the kitchen." Lizzy tugged my sleeve and nodded where Cook...Sam...gestured.

"He's ready. Tell everyone to find a table, and I'll help get the serving started."

Lizzy held onto my arm. "Be careful, Penelope. I don't know what is going on, but I'm glad Everett has extra eyes here. I won't let anything happen to you.

Never. Tina wouldn't want me to."

I blanched. Tina, who took a bullet for her lover, would know, just like my father did, everything I'd done. Just like Lizzy would know sooner than I intended if Mr. Snyder, Uncle Roy's attorney, had a chance to speak to her before I did. "Lizzy, no matter what happens, I want you to know I always meant well. You won't forget that, will you?"

Lizzy squeezed my arm, beautiful, in a different outfit from what I wore. I'd burned everything that matched. No matter how much Cook insisted Rudy's vile intentions had nothing to do with what Tina and I wore, I would forever distinguish myself from the innocent. Just in case.

I scanned the crowd for broad shoulders, dark hair and jacket. There were too many to spot Everett, the one who stood between me and harm...and who I would stand for also.

Lizzy raised her hand and called for attention in a sweet voice which thanked the faces that turned her way. She told them to please find seats and fill every empty space, since Eat Here was so full. I gave up my gawk for Everett when every eye turned our direction, and hurried toward the kitchen face down, my ears deaf to the St. Louis voice I couldn't let say, "Miss Archer."

The aroma of good food took the place of conversations as people settled into chairs and I, along with the servers we'd hired, brought full dishes of Mr. Brandt's entrees from the kitchen. Mr. Brandt had set us up well with the cost of this event. Each plate, full of exquisite beauty and flavor, drew pleased exclamations, which became lost with the sound of the clock that ticked in my head. Time marched Nicholas and me to the same point, the draw of weapons to see who could fire first, fire at just the right moment so one would win and the other lose.

A hand raised. Someone waved off to the side. Drat. The attorney, most likely. Or Mr. Brandt. Or his bride, who managed to reign like a queen as if we were in Better Times instead of Eat Here. I set my jaw and looked. Nearly gasped in relief at Lizzy's arm, raised and pointed toward Les, who neared the kitchen with the money box.

Drat. I gathered my skirts and rushed past tables and greetings, hurried to apprehend Les before he reached the kitchen. Drat, drat, and double drat. I'd let my fears get in the way of Everett's plan.

"Wait," I called. Heads turned, Les's included. "I need you to help Lizzy." It was all I could think of over my swishing skirts, my unladylike race between tables. At least I was obvious. Everett should be pleased with that, wherever he happened to be. "I'll take care of the money," I said loud enough for everyone to hear as I took the box from Les's hands. "Thank you, Les. We couldn't have done this without you." I threw an arm around him in spite of his baffled expression and sent him Lizzy's way.

I felt like a fool as I climbed the stairs, me and the money box exaggerated with each step. I felt obvious, the way Amber liked to be, good odors and conversation slow to resume after the disruption I'd caused. I closed the door to my room behind me, pressed my back against it, and held the box to my stomach. "Get a hold on yourself," I hissed in the dark. "You did what Everett said. Now you have a class to teach and a banker to ruin." I straightened, tripped over a rumpled rug as I toted the money box to my cot. I kicked at the rug, flattened it with a stomp, then tucked the box beneath my pillow. My room had never been a good place to hide something. It was too stark. Even my trunk hadn't been able to hide Jim from Cook. But it hid my wedding gown from Lizzy, mended for her, resewn and pieced together like a bridal puzzle.

A beam of light shone from the floor, from Cook's first bullet hole. A peephole to the dignified noise below, the sound and aroma of a meal, of expensive drinks, of friends, and at least two enemies. Maybe more, since Everett had brought in more than two deputies.

I bent and touched Cook's gun beneath my skirt and petticoats. Lizzy said she'd protect me, and I knew Everett would. And I'd die protecting them. I yanked my skirt up and removed the pistol from my boot. I'd never taken the time to practice or even learn how to aim and fire. What if I accidentally shot Lizzy or Everett? I dropped the gun to my bed, stared where it lay in the darkness. I picked it up again. Cook gave it to me for a reason. He said to keep it with me. But we had him back now. Slowly recovering from his own bullet wound while the memory of Tina, the blood on her blouse, a blouse I'd had made for her, remained. I dropped the pistol again. I wanted it with me, yet I didn't. I stared where it lay in the dark.

Chapter 35

Everett sat too far from the bottom of the stairs. Nowhere close to where I thought he should be as I descended to the dining room. His dark hair and attire blended too well with the pool of black Nicholas had invited…shadows. I shuddered.

Plates were cleared away as the meal wound down, coffee or whatever people drank refilled at their tables. For free, the way Mr. Brandt had arranged. I'd insisted Cook lock the back door, even though the shiny metal trigger protruded above his apron, and informed two of our servers they were to stay with him in the kitchen at all times if they wanted to be paid.

I watched Lizzy as I took my place at the front, my eyes on her back and her smile as she went from table to table and dropped off ink, paper, and pens, asking if anyone needed anything else. Everett surely watched also, he along with his invisible deputies, who were to keep a close eye on the crowd as my friend stood out in the open. I'd insisted Les should do that job, he being no one's target and too thin to hit anyway, but she'd refused. I'd told her to take a seat near Everett when she finished, but she'd refused that as well and insisted she be on her feet to watch me.

She had covered most of the tables. It was time to welcome the attendees, but I didn't. My friend, my twin Elizabeth, held my attention, her face and her smiles, her welcomes. I watched everything around her, monitored for any sign of trouble. Surely there wouldn't be any. Surely Mr. Brandt felt confident he had us over a barrel financially…and me over a barrel if he understood who Mr. Snyder was, in the audience. I took my eyes off Lizzy and did a quick scan of the room. I saw so much black, so many faces, many as handsome as his, and some wives almost equal to Amber…a sea of too much confusion.

"Oh, no, you must be mistaken." Lizzy paused at a table and smiled down at a man. At him, at Mr. Snyder. He smiled back at her, the same patronizing smile he used to give me in St. Louis. She turned to me and waved a handful of papers my direction. "That's Mrs. Strong. She's your teacher tonight." Lizzy's face shone the way Mama's had as she looked at me. She—both of them—trusted me.

"Welcome, everyone," I blurted before Mr. Snyder could blurt something worse. Faces looked up, and Lizzy moved on as Uncle Roy's attorney's studious look joined the others. "I want to thank you for…" My voice ran on, words spilled out, hopefully making sense while my mind tumbled in nonsense. "I want to do a quick review about contracts before we begin. We taught that in the first class, but many of you weren't here." Especially Mr. Brandt. "I'll cover quickly what makes a contract good, and what makes one bad. Then we'll go on to tonight's topic. When I am finished, we'll announce tonight's winners. A free meal at Eat Here to one winner, and tonight's meal paid for to the other."

"And a cash prize of twenty dollars."

I wheeled to the right, where the voice came from,

the opposite side of the room from where I'd last seen Everett. Mr. Brandt rose to his feet, Amber along with him. They were too near the stairs, too near the kitchen, had too many people between them and Everett for him to see…or shoot.

"Well, we didn't…" I hedged.

"Of course you didn't." Mr. Brandt smiled. "But it's only right, in a crowd this size, that more prizes are offered. It increases the probability of winning." Applause rose along with nods of approval between me and the frantic look from Lizzy across the room. She froze. Twenty more dollars, a fortune we didn't expect. A tighter noose if we failed. I saw it on her face.

"Something for everyone," I said. "Something special for a lucky few." Time ticked louder and faster, seconds I could no longer count to precisely predict how many it would take to flush Mr. Brandt out before he trapped me, him and any shadows with him. "Let's begin."

A man stepped through the door after I'd outlined the elements of a good contract and prepared to explain the bad. He dressed like Larned but worse, ragged, a face I didn't recognize as he inched toward the back. Another deputy? I spoke on as I looked toward Everett's side of the room until I spotted and watched his face. I wanted to tip my head toward the man who'd just entered. Everett watched me, his focus on everything except what it should be. Drat.

"This is an example of a good contract." I held up the one I'd written for Mr. Holt, his dollar investment easily returned with a profit. Everett watched the contract I held high, his attention there instead of the direction I waved it, where the man had walked…and vanished. He could be a farmer, late because he lived far out of town. I set the contract down and stared at the one I'd drawn up for Mr. Brandt. The one which should bring him to his feet, and hopefully Everett with him. "And this…" I set my fingers on the slighted form, one that left Mr. Brandt with nothing. "This is an example of…"

"Excuse me. Louise? Question, please."

Twenty-eight years of being Louise Archer brought my head up. Drat. Two hours of knowing a snake from St. Louis infested the room should have kept it down. Drat, drat, drat. Mr. Snyder stood, his hand half raised. Mr. Brandt rose also, his mouth a full smile.

"Questions will be addressed after I conclude. Now, this is a poor contract." I held Mr. Brandt's high, the white paper trembling, so I flapped it.

"I think it would be proper to allow high-paying guests to ask questions whenever they have them. I believe Mr. Snyder there has one…Louise." Mr. Brandt moved from where he stood and began to edge forward, as Amber sashayed with him. "Louise Archer from St. Louis." Two others stood, men I didn't recognize, both in black suits. I prayed they were Everett's deputies. The paper shook, the contract meant to ruin Mr. Brandt fluttered like a white flag…an admission of defeat.

The room became silent, every eye on me. I opened my mouth, sorted through lies which would save…spare Lizzy. I caught her gape from where she stood near the kitchen alongside Cook.

"Nothing makes a contract more void than falsifying your identity," Mr. Brandt continued as he sliced through the silence.

I fought for air. I needed to gasp but even that

wouldn't come. I stared at the man who'd drawn before I could, who'd outthought me, out planned me, outsmarted me. His bullets of truth took perfect aim and exposed me, ruining Eat Here. And Lizzy… I looked at her, at the white expression of unbelief which gaped at me. Then at the movement behind her, the ragged man who'd slipped in and slid past the laundry area.

Mr. Brandt had outthought and out planned Everett as well, his own people planted in even better disguises. He had outdrawn me, concocted something unethical faster than I had, but he wouldn't outdraw my gun. Nor would whatever villain he'd brought in to harm Lizzy.

I kicked my leg up, clapped my boot on the table next to me, hiked my skirt above my knee, and groped where Cook's pistol should have been. I pawed at my leg and my stocking through gasps as guests gaped at everything I exposed…except Cook's gun. I'd left it on the cot. Drat. I heard a scream, a shriek in my head, horror at what I hadn't done…and what I had. The scream came again, louder…Lizzy.

I dropped my foot to the floor. Lizzy stared at the ragged man who stood close to her…too close. "Stop!" I shouted as Lizzy stumbled and landed in his arms. "Let go of her!" I heard her sobs muffled by his tattered shirt, her blonde head burrowed below his even blonder hair.

I stopped and stared and listened. My goodness. I could have shot him. I could have shot the man to whom she had cried, "Phil!"

Part of the crowd moved their way, streams of brown as Larned came to its feet and swept around tables to welcome Lizzy's long-lost brother home. Puddles of black stood back, confused glances at each other and Mr. Brandt.

"Now, Miss Archer," a familiar voice hissed near my ear. "There's nothing more you can do here. Not for the two of them…or should I say to them. I believe Mr. Brandt has a case against you, and I intend to see he wins it." The fine food we'd paid for smelled less fine on Mr. Snyder's breath.

I took a step away, but his fingers had my sleeve. I didn't look at the face which had tried so many times to undo me and now finally had. Or I had. I gazed around the room. We were alone, everyone else who knew me mobbed around Lizzy and her brother. Those who didn't were clustered at the back. I searched for Everett or even Joshua, who'd been strangely invisible, prayed one of them was near, prayed I'd hear one kind voice.

"Ah, there she is." Mr. Snyder's "ah" filled the air with more fumes of Mr. Brandt's meal. I looked where his "ah" indicated and saw Amber at the top of the stairs, Lizzy's gown in one hand and the metal money box in the other. "You're a fraud, Miss Archer. A jilted bride. Your mother took ill when I told her."

"You what?" I wheeled, holding my breath.

"I'm thorough. There is a case against you that I have pieced together. Your family's mercantile money you took under the false pretense of going to marry, your fake identity, the missing body of Mr. Walters. And now that little display of indecent exposure which speaks very poorly of you and what little character remains."

"That money Amber has is Lizzy's." And Phillip's. I glanced where my friend stood…the woman who had been my sister in heart. Lizzy stood with her brother, who'd also be able to testify there had never been such a person as Mr. Strong, no arrangement which had brought me here.

"It's the court's money, if anything, though it rightly belongs to Mr. Brandt. He'll have it back soon enough, though. As soon as Mrs. Brandt brings it to me, you and I can go."

I watched Amber toss my gown back into my room. With the tin box high, she marched it down the stairs and vanished in a crowd which watched her as well. I prayed her greed would overcome her and she'd make a break for the back door. Cook would get her then.

Amber cut through the crowd like a schooner through water and appeared with the metal box still high. The crowd parted, clearing the way between me and Lizzy, Phillip, and Cook. The tin box hit the table in front of me.

Lizzy staggered forward, Phillip close behind. Both came my way until Lizzy heard "Louise Archer" spouted from Amber's lips. Lizzy stopped alongside her brother, Cook close behind, as Amber proclaimed the money as hers and Nicholas's.

Mr. Snyder let go of my sleeve and latched onto the box's handle. "We'll make that final before the judge, when he comes through."

"You can't do that." My voice sounded quiet, softer than his, far softer than Amber's.

"I'm afraid we can." Mr. Brandt appeared alongside Amber.

"No, you can't." I might have left Mama in utter ruin, but I could still save Lizzy. I reached behind me and slid Mr. Brandt's contract from the table. Then reached for another sheet. "Two reasons, actually.

339

One…" I held up the second sheet. Unsteady, I scanned the crowd and finally spotted Cook and Everett. Both now stood back. Both watched in a way and at a distance I didn't appreciate. I swallowed as the two who could vouch for me remained far away. "This is the contract between me and the people who invested in a class." I lifted the other sheet, Mr. Brandt's contract with Lizzy. "There's nothing fraudulent about either of these agreements. Lizzy signed each one. Not me. So did Mr. Brandt, on this one. And if you'll notice the date, this contract ended yesterday, the same day each contract ended. It is in the fine print. If terms weren't settled by midnight last night, all monies stayed in the hands they were in. Plus, note the clause referenced by these letters."

Mr. Brandt stepped forward as Mr. Snyder snatched the paper from my hands.

"What letters? What clause? You're a worse scoundrel than I thought." Mr. Brandt reached for the contract Mr. Snyder scanned.

"Those letters at the bottom reference another document you failed to ask for."

"Those?" He stared at the page, held it close to his face. "This conglomeration of nonsense?"

"They're Latin. They mean the end, final, irrevocable. So I will finish this class for the participants on tonight's roster, as agreed." I turned to Mr. Snyder. "I don't recall seeing your name there…unless you used a false one."

Larned gathered close, brown behind Lizzy, as black pressed toward the door. A door blocked by men I didn't recognize—deputies, no doubt. Another near the kitchen, behind Cook, Cook's grin a smile of not nearly enough teeth.

Everett appeared beside us, along with Joshua, a wad of money in the deputy's hand. Everett took the contract while Joshua took the money box, lifted the lid, dumped plain paper out, then stuffed the bills inside. "Thought you'd spot me when you tripped over that rug I messed up in your room." Joshua winked at me. "I emptied the box and filled it with blank paper."

I looked at Everett, who had stood back and let me defend myself alone. Then at Joshua who had watched me pull a gun from my boot and drop it on the cot. I couldn't look at Lizzy or her brother, not even Cook, who still grinned in the back.

"I think you owe some people a lot of money." Everett stepped to Mr. Brandt. "And you owe me some explanations."

I watched as Everett led Lizzy's banker away, Amber behind them. Joshua took Mr. Snyder by the arm, and two other black suits...shadows...were escorted out by Everett's men. The room stirred, abuzz and alive with chatter, people I owed a class to, two I owed apologies to, none of which I cared to face.

Especially Lizzy and her brother. I extended my unsteady hand. "Hello, Phillip. I'm Louise Archer from St. Louis. And I'm...I'm...sorry." I glanced at Lizzy, saw tears trickle down her face. Clement stood at her other side.

"Excuse me." I looked away from my friend's eyes. "I owe everyone a class," I said to the crowd as I held up the roster with everyone's names. "We have an agreement I intend to honor." Even though I wasn't honorable. I'd destroyed my mother's trust and likely let Uncle Roy ruin her business, since I left when I should have stayed.

No one moved.

"Please." I gestured to the empty tables. "I owe you this much."

"Consider yourself paid in full." Cook crossed his arms, the butt of his gun shiny above his apron.

"Same here," someone added, and a chorus of similar sentiments followed. There were more agreements, more thanks.

I gathered papers I could barely see through my tears, kept my eyes on them as I walked through the crowd, past Lizzy and her brother to the stairs. I made my way to the top, to what had been my room, and closed the door. It was time to go. Halfway to nowhere.

Chapter 36

"Ma'am? You look like a woman who could use a private seat."

I didn't look at Everett or ask him how he knew where to find me. I'd waited two days in my room, waited today until dark, then slipped to the train station and repaid a smug Julius Weston every last penny I had for the same half ticket again, to head halfway to St. Louis to face Mama, tell her the truth, and hold her up while Uncle Roy claimed Papa's store.

"A public seat will do." They were hard, just what I deserved.

"I thought you should know Mr. Brandt lost more than you managed to get from him. Thanks to Phillip's story, he lost his freedom as well. He's been locked up for not only the conniving he did, but the theft, the fraud, and the harm he caused Phillip and other men like him."

I could hear Everett's kindness, an offer which came too late...and that I didn't deserve.

"That attorney has been charged for his part in Brandt's scheme as well. He won't get nearly the trouble Mr. Brandt did. They're slippery, those lawyers. Harder to catch, and good at covering their tracks. So thank you," Everett said. "This town owes you."

I wanted to snort. Owes me? I could just imagine what each person thought. I owed them, if anything. A debt I could never, ever repay. My train whistled in the distance, a far-off announcement the fraud was about to leave town and head back to the only open door Louise Archer ever really had—her father's business…or what was left of it…instead of a husband.

"I should never have come here," I muttered to my hands as the whistle died down. "Better you just say what's true. I should never have lied. I should never have stayed once I got off here. I was an angry woman with a ridiculous plan. Angry at Jim who jilted me, at you because you interfered, even at God." The whistle blasted again…louder.

"You were meant to come here, Louise Archer from St. Louis. I figured it out. Haven't you?"

How dare the man who'd left me alone with my shame in front of the whole town try to slip out from under his part of the blame! His audacity brought me to my feet and face to face with the one who'd helped cause all of this trouble I'd caused Larned…and Lizzy. "I never meant to end up here. I intended to go on, force open the door that had closed on me. Not stay here and wreck good people's lives."

"Louise." Everett's hand bridged the gap between us and touched my shoulder. "This is your open door. You didn't make any mistakes."

"Of course I did. And didn't you as well when you stood back in silence at Eat Here? Just like Jim, who chose to smolder in it?"

"Jim missed the chance to know the woman capable of setting fires, robbing the rich, and moving heaven and earth to right a wrong. You set fire to everything you needed to, Miss Archer. It was my pleasure to let you, and to be there to clear away the rubble when you were done."

"But the other night at Eat Here…"

"I couldn't have said or done things better than you did. Cook said you were the best shot, and to let you have at it."

The train whistled again, closer this time, near enough the engine could be heard as well. I looked at Everett's face, the softened grooves which lined his kindness. "This can't possibly be my open door…" Engagements weren't supposed to end in ruin. Mothers weren't supposed to collapse because of what their daughters did or made of themselves, then live out their lives in destitution. "I can never fix or face…"

"Me? Your friends? Or someone like the person on that train who can't wait to see you?" Everett nodded toward the locomotive which struggled to slow for the station behind me.

"What?"

"Your mother. The woman I watched see you off in St. Louis, and who believed she was sending you forward to the right door. She agrees with us."

"Us?"

He glanced behind him. I squinted in the vague light at Cook and his gun, at the thin shadow Les made at his side, and at Phillip cleaned up and in new clothing. Then at Clement and the woman in white next to him.

I stared at my gown—Lizzy's gown I'd mended and she now wore—while, "Please say you'll stay," and words of thanks came from the crowd behind her. And from her.

"There will be more trains stopping here from now on," Everett said. "You can go whenever you want.

There will be more stages, as well. Lots of them. Turns out Mr. Brandt had choked the traffic through here in an effort to dry up the businesses so each would fold, and with money he made in cahoots with men like Rudy Walters, he could buy them up and take them over for himself. Then he would have opened everything back up and done the same thing you set out to do for travelers who would stream this way. It's opened up now." Everett grinned. "Thanks to you and that fiery passion of yours."

The train ground to a stop, the squeal of the brakes, the metal against metal, announcing another door was about to open. One Mama would step through.

"May I get your trunk and bags for you?" Everett looked down at me. I caught the glint that would let me go through the train's door if I so chose. Or escort me through the other door, the one he said was mine.

"If you hadn't been so eager to help last time, I would never have been here." I frowned enough Everett could see it even in the near dark.

"Yes, you would. This was your open door and you were theirs."

And his. I saw it in the kindness which looked down at me.

The train came to an exhausted rest. "Maybe you should get Mama's luggage instead."

"Let me. I'd be honored to tote any Archer woman's bags." Cook hobbled to my side and paused, Les close behind him. "Perfect aim," he whispered, which Les affirmed with a grin and a nod. "I knew you could do it…once we got pointed the same direction." Then he and his little shadow hustled on to the train while Everett held tight to my trunk.

I watched Cook's limp and Les's near mimic of it disappear in the cloud of soot and steam, then turned to the crowd, to Lizzy, to faces which welcomed me, that said, "Please," again, and prayed I'd stay. Two open doors stared at one another. Neither the door I'd imagined, neither one Jim. Not the wifely duties I'd thought would fulfill me, but business tactics, wily ones which outthought, out planned, and outsmarted the best. Not the companionship I'd envisioned, either, as Lizzy came to my side and buried me in her arms…a sister for life.

Nor the open door of kindness I'd expected, the real voice which spoke as it came close. "Like I said, it will be some very fortunate man who changes your Miss to Mrs. someday, Louise Archer. May I?" Everett extended his elbow.

I eyed the gesture I'd first opposed in St. Louis, one intended then, and again now, to say *I want you to be all right.* His expression added *Please…Please come…* as he beckoned me toward the door he wanted to walk me through. I took the arm I should have held onto to begin with and told Everett McCloud the truth…at last. "You certainly may."

A word about the author...

Colleen L Donnelly put her science education to use for years, and then put it behind her to pursue other passions. Her first love is writing and her second is hunting—hunting for that next good story, hunting for shed antlers or mushrooms in the woods, hunting for the next good author to read. An avid believer in work hard/play hard, Colleen splits her time between indoors and out, always busy at something.

http://www.colleenldonnelly.com/

Thank you for purchasing
this publication of The Wild Rose Press, Inc.

For questions or more information
contact us at
info@thewildrosepress.com.

The Wild Rose Press, Inc.
www.thewildrosepress.com